THE MAID AND THE CROCODILE

THE
MAID

AMULET BOOKS · NEW YORK

AND THE

CROCODILE

JORDAN IFUEKO

A note to readers:

The Maid and the Crocodile is a warmhearted fantasy set in the mystical world of Oluwan City, exploring themes of disability discrimination, permanent physical injury, emotional and physical abuse, reproductive coercion, and familial death. If you are sensitive to these themes, please take care . . . and prepare to embark on a magic and secret-filled adventure.

PUBLISHER'S NOTE: This is a work of fiction. Names, characters, places, and incidents are either the product of the author's imagination or used fictitiously, and any resemblance to actual persons, living or dead, business establishments, events, or locales is entirely coincidental.

Cataloging-in-Publication Data has been applied for and may be obtained from the Library of Congress.

ISBN 978-1-4197-6435-6

Text © 2024 Jordan Ifueko
Illustrations by Alex Foster
Book design by Micah Fleming

Printed and bound in the United States
10 9 8 7 6 5 4 3 2 1

Amulet Books are available at special discounts when purchased in quantity for premiums and promotions as well as fundraising or educational use. Special editions can also be created to specification. For details, contact specialsales@abramsbooks.com or the address below.

Amulet Books® is a registered trademark of Harry N. Abrams, Inc.

ABRAMS The Art of Books
195 Broadway, New York, NY 10007
abramsbooks.com

To the ants in a world of giants

BALOGUN INN AND PHILOSOPHY SALON: GROUND FLOOR

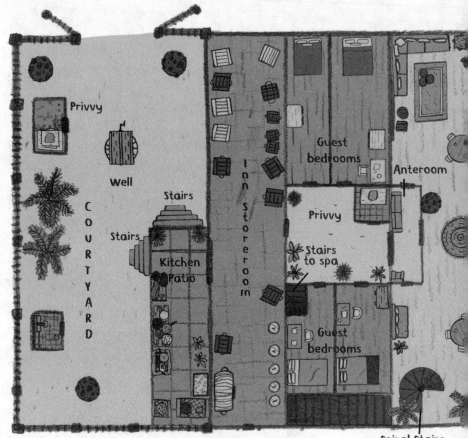

2ND FLOOR

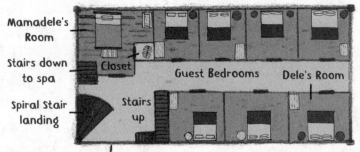

3RD FLOOR
SERVANT'S GARRET
& ROOFTOP GARDEN

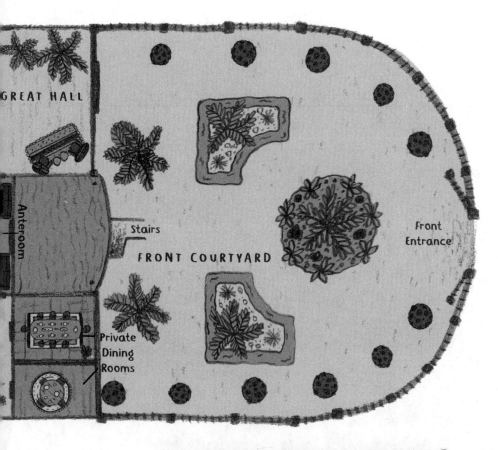

GREAT HALL

Anteroom

Stairs

FRONT COURTYARD

Private
Dining
Rooms

Front
Entrance

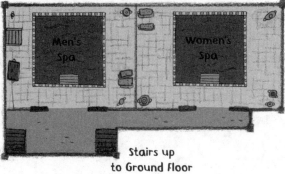

Men's
Spa

Women's
Spa

Stairs to
Upper Floors

Stairs up
to Ground Floor

UNDERGROUND SPA

Manservant's Quarters

Rooftop Garden

NAME PRONUNCIATION GUIDE

SADE: **SHAH**-DAY

YE EUN: YEH-**UN**

DELE: **DEH**-LAY

WAFA: **WAH**-FAH

KANWAL: **KUH**-VUL

HANUNI: HA-**NOON**-EE

FINNRIC: **FIN**-RICK

ONIJIBOLA: OHN-NEE-**JEE**-BOH-LA

LIAO: **LEE**-OW

INJAANA: EEN-**JAH**-NAH

TARISAI: **TAH**-REE-SIGH

SANJEET: SAHN-**JEET**

KIRAH: **KEE**-RAH

BISI: **BEE**-SEE

ZURI: **ZOO**-REE

PART I

CHAPTER 1

YOU ARE POWERFUL AND IMPORTANT, AND I AM ONLY ME.

But I am told you are a good listener, and if I do not look into your eyes, I am a little less afraid. So I will try to tell my story without lies.

When a god stalked me on my seventeenth birthday, the day I aged out of the orphan house, I did not see him. Not at first.

No one does, as immortals prefer to send signs ahead of themselves: a flock of herons making rude symbols in the sky, for example, or a pair of oxen that eerily resemble your town butcher and his wife.

In my case, it was a perfectly ordinary gecko: bright green, flecked with orange and ochre. It skittered across the outer courtyard wall of the Aanu Meji orphan house, making dust patterns on the whitewashed brick as Mama Poorchild and my foster siblings bid me farewell.

"I was kind to you," Mama Poorchild cooed in her singsong way, unaware of the agitated gecko inches above her head.

Mama Poorchild was my Mercy Auntie: the Realmhood worker assigned to me when I arrived in Oluwan City one year ago, an orphan still reeking of the countryside sweatmills. As I leaned on my cane, she straightened the pack on my shoulder and smoothed my threadbare red wrapper: all I owned in the world. "I was kind," she said. "Wasn't I, Small Sade?"

It was not truly a question, and so I gave her the answer she wanted: words I had repeated every day for the past year, meaning it a little less every time.

"Of course, ma!"

"And I did my best?"

I swallowed, watching the gecko on the wall to avoid Mama Poorchild's eyes. I sucked on the prayer pebble I kept beneath my tongue, hoping the Goddess of Earth would sweeten my ungrateful spirit. "I could not have asked for better," I said. "If they knew of your kindness, how you cared for this poor Small Sade, the Anointed Ones would kiss your feet. Even if I sleep on the streets tonight, I will remember your goodness and thank Am the Storyteller."

She beamed, especially when I said *poor*. Mama Poorchild was very proud of her name. Commoners in Oluwan take on the name of their first-born child. Mercy Aunties, who are mothers to the Realmhood's orphans, adopt names like *Mama Poorchild* or *Auntie Lostangel*—or the worst I'd heard, *Sister Sadwaif*.

There was a Mamasade, once. And a Babasade, assuming I was his firstborn.

But if you do not mind, I will not speak of them just now. You seem a happy person, and that is not a happy story. I would not dim the light in your eyes.

"You won't really sleep on the streets tonight, will you?" asked Beauty Bisi, a girl from my high-rise floor. She was nearly my age, though her mind was a bit slow. She had earned the nickname both for her winsome dimples and for her religious devotion to making plain things lovelier. This morning, her deft fingers had pressed my hair into shining cornrows that ended at the nape of my neck. She had tipped the ends with beads she made herself—pebbles dyed red from the iron-rich dirt of Aanu Meji Street and bored carefully with a needle. Now she scowled at me from behind Mama Poorchild's shoulder, as though my imminent departure had turned me, her roommate, into a stranger. "Promise, Small Sade. Say you won't sleep on the street and get sold to a body bazaar."

"Of course she won't," Mama Poorchild laughed, though she avoided my gaze.

She placed twenty-six zathulus in my palm, just enough rickshaw fare for me to reach one of the vast city's major markets. She also gave me the token I had asked for: a short reed broom to represent my trade as a house girl.

"I still think you should carry a scroll," she tutted. "After a few years' indenture, you could be a scribe's assistant at the Academy of the Realm. It's a lucky orphan who knows her letters."

I did not, as she put it, know my letters. I *had* worked at a sweatmill that produced those torture objects called books. Copier children did not need to know how to read. We only needed to work: stirring foul-foul vats of ink that singed our eyebrows and binding reams of paper with edges so sharp, they drew blood. Books were for people with soft minds and full bellies. I had been hungry since birth, and so I stuffed the reed broom snugly into my pack.

Edict brats—or Wards of the Raybearers, as the more sentimental liked to call us—suffered quickly if they weren't adopted, or in my case, hired when coming of age. Women and men with greasy smiles skulked outside orphan high-rises, quick to loan us newly homeless wards a bed and a bowl of stew . . . for a price, of course. The interest was never paid in coins.

If I was lucky, a merchant or housekeeper would not mind hiring an orphan with one strong foot and one weak one. If I was even luckier, they would reserve a back stoop for me to sleep on, providing a tarp in wet season if they were generous. But if fortune did not favor me, well . . .

By sundown today, I would have nothing.

I could have sworn the gecko winked from its perch on the doorframe. Only then did I recognize the symbol it was etching in the dust: the round, bumpy shape of a seed pod. The mark of a Clay spirit.

"Oh no," I blurted. "Not again."

I was not surprised to be stalked by a deity. Perhaps for important people like yourself, encounters with the divine are special. High gods, like Am the Storyteller and the Goddess of Earth, tend to visit high mortals—creatures as rare and perfect as themselves.

But low beings always outnumber the high, even among deities. Imps and wisps, demigods and bickering sprites . . . these are workers of everyday miracles, who cause fruit to sprout from seeds, and teach bees how to swarm, and guide unborn babies to form fingers and toes. These gods do not seek perfection. They seek entertainment.

These gods, you see, are bored.

In cookfire tales, deities are drawn to unusual beauty. But in true life, they are lured by unusual . . . well, *anything*. And that is where my story comes in. We Small Sades, with our speckled skin and dead parents and misshapen feet, have been fending off spirits since the day we were born.

Do not say them, please. Those words. I see them now, eager to be spat out, hopping across your tongue like cayenne pepper.

You should not say such things about your skin. You are looking so nice, Small Sade. Really, I did not even notice.

But you did notice, and that is fine. I like my face, and it has always been this way: light spots on dark, like clouds drifting over a moonless pond. I am this way all over, in fact. The high-rise physician called it *vitiligo*. It is blander than the phrase I hear most often: *spirit-touched*.

"What do you mean, 'Oh no?'" asked Mama Poorchild. "Not what again?"

I only shook my head, knowing she would not believe me. Most city people worshipped in the ways of Well or Ember, dismissing Clay gods as countryside superstition.

Besides, if I ignored the gecko messenger, perhaps the deity who sent it would get bored with me.

I will entertain you another time, I thought at the gecko, grinding the prayer pebble against my cheek. *Right now, if you please, I would like to focus on not being homeless.*

I waved up at the small unsmiling faces that dotted the high-rise windows and kissed Beauty Bisi goodbye. When I leaned in, she caught my face in her hands and whispered, "Beware the Crocodile God."

Mama Poorchild shuddered . . . for this, of course, was a deity that all city folks believed in.

"The Crocodile God only eats pretty girls," I reminded Beauty Bisi with a wink. "So I'll be just fine."

Beauty Bisi only frowned, fingering the beads she had strung in my hair.

CHAPTER 2

THE RICKSHAW LET ME OFF INTO A BUSTLING HIVE: THE SUN-bleached Lower Market of Ileyimo, the Academy District.

You know that Oluwan City sprawls into five massive boroughs, each devoted to a craft. What you may not know is that every district has both a High Market and a Lower one.

High Markets sell goods related to the trade of their district. In the case of the Academy District, that meant neat rows of talking drum and kora harp vendors, dusty scriptorium tents, and podiums where silver-throated griots sang the histories of our divine Anointed Ones.

Lower Markets, in contrast, were a crowded, chaotic collection of everything *else* a district needed to survive. Like food, and animals, and Am willing . . . house servants.

When I produced my zathulus to pay the runner, a hand snaked out from the crowd and snatched my money pouch.

I stuck out my cane to trip the phantom passerby, caught his wrist as he fell, and wrenched. He howled, but by then I had let him go, slipping the pouch safely between my breasts. As Oga Snatch-Purse ran away, he cast a look over his shoulder that was almost apologetic. As if to say, *I thought you were new.*

I smiled ruefully back. Poor man. I was new to the city. *But not, oga, to the gutter.*

I grunted fondly at my knobby cane, adjusting my grip on its raw wood handle, which my palm had worn smooth over time. My cane often attracted thieves, who thought me an easy target. So I had learned to make it a weapon. I was able to walk without it for short spurts. It meant moving slowly, but I had grown skilled at balancing on my uneven stance so as not to fall. Still, after a few minutes, my weak foot would begin to seize. Within half an hour, a burning ache would spread to my calf and up my thigh. When I used my cane again after such attempts, I would need to lean even more weight on it than usual, leading to strain on my wrist in addition to my foot smarting. So it was better to use my cane at all times, even when it attracted unwanted attention.

Back at the orphanage, I had wrapped the cane's bottom tip in a rag, so it thudded mutely on the floors instead of announcing my presence with an echoing tap. But here at the Lower Market, being quiet would do me no favors—not if I wanted a job.

Swelling music tempted me to close my eyes, so I could pick apart the rhythms and enjoy each one. I was unused to how many dialects filled Oluwan City. Every Arit, even bumpkins like me, knew that the Realmhood of Aritsar was thirteen countries vast, each land large enough to be its own small continent. But I did not understand what a Realmhood was, I think, until I saw those lands all hustling together here, in the faces and selling songs of the market.

"*Light of the ocean, shine-shine-shine. Sprites for your lantern, shine-shine-shine!*" A sea-wrinkled Oluwani man spun and sang, voice whining like the water sprites in his lanterns, which dangled from his outstretched arms.

"*Oga, are you tough? Not as tough as my leathers eyy! Madam, are you soft? Soft and black like my leathers eyy!*" A tanner from the hunting nation of Djbanti rapped from his stall, beating on the pelts for rhythm.

"*My empress was born in a mango grove,*" warbled a woman from Swana, a lush realm of farmers. Her hips swayed as she balanced a basket of fruits heaped high on her head. "*Bite a mango for the luck of an empress.*"

Most sellers were dark-skinned people from the center realms, like me. But as the capital, Oluwan City drew thousands from farther lands of the Realmhood too. A Nontish family with hair like straw, pale faces peeling in the sun, sang harmonies as they thrust flowers at passersby: "*A rose for her wrapper makes a girl smell sweet . . .*"

Not to be outsung, a golden-skinned old woman in wide skirts and a broad-brimmed hat belted from a stall of glittering ceramics: "*The brightest pot is Songland green, a trusty vase is celadon!*"

I touched the broom sticking out from my shoulder pack, feeling like a musician who had not tuned her instrument. Summoning courage, I spat out the prayer pebble I kept always beneath my tongue and tucked it into my wrapper for safekeeping. Then I thrust the broom above my head and charged into the pulsing heart of the crowd.

"*Let me be your maid, madam,*" I trilled with my whole chest. "*Oga, I will clean so well for you.*"

My voice said *I will clean.* But my heart? It sang, *I cannot sleep on the streets tonight, and a god is stalking me, but even if I had been born a queen, I would give anything for a place, just one place in this, your Oluwan City.*

I knew that divine leaders called Raybearers headed our Realmhood's government, along with their councils of Anointed Ones. But I did not like to think of them. For reasons I will not go into now, I preferred to forget the existence of Anointed Ones altogether . . . but in their terrifying benevolence, they had chosen to remember children like me.

When the Raybearers announced their Lonesome Child Edict, rescuing children from labor mills, I could have run from the government cart when it came for me. I had not needed to leave Dejitown, the countryside backwater where I lived before the orphan house. My home could have been the Bush, where my mother's ghost still sang. Or I could have hidden in the village slums, where at least I knew the streets and a face or two.

But I did leave. Because in villages you belonged to another person, or else you were barely a person at all. You had to be Togo the goatherd's son, or Mbisi the healer's wife, or Pele the trader's daughter. Small Sade Who Maimed Her Foot Grinding Paper at the Sweatmill, Such a Poor Little Thing, What a Shame had no place. I had lived in between names, changing shape like mashed fufu in a pot, forced to fit whatever crevice they jammed me in.

I left because in Oluwan City, you need not belong to something so unreliable as a father you would never meet or a mother who died coughing in your arms. Here, no one ever demanded, "Who are your people?"

Instead they asked, "What district are you from?"

You could be Osaze from the Academy. Or Adetomiwa from the Poultry Stall. Or Babareni, Who Works at that Dress Shop Down the Street. If you wanted, you could even simply . . . be.

I imagined Future Me bustling down the city streets, stopping to help awestruck tourists. *You're not from around these parts, are you?* I would ask, flashing a worldly smile. *Here to see the sights? Well, what you are looking for is just up that road. Though the best food stalls are near Palace Hill, if you can afford it. Oh, me? I am just Sade.*

Sade of Oluwan City.

And I could be. All I needed was a job.

I lifted my broom higher, in hopes that potential patrons could see it. But you see why I am well named, Small Sade? The gods who exchange a girl's legs for a woman's had forgotten me. Other brooms dotted the sky, along with cooking spoons, hair combs, and gardening trowels—tools of domestic trade.

"Fine-fiiiiine kitchen boy for your house!"

"Are you looking rough? Is your hair jaga-jaga? Best braider in Oluwan City, only fifty zathulus . . ."

"House girl, tent girl, anything-you-want girl . . ."

"Let me be your maid," I tried again, immediately drowned out by a chorus of more confident music. I wished that I had a griot's voice—rich and resonant, with the power to hush crowds as they sang great histories. Mine was high and fragile, prone to breaking when I grew too passionate, and teetering off-tune when I felt shy.

As I sang, my vision began to change. A metallic silt clung to every surface, even on the tops of people's shoulders and the folds of their starched *gele* headdresses. The silt gave off spores that shimmered as they drifted through the air, invisibly coating the lungs of every shopper in the market.

And now you know the worst of my secrets. I fear you were beginning to think well of me, and now you think me mad or a demon or both, for I see things that are not there.

Only it is there. Though few can see it, everyone feels spirit silt—the layer of dust and spirit creatures that lies atop living souls. For those at peace with their places in the world, spirit silt is as light as the air they breathe. But those who reject the roles placed on them by others, who chafe at the web into which they were born . . . well. They will feel the silver dust as cotton lining their throats, hands reaching up from the earth to grasp their ankles, weighting every step.

Me? I barely felt the silt. Life had slung me a rotting portion that I choked down without a sound, for at day's end, a meal was a meal.

The world had called my mother a nobody. She refused to believe them, fighting the silver every day she lived, and died unhappy for it. I learned then, you see, to call myself a nobody before anyone else could. Poison could not hurt me if I dosed myself first.

Through a break in the crowd, a woman with friendly lines around her mouth spotted my broom and beckoned. My heart leapt, and I lifted my cane singing as I shuffled toward her.

"*I will be your maid, madam—*"

Two girls, both about my age, elbowed their way in front of me. Both held brooms above their heads, twirling them, showing off the strength of their sinewy brown limbs.

"Why buy a broken pot, madam?" crowed the taller girl. "It is like having half a maid. How can she clean for you if she cannot stand?" She flashed crooked white teeth . . . and then swiped her foot beneath my ankle.

The red market dirt rose up to meet me, and my cane went flying. The other girl, small but willowy, stepped over me and preened in the woman's face.

"You don't want her," she declared, pointing at the girl who tripped me. "She's like a giant. Imagine her stomping through your house, *godun, godun*. But me, I am soft-soft and quiet, madam."

"It is a lie-o," bellowed the tall one, clapping in the other girl's face. "It is a lie! This cow has been mooing here all day. I swear by the Anointed Ones, if you take her, you will have no peace, madam . . ."

Wordlessly, I crawled to retrieve my belongings. Cruelty was weather to me—as dull and inevitable as rain in wet season. The prayer pebble had escaped the folds of my wrapper, bouncing onto the dirt. I wiped it off and popped it in my mouth, where it clacked against my teeth before settling back beneath my tongue.

From the ground, a streak of green peered up at me. It was the gecko from the orphanage, trembling as market traffic clattered down around us.

With a sigh, I scooped it up and placed it on my cane, where it clung in terrified gratitude.

"Your god may mean to torment me," I said. "But I will not see you flattened. Crushed limbs are no fun at all. Though I suppose you might do better than me," I added thoughtfully. "You can grow yours back."

The creature glanced down at my misshapen foot, then up at the bickering girls. I shivered when it *gestured* at me then, jerking its head over its tiny shoulder. As if to say: *Don't you have better things to do?*

"I do not," I said, as though gesturing reptiles were normal. "And how easy for you to say. You, who have a job already." I slipped one of Beauty Bisi's beads from the end of one of my twists, holding it out to the gecko. "There. Will this make your god leave me alone?"

It was a paltry offering, one that would insult a higher god. But if the gecko worked for a minor spirit—the imp of a well I had drunk from, perhaps, or the guardian of a front stoop where I had rested without permission—it might be content. "Please? It is all I have."

The gecko took the bead in its mouth with deliberate care, as though giving me an opportunity to recant. Then it swallowed my offering whole. Too late, I noticed that a coiling spring of my hair had looped around the bead.

My stomach dropped.

Now, every Realmhood child—even country bumpkins like me—knows that you never, *ever* offer a god any part of your body. I am not sure why. The cookfire stories vary, and it is a mystery that makes Academy godcraft scholars argue in the streets. But I do know that the moment my hair disappeared into that green rippling throat, a ball of heat stole over my skin, searching every peak and crevice with shameless curiosity.

Then the gecko scampered up my arm, lifted its fleshy pink tongue to my ear, and said in a high voice: "*Ixalix.*"

"Talking," I moaned. "That is new."

Spirit messengers did not talk, in my experience. They only made ominous noises as you tried to sleep, or scratched the ground with cryptic symbols, or exploded in a show of blood and feathers—all until you paid attention to the god who sent them. But the god had my hair now. Perhaps that meant it had my brain as well, and my eyes and ears, and could make me hear as it liked.

"Ixalix," the gecko repeated.

"I am very dull," I said with sweating palms. "All I think of is cleaning and eating. Your god would be bored with me. Go find someone else."

"Ixalix."

"Think what offerings I will bring once I have a job," I pressed. "Palm wine. Rice. Copper zathulus. Maybe—maybe even a silver kirah every now and then. All I need is a day. An hour . . ."

The gecko considered me with calm pity. Then it leaned even closer and spoke into my ear. My face went cold, and I knew then that there would be no job, no place in Oluwan City, no life for me at all. For the word it croaked into my ear was:

"*CROCODILE.*"

CHAPTER 3

THREE MONTHS AGO, FIVE MANSIONS OF IVORY BONE ROSE overnight from rubble—one house in every district of Oluwan City.

Cold leeched from their windowless plaster walls, even in the blazing Oluwan heat. On each front door hung a single adornment: the head of a crocodile, glossily preserved in resin.

Rumors about the houses' owners roared through the city. These days, animal heads hung on many households. The decorations had grown popular ten years ago, back when the Arit Realmhood was still the Arit Empire, and a series of vigilantes masked as different beasts had led the charge against corrupt nobility. But the heads on the bone doors, gossips decided, likely had nothing to do with Arit history but represented the avatar of the god within. They concluded that a shape-shifting spirit had built five shrines to itself. And as children bicker to name a stray dog, every religious sect rushed to claim the god. The idea of having a housed deity to bless trade and smite enemies excited neighborhoods everywhere.

Most city folk are People of the Ember, and so offerings of coal, newly minted coins, and volcanic ashes piled at each of the shrines' doorsteps. Next came the sides of fish, mother-of-pearl shells, and hunks of ambergris left by People of the Well. When the god ignored fire and water worshippers, the ascetic People of the Wing flocked to the shrines, flaying themselves and anointing the steps with pelican oil. Even I, an earthworshipping bumpkin of the Clay, shyly left a ripe tangerine at a shrine, in case the god wanted to protect me too. But every single gift rotted away in the sun, left untouched on the steps of the houses.

Then someone thought to bring a girl.

You know, of course, that human sacrifice is illegal in the Realmhood. It is a practice that died with the old Arit Empire, which appeased demons by sacrificing children to the Underworld.

But this girl had been both beautiful and poor, an unwise combination in any town. Her neighbors called her an angel. Then she refused to be wooed, marry, or have children, and so they called her a witch. In time, they broke open one of the shrine doors, tied a rope to her ankle, and thrust her into the shadowy mouth of the bone house.

She did cry out. But as soon as the door shut behind her, the wailing stopped. The rope, meant to drag out her body after the god killed or ravished her, fell slack. When the neighbors pulled it from the doorframe, there was nothing at the end of the line. No one dared enter the house, but when a few brave souls squinted over the threshold, they saw nothing but a smooth, windowless room.

So born was the legend of the Crocodile God, who ate pretty girls.

If that gecko had screeched "Crocodile!" into your ear, I think, you would have swiped it from your shoulder and fled. It would not have helped much, for no one outruns a spirit on two legs. Still, you would have done it, because you are not like me. You have a lioness heart: one that fights, against the odds, to keep beating.

But I had never been the hero of anyone's story, least of all my own. The silt lining my lungs had addicted me to peace. And peace, the silt insisted, meant accepting one's fate. So when the gecko pointed for me to leave the market, I obeyed. When it leapt from my cane to climb across the walls and alleyways of the Academy District, I followed, pausing only to admire slivers of the city that, in another life, might have been mine.

"Goodbye," I bid the stewmongers, as they beckoned hungry customers to sit on the curb. I blessed the pots simmering in open-air kitchens, scenting the air with clouds of spicy steam. "Be careful," I told the rickshaws that hurtled through the streets with bells and shrieking wheels, weaving around the wealthy in their palanquins. "Forgive me," I begged the towering murals of Raybearers and their Anointed Ones, the guardians of our Realmhood, whose eternal eyes stalked me on every block of the city-long Watching Wall.

The gecko turned onto the Way of the Crocodile—the name locals had given to each dead-end road on which a cold white house had arisen. A hush thick as smog fell over the air. It reduced the Oluwan City din to a murmur, so I heard the thud of my steps on packed dirt and cobblestone. Business teemed in Oluwan City at every hour of the day and night, and so a quiet neighborhood meant great wealth or great danger. Crumbling and dog-ridden tenements betrayed this place as the latter. The newly built house stood out at the end of the street, like a coal burning white in a pile of gray kindling.

As I mounted the cold plaster steps, I fantasized about someone seeing me. A flock of strangers to cry out: "You there, small girl! Get away from the door! Don't you know a god lives in there? Come back to the city and be safe. Come down and belong to us."

But locals had erected a high palisade wall in front of the house, just long enough to shield the entrance from view of the street. The wall offered privacy to those leaving offerings, and also to those with wicked intentions. Local officials had tired of searching for girls fed to the shrine. A wall meant no more witnesses, and no witnesses meant no missing girls.

The remains of past offerings—dry rice, tarnished coins, sticks of incense—crunched beneath my sandals. The crocodile head watched impassively from the door, sunlight glinting on its polished scales. Its hollow eyes froze me in place.

"Will it hurt?" I asked the gecko in a whisper. "When he . . . you know."

But the gecko said nothing, skittering through a crack in the entryway.

Thoughts could only slow me down, so I banished them, and with a sob, I lifted my cane and burst through the door, wailing my own funeral rite.

"*Tonight I may join Egungun's Parade,*" I sang, plunging into shadow. "*Tonight I may be purified . . .*"

My voice did not echo. It was as though I stood in an unlit box, barely larger than a peasant's hut. But that wasn't possible. From the outside, the shrine was several rooms wide, at least.

When my eyes adjusted to the darkness, I made out the gecko, who wriggled by my feet. It gestured to a line of chalk inches from my toes, where something appeared to be stuck in the smooth floor: a single human tooth.

The gecko raced past the line into the gloom, making it clear I should follow. My foot hovered above the chalk. "*Am who wrote my birth and death*," I warbled . . . and stepped over the line.

The world changed.

Sunlight stung my eyes and dappled across a small flagstone court-yard. The palm-dotted walls of a villa encircled me, and the sky stretched in a country-clear blue dome, untouched by city smog.

I whirled around to look back at the shrine door. It had vanished, though the chalk line on the ground, along with the human tooth, re-mained. It had glowed red as I passed over, then faded again to white.

In the courtyard's center, a mask hung several feet above the ground in thin air, suspended without strings like a star. The mask was made of crocodile skin, fringed in a halo of teeth.

Below the mask was a stone well, on the rim of which the gecko sun-bathed, looking very smug. Beside the well stood a man.

He was the handsomest person I have ever seen, and of course, this terrified me.

Beautiful people—especially ones like him, an Arit blueblood with cobalt-black skin and shining, toned limbs—were often unhappy to see me. They saw my spots and my foot and worried that whatever I had was contagious. Or else my very existence made them uneasy—a reminder of a privilege they had not earned and could lose by an accident of birth.

In any case, I could not be what the Crocodile God wanted. And this man *was* the Crocodile God. I knew it because I was still singing and could see his spirit silt. No one is covered in more spirit silt than a god.

An iridescent film, the weight of a hundred thousand whispered prayers and expectations, glowed across his chest and arms, his neck and bare shoulders. Grief-gnats sparkled hungrily at his ears, while lurid ambition-spores clung like burrs to his waist-length locs. Worst of all was his left bicep, on which a gaping wound festered with layer upon layer of slimy, silver despair-mold.

Despite it all, the Crocodile smiled, and that scared me more than anything.

"*Guide me to Core, the world without end—*" The funeral rite died in my throat, and with it, my vision of the spirit silt. What remained was a shirtless man, holding himself as though with great age, despite his youthful appearance. Scars—stab wounds?—rose in keloids across his broad chest. A gold cuff shone on his bicep, along with a scattering of green scales. Mud spattered his crisp linen trousers.

"Ah," he said in a voice like nettle leaves: velvet and stinging. "So they sent you after all."

I waited for him to take me in: my face and cane and threadbare wrapper. I expected him to recoil. That could be a good thing, if he only ate girls as lovely as himself. Then again, he might devour me out of sheer rage at my plainness, shape-shifting into a crocodile and swallowing me whole.

Instead he bowed, grimaced at himself, then swiped at his dirty trousers.

"Excuse the appearance," he said, dark eyes twinkling. "I am usually devastating, I promise. But I had a run-in with some cultists in the Agricultural District. There was a chase, and some goat pens got involved . . . Sade, is it?"

"Yes, oga," I rasped.

Of course he knew my name. He had probably eaten it, along with my body, the moment I stepped over that line. How kind of him to make my death so painless.

"Don't call me that," he snorted. "I'm not an oga or a sir. I'm useless and covered in mud."

"Sorry, oga," I said, just in case it was a test.

I realized then that I could not be dead. Human souls passed on to Egungun's Parade, dancing to ghostly drums as they marched to their final rest at Core. I could not hear any music, and besides the Crocodile, I was the only soul here.

So where in Am's name was I?

The villa courtyard was eerily lifeless, empty of dogs or chickens. Absent even was the buzzing of flies. Aside from the gecko, the closest thing to an animal was the crocodile mask floating above the well. On the breeze I smelled mangos, as though an orchard blossomed nearby. In addition to the line with the tooth I had stepped over, four other lines of chalk glittered around the yard's perimeter.

"I see you came through the Pointy Molar Door," the man said. "So you came from the Academy District?" When I nodded, he continued, "I am glad it was not the Chipped Molar Door. Palace District people are insufferable. I assume Ixalix filled you in on the details?"

Ixalix. He must have meant the gecko. I glanced at the small creature for help, but it only flicked its tongue, sunbathing on the rim of the well.

The man took my paralyzed silence for assent. "They should not have dragged you into this," he continued. "Personally, I would have let you be, but it appears the decision was made for me. Your face excited a lot of people, not least of all the Boss Almighty. Tea or mango wine?"

At this point, I began to suspect that he was mad. Many gods were, by human standards, and in such cases it was best to agree with whatever nonsense they said. The same madness that made the Crocodile eat girls, you understand, might just trick him into setting me free.

So I squeaked, "Tea, please."

He touched the cuff on his arm and closed his eyes. Discomfort crumpled his features, and I imagined that invisible wound above his bicep, teeming with despair. Then his face cleared, as chiseled and beautiful as it was before.

"I am not supposed to do this," he said. "But I wanted to impress you."

A hunk of clay lifted from the ground, shaped itself, and burst into flames. It cooled and burned several more times before resting daintily on the well: a green-glazed earthenware mug. A jet of water leapt from the well and splashed into the newly made cup, joined by fragrant leaves that freed themselves from a nearby tree and looped in a breeze across the courtyard. At last, a faded rug unfurled, and a stool rolled across the flagstones and righted itself inches from my feet.

I sat. He strode over, making me shiver with each step. When he placed the steaming cup of tea in my trembling hands, I planned to say *thank you*. I wanted to say, *If you are going to make things fly and set themselves on fire, please warn me in advance, oh powerful and insane Crocodile God.*

Instead I blurted, "How in Am's name would you have made the wine?"

The man laughed—a low, musical sound that appeared to surprise us both.

"Cheating," he admitted. He indicated some barrels against the villa wall. "The wine's already made. I need only have conjured the glass."

The wine's already made. Did he have servants? I didn't see anyone.

I sipped at the tea, willing the mug not to slip from my sweating palms. "Where am I?" I asked, doing my best to sound casual.

"My home, of course. Well. Sort of." He spread his hands. "Like many things in my life, this place is on loan from the Boss Almighty. She didn't want it, and I needed somewhere to mope and get drunk, so . . . here we are."

"But where is *here*?" An edge crept into my tone. My head was beginning to hurt, and I doubted his magically conjured tea would soothe it.

The man's brow wrinkled, then lifted, as though he had found a perfectly clear way to explain. "Nowhere," he said. "Though also, it's a remote savannah in Swana. And four other places, including that street in Oluwan City. But also, nowhere."

With great effort, I managed not to hurl the cup at his head.

"Right," I said, setting down my tea. "Well. This has been *very* nice, oga, but I think it is time I went back to Oluwan." I stood and backed away toward the chalk line, gesturing vaguely around me. "I have so enjoyed your well, and your fine-fine tea, and your lovely . . . stools, but I fear I have tired out my welcome, and so—"

"You're leaving already?"

I froze, waiting for wrath to simmer in the god's eyes.

He only looked at me blankly, then raised his arm, pointing to the cuff and its invisible wound. He asked, "Aren't you going to try and break my curse?"

My fingers clenched, digging into the grooves of my cane. But I smiled and said the only thing I could say.

"Of course, oga."

CHAPTER 4

IT WAS NOT THE FIRST TIME SUCH A THING HAD BEEN ASKED of me.

Curse-eating is a very old profession. It is born of an idea that unfortunate people attract bad spirits away from wealthier, more fortunate ones. As a result, Curse-Eaters are both shunned pariahs and celebrated luck charms.

Daughter getting married? Pay a jilted spinster to touch the girl's wedding clothes. Foul spirits, people believed, would leave the bride, seduced away by the Curse-Eater's loneliness. Buying a new cow? Have a dying person clean its stables. Demons would flock to the Curse-Eater's broom, leaving the heifer to calf in peace.

As a child, I had been a popular choice for curse-eating in Dejitown. Being a limping, spirit-touched orphan will do that for you. The previous Curse-Eater, a near-toothless man named Popo who always reeked of palm wine, was getting old, and so the village was eager for him to train an apprentice.

I worked for Popo on my days off from the sweatmill. The first question I asked him was, "Can you see the silt?"

To which he yawned and replied, "Eh? You are talking nonsense, small girl. Go and clean the yam farmer's house; they are expecting a new baby any day now."

I learned quickly not to bring up my sight again. Being *Small Sade Whose Foot Got Smashed in the Sweatmill, What a Shame* was hard enough, without having *addlebrained* added to my title.

Mamasade had explained my singing sight to me. At first, when I spoke of silver slush and glowing spores, she had been as confused as I was. But the closer she got to death, cheeks burning as I held her in my arms, the more she caught glimpses of what I saw.

Perhaps teetering on the ledge between life and death gives you special knowledge. Or perhaps it was the kiriwi tea I made to soothe her fever, steeped in boiled water from a stream in the haunted Bush. In any case, when I sang to her for the last time, she gasped and clawed at the ground around her, where oily pools of silver oozed from her frail body.

"What you see, my Strong Sade," she said, "is the stuff hope is made of. Wishes we dream for ourselves. Roles that others make for us. We shed them wherever we go, and the stronger those hopes are, the more we drown in them." It took me years to figure out what she meant, and even longer to come up with a name I felt was suitable for the pulsing, living substance that covered all humans and their dwellings.

I decided on *silt*: named for the powdery eroded minerals that filled the dirt and streams of the Oluwan countryside. Silt, most village children knew, could make the ground fertile, causing crops to thrive in its rich, life-filled mantle. But silt could also poison—muddying rivers and clogging streams, suffocating fish and any other life.

For most Curse-Eaters, I learned, the job was a grift. When Popo cleaned a house, nothing truly changed. A baby was born breathing or it wasn't. A marriage succeeded or failed. And as long as Popo made a show of muttering nonsense incantations while he pushed a broom around, sometimes pausing to mime catching imaginary pests and dropping them down his throat . . . the patrons would be satisfied, basking in their new false cloud of good luck.

But when I worked, singing out of habit . . . something actually happened. Piles of lurid spirit dust moved when I scrubbed with a soapy rag. It shifted even more quickly when I used bits of my hair or wet the ground with my spit or tears. When I cleaned a house, the couples who lived in it quarreled less often. Their elderly slept soundly, their children laughed more often . . . even babies seemed more eager to be born.

At first, I mumbled nonsense incantations like Popo, just so my patrons felt like they were getting their money's worth. But after a while,

I experimented with new sounds. Songs with tongue clicks scared away spirit beetles, while nasal songs helped scour away greedgrime and egorust.

Some spirit muck would not disappear on its own, no matter how hard I scrubbed. Trying to relocate the stubborn stuff did not work either. If I tossed a dustpan of silt off the edge of a patron's property, it would whip itself up in an iridescent cloud over my head, settling peevishly back on the house again.

In these cases, the only option was to hold the spirit silt in one hand, pinch my nose with the other, and swallow the stuff in one miserable gulp. The first time I tried this, I clutched my stomach all night, waiting for brutal cramps and an explosive death. But as far as I could tell, eating spirits in small amounts had no effect on me at all—except for strange and vivid dreams, and strands of hair that stood out from the rest of my coils, metallic silver against the cloud of black.

No cleansing had permanent results. Like dust, spirit silt settled back on floors and objects over time, shedding from any human souls that roamed near. The only time a house remained clean was when its people changed—adjusting their expectations of themselves, or each other. That rarely happened, and so my services remained popular.

They called it curse-eating. But I believed spirit silt was neither a curse nor a blessing. It was simply what one made of it . . . and that was why I never tried to cleanse the silt that covered my own body, even as it lined my lungs and wept from every pore.

"I'll need some hot water," I told the Crocodile God. "Towels. Rosemary for disinfectant. Soap, honey. You . . . might want to sit down for this."

He sank obediently onto the rug, and the items I had asked for sailed down from various windows of the villa, arranging themselves neatly in baskets before us. I crushed the rosemary branches over a bucket of scalding water, then lathered and dipped a washcloth. I spat in the cloth too, for good measure. Then, heart pounding, I resumed the stool beside him and placed the towel across my lap.

He watched and asked: "May I?"

When I nodded, he placed his forearm in my lap. The weight of him sent a jolt up my spine. He felt substantial. I had half expected his perfect chiseled arm to fall through me, like a wraith's or a demon's. I worried the prayer pebble against my teeth.

"This is going to hurt," I warned.

"Most things worth doing do," he said.

With effort, I pried the wide gold cuff from his arm. Immediately I dropped it, recoiling. Two stones—one metallic, the other green and glittering—lay embedded in his smooth, dark skin. Veins spidered out from the wound, and the skin puffed and puckered with slowly spreading infection.

"What is this?" I demanded.

"My doom," he sighed, and closed his eyes.

Carefully, I removed the prayer pebble from beneath my tongue and folded it into my wrapper. Then I sang, blurting out the first tune that came to mind. With the first few notes, my sight returned, and the wound festered to life. The gurgling silver sludge of despair-mold covered his arm so thickly, I could no longer see the infected stones underneath.

"Some say a god is made and remade, praise the maker!
Some say a god is born. Tell me where! Praise the mother . . ."

I balled the washcloth and passed it over his skin.

He stiffened—but his eyes remained closed, and as I wiped and dipped, rung and re-rung the scalding cloth, he did not make a sound. The mold began to melt away, receding in sheets from his inflamed skin.

"Tell me your name, hungry god, deathless oga . . ."

I could see the stones again but sensed with a chill that any attempt to remove them would be fruitless. Instead, I covered the wound with honey, willing the poison of despair to stay away for as long as possible.

"Tell me your name, or I'll pick it for, pick it for you."

I held out the last note, pressing his arm with both palms. He had relaxed, leaning into my touch, though by now my task had so absorbed me, I barely noticed. I have always found cleaning gratifying. I attacked dust and grime with more ferocity than I had ever shown another human being. In a world ruled by dirt and decay, a well-swept corner felt like rebellion.

Then the song finished, and I remembered that I held a god. I shuddered and pushed him away, shaken from a dream.

"All finished," I said, breathing hard as I replaced the prayer pebble beneath my tongue.

Slowly, he stood and flexed the rippling muscles of his arm, blinked, and then stared down at me, expression unreadable.

"It will not last more than a few days, but it should hurt less," I babbled. "That is all curse-eating is, really. Not healing, just . . . a chance at more time. I hope it is what you were looking for. You were not expecting—"

"I can't tell you," he whispered.

"Oga?"

"Your song. You said I should tell you my name, or you'll pick one for me. But I can't." He paused. "Though I would not mind a new name, I think, if you chose it."

"It didn't mean anything," I moaned. "Songs come to me when I clean. They let me see the silt—the spirit muck—but they're nonsense. Really. Ignore what I said."

He smiled, looking startlingly younger than when I had first seen him. Before I cleaned his wound, he had moved with the rigidity of iron, something I had attributed to his ancient years as a god. Now he seemed barely older than I was. The stiffness of his shoulders had not come from age but from brutal, unending pain.

"What would you have of me?" he asked, pinning me with those unreadable black eyes. "I am in your debt. I find it is a burden I do not mind."

Beneath that gaze, every coherent human thought fled from my poor Sade brain.

"I suppose . . ." I said, after regaining my senses, "I suppose this means you are not going to eat me?"

He chuckled. Then he realized I was not joking, and the good humor drained from his features.

"Is that what Ixalix said I would do?" he demanded. "Her sense of humor has always been inappropriate, but that is a line too far, even for her."

"Actually, your servant didn't tell me anything."

"What?"

"Ixalix. Your messenger." I pointed at the suddenly sheepish-looking gecko. The Crocodile's confused expression deepened.

"Ixalix," he said slowly, "is a twelve-foot-tall alagbato—the immortal guardian of a rainforest two-thousand miles from here. She is not anyone's servant, least of all mine, and she is most certainly not a lizard. That"—he pointed at the gecko— "is merely a spy. A Clay spirit who Ixalix created specifically to be my nanny. He accepts offerings on my behalf, whether I want him to or not. He does fancy himself my messenger, though he can only say the names of people he's met before."

"Small Sade," chirped the gecko.

"Helpful," the Crocodile deadpanned. "It is how I learned your name, after all." He paced, gathering his thoughts. "Sade, I am extremely confused. If Ixalix did not appear before you and tell you about my curse . . . why did you come here?"

"Because you would hunt me if I did not!" I burst out. "You think I wanted this? I was trying to find a job. To find a place to *sleep* tonight. Then along comes your gecko, drawing patterns and croaking 'Crocodile,' making it seem as though you had summoned me, and so . . ."

"And so you came? Even though you thought I'd eat you?"

I opened my mouth. Closed it. "It seemed easier," I mumbled at last. "None of the other girls got away, so why would I?"

"But they were tied up. Thrown in. You just . . . walked."

Well. It sounded foolish when he said it like that.

But it wasn't. My pulse throbbed fiercely. Any ant who lived in this world of gods and giants knew that accepting one's fate was not foolish. The cost of fighting power was to limp away in pieces.

I had tried it once.

As a much younger, much Smaller Sade, I had stood my ground and said *no* to power. It had cost my mother her place in our village. My *no* banished us both to the haunted Bush, where bad food and tainted air had stolen away my mother's life.

My *no* had killed her.

"I am not sure I believe you," the Crocodile said evenly. "If you didn't want to come here, why would you bond our souls?"

I blinked in confusion. He stared into the distance for a moment, balling his fist. When he opened it, the bead and coil I had given to the gecko rested in his palm.

"You gave me your hair," he said. "I assumed you did it to strengthen your power. That perhaps that link was necessary for you to heal me. But . . ." For the first time, he appeared to take in how terrified I was. "Am's Story," he breathed. "You mean to tell me it was a *mistake*?"

"Yes!" I threw up my hands. "The offering was the bead. I thought you were a stoop guardian. A minor spirit. Not . . ." I gestured at him. "Whatever you are."

"Take it back." He held out the coil-wrapped bead, a vein throbbing in his forehead. "For Am's sake, take it back!"

I did. He waited a moment . . . and then that *presence* darted through me again, an invasive consciousness.

His consciousness.

It retreated as quickly as it came.

"It didn't work," he murmured. "We're still body-bonded." His expression was stony. "I am . . . new to the rules of spirithood. I will have to consult Ixalix on what can be done. From what I've seen, these bonds are like salt dissolved in water. Possible to reverse, but not easy."

"What does that mean?" My chest began to heave. "Can you . . . can you possess me?"

He swallowed hard. "Parts of you."

"And read my thoughts?" I demanded shrilly. "Can you tell what I'm thinking right now?"

"No." He lifted his hands in placation. "I swear, Sade. And even if I could, I would not try. Look—" He pinched the bridge of his nose. "More than anything, our link means you have my attention. As long as I live, your needs will be . . . difficult for me to ignore." He paused, touching the green scales embedded in his arm. "The trouble is that I am changing into something whose attention you will not want. You call me a god, but I have not always been as I am. My power is a curse that I gave myself. And someday, it will turn me into a mindless monster from the pit of the Underworld."

CHAPTER 5

"SO," I SAID SLOWLY, "YOU WILL END UP EATING ME AF-
ter all."

"No!" he shot back, but then his expression grew uncertain. "That
is . . . *I* would never hurt you. But in a few months, perhaps a year's time,
I do not exactly know what *I* will be."

"But you will be drawn to me."

"Yes."

"And you cannot break our bond."

He smiled grimly. "I am about to spend every waking hour trying to
find out."

Before my shock could spiral into panic, a chalk line across the courtyard glowed crimson.

"Yellow Molar Door," the Crocodile observed. "Agricultural District."

A lone sandaled foot appeared on the ground, then above it, a grass-
stained pant leg. By the time I roused from shock, an entire new person
had materialized in the courtyard.

"Am's Story," the woman swore when she saw me. "Croc, did those
idiots sacrifice another girl?"

She held a bundle of wildflowers in both arms, blocking most of her
face from view until she set the blooms down with a grunt. Her ethnicity
was Songlander, and she looked to be in her early twenties. A leafy flower
crown sat atop spiky cropped hair and dipped over black half-moon eyes.
She wore the sturdy canvas clothes of a garden worker, and a faded lattice
of purple geometric patterns—or were they birthmarks?—crept across
her sweaty golden skin.

"No," she gasped, peering at me. "You're the girl from the tapestry." She grinned and whirled on the Crocodile, hands on her hips. "You said you weren't going to pursue her."

"I didn't," he replied flatly, jerking his chin at the gecko. "Someone saw the tapestries, figured out where she lived, and went on a little retrieval mission of his own."

"And? Did she fix you?" She grabbed the god's arm with a casualness that made me shudder. "Hmm. The scales are still there, but it seems less swollen now. Loads better than before." She faced me. "Nice work . . ."

"Small Sade," the gecko supplied.

"Small Sade," the woman repeated. "Well, I've no idea why you let yourself get dragged into this mess. But let me tell you, if you pull this off, a lot of powerful people will thank you. The Anointed—"

The Crocodile cleared his throat obnoxiously, and the woman rolled her eyes at him. "Right. We're pretending they don't exist. Small Sade, has he told you who he is?"

"I told her," the Crocodile cut in, "that I am a doomed fool. For the security of the Realmhood, that is all she needs to know. She should not be here, and neither should you. Ye Eun, how many times have I told you to stop using this place as your personal lodestone?"

"It was an emergency," said the woman called Ye Eun, looking unapologetic. "Dele's mother ordered some coneflowers. If I'd walked all the way from the Agricultural District, they'd have wilted."

"Impressing your girlfriend's mother is decidedly *not* an emergency. What if someone sees you leave one of my houses?"

She took a flower from her crown and bopped his nose with it. "I'll say I'm a sacrifice that you rejected. Besides, if you really hated seeing me, you'd lock the doors."

"I've considered it," the Crocodile muttered. "Of course, if I did that, they'd find another way to get rid of those girls. At least when they show up here, I can give them half a chance at life."

My heart pounded. What *had* he done with those girls? Ye Eun seemed mortal enough, and it was clear she had no fear of the Crocodile.

I began to hope that he had never eaten anyone. But none of those girls had ever been seen again. And from the eerie silence of the courtyard, the mysterious villa appeared to be empty.

I am sure you would have demanded to know the fate of those girls. You, with your brave tongue and lioness heart.

But me? I only dared say, "You are mistaken, madam. I have never sat for a portrait." When Ye Eun raised an eyebrow, I pressed, "You said you've seen me in a tapestry. But it must have been someone else. Oga Crocodile is right; I should not be here. I'm only a maid, madam. A Curse-Eater."

Her face brightened. "Are you really? What are you up to this afternoon?"

Well. Until a moment ago, I had planned to be dead.

"Finding a job," I said. "If Am wills it, madam."

She rubbed her hands conspiratorially. "Look no more, Small Sade. You're coming with me to Ileyoba: the Luxury District."

The Crocodile groaned. "Really? A job in that insufferable neighborhood? Ye Eun, you can't be serious."

"Curse-Eaters are all the rage there right now. And it's not as though she'd be happier here," Ye Eun retorted, waving up at the villa and the crocodile mask that hovered above the well. "Surrounded by creepy decorations in your haunted bachelor mansion. And Am knows you've no better job connections after vanishing from existence for nine years and then moping around for one more. Unless you plan to ask—what is it you call her?—the Boss Almighty—"

"Stop it," the Crocodile hissed. "You know I don't ask her for favors."

By *Boss Almighty*, I now assumed that the Crocodile meant the alagbato called Ixalix. It made sense. Who else could command a god?

Relief flooded my insides when he declined her assistance. I had only heard of alagbato in cookfire tales. Known to some as fairies, they were the deeply reclusive guardians of lands, rivers, and mountains and were said to be as old as the earth itself. One generally did not hear of them until some foolish group of humans polluted a lake, burned down a forest, or depleted a mine, bringing on alagbato wrath in the form of floods, earthquakes, and volcanoes.

"If you really don't like Mamadele's," Ye Eun said, considering me, "I have some connections at An-Ileyoba Palace. It's a little stuffy for my taste, but my little sister likes it well enough. The staff is very well paid—"

"No," I cut her off with alarm, and then remembered my manners. I sucked on my prayer pebble. "That is . . . I will be very happy at this Mamadele's house. I am sure of it. Please do not send me to the palace, madam. They would not like me at all."

"You find the palace distasteful?" the Crocodile asked, watching me curiously. "Why is that?"

"I've never been. Truly. It's just . . ." I swallowed a lump in my throat and tried not to think of a night festival many years ago. Faces gold with firelight, staring down at me with terrible beauty and benevolence as I mewled:

I don't want to.

"I do not wish to see the Anointed Ones," I said simply.

Ye Eun laughed. "Do you know how big An-Ileyoba Palace is? It's practically its own town. You'd be lucky to see an Anointed One after working there a whole year. Besides, after the Raybearers dismantled the imperial monarchy, they opened most of the palace to the public. It's mostly community buildings now. Teaching hospitals, meditation gardens. Even soup kitchens." When my face remained stony, Ye Eun shrugged. "All right then. Mamadele's it is."

I collected my broom and cane, and she heaved the flower bundles back into her arms. Before leaving, Ye Eun sniffed the air, searching the courtyard suspiciously. When she noticed the slightly shimmering earthenware mug, she shot a look at the Crocodile.

"Did you use Pale Arts again?" she demanded. "After everything Ixalix said? You know using magic makes your curse work faster."

"Sade was thirsty," the Crocodile said, rubbing the back of his neck. "And I wanted her to like me."

Ye Eun groaned in exasperation, then waved for me to join her by a third chalk line. Like the first, this line had a tooth in its center, though this one glinted with a jagged chip. I shivered.

Had it once belonged to a girl?

Ye Eun stepped over the line, vanishing into the golden courtyard air.

Before I stepped, I looked back over my shoulder but did not raise my eyes from the ground.

"Goodbye, oga," I said.

"Try again." His voice murmured across the courtyard. "Useless and muddy, remember?"

"Goodbye . . . Crocodile." I dared steal a peek. He was holding the mug he had made for me and lifted it in a toast.

"To Sade," he said. "The girl with worlds on her skin."

With a gasp, I stepped over the chalk.

My vision plunged into shadow. I was in the shrine house again—back in the inky box room. This time I faced a door, its edges rimmed in sunlight.

"Get out of there," Ye Eun's voice floated in from outside. "Quick! While no one's watching the shrine."

I burst through the door, breathing hard.

There lay the cold white landing and the shrine steps, just as before. But everything else looked different. Over the high house fence, instead of the scrap-ridden alley of the Academy District, I made out a broad, quiet cul-de-sac, lined with manicured palms and marble public squares. The air smelled like nothing, which of course meant wealth: palanquins instead of pack mules mucking up the streets, and an army of servants to keep the gutters clean. Even the shrine step offerings hinted at luxury: piles of fried plantain instead of meager bowls of rice, and silver kirah and ai-ling coins instead of copper kamerons and zathulus.

"Come on," Ye Eun goaded, shifting the flower bundle to one hip and tucking my arm in hers as we hurried from the shrine. "Easy breaths now. You look like you've just seen a demon!" She chortled to herself. "Though I guess in a way, you have."

"What is he?" I whispered. "The Crocodile? And how do you know him?"

Ye Eun chewed her lip, shooting a conspiratorial look at me. "I'm not allowed to say everything. *Security of the Realmhood*, and all that. But I'll say this: Croc hasn't been a house-conjuring wonderworker for very long. I knew him when I was a child. He was your age then, or a few years older, and completely human—except for that reckless experiment he did with his arm. Then he was murdered."

Shock made me lose my balance, striking my cane on a strip of uneven cobblestone. "Then he is a shade?" I breathed. "An undead spirit?"

"We thought he was murdered," Ye Eun amended. "Apparently, those enchanted stones wouldn't let him die. They sent him somewhere—out of Aritsar, out of time itself, who in Am's name knows? But he was gone for nine years. Then *splat!* A year ago he appears again, face down in the mud of some distant realm, exactly the same age as when he disappeared. In his mind, no time had passed at all. He was still alive. Still eighteen years old. But the world he knew had aged without him. We were all grown up, thriving in the new Arit Realmhood. And he was still a child, bloody from the end of an empire."

We were all grown up. Perhaps she and the Crocodile had belonged to some sort of sorcerer's cult. While Ye Eun appeared ordinary enough, except for her birthmarks, the Crocodile's arm was a clear sign of Pale Arts—Underworld magic, which was strictly illegal. That would explain the threat to Realmhood security.

"He is going to eat me, you know," I said.

She chortled, not pausing in her stride. "What in Am's name do you mean?" But when I explained about the body-bond, she stumbled, frowning. "You mean when Croc goes full lizard beast, he's dragging you along with him?"

My shoulders hunched. "It is not his fault. My bead—"

"Of course it's his fault!" Ye Eun howled. "This is what happens when you enchant yourself immortal instead of dealing with your trauma like a normal person. Twelve *Realms*, Croc. As if that wretched curse wasn't complicated enough. Well, I expect he'll ask that swamp alagbato for help. If anyone can break your bond, she can."

"He called me something strange," I said. "'The girl with worlds on her skin.'"

"Did he now?" Ye Eun's frown lifted into a smirk. "Interesting. He said the same thing when he saw your tapestry."

If Ye Eun and the Crocodile belonged to some Pale Arts cult, perhaps there *was* a tapestry of me somewhere, conjured for some reason I could not even begin to guess. Was my image hung alongside portraits of other girls—girls whose teeth the Crocodile found attractive?

"What did he mean by it?" I asked, my shoulders sprouting with goosebumps.

"Well . . ." Ye Eun nudged my dappled arm. "You've seen a globe, haven't you?"

I had, once. In the brief year I'd been allowed to go to village school. A parade of majestic continents had floated across a painted blue sea. The tutor had explained that while Aritsar was made of many continents, they were each so vast and teeming with stories, they could be worlds unto themselves. My eyes fell to the milky patches shining on my arms and breastbone.

"That's what Croc sees when he looks at you. An ocean of stories. Of potential." Ye Eun smiled distantly, crinkling one of the geometric shapes on her cheek. "I had a map on my skin once too. You can barely see it now, but it told of my pain, not my potential. I much prefer the map on yours."

I was not quite sure I wanted to be an ocean of stories. Gods thrived on novelty, and so if I was to be linked with a beast-god, my salvation might lie in being as boring and unremarkable as possible. All the more reason to beg this Mamadele for a nice, lowly maid's job. What god would be drawn to the tedious activities of a scullery girl?

We passed by a long, stately avenue murmuring with fountains and glinting with statues of Enoba Kunleo the Perfect: conqueror of the continent, and first emperor of the now bygone monarchy. To my surprise, in this particular stretch of road, the sweeping *agbada* kaftans and starched *gele* headdresses typical of Ileyoba residents were scarce. Instead, bareheaded commoners picnicked on mats while their children squealed and splashed in fountains. People in plain wrappers and worn aprons gathered by a pedestal, where a robed scholar gave a lecture. Wet laundry hung from the Enoba statue's outstretched arms, and servants snored in his looming shade.

"Unity Square," Ye Eun said, when she saw me gawking. "A few months ago, it was Crown Park, and was gated off to anyone who wasn't from the neighborhood. Then the Anointed Ones declared it public property. I bet that rankled the nobles."

We turned a corner, then stopped before a building of sandstone with elegant arched windows and a fragrant rooftop garden, walls adorned with creeping green vines. Servants in starched linen wrappers waited by the latticed entryway, helping well-dressed guests down from palanquins.

"Welcome to Balogun Inn and Philosophy Salon," said Ye Eun. "Rest stop for the traveling elite." Her words were sardonic, but when she stared up at a certain blossom-framed window, her face flushed pink.

From her gardening clothes, I had thought Ye Eun to be a commoner. I must have been wrong. Only a fine-fine lady could court the daughter of a grand house like this. To my confusion, however, she bypassed the front of the house, leading the way to an enclosed yard behind. Kitchen awnings stretched out from the villa's back wall, under which servants hauled water, and meals sizzled on beds of coal. They paused their laughing chatter to greet Ye Eun and stare at me askance.

When Ye Eun approached the servant entrance, I stopped her.

"Please do not enter this way on my behalf," I said. "Go and greet your lady-maiden at the front. I will wait for you here."

When I said *your lady-maiden*, the kitchen maids burst into hoots and whistles, wiggling their eyebrows at Ye Eun.

She reddened, stifling a smile as she shushed them. Then she turned sheepishly to me.

"A detail," she said. "Mamadele doesn't exactly . . . know about Dele and I. We will tell her of course. Eventually. But for now . . ." She held up the tangle of coneflowers, then reached into the air, muttering under her breath. Before my eyes, the coneflowers perked and flushed with color, solidifying my impression that she belonged to some sort of cult. At the look on my face, she laughed. "Don't worry, it isn't Pale Arts. It's called *sowanhada*—a Songlander trait, runs in my people's blood. I drew water from the air to freshen up the bouquet. After all"—she nodded at the inn door—"it's important that you and I make a *very* good impression."

CHAPTER 6

WE CREPT INTO THE VILLA. A BLOCK OF STOREROOMS HEAPED with sacks and linens led to an airy front hall. A spiraling stair curved up to more levels. Sunlight and dust motes fell in solid beams from the high unglazed windows, causing my head to spin.

Back in Dejitown, no structure stood taller than two men high, not even the sweatmill. Still, you would think I would be used to Oluwan City buildings after living for a year in the orphan high-rise. And I *was* fond of them . . . from the outside. They were brilliantly designed, each long-windowed tower bristling with porcupine-like wooden rods that caught the wind, forcing air into the building and cooling each floor. The towers reminded me of whitewashed mountains, lifting in a great jagged crown to the sky.

But inside the giant structures, my stomach churned. When I first arrived in the city and learned that some high-rises had six floors—six, more than a *hand* of fingers!—and that they expected me to live in one . . . I had nearly run straight back to the haunted Bush.

I am watching the expression on your face, and I worry that you think me ungrateful. So let me say this: The orphan high-rise provided by the Anointed Ones was much nicer than my slum in Dejitown. It was mostly roachless, and I shared my chamber with only four other girls—a boon, after sleeping back-to-back with thirty children in the sweatmill.

But every night, the ceiling closed in. I pressed my body into the straw pallet beneath me, paralyzed with fear until morning blushed through the tall slit windows.

Ordinary people, or at least Small Sades, were not meant to have sheets of rock between themselves and Am's sacred sky. For months, I was certain the stories above me would crumble, or that even my small-small weight would collapse the floor, killing my fellow edict brats in the rooms below.

But I would have to be brave at the Balogun Inn. If I couldn't bear to live here, where else could I go?

Floor cushions, dyed mats, and kneeling tables heaped with refreshments lay invitingly across the inn's front hall. But aside from the staff and a few tired-looking gentry, the Balogun Inn and Philosophy Salon appeared mostly empty. A lady in an elaborately starched gele headdress lounged on a cushion in the room's center, looking desolate as she nibbled from a bowl of dates. An old servant woman knelt blank-faced at the lady's side, fanning her with a woven palm frond.

"Isn't it sad, Simple Hanuni?" the lady moaned, glancing listlessly around the hall. "My eye for atmosphere. My tasteful decorations. My cold hard *money*. All gone to waste."

"You are hardly destitute," droned the old servant, who did not look at all simple to me. "Not yet, anyway. Calm your nerves, madam. It is like any business—the guests will come when they come."

"It's no coincidence that these rooms are empty," retorted the lady, words muffled as she sucked a date pit. "You know that as well as I do. Ever since those bleeding heart Anointed Ones opened Unity Square, nobody who is anybody will set foot on Balogun Street."

The servant Hanuni paused. "But surely you are happy, Mamadele, that the young ones have a place to play. That those with no schooling can attend the lectures, and those who walk instead of riding in palanquins have benches to sit on. The square has been good for people."

"Not my kind of people," muttered Mamadele.

When Hanuni's features tightened, the lady tittered, reaching to squeeze her servant's shoulder. "Am's Story, Simple Noonie. I keep forgetting you do not understand sarcasm. Of course the little urchins need a place for their games. Do you know how much I give to charity every year?" She waved around at the salon surroundings. "All I meant was . . . what about the rest of us? The thinkers? The jobmakers? Don't *we* deserve a place to play too?"

Then her eyes fell on me and Ye Eun.

Ye Eun jumped and cleared her throat, setting down the flowers. "Ah . . . Am bless you, madam. You wanted arrangements for the great room?"

"I didn't order flowers." The lady called Mamadele squinted at Ye Eun as though trying to read a crumpled note. "You are the woman who prunes our vines."

"That's me," Ye Eun replied, her voice a note too high. "I also run a business, like you. We've met before? A few times now, actually . . ."

Mamadele looked blank. Ye Eun hurried on.

"Rumor has it you're in need of some fresh accents, something to lure people into the salon. So when I received these rare imported cuttings at my store in the Ilemalu District, I thought, who better to appreciate them than Mamadele of Balogun Inn? Your taste is famous, and we industry women must stick together, you know . . ."

"I'm not paying for them," Mamadele said.

"Of course not." Ye Eun's smile wavered. "They're a gift."

Mamadele's expression softened, considering the blooms in a new light. "I could see them in the archway. Perhaps by the celadon vase." She stood to examine the flowers more closely, then waved her fingers for Hanuni to fetch them. "Very well then, gardener girl. You have my thanks."

"Ye Eun," said Ye Eun, but Mamadele wasn't listening anymore. She had turned her attention on me, brow wrinkling with alarm.

"And what exactly," asked the lady, "are you?"

Even with the frown, Mamadele looked winsome, even sweet. Her polished brown skin, glossed lips, and heart-shaped face would have stunned the Small Sade of this morning into admiring silence.

But this Small Sade had just spent an hour scraping despair-mold from a deathless sorcerer god.

"I am Small Sade from the orphan house," I said firmly, meeting her eye. "Ileyimo District. Am bless you, madam. I am here to be your maid."

"Your curse-eating maid," Ye Eun added, and Mamadele's expression changed from alarm to curiosity.

"Praise the Anointed Ones! I was just telling my daughter that this salon needs a hook. Something we have that nobody else does . . . at least, not in the city. In the countryside, lords and ladies keep curse-eating girls on retainer." She peered down at me. "How did you know I'd be interested?"

When Mamadele mentioned her daughter, Ye Eun stiffened. I jumped in to save her.

"Because you are a thinker," I said, leaping onto her word from earlier. "Everyone knows it, madam, especially Madam Ye Eun. She could have kept me for herself, but she is so generous. She said, 'Why work for me when you could have a mistress as kind and successful as Mamadele Balogun?'"

Ye Eun stared at me, grateful but clearly surprised. She should not have been. Gutter girls are very good at lying to wealthy people, and I was no exception.

"You have the right look for it," Mamadele said, scrutinizing me. "That's rare, I've found. Some people trying to pass themselves off as Curse-Eaters don't look unlucky at all. One girl I interviewed was even *pretty*, for Am's sake. You are . . ." She eyed me up and down, her gele headdress bobbing with approval. "Much more suitable."

"I have been told so, madam."

"Don't lose hope," Mamadele said quickly, reaching out to give my cheek a pitying pat. "You'll get handsome one day. Some girls are late bloomers."

"Not me," I said, trying not to laugh. "Do not worry. My bad-luck face is guaranteed."

Relief washed over Mamadele's features, though she had the decency to try to hide it. "Let's see it then," she gushed, bangles jingling on her tapered arms. "Do you see curses in this room? Can you eat them right now?"

"No," I said, taken aback. Immediately, I regretted telling her the truth. Perhaps it would have been better to put on a quick but convincing show, waving my arms and rambling like old Popo. If I fooled her with fake curse-eating, then I would never have to use my true gift. And if I never used my gift, any gods stalking me would soon grow bored, as there was nothing interesting about a scullery maid babbling nonsense.

But if Mamadele was not fooled, I would not get the job at all. If she had interviewed Curse-Eaters before me, she had seen false performances already and might recognize mine.

I had come to Oluwan City for a place, not a performance. So I would convince her I was worth keeping.

"I have to sing," I explained. "And you'd see the results sooner if I started on a smaller room."

"Very well." She floated across the room and was halfway up the mud-stone spiral staircase before I reached the bottom. Ye Eun and I followed, with me bringing up the rear as I puffed up each stair with my cane. Mamadele pouted down at me from the landing above.

"Oh dear, that *is* a struggle for you, isn't it? You poor thing." She played with her bangles. "Of course, if you can't handle stairs, I can't imagine how you'll manage the rest of the job . . ."

"I can handle stairs," I said grimly and marched the remaining steps, shoving down both the ache in my foot and my fear of multistory buildings.

"How old are you, anyway?" Mamadele asked as she bustled down a hallway. "You're wise around the mouth but very small. Should you be working? Didn't the Anointed Ones pass a law protecting babes like you?"

"I am seventeen, madam. That is when we leave the orphanage."

"Orphanage?" Her eyes widened with a little gasp. "I didn't know we still had those. These days, one can barely hold a salon without some couple being fawned over for *opening up their homes* and *rescuing an angel.* Ever since that Lonesome Child Edict rolled out, foster care has been all the rage."

"Some of us were not taken into homes, madam." Some of us, I thought, sucking my prayer pebble, were not the kind of children adults could show off to their friends. Children like me and Beauty Bisi, left behind in the shelter high-rises, were said to be the unfortunate ones. But sometimes I wondered about the others. What happened when they tired of being a rescued angel and wished simply to be a human child?

But that was ungrateful, I chided myself. What right had Small Sades of the world to look down on the kindness of their betters? Of people who could read and write and sit around inventing words like *edict* and *administration* and *foster care*. Words that could change the life of a village girl with one stroke of a pen?

Remember your place, I thought. *Remember what happens when you don't.*

Doubts and questions belong back in the countryside, along with fleas, and hunger, and dead mothers.

"Fostering is of course very noble, if you don't have any children of your own," Mamadele said, as though I had not spoken. We had stopped in the hallway and now stood before a door. "But Am knows I've got my hands full with this one."

Then she threw aside the thick embroidered doorflaps, revealing the most colorful chamber I had ever seen. At its base, the room was draped in the same pale gold linen as the rest of the inn. But here, floral embroidery covered every inch of the fabric. Tangles of milkweed, lilies, and blooming kuso-kuso climbed the curtains in rainbow threads. Daisies dotted the floor mats, while primrose and pink clover choked the bedclothes in joyful thread graffiti. Even the mosquito canopy, hanging in frothy netting from the ceiling, winked with saturated violets and cheeky birds of paradise.

In the middle of it all, a young woman stood poised to climb out of the room's single window.

"Mother," she screeched, eyes growing wide. "How polite of you to barge in. Weren't you just doing the inventory with Hanuni?"

I felt Ye Eun's breath catch at the sight of her. The woman was a younger, plumper version of Mamadele, though she radiated cunning instead of her mother's practiced naivete. Hair floated about her in a shining black haze of coils. A pink silk wrapper embellished with sunflowers hugged her figure, and a belt of half-finished embroidery hoops rattled at her waist. One elegant sandaled food rested on the windowsill, and a knotted sheet rope lay slack in her hands.

"I could just as easily ask," Mamadele cooed through gritted teeth, "why you are scaling the walls like a demented reptile, when there are perfectly good stairs outside your door."

Dele shot a significant look at Ye Eun, whose face flushed.

When we arrived at the landing, I had caught Ye Eun eyeing a second set of stairs. Ah. So these two were supposed to have met in the rooftop garden. I noticed then that in addition to the threaded flora, potted plants and vases of blossoms rested on every surface in Dele's room. Excuses, I gathered, to visit a certain florist stall in Ilemalu District.

"I'll board the window," Mamadele said quietly.

"I'll scream and scare the customers," Dele replied, just as calm.

They smiled at each other, freezing the air in a stalemate until I tapped my cane on the doorframe, clearing my throat.

"Is . . . is this the room I am to clean, ma?" I asked.

"Immediately," said Mamadele, ignoring Dele's scoffs of protest. "If any room in this house is riddled with curses, it's this one. How does it work? Do you need a drum, or music?"

"Only my voice, madam. And it is just an inspection for now. After that, I will need cleaning supplies."

"A Curse-Eater, Mother?" Dele laughed bitterly, plopping down on the silk-swathed bed platform. "Really?"

"Not just for you," Mamadele retorted, looking a little defensive. "She's for the inn. If she passes probation, we can rebrand the villa, offering curse-cleaned rooms as a service. As usual, I am thinking of your future. I am working to keep this family off the streets."

Dele's gaze slid resentfully to me but softened when she noticed Ye Eun's hand on my shoulder.

Please, Ye Eun mouthed.

Dele raised her eyebrows but then shrugged and unhooked an embroidery hoop from her belt, whipping out a needle and stabbing the cloth with cheery aggression. "I'll just sit here for my exorcism, shall I?"

When they all stared at me, I gulped, brandished my short hand broom, and dragged it around the room's perimeter. It strained my back and had taken a while for me to master, but I was adept at leaning weight against my cane in one hand while bending to sweep the floor with the other. A song lifted from my lungs, mingling with the dust.

> *"Mother, may I burn the garden?*
> *Father, may I cut the roots?*
> *Shall I salt the seeds you planted?*
> *Sha, sha, sha!"*

The level of spirit silt stunned me: an ankle-high pool of glowing muck that covered the chamber floor.

> *"Mother, is this spade my virtue?*
> *Father, is this rake my worth?*
> *Shall I blunt the tools you sharpened?*
> *Kraa, kraa, kraa."*

The disappointed hopes that Mamadele had pinned to her daughter grew like silver mold up Dele's walls, shedding spores that floated in the air, revealing Dele's lovely room to be a suffocating den of pollen.

I steeled my face into a calm mask. It would not help to seem overwhelmed.

"Well?" Mamadele asked, sweeping a slender hand. I could tell she took pride in the bedchamber. I wondered how many times she had trudged through the spirit silt to arrange Dele's furniture and plump her velvet cushions, unconscious of the sloshing swamp around her. "How long do you need? I know it doesn't *look* particularly cursed, but at this point . . . I'll take any help I can get."

I inhaled sharply. The floor alone would take days to drain and resurface. As for the plaster damage on the walls, and the grief-gnats infesting the drapery . . .

"A month," I admitted, wincing as I said it.

"Ah-ah!" Mamadele exclaimed. "She is really joking now. One whole month, for one mere trial?"

"I can do regular scullery too," I said quickly. "To earn my keep. And you would barely have to pay me anything! A kirah a week." When Mamadele frowned, I forced myself to stand tall, squaring my chest.

"I am the best you will find, ma. The only true Curse-Eater in Oluwan City."

And that, as far as I knew it, was the absolute truth.

"Show me your hands," Mamadele commanded, and I set down my broom and cane to offer them.

She held my rough fingers in her manicured ones, hemming at my calluses. "You're not lazy, at least," she mused. "Well then, listen closely: You can sleep in the garret with the other maids. You'll spend the mornings on Dele's room, and the evenings on whatever tasks Simple Hanuni gives you. No days off. And a kirah every two weeks, not one."

My heart leapt to the ceiling. "Oh, thank you, ma! I swear on the Anointed Ones, you will not regret—"

"But for such a fee," she continued, "I expect an *extremely* lucky house. If you want a permanent place in this house, Small Sade, then by the end of this month . . ." She flicked a stray piece of date from her teeth. "The inn will be full of guests, and Dele will be engaged to a man."

CHAPTER 7

"DON'T PANIC," YE EUN WHISPERED IN MY EAR BEFORE SHE left the inn, and that night as I followed Hanuni to be fitted for my servant livery, I tried to follow Ye Eun's advice.

My bowels twisted all the same. Mamadele's first request—to fill the inn with the guests—would be difficult enough. Still, there were things I could do. Cut down on spirit silt in the front great room, perhaps, so the inn as a whole felt more inviting. Offer my curse-eating services to passersby in Balogun Street, provided they stay a night at the inn.

But the second request was impossible. Even if Dele was interested in men as well as women, she was clearly in love with Ye Eun. What was more, the only curse in Dele's room was her mother's disappointment.

If anything, cleaning the silt in Dele's room would make her *more* likely to run off with Ye Eun, not less.

"Don't panic," I muttered to myself. Maybe I could sneak a cleaning of Mamadele's room. I was sure it crawled with silt, like everywhere else in the inn. If Mamadele felt better about her own life, even temporarily, maybe she would be less eager to change her daughter's.

The long-gabled storeroom clearly served as a watering hole for the inn staff. After hearing Dele's outburst at her mother's declaration, the servants must have gathered to gossip, because when I walked in, four heads turned to gawk at me.

"I see you are all hard at work," droned Hanuni, who I had since learned was the inn stewardess and former nurse to both Dele and her mother. Her voice was stern, but amusement danced across her features as the staff barraged her with questions.

"Is it true, Hanuni?" chirped one girl over the rest. She twirled with a sheet, nearly upending a basket of clean folded linens. "Is Dele really getting married?"

"She wouldn't," another girl panted. She was as grim as the first girl was bubbly, and she pounded cassava with a wooden pestle as tall as she was. "And good for her. Ileyoba men are useless."

"I'm an Ileyoba man," a pale-skinned servant in his early twenties retorted, puffing out his chest. "And I have plenty of uses."

The two girls dissolved in laughter. Hanuni said, "Now, now, girls," but her lips twitched too, and the man turned bright red.

"Remind me, Finnric," said the pestle girl, "just how long ago you were shoveling sheep dung in the sunless northern realms. One year? Two?"

"If working at an inn makes you an *Ileyoba* man," said the twirling girl, crowning herself with a bucket, "then as head laundress, I am practically an Anointed One."

At her last words, an old Oluwani man who lay snoring against a cupboard lurched awake. "Eh? Anointed? Praise the Idajo," he blurted, dropping something he had cradled to his chest. The object, an effigy, skittered across the floor and glinted in the light: a woman carved from dark polished wood, crowned with a blazing disc of gold.

"Oh. Oh, no," he gasped, and scrambled to retrieve it.

"See what your teasing has done, girls?" scolded Hanuni. "Now you've gone and set off Onijibola."

The old man kissed the effigy and clutched it with both hands, rocking as he whispered in prayer. "Forgive me Idajo, woman-born and spirit-sired, Empress Redemptor and Raybearer undying; holy is she who fought death in the Underworld, and blessed is her right hand, Ekundayo, and righteous are her Anointed Ones, so forgive me, Idajo, woman-born and—"

Hanuni left my side to squeeze his shoulder, and he trailed off, still rocking. I froze in fear. The only people who scared me more than the Anointed Ones were the cultists who worshipped them. My shoulders eased a little, though, when I counted his fingers and found ten. He was devout, but not a fanatic.

True members of the Cult of the Empress, as you may know, amputated half the index finger of their left hand. I had seen them in the streets, holding up mutilated hands that they had gilded and painted with henna. They beamed as they sang of their "Idajo" and how she had descended to the Underworld, losing a finger as she defeated the armies of the dead.

"You will have plenty of time to praise the Idajo after we welcome Madam's new trial hire," Hanuni told Onijibola, who continued to clutch the effigy. "Everyone—meet Small Sade. She will be curse-eating for Madam."

"Mamadele finally hired one, huh? Kanwal," said the pestle girl by way of introduction, wiping her hands on her wrapper and nodding once at me. Her warm-toned features and musical accent revealed her to be from Dhyrma, a realm lying far-far, somewhere south of Oluwan. She pointed at the other girl. "And that's my sister, Wafa. We help Onijibola run the kitchen. We also do everything else, when Finnric can't be bothered."

"Do you sing, Small Sade?" Wafa gushed, dropping the sheet to come and clasp my hand. "I hope so. They say Curse-Eaters have Hallowed voices. Or maybe you're the kind who only yells and dances around. That's all right. It's all a show, isn't it? I'm a dancer myself, and I love a good—"

"Should you be touching her?" interrupted the Mewish man named Finnric, eyeing me warily. "What if whatever she's got is contagious?"

"Don't mind him," Wafa told me, sucking her teeth at Finnric. "He only trusts rich people. Besides, Madam would not have hired you if you were dangerous."

"She's bad luck," Finnric protested. "Isn't that the point of Curse-Eaters?"

"The point of Curse-Eaters," sighed Hanuni, "is to help the comfortable continue to feel comfortable. Now stop the chatter, all of you, and fit Small Sade with a maid's kit."

Kanwal demanded, "Have you eaten?" and I shook my head. Without a further word, she disappeared outside to the courtyard, where I heard pots of stew bubbling on the coals. I cringed when Onijibola came near, but he only helped Hanuni show me where to find rags and cleaning supplies. I noticed that his fingers were gnarled and swollen. His hands resembled my foot, after a day of labor. I wondered if they had always been that way, or if Onijibola had met with misfortune like me. When his eyes met mine, we shared a jolt of kinship. We both of us fought to work in a world not built for our bodies.

Wafa presented me with a neatly folded wrapper, pale gold to match the rest of the staff.

"You might have to soil it," Wafa said apologetically, and I winced, realizing what she meant.

Patrons preferred their Curse-Eaters to look the part, as if it might enhance their unluckiness. Not truly dirty, mind you, but with stained clothes and mud-matted hair, and perhaps a pathetic swipe of soot on one cheek, like an orphan in a morality play.

I lifted my chin defiantly, putting the new wrapper on over my old one. "I don't like stains," I said, smoothing out the wrinkles. "This will do as it is."

Mamasade had loved cleanliness. Even when we lived in a cave, the dirt floor was swept and packed with rushes, our shifts scrubbed with plantain ash and rinsed in a stream. When it came to curse-eating, hygiene was bad for business, but that was one practicality I could never bring myself to accept.

When Wafa offered a bucket of cool rosemary water, I accepted eagerly, washing the sweat from beneath my arms and the dust from my soles. I always kept the front half of my injured foot wrapped in a thick cloth bandage, which served as a cushion before I jammed on my sandals. When I removed the bandage to wash, Wafa snuck a curious glance.

While the pain of my injury had improved over the years, its appearance had not. The trouble was, after the accident, my foot had still tried bravely to grow. The result was an array of stretched skin and puckered scars. My two smallest toes had needed to be amputated, while the remaining three splayed in different directions. The absent toes caused me to balance on my heel and inner arch, and so both places had sprouted thick, ashen calluses.

No serving girls had pretty feet. Still, for years after the accident, the sight of my injury had filled me with shame. I would fantasize about the foot disappearing completely, as though I walked on air, or imagine falling asleep and waking to a brand-new body part, royal brown and sleek with muscle, crowned in a fan of five plump toes.

But as time passed, I grew fond of my stubborn, lumpy companion. It had gotten me this far, after all, swelling and bristling and knitting itself together, fighting to remain a *foot*, no matter how motley its parts.

Wafa shyly offered me a fresh bandage to replace the old. I thanked her and washed as though the earlier part of the day—the Ileyimo market, the gecko, the Crocodile—could be removed as easily as dirt. The more I stayed in that storeroom, pulse easing beneath the friendly commotion of the inn, the more my harrowing morning seemed like a dream.

You will think me foolish, but I dared hope that I would never see the Crocodile again. That perhaps he had forgotten me already, like most gods did after a mortal amused them. I could be normal—at least, as normal as a Curse-Eater could be, anyway. All I had to do was work hard and keep my head down. Remember my place. Then maybe . . . a hill formed in my throat as Wafa beckoned me to sit with her and the other servants, her large brown eyes twinkling with welcome.

Maybe I could be Sade of the Balogun Inn. Sade of Oluwan City.

Kanwal burst back into the storeroom and placed a tray on my lap. "Eat," she commanded, and I obeyed. The tray held a steaming bowl of something red and savory, topped with neatly shaped balls of cassava fufu. After removing my prayer pebble, I scooped the stew with a ball of fufu, carefully avoiding the hunks of meat, and placed it in my mouth. A moan escaped me.

"That's incredible," I murmured, scooping another helping.

"It's Kanwal stew," said Kanwal, entirely straight-faced. "Of course it's incredible."

Onijibola watched me with rheumy eyes as I continued to eat, and I tried not to cringe away from his gaze. He seemed kind enough, when he was not whispering over his effigy. Still, I jumped when he observed: "You are not eating the goat."

Everyone's attention turned suddenly on my bowl, now drained of stew but still rattling with cubes of brown meat.

"You need not worry that it will make you sick," said Onijibola. "All meat that Finnric brings from the market, I bless with the eye of the Idajo."

"It is not that," I said, wiping my mouth and stealing an apologetic look at Kanwal. "It is only . . . I am of the Clay. People who worship the Goddess of Earth do not eat land animals."

Kanwal shrugged. "You should have said," she reprimanded kindly. "Hanuni is of the Well. Her people eat everything with fish. Next time, I'll dish up something for you both."

"I've never met a Clay person before," Wafa mused, resting her chin on her hands. "You're mostly farmers and country folk, right? Kanwal and I were raised Well and Ember, like most in the city, though I've considered converting faiths. The Goddess of Earth sounds a lot friendlier than King Water or Warlord Fire."

"That's backward," Finnric snorted. Apparently having overcome his fear of my spirit marks, he leaned over me, helping himself to the meat in my bowl. "You listen to me, Small Sade. Wafa's got it all wrong. I was like you once—a country bumpkin. A mud-worshipping peasant of the Clay. But once I set foot in this city, I left all that behind. Earth dries up, water floods. But you can always rely on the fruits of the forge. All hail Warlord Fire!" He lifted a pendant from beneath his tunic: a bright golden coin, suspended around his neck from a piece of twine.

I gaped, impressed. "Is . . . is that a taridayo coin?"

"It's fake," Hanuni droned, before Finnric could answer. "If it was real, he wouldn't be here, scrubbing floors for kirahs and zathulus like us."

"I'll get a real one someday," Finnric shot back, nibbling sulkily from my bowl. "I'm not like the rest of you. I'm willing to work hard. To grind. To—"

"*Pull myself out of here by my own sandal straps*," Wafa and Kanwal finished with him in a high-pitched singsong, pealing with laughter, and I covered my mouth to stifle a giggle.

"Oh, Finnric," Wafa cooed as the Mewish man turned red again. She patted his knee. "Don't mind us. I'm sure someday you'll make a very nice, very handsome slumlord. But for now, you are an Amenity just like us. So why not embrace it?"

"Amenity?" I echoed, and Wafa clapped her hands.

"Right, you don't know yet! Hanuni, is it too soon to make Small Sade choose a name?"

Hanuni pinched her nose bridge. "Must we drag her into our nonsense this early?"

"It's not nonsense," Kanwal said, flipping her thick, shiny braid. "It's *us*. A Balogun Inn staff tradition."

"Amenities," Wafa explained, "are objects an inn takes for granted but could never go without." She swept a grand curtsy. "My Amenity name, for example, is Feather Pillow."

"Breakfast Tray," Kanwal said, tapping her chest.

"Bathwater," Finnric said with a mocking bow.

"Chamber Pot," wheezed Onijibola.

They all looked expectantly at Hanuni, who rolled her eyes but smiled and said at last: "Baby Rattle."

"Because," Wafa explained in a stage whisper, "she's been quelling tantrums from Mamadele and her daughter since both of them were born."

"You do not have to pick a name now," Onijibola told me, his lined face twinkling. "Take your time. It is a big decision."

"She can't pick it now," objected Finnric. "In a month, she might not even be here."

Out of all the jabs thrown my way today, this was the only one that stuck. Because as I sat cross-legged in that storeroom among the barrels and herb-scented linens, watching the Amenities banter with my feet freshly washed and my belly full of Kanwal stew . . . a terrifying thought occurred to me, making me gnaw my prayer pebble for comfort.

I loved it here already.

And the only thing worse than living nowhere at all was to love somewhere—to *fit* somewhere—and then, after trying your very hardest . . . lose it forever.

CHAPTER 8

THE MOON CAST A SOLID WEDGE ON THE FLOOR OF THE SER-
vants' garret where I lay on a sleeping mat beside Wafa and Kanwal. In the
rooms on either side of us, Hanuni had a chamber to herself, while Finnric
and Onijibola slept in the other.

Instead of saying good night, Wafa splayed out on her bedroll and
called into the ceiling: "Feather Pillow."

Kanwal mumbled, "Breakfast Tray," and replies echoed through the
thin walls.

"Baby Rattle."

"Chamber Pot."

"Bathwater."

An awkward silence passed. Then I peeped: "Small Sade," and five
voices cheered quietly, with Wafa rasping *"one of us, one of us,"* until my
cheeks burned happily.

"The council of Amenities has convened," Kanwal yawned. "And we've
decided that we're rooting for you, new girl. So don't screw it up." Then
she winked at me, threw an arm over her face, and dropped asleep. In
time, snores filled the garret, buzzing atop the faint roar of Oluwan City.

Until now, I had managed to forget my fear of tall buildings. But now,
as two stories creaked beneath me and a very near, very heavy roof creaked
above, my breath grew shallow.

You did not die in the orphan high-rise, I reminded myself. *You learned to
sleep there eventually.*

*But what if that giant building was the only safe giant building in the entire
world?* Fear asked. *What if this one is nothing but a huge, teetering mistake?*

That is foolish, I said.

Unless you die, Fear replied reasonably.

I twisted beneath my mosquito net until my sleeping scarf came undone. My beaded cornrows pressed onto the mat, now unprotected and drenched in sweat. It grew so late that the moon changed places, and the chorus of cicadas quieted. I had just begun to resign myself to starting my first day at the Balogun Inn on a night of no sleep when something skittered by my ear.

At first I batted it away without looking. Roaches were common enough in any servants' quarters, after all, and impossible to find in the dark. I would ask Hanuni if I could put out traps tomorrow.

Then a tiny tongue flicked against my ear, and a high voice croaked: "*Crocodile.*"

"Oh no," I moaned and shut my eyes tight, ignoring the gecko.

You are dreaming, I told myself as my palms beaded with sweat. *There is no spirit gecko. There is only Wafa, and Kanwal, and me, and . . .*

. . . and I was hovering in midair.

I whirled to look beneath me, just in time to see the messenger gecko disappear. My limbs flailed but struck only the mosquito net, as my bedroll was now several inches below. I jammed my fists into my mouth to keep from screaming. This was only a dream. Besides, if I woke the entire house on my first night, I would be fired for certain.

A force pulled me to the window, bouncing me like a leaf on a breeze, and expertly turning my body so no part of me struck the sill as I passed through.

A low wail escaped me as I hovered above the deserted courtyard. The force pinned my hips to the cold stone wall of the inn, holding me upright. Then a figure descended before me, locs floating around his face in a shadowy halo.

"You cannot sleep," observed the Crocodile. Irritation pooled in circles beneath his black eyes. "Therefore, I cannot sleep."

"Ah," I squeaked, my throat dry. "Sorry."

I had not made it all up, then. The previous morning, the shrine, the bond that linked my body with his . . . it had all been real.

I spread my hands. "I did not mean to keep you up, oga. I promise I will not make it a habit. Only I have a lot on my mind."

"Care to share?" He sounded as though we stood chatting in a corridor, instead of dangling three stories above the ground. The absurdity of it all made me strangely calm.

"Well, there's curse-eating," I said. "And impressing Mamadele, so I do not get fired. And . . . *you*, for Am's sake."

Wondering how long I have until you take my teeth and then eat me.

"Ah." He peered past me into the garret, nose wrinkling with distaste. "Is that your bed? No wonder you've been thrashing all night. I can make you a new one, if you like."

"It is not the bedroll," I shot back. "It is the inn. Multiple floors. I do not do well beneath ceilings."

He lifted me from the wall. We floated to land lightly in the rooftop garden, his invisible power arranging us side by side on the terrace. The perfume of night-blooming jasmine and lemongrass wafted around us. Beneath my head, a tangle of soft ferns grew in seconds, curling themselves into a pillow that nestled my neck.

Despite everything, my body relaxed. With soft leaves beneath me and the sky above, I could have been stargazing with my mother again, outside our cave in the Bush.

"Better?" he asked. Moonlight bathed his broad chest and shoulders, lending a blue glow to his scarred black skin.

"Yes, but . . ." I swallowed hard. Was I really about to scold a god? "You will become a beast even faster now. Ye Eun said casting enchantments will speed up your curse, and here you are flying over buildings and making pillows."

"I had no choice," he insisted, flopping onto his back. "When it comes to curses, the only accelerant stronger than magic is madness. And if I had felt you twist and turn for one more hour . . . I would have gone insane."

"I cannot sleep here," I pointed out, though thanks to that cushion of ferns, my lids had already begun to droop. "If I am not in the garret tomorrow morning, the others will be suspicious. Besides, you will take my teeth when I nod off."

Exhaustion had betrayed me. I had not meant to say that last part. But before I could take it back, he propped himself up on his side, gazing down on me with interest.

"That's a new one," he said. His eyes danced. "Is that the latest crime the gossips have laid at my door? Tooth Burglar, in addition to Cannibal of Maidens?"

I scowled, curling my knees to my chest and tucking my head to shield my mouth. "If you did not eat those girls," I demanded, "then what happened to them?"

"They left." The levity drained from his features. "You have my word, Sade. Every time a girl stumbled through those doors, I cut their bindings and they left. Some stayed for a while. But in the end, they always picked a door." He hesitated. "I . . . changed their features, sometimes. So they wouldn't be recognized by the people who sacrificed them. Some girls tried to return through the same door they came through, but I did not allow it. It seemed dangerous. Why return to a place that discarded you?"

"Because you have nowhere else to go," I retorted. My feelings were a confusing whirl of relief and anger. I was happy that none of the girls had been killed. Still . . . "What about their homes? Their lives, their families? How were they supposed to survive, after you changed their faces and sent them to districts where they knew no one?"

"I gave them everything I could," the Crocodile said. "Food, clothing. Whatever coins people left in front of my houses. I would have given more, but my powers don't conjure things, only move them. Lift objects, speed their growth, slow them down. Make them hotter or colder. Perform illusions."

You still should have let them choose, I thought. But the words died unsaid in my throat, evaporating into night air.

Of course the Crocodile had decided for those girls. Just like their murderous neighbors had decided for them and would continue to decide for nameless girls the whole world over. That was the way of things. I knew it, and knew better than to think my small, nobody-person rage could change it.

"I am still astounded that you walked in," he mused. "How did you even know to follow the gecko? To give it an offering?"

He spoke as though I were a clueless babe. I felt the reins of my patience slipping, so I waited a moment before answering, massaging the palm and wrist of my cane-using hand. It often ached after hours of gripping a wooden handle, and the pain did not help my mood.

"Common people," I said, "have to deal with gods all the time. Spirits often live in in-between places. Cracks, closets, shadows, and edges. The sort of places one only goes to hide or to clean. Powerful people do not visit such places, oga." I added the honorific, though I knew it would irritate him. I uncurled to sit upright, ticking off items on my fingers. "And why would they? Their linen wrappers are brought by servants in the morning. Their stew in the afternoon. Their children in the evening, after the nurse has changed their nappies and polished their heads with oil.

"But girls like me? We scrub those linens in the stream behind oga and madam's house. We tie blessing knots with our sandal laces so water imps don't drown us and steal the laundry. We mist the kitchen coals with salt water so ina sprites don't nest among them and burn the stew. When madam's infant fusses in their fine gilt cradle, we strap them to our backs and find a window facing the Bush, for nothing calms babes like the song of a haunted forest.

"So yes, oga. I walked into your shrine and made offerings to your messenger. But you need not act as though I had lost my senses. I may be common, but I am not a fool."

"No," the Crocodile murmured, with a heat that surprised me. "No. You are many things, Sade, but simple is not one of them."

I sat up then, staring at him. The anger drained away, replaced by wariness. At last I said, "Oga. I cannot figure out what you want."

"Want?" In his velvety voice, the word doubled in weight, pregnant with meaning.

I swallowed hard. "Yes." It was my experience that gods wanted one of two things: worship or amusement. Gods who were happy wanted mortals to admire them. Gods who were miserable wanted mortals to distract them.

Judging from the sheer amount of grief in the Crocodile's spirit silt, it seemed unlikely that he craved my admiration. But he had not hexed me, or sent me on a quest, or any of the other petty tortures typical of a god bored with eternity.

"If you did not want sacrifices," I asked, "why build five bone houses? You must have known it would make people worship you."

He steepled his hands. "You will laugh at me, and I will deserve it. But I actually hoped no one would notice."

"Not notice?" I exclaimed with a snort. "Not notice mansions that grew overnight?"

He frowned. "They were not supposed to grow that fast. Or look so obviously enchanted. But that is Pale Arts for you: unpredictable, and always a bit conceited. The buildings were illusions, mostly. A way to anchor my tooth portals to the savannah house. I needed a way to get around town quickly, without being seen."

When I looked suspicious, he continued carefully: "I run errands for someone. The Boss Almighty. I call her that, but she's . . . well. An old friend. And I owe her about a thousand favors, so occasionally, I act as her agent in delicate situations. Areas where she cannot publicly intervene."

So he worked for that alagbato, Ixalix. What business could a swamp guardian have in Oluwan City? I decided it was better not to ask, and instead squeaked, "Tooth portals?"

"Homegrown." He hooked his finger in his cheek, revealing the back of his mouth, and four gaping holes where his wisdom teeth would have been.

"Oh." Relief coursed through me. "Then those teeth on the ground . . . they were—"

"Mine. I use them as lodestones. So you can stop hiding that adorable mouth of yours." He flashed the remainder of his brilliant teeth, and my heart annoyed me by hammering.

The only lodestone I had ever seen was massive, a rock ten men wide outside of the city gates. I had never used one but knew that dozens lay scattered throughout Aritsar, allowing wealthy people to travel thousands of miles in the blink of an eye.

He shifted his arm cuff to reveal the veiny wound and pointed at the gray stone covered in symbols. "Do you know where lodestones come from?" he asked, and when I shook my head, he said, "Tunnels in the Underworld, hundreds of years ago. Monarchs sent mining expeditions, back when breaches in the earth connected the spirit world to the living. They used Pale Arts to connect the stones, creating a rapidly efficient, occasionally lethal way to travel across the continent."

He tapped his arm, looking coy.

"Certain . . . influential families broke chunks from the larger stones and kept them for themselves. Small pieces are not bound to specific locations. That allows for freer travel but requires a much higher dose of Pale Arts, and all the toxicity that entails. I used to travel simply by vanishing, but it's no longer safe to do so. The more I indulge in enchantments, the faster my humanity dissolves.

"When the poison spread to my bones, however, it enabled me to use my teeth as external lodestones. Stationary lodestones are less volatile than mobile ones, you see, and require less power. By removing my bones and anchoring them throughout the city, I could continue to travel while slowing down my transformation. Into . . ." He picked at the scales in his skin. "Whoever *he* is."

Quiet despair flooded his features, a feeling so familiar to me, I reached out to comfort him. The god stilled, staring at my hand on his arm.

"Perhaps it will not be so bad," I suggested. "Whatever is happening to you. In case you have not noticed, I do not look very normal either. Some people think it is a curse, but it is not. At all, really. It is only . . . different."

When he spoke again, his voice was strained. "You are very kind," he said. "But we are not the same. I am the product of my own foolish hubris. As for you, Sade . . ." He fixed me with those unreadable dark eyes, closing his hand over mine. "No sane man could see that face and think of curses."

I withdrew sharply, as though waking from a trance. "Small," I mumbled, turning my back to him.

"Beg pardon?"

I had removed my prayer pebble when I went to bed, but now I found it in my wrapper and wedged it inside my cheek. "Small Sade," I said. "That is what everyone calls me. You forgot."

"I did not forget," he replied, floating his body around mine so he faced me on the terrace again. "I disagreed."

A warmth blossomed in my chest then—one that felt dangerously like happiness. I stood in a panic. Of all the risky games this god could play with my life, the most lethal one of all was to convince me I was something I was not.

Know your place.

"I am sorry for keeping you up, oga," I said sharply, collecting the woven ball of ferns. "I would not deny you rest any longer. Thank you for the pillow. Goodnight." Then I paused. "If my feelings affect you . . . will yours affect me?"

What if his needs consumed me while I cleaned for Mamadele? Would I know if he was tired? Angry, bored, or hungry? Did gods even get hungry?

"No." He smiled wanly. "That part of our bond is one way only."

"That hardly seems fair."

"It isn't." He hesitated, avoiding my gaze. "But not in the way you think."

He chewed his bottom lip, making me watch his mouth. I found myself wanting to touch him again.

The Crocodile stilled, glancing up. His eyes shone with amusement. When I remembered his words from the shrine, horror froze every one of my bones.

Your needs will be difficult for me to ignore.

My hands flew up to my burning face. I continued to cover my eyes as I felt him come near. Solid arms encircled my waist, and we lifted lightly from the ground.

When I dared peek again, I was back in the garret, atop my bedroll. The mosquito net hung around my body, and the gecko was nowhere to be found. My sleeping scarf, formerly lost to the darkness, had been smoothed of wrinkles, folded neatly, and placed by my head. Wafa and Kanwal snored beside me.

Could it all have been a dream? I clung to that hope like a girl drowning, and hugged my bedroll, letting all fantasies of gods and crocodiles fade into the night.

Moments before sleep took me, a lump beneath my mat made me squirm. Groggily, I reached to remove it.

A pillow of ferns splayed across the floor, leaves pale as feathers in the sinking moonlight.

PART II

CHAPTER 9

I ROSE EARLY, KNOWING IT WOULD TAKE ME A WHILE TO haul cleaning supplies up the stairs to Dele's room. My cane left only one hand available. I cleared my throat loudly outside her doorflap and fidgeted, worrying she would be unhappy to see me instead of Wafa, her usual morning attendant. Since Mamadele had assigned me the bedroom, I was also expected to take over Dele's toilette.

I called out a shy greeting, balancing a breakfast tray on my hip. There was no reply. So I crept through the embroidered flap . . . only to find Dele sprawled across the bed platform, still fast asleep. She squinted awake when I placed the tray of honeyed porridge and neatly cut orange slices on her bedside table.

"Oh," she groaned. "Have you come already to cure me?"

She sat up, and her coiling mass of hair, temporarily flattened by her silk sleeping bonnet, expanded in a haze around her plump, dark shoulders. Even groggy, lashes crusted with sleep, Dele looked lovely. Her pert, turned-up features shone in the late morning light.

"I cannot cure anything, madam," I told her, drawing aside the violet-covered mosquito canopy. "I am a maid, not a healer, and I do not think you are sick."

"No," she grumbled. "Only cursed."

"Yes," I said lightly. "Cursed with many fine-fine clothes and pretty things. I do not know how we shall keep them all clean."

She smirked. "I can see why Ye Eun likes you," Dele said, standing to stretch in a nightshift covered in creeping violets. "She always tells me I 'whine entirely too much for a girl with seasonal outfits.' I suppose she's right. What's Mother told you to do? Are you stuck with me all morning?"

"I am to help you dress," I said. Wafa had given me a rushed tutorial on being a lady's maid the night before. "And attend to your hair. But you don't have to stay while I spirit-clean." I scanned the room, remembering the grief-gnats infesting the curtains and wincing at the sheer amount of fabric swathing the furniture. It would all need to be washed and boiled. "Why don't I start on the drapes, while you visit the bathing spa?"

At the last phrase, a note of awe stole into my voice. I'd heard rumors that fancy houses in the city had miniature bathhouses in their cellars, but I had not believed it until Hanuni showed me this morning. Two tiled chambers, one for ogas and the other for madams, lay beneath the inn. In each room, a marble pool sunk into the floor, fed by gushing pipes that led to an underground reservoir. Another pair of pipes drained to the sewer, ensuring a constant flow of fresh water, a feat I had not thought possible outside of a countryside stream.

I was both relieved and saddened when Hanuni told me that the spa was for guests only, except for when servants washed the laundry. On the one hand, the idea of a daily, full-body wash instead of sponging from a bucket filled my cleanliness-loving heart with something like lust. On the other hand, an underground spa sounded suspiciously like a death trap. If the inn's many floors were to crush me, I would rather not be naked when it happened.

Dele sank onto her dressing stool, and I sectioned her hair, cleansing her scalp with tufted cotton balls and jasmine-scented vinegar.

"You're barely more than a child," she observed, grazing at her breakfast. "What a world, where people like you are sent to babysit grown women."

My fingers hesitated, confused. "Do you still want me to twist your hair, madam?"

"Yes," she admitted, and I resumed sectioning. She picked at the silky stems on her night shift. "It's only, Ye Eun told me that until yesterday, you were homeless and an orphan—"

Still an orphan, I thought wryly.

"And now the roof over your head depends on the whims of people like Mother. People like me. It just isn't fair."

Uncertain of what she wished me to say, I only smiled, coating the twists with flaxseed paste.

She continued, "We're disgraced, you know. The Baloguns. Mother tells everyone we have a large villa in the country and that we only host an inn to 'provide an intellectual hub where the cultured minds of Oluwan City may engage in a bazaar of ideas.' But everyone knows it's a lie. When I was younger, my father was a lord. For generations, our family were stewards to several quarries belonging to the imperial family."

My eyebrows rose. That explained all the marble in the spa and the shining tiles in the inn's front rooms.

"Then all that chaos happened with the emperor and empress deciding they no longer wanted their imperial titles. That they only wished to lead the Realmhood as Raybearers. And when they disbanded the monarchy, ceding their quarries to the people . . . well. My father *intellectually* disagreed. He tried to seize some of the quarries, claiming they'd belonged to us all along. The workers weren't too happy about that. Apparently over the years, the Baloguns were less 'stewards' of the quarries and more 'slave drivers.' So they ran us out of the countryside, and the Raybearers stripped my family of our titles, as well as of our ancestral lands. The only property we had left was this house in the city. Father died soon after, of shame, they say. But Mother never quite accepted what happened. To her, this inn is our key back to high society. Of course, thanks to our disgrace, the truly influential of Oluwan City would never darken our door. But she thinks that can change. She thinks . . . *you* can change it." She winced at me. "No pressure."

"The flaxseed paste in these twists should be dry in a few hours," I squeaked, wrapping her head in a bright yellow scarf. "Then you can wear your hair out, the way you like. Your curl pattern will look so very nice, madam."

"Thank you. And . . . I don't know. Sorry, I guess. For all of this." She pulled on an airy robe to cover her nightshift and made to leave for the spa. I began collecting my cleaning supplies to start on her room. But she stopped at the door. Her brow wrinkled in worry. "This curse-eating business . . . it's all a show, right? If you clean my room, you can't really change how I feel, or what—or *who*—I want. Right?"

I inhaled. "It is . . . complicated, madam." I cast about for the right words, then settled on her breakfast. "Spirit-cleaning is like this," I said, retrieving a square of linen from beside her porridge bowl. "You see this as a napkin because Kanwal placed it on the tray, and you are unlikely to use it as anything else. But if I wash it and place it with your hair linens . . ."

Shyly, I halved the napkin into a triangle and tied it around my head like a kerchief. Dele giggled.

"You will see this napkin as another object entirely," I explained. "You'll start wearing it every day. Or . . . you won't. Perhaps, no matter how soft and pretty this cloth is, you do not *need* a hair accessory. You need something to wipe your face. And so it does not matter if I clean it, or if I press it with rosewater, or trim it with ribbons." I placed the cloth back on her breakfast tray, giving her a reassuring smile. "The napkin will always be a napkin. Because that, madam, is what you need it to be."

Dele's features softened in relief, then sparked with determination. "Then I'll help you," she said, rolling up the sleeves of her robe.

"Sorry?"

"I'm not like my mother," she insisted, almost to herself. "I don't think I'm better than you just because you're my maid. So tell me what to do."

A sense of unease rose in my belly. She would not truly help, of course. She could not see spirit silt, and from the sight of her manicured fingers, I would be surprised if she knew how to hold a broom. What was more, if Dele amused herself by scrubbing floors, Mamadele could find out and blame me, thinking her daughter more cursed than ever.

Now, what I am about to say may make you uncomfortable. But when speaking with wealthy people—even kind ones like yourself—it is safest for poor people to have a strategy. We must approach powerful humans in the same way we do touchy godlings: That is, we must make them feel like good people, and keep them entertained. That meant letting Dele help, though it might make my task take twice as long.

"Very well," I said, shoulders slumping in resignation. She could not spirit-clean, but there was plenty to do before that. I pointed up at the window drapery and wall hangings. "When cleaning any room, it is best to start high and end low. So we should take those down."

I had mastered balancing on crates and using my cane to dislodge objects from high places. Still, this part of maid work had always been a challenge. I expected Dele to balk at the task, but instead she brightened.

"Sure. I've pulled the drapes loads of times to embroider them. We could use a ladder from the storeroom, but it would be simpler if I gave you a lift—don't you think? Here, get on."

She crouched in front of me, cheerfully patting her shoulders. My mouth fell open.

"Madam," I sputtered.

"You can't weigh much," she said reasonably. "And I'll hold your ankles, so you won't fall off. That's it," she grunted, "there you go."

In a daze, I straddled her shoulders. She stood, and a disbelieving laugh escaped me as we wobbled together, two women high.

"To the curtain," she crowed, and I windmilled my arms for balance as she marched across the room, praying no one would peek in from the hallway. Several minutes of stifled screams and swaying later, we had managed to strip the walls, and a small fabric mountain rested in the room's center.

Dele knelt, allowing me to climb down, and then collapsed onto the pile of drapery, grinning as her chest rose and fell. "Phew!"

"Well done," I told her, and meant it.

"You too." She gave me a wry salute, and then brushed her hand over the mountain, tracing the colorful patterns. "Do you know why Mother hates my needlework? It's because I only embroider weeds. I do it to annoy her, I suppose. But also to remind myself that no plant is truly useless. Only unlucky in where they bloom. Surrounded by people who deem them untamable and a threat to the rest of the garden." She glowered into the distance, then smiled up at me. "Time for a break, I think. I'm dusty everywhere, even my insides. Shall we head for the spa?"

I stared in surprise. "We, madam?"

"Don't bother about the inn rules. You're allowed to use the pools if you're with me."

"No, I mean . . . I can't leave. I am not done." I gestured around at the furniture. "I only have the mornings to spirit-clean your room, and we have barely begun. There is the cloth to be sorted by type for proper laundering, and the cobwebs in the eaves, and silt to dust from the ceiling, if there is time . . ."

With every task I listed, Dele appeared to deflate.

I stopped, smiling gently. "It is all right, madam. You have been very kind, and I am sure you're tired. Just go to the spa without me—"

"No," she insisted, frowning to herself. "I said I'd help. So I'll help."

And she did, for another half hour, throwing herself into sorting the linens as I sang and spirit-dusted, peppering me with questions and telling jokes to pass the time. Then her focus began to wander. More than once, I caught her lounging on the bed platform, playing with bottles of her thread dyes instead of cleaning. She would jump beneath my gaze and sheepishly return to our task. But soon enough she'd get distracted again, emitting heavy sighs and looking dolefully out the window.

On one of these occasions, a gaggle of fashionable ladies in the street noticed Dele and called up to her. Dele perked up, waving back.

"Still abed, Dele?" the young women hollered, geles bobbing like giant cloth flowers. "We're going to the Textile District. A ship docked from Moreyao, so the silk stalls are filled to *bursting*!"

"I could use some new silk thread," Dele murmured, and then glanced at me, having the decency to look embarrassed. "Not today," she called down.

The ladies protested in disapproval. "Am's Story, Dele," one of them swore. "It's the chance of a lifetime. And you never come out with us anymore. Not unless it's the Ilemalu District to see your pretty flor—"

"Shh!" Dele hissed. The ladies erupted into chortles, and Dele bit back a smile. Her eyes slid back to me, and I nodded at the door.

"Go on, madam. You know you want to."

"I'll help more tomorrow," she babbled, tearing off her sleeping clothes and donning a bold fuchsia wrapper. "And tell you what—I'll bring you back a present. What's your best color? Green? I bet it's green. Don't work too hard, all right? And don't worry about Mother. You're a brilliant maid, and she'd be a fool to fire you; back soon!"

And in a flurry of fabric and hastily applied perfume, Dele was gone.

Rolling my eyes to the ceiling, I began gathering the clothing she had left on the floor.

Despite Dele's short-lived assistance, I could see why Ye Eun fancied her. Staggering beauty aside, Dele made declarations in a way that drew you in, like a moth to blazing lamplight. Most importantly, beneath all that charm . . . her kindness felt sincere.

I wondered if Ye Eun had been honest with Dele about her past. About the Pale Arts cult she had lived in with the Crocodile, assuming I had guessed correctly about his history with Ye Eun. It was clear Dele did not know about the Crocodile. From what I had gathered as we cleaned, Dele appeared to believe that Ye Eun had met me at the orphanage, where Ye Eun just happened to be delivering flowers.

I understood the secrecy but suspected it was not necessary. Whatever skeletons hid in Ye Eun's closets, Dele would be delighted by another scandal to hide from her mother.

I picked up a basket of drapery to launder in the spa, then paused at the bedroom doorflap. Until now, I had guiltily considered faking my spirit-clean. It would be simple enough, going through the motions of cleansing Dele's room but leaving most of the spirit silt behind. After all, the more Dele rebelled, the higher my chances of getting fired. Of losing everything.

But after wobbling around that room on Dele's shoulders, surrounded by weeds, the rainbow tapestry of Dele's love for the strange and unwanted . . . I sighed, hoisting the basket up on my hip and retrieving my cane. I would spirit-clean Dele's room as I had promised. But in the meantime, I would need all the help with Mamadele I could get.

"Small Sade," piped a splotch of green from my basket.

I started, nearly dropping the heap of curtains as I stared down at the bulbous eyes of the messenger gecko.

"Is he here?" I demanded. "Now, in broad daylight?"

"Crocodile," the gecko affirmed.

"That is not," I moaned as I headed for the stairs, "the kind of help I meant."

CHAPTER 10

I HAD BEEN FOOLISH TO FEAR BEING CAST OUT ONTO THE streets of Oluwan City when it was clear the stairs down to the Balogun Inn spa would kill me long before I was fired.

The spiral staircase in the front hall had been difficult enough, and those steps were wide. Not only were the spa stairs steep and narrow, but each step shone slick with condensation from the baths below. When I had visited last night with Hanuni, I had held my cane with one hand and gripped the slippery railing for dear life with the other. Even still, a spasm in my foot had nearly ended my story then and there, sweeping my legs from beneath me before Hanuni caught me by the shoulders.

Now, with a load of laundry, my least lethal choice was to stash my cane in the basket, and descend the stair seated on my bottom. Cold wetness seeped into my wrapper as I half slid, half crab-crawled down each step, dragging the basket along behind me.

A feeling shot to my stomach then. A sad, churning anger that I had grown skilled at shoving down with words, phrases drummed into me by priests and physicians and Mercy Aunties.

It is good to be grateful. It is good to know your place.

But—

Let me put it like this: If I pointed to any building in Oluwan City and asked, "What is that for?" no doubt you would say, "For someone to live in." But if a place for *someone* is suited only for those with two working feet, then people like me are not someone.

We are no one at all.

As I worked my prayer pebble against my cheek, muting my starved rage as one buries a scream in pillows, the gecko wisely abandoned the laundry heap, hopping out to crawl along the wall beside me. His feet made tiny *schlooping* noises on the stone.

"Where is your master, anyway?" I asked him. "Hovering outside the inn? He had better not be reckless enough to make me fly to him in the middle of the day. Whatever he wants, it will have to wait. I have a lot of washing to do."

"Ixalix," the gecko replied affably.

I cocked my head. "You know," I said, considering him in the muggy dim of the stair, "you have never told me your name."

The creature slowed his walk and hunched, as though suddenly self-conscious.

"No," I breathed. "You don't mean that alagbato Ixalix created you to say the names of others but never gave you your own?"

The gecko nodded, looking sorry for himself. I placed my hands on my hips to show offense.

"Then we will give you one right now," I said. "Something handsome. Or strong. Or . . . what do you like to do, in your free time?"

The gecko licked each of its turquoise-rimmed eyes, savoring the question. He curled its body in a thoughtful crescent, as if considering the keenest pleasures of the universe.

Then, concentrating with great difficulty, he piped: "Clem-eh."

"Clem-eh?" I straightened with understanding. "Oh—climb! Is that your favorite thing to do?"

It nodded several times. *"Clemeh!"*

"As it should be," I told him seriously. "You are very good at it. Clemeh it is." And newly christened, Clemeh looped in delighted circles on the wall before wiggling, puffed with pride, down the stairway.

As I neared the bottom, my shins sore and damp, voices echoed out from the women's spa. I hesitated. It would not do for me to disturb bathing guests.

But when I listened closely, I recognized Wafa, Kanwal, and . . . Finnric? Gripping my cane to stand, I hoisted the basket onto my hip and entered the chamber.

The women's room of the Balogun Inn spa shone with white marble tile, tinted gold by flickering oil sconces and shot through with crystal veins of blue. Additional lamps dotted the rim of the long pool sunk into the tiled floor. The nutty scent of plantain ash soap and almond bathing oil hung in the sultry air. To my surprise, baskets of linens lay scattered across the tile. Wafa and Kanwal also had brought down washing, and they knelt by the pool scrubbing bedclothes, voices muffled by the constant gurgle of water, which fed the pool from elegant spouts on each wall.

On the far side of the chamber, Finnric leaned over the edge, talking down to a short-haired stranger who stood submerged in the pool.

"Let me know if you need help down there," Finnric called, flexing his narrow arms. "Madam usually has me clean out the filters, and these pools are luxury city technology, so you might need a sharper pair of eyes."

"Don't listen to him! Finn's never done more than scrub scum off the tile," Kanwal called out as Wafa melted in giggles. When the two of them noticed me at the door, Wafa waved me over.

"Small Sade! Come and watch our latest entertainment. Madam hired a plumber to clean the pool filters, and Finnric is hoping the handsome man will adopt him."

"I am not," Finnric retorted, then explained to the plumber. "I'm just offering my knowledge. I do not spend my days off mooning about, like other youths of my generation. I exercise. I *plan*. I improve my mind. I—"

"Exactly the skills," Wafa said innocently, "that one needs to change pool filters."

I chuckled, about to join her with my basket, when the plumber rose from the pool. I froze at the spectacle, while Wafa and Kanwal sighed beside me.

The man had cropped hair and a thick, curling beard that concealed his face. But beyond that, no hint of age weakened him as water rolled from his back and rippling limbs, glistening on his broad black shoulders.

My pulse quickened. In the humid stairwell, my wrapper had grown damp, clinging to my torso. I was suddenly conscious of every place it chafed, teasing the tops of my breasts and thighs.

I indulged that feeling for several beats of my heart—*one, two, three*—and then chased it soberly away.

For you see, romantic fantasies did not often end well for girls like me. My experience of men included boys at the sweatmill, flirtatious vendors on Aanu Meji Street, and the occasional roving-eyed son of countryside gentry. Most avoided girls who were spirit-touched, though curiosity had enticed a few to try to kiss me, an experience I sometimes enjoyed. Still, wealthy men did not claim commoners as sweethearts, and poor men were unable or unwilling to buy the herbs that prevented pregnancy. For those reasons, I had found it best to treat attraction like a head cold: coddled for a day or two, then washed away with a bath and a sensible cup of tea.

"He is too gentlemanly to flirt with maids," Wafa murmured, as if I had spoken my thoughts aloud. "Nice to look at, though."

"Just my luck," whispered Kanwal, "to be scrubbing madam's cycle blood from sheets when someone interesting comes along."

The plumber kept his head down, studiously attending to the water spigots. "Don't mind me," he said in a strange, muffled voice. "I'll be out of your hair in an hour or two. Pretend I'm not here."

"Now that is a professional," Finnric told us, resuming his scrub of the floor tiles and then shaking the brush at us for emphasis. "If I were him, I'd take that expertise and build my own bathhouse chain. He could be a rich man, with a little more drive."

"Of course," Wafa goaded, spreading her arms wide. "Ogas and madams must be full of drive, to boss us about the way they do. Why, this morning, madam had so much drive, she made me arrange her hair three different ways. It tired her so much, she had to nap for an hour."

Finnric crossed his arms. "Has it ever occurred to you that the owning class *deserves* what they have? We may be working hard, but they are out there being daring. By buying property, they are taking on all the risk—"

"Risk?" Kanwal scoffed. "Of what? Being slightly less rich? Finn, the only people buying property have their basic needs met already. If an oga's investment falls through, will he starve? Will he sleep on the street? Of course not. The worst thing that can happen to a rich man is that he has to get a job like the rest of us."

"Well, you will never know," Finnric shot back, obviously feeling cornered. "You can't even get a promotion here."

To my surprise, Kanwal looked wounded.

"That is not her fault and you know it," Wafa said, patting Kanwal's knee before turning to me. "Kanwal's basically run the kitchen for years, ever since Onijibola's joint trouble got bad. She should be head cook. But we can't tell madam about Onijibola's health problems, or she'll fire him, and where else could a person go at his age?"

"That's why the old man prays so much," Finnric added. "Once Mamadele figures out he can't earn his keep, only the Raybearers can save him."

"Finn!"

"I'm as fond of Onijibola as anyone else," he protested, raising his hands in defense. "I'm just saying, some people are just small-minded. If he'd started his own inn instead of working for one . . ."

"The real shame," said Wafa, "is that a person can work for forty years, then be tossed out with nothing. Still . . . Kanwal deserves that promotion. She could cook circles around Onijibola, even before his illness."

"It's true," Kanwal grunted, wringing out a towel. "But Mamadele wouldn't make me head cook in any case. Doesn't like the optics of a woman in charge. Not one younger than herself, anyway. If we sold out Onijibola, she'd just hire another man."

Finnric eyed me with interest. "Do you have any ambitions, Small Sade?"

Across the room, the plumber stilled suddenly.

I blinked at Finnric in surprise. "Me?"

"Yes, you. This 'resident Curse-Eater' idea of madam's is unusually clever," Finnric said, stroking the orange fuzz on his jaw. "I'm surprised I didn't think of it. Maybe I'll poach you when I start my own inn. What do you suppose your rates will be?"

"I haven't given it much thought," I said, laughing a little. "I suppose—all I really want is . . ."

At my pause, I could have sworn the plumber's neck craned ever so subtly, as if desperate to hear what I said next.

Visions of that future girl, Sade of Oluwan City, flashed before me. She didn't look wealthy, really, as she glided through the markets, giving directions to tourists. She just looked . . . radiant. Glowing with the rare peace of someone who belonged.

"A home," I said. "But not just anywhere. Somewhere a person could get lost in. A place that always changes, yet somehow stays the same."

"How poetic," Wafa said kindly, but Finnric tsked.

"You're thinking too small," he chided. "But at least your goal isn't imaginary. Unlike dreamscape Wafa here."

Kanwal fashioned the wet towel into a whip and caught Finnric's arm. "There's nothing imaginary," she said as he howled, "about my big sister's goals. So you keep her name out of your mouth."

I asked, "What's a dreamscape?"

Wafa gave an embarrassed laugh, her large brown eyes crinkling at the corners. "It's nothing," she said. "Just . . . an idea I've had since I was little. Back when the Raybearers were young and their Anointed Council went on a goodwill tour across the continent. When the Anointed Ones visited our hometown back in Dhyrma, they used their blood powers to entertain the children.

"One of them, Anointed Honor Theo, made illusions appear by playing his lyre, and a griot accompanied the music by telling a story. It was only a common cookfire tale. But I started dancing without knowing it—don't laugh! I was a child, and I could never help moving to music. Next thing I knew, the Anointed Ones invited me up in front of everyone. I acted out the story as I moved, even giving all the characters different dances. I've never forgotten how that felt. Not just the attention, but the immersion of the music, the illusions. It's like I was *in* the story. Like I lived in a dream.

"Now every time I hear a griot in the streets, I think . . . what if, just for an hour every day, you could go somewhere else? Visit another world.

Live someone else's story?" Her expression went hazy. "For a while, I considered starting a theater troupe of some kind. Putting on plays, like mummers do at festivals. But mine would be more immersive. I could decorate rooms and add effects with shadow and lighting. Maybe the audience could be characters somehow." She smiled ruefully. "The only problem is, I'm only good at dancing. I'm useless at making up stories, and so is Kanwal. Our patrons would get bored in ten minutes."

Sadness looked so out of place on Wafa's cheerful features, my heart melted. I racked my mind for ideas. "Maybe you don't have to make up stories," I said. "Maybe your dreamscapes could be about things that actually happened."

"Like ancient history?"

"Like anything," I said, smiling at her. "What's something exciting that ever happened to you and Kanwal?"

"Oh!" Wafa's lashes batted rapidly. "I suppose—that would be back home in Vhraipur, when we almost got arrested by the Dhyrmish Royal Guard."

"Arrested?" I gasped, and Kanwal grinned.

"We were only children," she said. "Our parents had taken us to see the enchanted Royal Garden of Vhraipur. It's this famous part of the Maharani's palace, open to commoners only a few times a year."

"There are trees made of gold and silver," Wafa put in. "And real, living flowers with jewels for petals. But the moment someone plucks a blossom or breaks off a leaf . . . the precious stones turn to ash. The garden's enchanted against thieves, you see."

"But that doesn't stop people from trying," said Kanwal. "'People' meaning us, when we were six and eight. We found this marigold—a tiny one all by itself, made of sparkling citrines. We didn't want to sell it. Only to take it home, where we could look at it all the time and fight over who got to wear it in our braids."

"Wait," I told them, emptying one of the baskets and turning it upside down. They giggled as I drummed on its woven bottom, and though Finnric rolled his eyes, even he cracked a smile.

"You'll have to imagine the other musicians," I said. "Someone could clink bottles together to show the jewel flowers tinkling as the breeze rushes through."

"And shaker gourds," said Wafa, perking up. "For the clatter of leaves on the metal trees. And we'd light the room with colored glass, so the audience would feel like me and Kanwal, surrounded by all those jewels. And I would dance." She stood and began to wind her hips, which made Finnric look uncomfortable.

"The floor's damp," he muttered. "You'll fall."

"I don't fall," Wafa said simply, and she didn't.

I picked up the drumming pace. Then I summoned that deep part of myself, the one that made up songs without trying, drawing on the energy of any place that I spirit-cleaned.

"*Kirin-keh, kirin-keh, chime crystal flowers,*" I warbled.

> *In a forest of silver and gold,*
> *Two sisters spy it:*
> *A bright yellow blossom.*
> *It's mine!*
> *It's mine.*
> *Cried the girls in Her Majesty's garden.*

"Catchy," Finnric quipped, and Kanwal tapped a counter beat against her soap bucket.

"Small Sade makes us sound like romantic heroines." Wafa laughed, still dancing. "But she hasn't heard the rest."

"*Then go on,*" I sang, and she did.

"Kanwal gets the brilliant idea to dig the marigold out by its roots. She figures that won't actually count as picking it. So we wait for our parents to wander away, and then we claw around the flower with our bare hands, like tiny feral wolf cubs."

"*A thief plucks the petals and sits in jail,*" I trilled.

> *But a mole takes the roots and feasts in his den.*
> *"Let's be moles!' said the girls in Her Majesty's garden.*

My spirit sight filled the spa with silt as I sang, but I ignored it, closing my eyes to imagine Wafa's story.

"Skret-tu-keh, skret-tu-keh—their nails dig the earth.
"It's mine!
It's mine.
Cried the girls in Her Majesty's garden."

"All of sudden, a palace guard rounds the corner. Kanwal scoops up the dirt clod with the marigold, and I stuff it under my dress. We take off running but don't get far."

"'Who goes there?'
"'Small girls with dirt on your hands? Who digs in Her Majesty's garden?'
"Pit-tah-pah! Pit-tah-pah.
"On the silk grass ground
"Beat the feet of two small fleeing thieves!"

"I trip over a boulder made of diamonds and tumble into a pond, dragging Kanwal with me. I brace my belly to protect the marigold . . . but it's gone! Nothing but a ball of mud beneath my soaking dress. We had not outsmarted the enchantment after all."

"Plish! Pah!
With a splash and a drop
Drown the dreams of their marigold sister."

"We're banned from the Royal Gardens of Vhraipur for life," Wafa finished with a grand twirl. "But we don't get arrested. The guard didn't actually see us take the marigold, and the pond covered us both in mud, concealing the evidence. We go home, accept spankings from our Amah, and swear off a life of crime."

"*Moles feast in their dens,*" I sang out, and this time both Finnric and Kanwal joined in for the refrain, finishing the song brash and loud.

> *"It's mine!*
> *It's mine.*
> *Cried the girls in Her Majesty's garden."*

We finished with a cheer, and Wafa gave a little bow. Slow applause echoed across the spa.

We stopped, having forgotten we weren't alone, to find the plumber clapping, bearded features alight with amusement. Then that arresting dark gaze fell on me, and my face slackened.

I had seen those eyes before.

"I believe," said the man, as realization dawned over me, "that I've left a tool back at my workshop. I will have to go and get it."

"And I," I said through gritted teeth, "must fetch another load from Dele's room."

"How convenient," he replied, in a familiar drawl that filled my foolish stomach with butterflies. "I'll help you up the stairs."

Then without another word, I seized my cane and marched from the spa, with the disguised god chuckling quietly behind me.

CHAPTER 11

"I SEE NOW YOU WERE TRYING TO WARN ME," I TOLD CLEM-eh, who scampered along the wall outside the spa, chittering when he saw me emerge with the plumber.

The man's thick beard melted away. Locs burst from his scalp to replace the short curls, and his skin puckered to reveal his cursed arm and stab scars. He scowled at the narrow stairs back up to the house. "Do they really expect you to take those every day? It's a death trap."

"It's a job," I said.

He extended his arms, an offer.

My face heated, but after another look at those stairs, I sighed and nodded. With an arrogant grin, the Crocodile scooped me into his arms. His warm skin, still damp from the pool, clung to mine.

"I should give you a way to summon me," he said as we climbed the stairs. "Our bond tells me when you need something, but it's fairly vague as to what . . . why are you laughing?"

I only shook my head, unable to contain the chortling fit that had seized my body. I did not explain to him that I was not happy but tired. Exhausted by the enraging silliness of a world where I could summon a god to carry me but could not find work in a house without stairs.

"Did you really go through all this trouble to help me with my chores?" I asked, once I had recovered. "You can't enchant yourself as a plumber every time I need to carry a basket."

"No," he mused. "I could be a roofer next. Or an egg peddler."

"You will be a beast next, if you do not stop using Pale Arts."

He paused, looking less jovial. "That is actually why I came to the spa," he said. "I needed to ask Ixalix a few questions about my curse—namely, if we can break the bond between us before I transform for good. Ixalix is a rainforest alagbato, so aside from building a portal to Quetzala, the fastest way to reach her is to speak her name in a cenote. It's a sort of lake that forms underground. Seeing as there are no cenotes in a thousand-mile radius . . . I thought an underground spa might do. So I donned an illusion, took a job as a plumber, and whispered a message into the pipes. With any luck, she'll find a way to get back to me."

"There's an alagbato listening to the bathhouse?" I asked.

"I certainly hope so," said the Crocodile.

My shock lasted for only a moment. Spirits listened everywhere—I knew that more than anyone. The real trouble was getting them to care when you wanted them and leave you be when you didn't.

When we neared the top of the stairs, he paused. Against my cheek, his heart thudded just a little faster.

"Do you mind that I came?" he asked, voice carefully neutral. "I won't make myself a nuisance."

"I'm the nuisance," I replied, avoiding the question. "My needs being yours and all."

"It's more than that. I enjoy being near you quite a lot." He smiled, glancing back down the stairwell. "And I envy those who get to be your friends."

I froze. "In the mouth of a man," I said slowly, searching his eyes, "those words would be sweet. But in the mouth of a god, they are a threat."

He recoiled. "I . . . understand. Forgive me." He set me down firmly. "Sade, I will never harm anyone you hold dear. You have my word. But seeing as I've already tripped over my tongue . . ." He bowed with a grim little flourish. "I will leave you be."

But before he disappeared through the door at the landing, I blurted, "I don't mind. But you will have to get better at disguises. You speak like a lord. That makes you seem wealthy, which is why Finnric wouldn't leave you alone. Also—if you want to blend in—" My last words were a mortified rush. "*Don't-be-so-handsome-next-time-it's-distracting.*"

Then I pushed past him, ignoring the delighted heat of his gaze as I fled.

MY ONLY CHANCE AT KEEPING THIS JOB WAS TO CHANGE Mamadele's mind about what she wanted . . . or at least, to make her happy with what she had. So in between attending to Dele and working on her room, I waited for chances to steal across the hallway to spirit-clean Mamadele's chambers in secret.

The problem was, Mamadele spent an extraordinary amount of time in her chambers, even during the day. Most fine-fine ladies, in my experience, spent the morning and afternoon away from home, attending social gatherings and sampling market wares. But those activities required both friends and money, and compared to their gentry peers, the Baloguns did not have a great deal of either.

So I bided my time, working each day, and collapsing in a full-body ache each night. I had built some stamina for stairs at the orphan high-rise, but not much, using them only at the beginning and end of each day to reach my room. Now, I made several trips per day and had developed more blisters, and later calluses, than I had even known was possible.

My first chance at securing my place arose two weeks later, the night of Mamadele's intellectual salon. I had never heard of a salon before coming to the Balogun Inn. From what I could piece together, it was a party at which gentry sipped wine from pearl-rimmed tumblers while discussing art and poor people, often in the same breath.

Hanuni had mentioned in passing that these events took hours, keeping Mamadele out of her room late into the night. Like the other Amenities, I was expected to sit up in the storeroom, on call to serve guests until the salon was over. To reach Mamadele's chambers, I would need to use the spiral staircase, sneaking past the party in the great room.

Satiny voices and kora harp music echoed across the tile as I crept toward the stairs. Most of the guests had their backs to me. In one hand

I gripped my cane, and in the other I held a sloshing bucket of water. Strapped across my back was a bundle containing my hand broom, scouring brushes, and cleaning tonics. I prayed none of them would drop, clattering on the marble and giving me away.

I reached the stairs, lifting my stronger foot to mount them . . . and then my cane struck an uneven square of tile, sending a pinging sound to the rafters.

A crowd of coiffed hair and immaculate geles turned sharply my way.

I expected death glares and a quick exile to the storeroom. What happened instead was much worse.

"Small Sade," Mamadele sang out. She lay poised on a chaise surrounded by some ten other guests, including a dour-faced Dele and a grandly dressed lord who hovered at Dele's shoulder. "Just the person we need," Mamadele gushed, slurring as she lifted a wine chalice. "Come here."

My heart sank to my sandals. Quickly, I stashed the bucket on the bottom step and hurried over, praying she wouldn't ask about my errand. The patrons parted to let me in, then closed again, trapping me in a cloud of wine-soaked breath and expensive perfume. Against the grain of my cane handle, my palm prickled with sweat.

"C-can I fetch you something from the kitchens, ma?" I asked Mamadele, but before she could answer, an older lady spoke up.

"Is this the infamous Curse-Eater?" she demanded, tossing a fall of graying loced hair over her dark, bony shoulder. The party guests were diverse in clothing and skin color, united only in wealth: a smattering of gentry from several different realms. From her accent, which seemed a posher version of Hanuni's, the older woman hailed from Djbanti. Resentment lined her features, and I gulped.

Years ago, news of Djbanti's commoner uprising had burned across the continent, inspiring revolutions to rise in other realms. It had happened when I was very small, so I didn't know many details. But after their lands were seized, many Djbantian lords and ladies had fled their country altogether, living out the rest of their days as jewel-encrusted refugees in Oluwan City.

"You'd better not be a charlatan, girl," said the old lady.

"Oh, don't scare her," said the lord near Dele. He was middle-aged with a long mustache and a jovial jowled face. His tan skin and sweeping robes hailed from the distant realm of Moreyao. "Poor little dear. She's shaking like a leaf."

"Don't coddle her, Lord Liao," the Djbantian lady retorted, and then to me: "You needn't be scared. We're all *enlightened* here. But I don't take kindly to those who waste intelligent people's time. And if any family could use a true Curse-Eater . . . it's mine."

"Are you threatening to poach her, Lady Injaana?" Mamadele giggled, shaking a finger at the lady in mocking reproof. "Ah-ah! That is my orphan. Go get your own."

"Do—do you want me to eat curses for you?" I stammered, voice rising in panic. "Now?" I could not possibly clean the entire great room in the space of a single evening, especially when it was crowded with guests. Perhaps I'd have to do some scam song and dance to entertain them, like old Popo from Dejitown.

"No, no," assured the man called Lord Liao. "We only wish for you to settle an argument."

"Small Sade," said Mamadele, "we wish to know what you would do if you weren't working."

I blinked. "Beg pardon?"

"It's a simple question," she said, gesturing so the wine in her chalice sloshed. "If you had no rooms to clean or pots to scrub or curses to eat . . . what would you be doing this very moment?"

I considered, fidgeting beneath all those kohl-lined stares, and cast about for answers that would get me safely out of the room.

"Well," I said through a shaky breath. "It is dark out. So it probably is not safe for a walk in the square. And I have had my supper. So . . ."

A vision of spinning dreamscapes with Wafa, Kanwal, and Finnric flashed through my mind. But now, as I cowered before these eloquent, well-dressed, worldly people . . . our whispered true-story games felt small and foolish. Besides, speaking of the dreamscapes felt like a betrayal of the Amenities, and I could not think to explain them in a way the gentry would understand.

89

So instead I said plainly, "I would probably go to sleep, madam."

Half the guests groaned in disappointment, while the rest crowed in laughter.

"And that," said Lady Injaana, "is exactly the point I have been making all night. Commoners, bless them, have no interest in pursuits of the mind. They don't study art or debate philosophy. So why try and involve them at every level of politics? Why not keep them where they're happy?"

"In the dirt?" Dele spoke up. "Serving us?"

Her tone was sardonic and her expression blank. It was the first time I had seen Dele bereft of color, clothes unadorned by the rainbow of weeds defining her typical wardrobe. She wore a wrapper that matched her mother's, yards of ivory ashoke cloth, a luxury weave shot through with gold and silver.

The threads caught in the lamplight, causing Dele to sparkle like a fallen star, though in contrast, her face looked dull and ashen.

Mamadele gave a tinkling laugh and patted Dele's knee, though her eyes held a dagger of warning. "Last time I checked, you were more than content to let Small Sade fetch your breakfast."

"Surely it's a matter of education," said Lord Liao, gesturing at me. "Girls like this one never had a chance at decent schooling. It's obviously too late for her *now* . . ." He eyed me with pitying amusement. "But before . . . who knows? With early enough intervention, her tastes could have bent toward higher things."

"You can't put everyone in school," Mamadele said. "You would bore them to death. Small Sade, when you were younger, would you rather have plucked a chicken or read a book?"

"The chicken," I said, though the true answer was more complicated. I worried my prayer pebble against my teeth. My accident at the sweatmill was enough to set me off books forever, but my distaste had formed before that. Every time a village schoolmaster had tried to teach me to read, the characters had swum, switching places before my eyes, causing me to sound out gibberish. Before long, the tutors gave up, pronouncing me a dunce. I wondered, sometimes, what sort of person I'd have been if they had tried a little harder. Perhaps the same. Perhaps not.

90

But though I hated the written word, I did love stories.

I hungrily inhaled the knowledge of griots, who shared intricate histories through song. Even those great storytellers, however, rarely spoke of girls like me. The words that truly set my mind alight were tales like Wafa's—shifting yarns of living memory, unsuited to grand recitations or static lines on a page.

"They talk of maids envying their mistresses, but in truth, you would hate switching places with me." Mamadele sighed dreamily. "When I was a girl, I'd spend hours in the Imperial Library. And art—oh! I couldn't get enough of it."

"And that," said Lady Injaana, raising her glass to Mamadele, "is why the gods made Small Sade a maid, and you a gracious lady. Let us all be rewarded for our different strengths."

"The Baloguns didn't obtain wealth by admiring art," Dele snorted. "We got it by enslaving children in a mine that we barely set foot in. Did you forget, Mother?"

The room froze, then burst into tipsy snickers. Mamadele joined in, though her grip on her chalice tightened.

"Such a wit," Lord Liao chuckled, gazing down at Dele indulgently. "And you're certainly right. There's being a lord, and then being a slave driver."

"Are lords really any better?" Dele retorted. "Even without slaves, you sell the fruit of lands you did not harvest. Why should you reap most of the rewards, when you did so little of the work?"

This caused shrieking outbursts across the room, birthing a new round of debate. The party seemed to have forgotten me altogether, and so I bobbed a good night and ducked slowly out of the crowd.

Cleaning kit in tow, I stole up the spiral staircase and slipped into Mamadele's room.

CHAPTER 12

MAMADELE'S BEDROOM SMELLED LIKE HER: COSTLY AMBER-
gris and fresh sunflower oil, laced with a date's sickly sweetness. Moonlight from windows recessed in the ceiling glinted on the marble bed dais,
winking across beaded seat cushions and painted end tables.

I removed my prayer pebble and sang in a whisper. My sight only
worked when I sang out loud, but I wished that I could summon my spirit
sight by singing in my head. It would lower my chance at being caught, for
one, but it would also make for less coughing and sneezing in general. I
liked my little songs, but inhaling a ball of dust and soap fumes with every
new stanza was hard on the lungs.

> *"A palace to a goatherd girl's*
> *A hovel to a queen.*
> *Is it not a silly tale?*
> *Shame, shame, shame."*

Spirit silt covered the chamber in a shifting, lurid haze. I looked for
an area to focus on. I could not be too ambitious. The salon would not last
forever, and besides my tools and tonics, I had only one bucket of water
with which to clean and would not risk sneaking down to the spa for more.

The surest way to impact Mamadele's desires would be to clean an
area she used the most. The bed?

I stared askance at the heavily draped platform, which swarmed
with grief-gnats and glowed with mildewing ambition-spores. I could do
nothing about the mold. In the short time I had, I would barely be able

to smoke out the gnats with incense, and then the smell might spread through the inn, alerting Mamadele to investigate.

Then, partially concealed by a folding screen, a vanity and stool caught my eye. Mamadele must have spent hours there every day, for even without the added sight of spirit silt, the area was hopelessly cluttered, with spilled bottles of hastily used cosmetics dripping onto the woven carpet. Determination sparked in my belly.

That, I could clean.

Still crooning the nonsense lines under my breath, I dragged my supplies to the vanity and began to remove Mamadele's sticky collection of bottles, rags, and used tufted cotton balls. I hesitated at her earrings and bangles and at her boxes of intricately braided hair extensions. Such items were very valuable, and if caught touching them, I risked losing my hands as well as my job. But shimmering silt covered everything, and if I didn't clean it all, my effect on Mamadele would be weakened. So I moved them too, working quickly, as if the items would burn me.

The jewelry I polished with a rag dipped in salt and ash, removing both the real-world tarnish and the spirit-world stains. The hair extensions I brushed free of dust, then sprinkled with scented vinegar, banishing any envy-beetles that hid in the braided coils.

"Is it not a silly tale?
Shame, shame, shame!"

You will wonder at the levity in my song, when all it would take for me to be cast out on the streets was for the wrong person to pass by Mamadele's door. But as always happened when I cleaned, a warm trance had come over me, flooding my heart and hands with spell-like focus.

I hummed as greedgrime came off the table in greasy sheets, and trilled rhymes as egorust melted from the mirror. My bristle brush banished shed hairs and worry-lint from the vanity stool and exorcised despair-mold from the soiled floor mat.

The last step of any deep clean was to organize. Here I stopped, scanning Mamadele's possessions with wired indecision.

Injaana had said that girls like me have no desire to make art. But I didn't know what else to call the itch possessing my hands to arrange those pots and powders.

I could do nothing of this sort, of course. To avoid detection, I had to put Mamadele's things back exactly as she'd left them, and so I did.

But I let myself fantasize about how I would do it.

First by size: round, fat cosmetic jars arranged like lanterns along the back, then the pressed pats of powder stacked in glittering towers, and at last the bottles of perfume, decorative stoppers neatly lined in a parade of cheery crystalline animals. Second, I'd rearrange everything by color: tonics and lip paints glittering in an intricate ombre pattern from light to dark, down to the minutest hue.

Panting with satisfaction, I stepped back to survey my work. The rest of the chamber was still a mess, spiritually, but already, this small corner of the room felt airier and brighter than before. Perhaps Mamadele would sit here and consider, just a moment, how lovely her life was, even if it was less grand than it once had been. I collected my things and turned toward the chamber doorflap.

Just outside, footsteps echoed on the floor.

I realized belatedly that the murmur of voices from downstairs had long quieted. The salon had ended sooner than I thought. Heart pounding, I raced back across the room, grateful for the cloth wrapping the bottom of my cane, muffling its tap on the floor. I crouched behind the vanity just as Mamadele swept through the doorflaps, towing Dele by the wrist.

"I hope you're happy," she hissed, flinging her daughter around to face her. "Antagonizing him like that. You'll be lucky if he ever looks your way again."

I watched them through a slit in the dressing screen. Mamadele's former tipsy glow had vanished, replaced by bleary-eyed rage.

Dele snorted, removing the pins from the shining folds of her gele, which splayed in a crisp fan about her head. "If that's the point of these parties, you might as well leave me out of it. I'm not going to flirt with Lord Liao."

"It was not just a party," Mamadele screeched. "It was a cultural event. An intellectual salon."

"In that case," Dele said lightly, "you should have appreciated my humor. But if you don't like my political jokes, I'll tell bawdy ones next time. Suppose I told Lord Liao the one about the mango seller with the juicy, ripe behi—"

Mamadele seized Dele's chin, wrenching it to face her. But when she spoke, her voice was chillingly gentle.

"You think I am your enemy," Mamadele said. "But I am not. Those streets outside this inn, the ones that crawl with pleasure bazaars and night merchants who have but one use for unskilled girls who have never worked a day in their lives . . . those, my dear, are your adversaries. And if tonight's salon, and the one after that, and every one thereafter does not fill our home with paying guests, we will live on those streets. The inn will go to your father's creditors, and your few friends who have until now found your crass antics charming will shut their doors in your penniless face. So," she murmured, tucking a coil behind Dele's ear, "you will smile for the guests. You will make elegant conversation. And you will do what you can to make any lord who enters this building believe he has a chance at marrying you. Have I made myself clear?"

Fear and uncertainty passed like a shadow over Dele's features. She was some five or six years older than me, but in that moment, she looked a mere child in Mamadele's grasp. Then she wrenched her mother's hand away.

"The only reason," she spat, "that we are strapped for funds is because you're still determined to be gentry. We could pay off our debts by moving to another district. We could live on less."

"Could we, now?" Mamadele gave a light little laugh. "And do you plan to scrub your own clothes? Cook your own meals? You, who have never touched a pot or pan in your pampered little life? You know good and well your only future lies in marriage. In convincing some wealthy idiot to throw their lot in with yours."

"Maybe," Dele said after a pause, her voice small and broken. "But why does it have to be a man? You know that isn't what I want. Queens and high ladies take brides all the time—"

"Yes," Mamadele snapped. "Powerful women take brides. Women so consequential to society, it does not matter who shares their beds. But those of us without status must bow to convention."

She clenched her fists, then exhaled, regaining her composure.

"My dear," she said evenly, "if you were sneaking out to woo some unwed heiress encrusted with taridayos, I would not stop you. On the contrary. I would pay both of your bride prices and dance at the wedding. But you are not." She leaned in close, voice lowering to a hiss. "You think I don't know you've been galivanting with some commoner across the *cow dung* district?"

Dele's face went slack with dismay, then hardened. "Mother, before you say another word . . . promise me you'll leave her alone. Promise me you've *left* her alone—"

"I do not know who she is," Mamadele said as she pulled off her jewelry, pacing dangerously close to the screen where I hid. "I only know you've been seen. Really, I could almost feel sorry for the strumpet. After all, you are far more dangerous to her than she ever could be to you."

Mamadele flung her bangles onto the vanity table without looking. A slight turn of her head, and she would have seen me. I nearly swallowed my tongue. One of the bangles Mamadele had thrown teetered on the corner of the vanity table. I begged it not to fall.

"You make me out to be your jailer," she continued airily. "But we both know I am not. The truth is, you could have left years ago. Your window is not barred." She gestured toward Dele's room. "If you truly wished to spend the rest of your life playing house in the slums, you could run off with your sweetheart, leaving me to shoulder the family name you find so burdensome. But you have not." She smiled in cold, cruel triumph. "Because you would not survive, and you know it. For all your self-deprecation, all your praise for the *noble working class* . . . you love security more than you love her."

The words appeared to strike Dele like a slap. Tears simmered in her eyes, but before they could fall, she fled from the room.

As Mamadele sank onto her bed, voices floated up to the room from outside the window. On the street below, those salon guests who were not staying overnight in the inn conversed as they waited for palanquins.

"These little salons were amusing at first," came a lady's voice. "Especially when the daughter gets involved. But I begin to find them tiresome."

"I believe the word you're looking for," came another voice, "is *desperate.*"

"And she isn't Lady Balogun anymore," someone else put in. "She can't even go by her maiden name, Simi of the Idowus. Now, she'll only ever be Mamadele."

Mamadele's hands clutched the bedclothes. Then, with a stifled scream, she ripped off one of her beaded sandals and hurled it toward the window. She missed, striking the vanity instead . . . and the bangle clattered to the floor.

Her eyes, now adjusted to the shadows, fell on me.

"Forgive me, madam," I squeaked, standing up as she yelped in fear. "I was—I was cleaning—"

"What are you doing near my jewels? Thief. Thief!" she rasped, marching to seize me by the ear. I cried out but did not resist as she searched the folds of my wrapper for valuables. Though she came up with nothing, her anger did not abate, and she hurled me toward the door.

"Did my rivals send you?" she demanded, kohl running around her eyes. "Were you a spy all along, sent to humiliate me? Pack your things. I should have known you were trouble the moment you entered that party."

"No. Please," I pleaded. "I—I was just trying to help." When her eyes still flashed with malice, I knew I would have to get creative.

I pointed at her vanity, then did my best impression of old Popo, the fake Curse-Eater from Dejitown. I showed the whites of my eyes, then groaned and gestured wildly. "There were demons, madam. Demons and bad-bad luck, sent by your enemies, everywhere in the room. So I lured them to the window and banished them. See there, ma! Look at yourself in the mirror. See how your fate has changed."

Mamadele gave an indelicate snort, but she looked back where I pointed. She frowned curiously, noticing how much brighter her vanity seemed, now scrubbed spotless. With a look, she told me to stay put. Then she glided over to the mirror and peered into it.

Ever so slightly, the lines on her brow smoothed. Perhaps my polishing the glass with vinegar had clarified the mirror, and that pleased her. Or perhaps the removal of egorust, though she could not see it, had made the mirror less addictive, freeing her from the impulse to sit and preen for hours. Or perhaps my old Popo performance had simply been frightening enough to sway her. In any case, I could see she was convinced of my power.

Still, I had been caught in her room uninvited. To avoid punishment, I would have to do more.

"You are unhappy," I blurted out. "And I can help."

I had a theory about spirit silt. I knew that it came from humans. But until I had cleaned the Crocodile's wound, I had only ever dealt with spirit silt after it left the body, covering floors and furniture. After I had sung, the rigidity of the Crocodile's body had eased, changing his entire demeanor . . . and an idea had begun to form. What if, instead of spirit-cleaning places, I purged silt from the people themselves? Both kinds of cleaning would still be necessary—a clean person would not stay clean in a dirty home, and the same was true in reverse—but so far, I had only tried one.

Mamadele laughed derisively, though she did not order me out of the room. "Can you convince the Raybearers to restore my title? Conjure up lands and a country villa?"

"No," I admitted. "But—if you'll excuse me for saying—those are not the only things that plague you."

When I had sung to reveal the spirit silt of Mamadele's room, an unusual amount of one pest had covered the floor, writhing among her bedclothes and boring holes in the furniture: guiltworms.

Slowly, I retrieved an empty fruit bowl from Mamadele's nightstand, then joined her at the vanity, placing the basin in her lap. I knelt before her.

"I am going to sing now," I said. "And when I do, I will cover my ears. That way, you can say things you might not want me to hear."

Her gaze narrowed. "What sort of things?"

"Whatever plagues you. Whatever you have done, or seen, that you might"—I cast about for words that would not make her angry—"regret. I will not hear them," I told her again, when her hackles rose in suspicion. "I will help you, madam. I will make you feel better."

I hoped. But all I could do then was sing.

This song had no words, only sound—a low, undulating wail that wrapped around us both. Unlike my other songs, this tune felt unnatural and did not come easily. Worst of all: Though I covered my ears, I could still hear Mamadele. The notes soured in my mouth as snippets of Mamadele's words stole into my head, turning my stomach.

". . . the children in the mines were so small, but how were we to know? They did the job and took lower pay, and that's just good stewardship . . . terrible for those commoners, but it's not as though we *personally* were whipping them . . . I might have made the *occasional* comment about Dele's body when she was little, but what mother doesn't? . . . of course Simple Hanuni had children of her own, but my family paid her salary, and I needed her more. It's not my fault her children don't talk to her anymore . . ."

Iridescent white worms spewed from her throat as she spoke, dribbling down her heaving chest and filling the basin in a pale, writhing mass.

The guiltworms would not stay in the basin long. Already some had escaped, reattaching themselves to Mamadele, suckling like leeches before absorbing, once again, into her skin.

So I had to move fast. Still wailing, I groped about for my cleaning kit. My hands closed around something hard: a box of scouring salt. I seized it, dumping its contents into the basin, and the ball of guiltworms hissed, shriveling down into silvery dust before vanishing altogether.

Still, some stragglers remained: slow, bulging grubs that held the worst of Mamadele's guilt. Living tumors filled to bursting with the worst things she had done.

I grimaced and wrung my hands, wailing louder. But I knew what I must do. One by one, I scooped up each slimy worm, shoved it past my lips, and choked it down.

Revulsion flung me to the ground. I stayed there, braced onto my forearms, concentrating on the grain of the wood floor so I would not vomit. When at last the bile receded from my mouth, I turned my head to peer at Mamadele.

She beamed down at me, cheekbones glowing angelically in the moonlight, as though she had not confessed a glut of atrocities just moments earlier. She sighed, serene as a milk-sated baby.

"You darling girl," she murmured. "I feel . . . why, a full five years younger. Ten, even. How long will it last?"

I struggled to shake my head. Even that small movement sent stars across my vision. "Not . . . long, madam. Unless the shape of what you have done changes . . . then the guilt will return. And I will have to sing again."

She left the chair and took my face in her hands, pressing a cool, damp kiss on my forehead.

"Well then, my Small Sade," she said, stinging my nose with wine-laced breath. "You and I will be friends for a very, very long time."

CHAPTER 13

DAYS LATER, MAMADELE STOOD IN THE STREET OUTSIDE the Balogun Inn, stuffing me into a rickshaw. The old cook Onijibola looked on while Finnric, wearing freshly starched livery and a haughty expression, stood ready to pull the vehicle. Its carriage seat was draped in bright festoons, which were painted with characters I could not read. Mamadele, however, had told me their meaning:

THE CURSE-EATER OF BALOGUN INN
CAN SING YOUR SINS AWAY.

"A palanquin would command more attention," she said, adjusting the blue gossamer veil she had placed over my head and secured with a saintly circlet of eucalyptus leaves. "But I couldn't spare the expense, and in any case, it's best you look a little humble."

I still wore my pale gold wrapper, identifying me as a servant of the Balogun Inn. But she had coated my arms and collarbone with gold powder so I resembled a living idol. She had also insisted I hold an irukere, a short totem made of horsetail hair, which I was to wave at passersby in silent blessing, showing off my otherworldly power.

Finnric was to pull me through the entire Ileyoba District, ending at the luxury High Market, advertising my services. The old cook Onijibola was to walk beside us, charged by Mamadele to sing my praises with the same sonorous tones he used in his fervent prayer to the Idajo.

"Don't say anything," Mamadele instructed me. "Only sit and look divine. Smile, but not too much. Keep an air of graveness about you."

"But I'm wearing a veil, ma," I pointed out. "No one can see my face."

"The smile will show in your bearing," Mamadele insisted, and a snort echoed from Dele's window above us. Mamadele shielded her eyes to squint up at the building.

"Daughter," she crooned, "are you going to wish Small Sade luck? Or only stand there making sow noises?"

Dele gazed down at me, expressionless. "I'm happy for you, Mother," she said. "You found it, what you've always wanted: a child who exists only to make you love yourself." And with that, she disappeared into the inn.

If the words hurt Mamadele, her features did not show it. She still had that milk-sated glow about her, still floating from the service I had done for her nights before.

"Don't forget to mention the Sin Salon!" she called out after us, and Finnric pulled away from the curb.

"Praise the Storyteller!" Onijibola caterwauled as we paraded down the street, rickshaw wheels skimming the flagstones. "Have you demons in your past? In your present? Let the Hallowed Maid of the Balogun Inn sing away your censure! Sleepless at night? Haunted by the shameful missteps of your youth? The god-blessed girl of Balogun Inn will make a stained soul pure again!"

We passed first by Unity Square, where commoners left their chores to line the street and watch us, hollering out questions and murmuring with curiosity. But Finnric rolled past them and told me to put my horse-tail down.

"Those are not the kind of salon guests Mamadele is looking for," he said curtly, and he did not stop until we had reached the Ileyoba High Market, which rested at the base of Palace Hill.

I sucked my prayer pebble until it chafed the roof of my mouth. The gentle murmur of the pristine square scared me more than the roughest low street bazaar. Instead of brawling goods hawkers and mazes of colorful stalls, matching storefronts with wide awnings lined the fountain-dotted boulevard. It could not have been more different from the Ileyimo Lower Market, where I had first plied my trade after leaving the orphan house. Did a district as fine as Ileyoba even *have* a Lower Market? I supposed it must, for though things like eggs and floor polish and sides of goat were unsightly, the manors of Ileyoba still needed them to run. You would not know it, though, from the elegant throngs of people bustling through the High Market, urgently browsing perfume and jewelry displays as though the baubles might feed their children.

What scared me more than anything, of course, was An-Ileyoba Palace, its sandstone walls and gold-capped towers looming in the near distance, home to the divine Raybearers and their Anointed Ones.

I tried to pretend it wasn't there as Finnric stopped the rickshaw near a fountain, and Onijibola gathered shoppers to gawk at me.

"Take a moment, ogas and madams!" he begged the slowly forming crowd. "Think of the worst thing you have ever done—yes, even that! The sins that have haunted you forever. I ask—what if the weight of those sins vanished in an instant? Scrubbed away by the voice of a divinely blessed scullery maid?"

"What other services does she offer?" leered a well-dressed nobleman, and his pack of attendants chuckled.

"Only the purest kind," Onijibola retorted, pinning the man with his fervent rheumy gaze. In general, Onijibola's bearing was so solemn that the crowd seemed chastened, eyeing me with equal parts doubt and wonder. I was deeply grateful for the veil.

"If any among you are completely free of transgressions," Onijibola continued in a theatric rasp, "such that you sleep with the peace of a blameless child, then pass us by! You have no need of the Balogun Inn's Hallowed Maid. But if, like many of us, you are haunted by past indiscretions . . . reserve your spot for Mamadele's Sin Salon, an event that takes place in just seven days' time! I will give you a token that you may redeem at the Balogun Inn for further details. But I warn you to make haste! This experience is open to only a select few."

The crowd swarmed Onijibola with questions, and I shot a nervous glance at Finnric. At the rate at which onlookers were appearing, it seemed unlikely he could pull the rickshaw away if the crowd grew unruly. He, in contrast, only puffed out his chest, basking under the attention of the well-dressed throng.

Just because they're rich, I wanted to hiss at him, *doesn't mean they won't rip us to pieces.*

But before I could form an escape plan, clanging symbols and a chorus of chanting echoed close by.

A parade of cultists had entered the square.

"Here come the loonies," Finnric snickered, but I did not laugh. In my experience, those who devoted their lives to worshipping the Raybearers were chillingly sound of mind. They had merely decided that people who did not share their fervor were enemies of truth—of goodness itself.

Shoppers groaned in annoyance as the cultists' voices drowned out Onijibola's, wailing hymns and lifting their mutilated hands to the palace in worship. The worshippers wore sweeping white cloaks, and lacy purple tattoos covered their skin.

"Praise the Idajo, woman-born and spirit-sired, Empress Redemptor and Raybearer undying; holy is she who for our transgressions fought death in the Underworld, and rose again victorious, to sit by her right hand, Ekundayo, in the righteous light of her Hallowed Anointed Ones . . ."

A few of the cultists stopped singing when they noticed my rickshaw and the crowd that gathered around it.

"You there!" cried one of the white-cloaked figures, striding toward Onijibola. They wore a sun-shaped mask that concealed their face. "What's this you're peddling about a girl absolving sins? Are you claiming this girl is a new Redemptor?"

"N-no," Onijibola stammered, his wrinkled hand going to his trouser pocket, where I knew he kept his worry-worn effigy of the Idajo.

"I should hope not," droned another of the cultists, this one with a mask shaped like a moon. He gestured to Palace Hill with an almost comical flourish. "That title belongs to the empress alone. Do not make us defend the honor of She Who Fought Death."

"Defend her honor?" Finnric snorted. "Didn't the Raybearers publicly disavow you fanatics? And they dropped those *emperor* and *empress* titles years ago. If you love Tarisai Idajo so much, why don't you listen to her?"

While I wished Finnric would shut his smug mouth and get us out of that square instead of grandstanding . . . as far as I knew, he was right.

I feel foolish now, speaking on things that you know more about than I ever will. But here is the average gutter girl's knowledge of Realmhood government: As long as anyone can remember, our continent has been ruled by leaders imbued with a power called the Ray, which binds their minds together and protects them from dying, except of old-old age. These Raybearers rule through a council of fearsome humans called Anointed Ones, who are chosen as children. Once, the Ray was bound to an imperial family, limiting those who ruled to those born in the royal line. But ten years ago, out of great kindness or great madness—the population had still not decided—the current Raybearers had dissolved the imperial dynasty, making it so the Ray could pass to any person worthy of leading the continent, even a peasant.

Finnric's retort did not ruffle the cultists at all. "Like all gods of old," intoned Sun-Face, "the Idajo speaks in riddles, and her perfect truth is revealed only to those who truly seek it."

"With her mouth," shouted Moon-Face, leaping onto the ledge of the fountain, "she disavows us! But with her heart, she embraces us and claims us as her true children, destined to sit beside her in Core and share in her immortal throne! By doing the opposite of what she *seemingly* says, we prove ourselves most faithful of all."

I squinted at Moon-Face. For just a moment, his reverent tone and grand gestures had held a hint of . . . mockery. As though Moon-Face was secretly laughing at his own cultist brethren. But I must have been wrong. His fellow worshippers clearly appreciated his speech, nodding and patting Moon-Face's back as he descended from the fountain.

"I would never disrespect the Idajo," Onijibola protested. "I . . . I'm only doing this because our mistress bid me to. And I must make a living somehow." He held up his gnarled fingers. "By trade, I am a humble cook. But though I have prayed to the Idajo for years, she has not yet, in her wisdom, seen fit to restore the use of my hands."

Sun-Face tutted gently. "My dear man," they said, "have you considered that the Idajo has withheld your healing on purpose, in order to lure you to a higher calling? Perhaps she will only commit to those who commit to her." They held up their left hand, revealing their amputated index finger. "Perhaps you must give, to receive in return."

"No!" snapped a voice, and I realized, belatedly, that it was mine.

The masked faces turned to glower at me. I ignored them, ripping off my veil and leaf crown to see Onijibola properly. "Don't do it," I pleaded, reaching to take the old man's soft, wrinkled hands in mine. "There's nothing holy about missing a limb. Believe me. I would know."

People like those cultists had tried to convince me otherwise my whole life. As if what happened to my foot in that sweatmill had been a blessing in disguise: some grand, mysterious lesson that the gods meant to form my character.

I had wanted to believe it. Truly, I did. For while I didn't relish the thought of divine beings maiming the foot of an eight-year-old, the idea of everything being my fault had been strangely comforting. Because that meant I could have done something to stop it. It meant that the world had rules.

It meant I had some semblance of control.

If I had been a better child, an obedient child who *knew her place*, then my mother would not have died, and I would never have gone to work in the sweatmill, and I would have two strong feet, and everything would be nice and right again.

I wanted to believe it. And most of the time, I could convince myself I did.

But deep down, a small, irritating voice whispered inside me: *Sweatmills do not need to exist at all.*

Children do not need to clear blockages from a water-powered stamping press meant to pulverize fibers into thin pages. Overseers do not have to drink on the job, making them careless with the safety lever holding the press in place. An eight-year-old does not need to scream, fruitlessly, for her mother, as a fifty-pound mallet maims her foot forever.

Sun-Face lifted his hand to rebuke me. "What place have you to reject the gifts of the Idajo—"

But before he could finish, chaos took the market as a shining squadron of armed warriors entered the square, arm and shoulder padding emblazoned with the dual-sun emblem of the Anointed Ones.

"This is an unauthorized gathering," announced a tall woman who appeared to be the squadron captain, placing a hand to the sword at her waist as she marched toward us. "Cultists, you are well aware the Anointed Ones have outlawed proselytization. Disperse in the name of the people!"

"It's the Raybearers' Guard!" squealed a gentry woman, giggling with excitement as the crowd and cultists fled in several directions, sweeping Onijibola and Finnric with them, and leaving me marooned in the rickshaw.

CHAPTER 14

MY HEAD SWIVELED IN PANIC. I COULD NOT RISK BEING trampled to death, and I would never make it back to the Balogun Inn fast enough to evade the Raybearers' Guard.

Then a white cloak flashed above me: Moon-Face had leapt over the crowd to seize my rickshaw. With inhuman speed, he towed it across the square, hurling us down a side street.

"Stop," I screeched as my seat bucked and bumped, the carriage nearly capsizing as my abductor careened through multiple alleyways. "Where are you taking me? I said—*stop!*"

Bracing myself for balance, I lifted my cane, leaned forward, and struck Moon-Face across his rippling cloaked shoulders.

The cultist howled, dropping the rickshaw and sending us both sprawling in the alleyway. We landed together in the gravel, and I scrambled away from his groaning form, waiting for him to seize me. Then a streak of green darted out from Moon-Face's cloak, stealing across the alley to perch on my knee.

"Clemeh," wheezed the gecko.

Slowly, I looked from Clemeh to the groaning, cloaked heap on the ground.

"Oh," I breathed. "*Oh.*"

I crawled over to the man and peeled off his leather mask. The Crocodile's chiseled features grimaced back at me as purple tattoos melted away from his dark skin.

"Nice hit," he chuckled with a pained cough. "Also, you look lovely in gold powder. The glow of a living idol suits you."

"But it cannot be you," I protested. "Your finger!" I seized his right hand. Before my eyes, his missing index finger reappeared . . . for of course, it had been an illusion.

My horror lessened only a little. The Crocodile could still be a cultist, even if he had faked the amputation. Reading the disgust on my face, he grunted and struggled to sit up.

"You will remember," he said, "that occasionally, I do favors for a friend of mine. Well, those favors include infiltrating groups on her behalf. The Boss Almighty is not fond of cultists. So I join their meetings to keep her updated on their movements, and I undermine them whenever possible."

My shoulders sagged in relief. "Then you are only a spy."

"I prefer the term *part-time professional nuisance*, but yes. It is . . . not as fulfilling as my old job. But it passes the time."

"What was your old job?"

He gave a sad, arrogant smile. "Changing the world." Then he winced again, shifting his shoulder blades.

"Sorry about that," I mumbled. "We should get you to a healer."

"No need," he said, struggling to his feet. He shed his cloak, retrieved my cane, and came to help me stand. "A perk of being cursed with immortality: one heals very quickly. I learned that after a year of looking for ways to die."

Before I could demand to know what he meant, the yells of the Raybearers' Guard echoed in the near distance. I froze.

"We have to get out of here," I whispered, seizing his elbow. "Come on."

"Don't worry," he murmured, though he tucked my hand snugly in the crook of his arm. "The Raybearers' Guard has more important things to do than comb the streets for stragglers."

"I won't risk it," I snapped.

"You've had run-ins with the Guard before?"

"No. But they work for the palace, and if we get arrested, they might bring us there, and . . ." I swallowed hard. "I won't go anywhere near the Anointed Ones, all right? I just won't."

His brow rose, but he relented, leading us around the corner and down another alleyway. This one contained a locked back door into one of the buildings.

"Shall we try hiding in here?" the Crocodile suggested. "The commotion with the Guard should die down in a couple hours."

Clemeh, who had followed us skittering along the walls, slipped under the door, then reappeared and chirped, "Clemeh!"

"He keeps saying that," the Crocodile said irritably. "I can't figure out what he means."

"That's his name," I said, leaning down to pick up the gecko. "You should have asked him for it long ago. All clear in there, Clemeh?"

The gecko scampered up to my shoulder, stuck out his tiny pink tongue at the Crocodile, then turned to me and nodded.

The Crocodile passed his hand over the lock. The veins in his cursed arm pulsed as the gears in the door came undone.

I hesitated, then asked, "You keep using your powers. When Ye Eun said it made your, ah, infection spread faster . . . was she wrong?"

"No. She was, as she has a habit of being, mercilessly correct." He gave a self-deprecating smirk. "But I have few useful skills. They were not encouraged in my past life, you see. So I have embraced the art of cheating."

"A picked lock is not worth turning into a beast for," I scolded.

His jovial expression remained, though it did not reach his eyes. "You do not have to worry about that anymore. I have made . . . arrangements so that when my final transformation is complete, you will be safe."

"What kind of arrangements?"

"Ones that will take me somewhere far from you. A place I cannot easily escape. You need never see me again."

"But what about you? What about ending your curse?"

He refused to answer, leaning over me to hold the door open. We passed into a cozy square room lit dimly by shuttered windows on the opposite wall. We had entered the closed storefront of a hair artisan. Braids, buns, and puffs made from dyed yarn and human hair extensions lined the walls on wooden display busts. Wide-toothed combs and pots of pomade lay neatly arranged on low tables. The space contained only three stylists' stools and velvet floor cushions, as though the store opened for a few select patrons at a time.

"Fancy," I muttered.

The hair artisans I knew and loved were the foulmouthed braiders who crowded in the muggy Ileyimo Lower Market, sweltering on stools beneath flimsy awnings. Their fingernails clacked with expert speed as they wove plaits and locs, gossiping cheerfully over the heads of their clients.

A tall, bronze-edged looking glass leaned against one wall of the studio, and I started in surprise. I was unused to my own reflection, as orphanages and sweatmills had little need for mirrors, but the girl in the glass looked . . . otherworldly. And not necessarily in a bad way. Gold powder had gilded the patches on her skin, so they shimmered like constellations across her dark face and shoulders.

In every other aspect, though, I found her wan and mousy, especially next to the man beside her. We looked absurd, side by side. I barely came to the Crocodile's shoulder, while his head grazed the frame. Where my features were snub and round, his were haughty and angular. My hair was plainly cornrowed, pinned to the nape of my scalp and unadorned even with Beauty Bisi's beads, as Mamadele had deemed them "too vain for a Curse-Eater"—while the Crocodile's locs hung in a thick jet fall to his waist, winking with tiny gilt cuffs and smooth cowrie shells.

But strangest of all was how the man gazed down at that girl, drawing unconsciously closer so the backs of their hands brushed, his dark eyes brimming with something warm and unreadable.

Then he noticed the mirror too. The Crocodile sucked the air through his teeth, touching the front of his scalp, where coiling new growth obscured the base of his locs. "This place is making me self-conscious," he said. "My roots are a mess. I have been so busy trying to manage this beast curse, I have not found a proper loctician."

I snorted in exasperation. He would look equally handsome bald or covered in a tangle of bird's nests, as I suspected he was well aware.

"I am very vain," he admitted, as though sensing my thoughts. His eyes met mine in the mirror, laughing. "It was an act at first. A persona I donned to lower the guard of my enemies. But I pretended so hard, the vanity became real. I now require myself to be devastating."

"Well," I laughed, "if you are suffering that much, I could help you retwist a few rows. We have hours to kill, after all."

The suggestion surprised us both. But the more we had watched each other in that mirror, the more I found myself desperate for something, anything to keep busy.

He looked on, wordless with amusement as I retrieved a comb, a wooden looped needle, and a water pitcher smelling of peppermint from the stylist's table. Schooling my face to be businesslike, I sank onto one of the low stools and nodded at the cushion beneath me.

"Sit," I ordered, and he obeyed, leaning so his rippling back rested between my knees and his shoulders pressed between my thighs.

When warmth stirred in my belly, I ordered it away in a panic.

He can sense when you are aroused, Sade. Do not embarrass yourself.

"Shouldn't take long," I chattered, dipping my fingertips in the tingling water before tracing the lines along his dark hairline. He shivered, as though with pleasure.

I split the coils into sections. "Interlocking is easy, when you have the right tools. I learned from some older girls in the sweatmill. They did hair on the side, when we were not working the paper press. It's good for spare—"

"You worked at a sweatmill?" he interrupted, jerking his head.

I turned his head back impatiently. "Yes. It is how I injured my foot, many years ago."

He was quiet for a moment, voice low with horror. "You would have been a child."

"Well," I said, beginning to loop the interlocking needle through his roots, "the Raybearers had not passed their edict yet. They did not find me in time. And I had to make a living then, just as I do now."

"Indeed," he said, his voice turned to gravel. "What is this nonsense I hear about a Sin Salon? I did not believe the rumors at first, but when I saw them drag you through that square . . ." He stiffened, a vein ticking in his brow. "In what way exactly," he asked, "does Mamadele expect you to make a bunch of lecherous rich pigs feel *innocent* again?"

"You have seen what I can do," I said, after a pause. "I . . . see something called spirit silt. It's like mud, or a pestilence, and we shed it everywhere—the stuff hopes and dreams are made of. That includes remorse. Regret for things a person has not achieved . . . or for what they have done."

"And those sods," the Crocodile said, "expect you to rid them of remorse for what they have done? Are you to wash their wounds, as you did mine?"

"No," I said.

My mouth had gone dry. Ever since Mamadele had explained her plan to me, I had put that upcoming evening from my mind, trying not to feel the slime of worms wriggling down my throat, invading my body forever.

"They are not like you," I said. "They are not wounded, only . . . dirty. Filled with—with something awful. And when Mamadele holds her Sin Salon, she plans for them to—well—give me all their awfulness at once. Then I am to get rid of it."

"How?" the Crocodile demanded, turning around completely and gripping the base of my stool. "Sade, what is Mamadele planning for you to do?"

My hands trembled in my lap. "Eat it," I whispered. "So they don't feel guilty anymore."

He laughed shortly—a harsh, enraged sound.

"For all that has changed since I stepped out of this world," he said, "I am newly horrified by how much it has stayed the same."

My gaze remained on my lap. His hands reached to cover mine.

"I am sorry they asked that of you," he sighed. "But at least you're not going through with it,"

I blinked at him. "What do you mean?"

His expression was disbelieving. "Sade, you can't possibly be considering doing as Mamadele asked. It's preposterous."

"It's a job," I retorted.

He stood. "They are asking you," he growled, "to bear the pain of the ones who *made* your life a living hell. The kind of people who own sweatmills. The kind of people who built their fortunes on the limbs of children."

"And what else am I to do?" I shot back, rising from the stool. Hair supplies tumbled from my lap to the floor. "Let Mamadele, the only one who offered me a home, throw me out onto the streets? Hope that someone, somewhere, won't mind hiring a spirit-touched edict brat with a foot that barely works?"

"Anything." He stared down at me coldly. "Anything would be better than letting those bastards . . . violate you like that."

I glared up at him through angry tears. "Spoken like someone who has never gone hungry a day in his life."

His chest deflated, and he lowered his gaze from mine.

"Things have changed since you were a child," he said. "In the old regime, the poor had nothing. But these days, there are . . . resources for people like you. The Mercy Aunties at those orphanages are terrible at teaching children what their options are, especially when they don't get adopted. But we can get help. Appeal to your district's justice council. The Anointed Ones—"

"No," I cut in, my voice shrill. "No Anointed Ones. I told you already, so just let it be, all right?"

His features narrowed in confusion. "Sade," he asked, voice softening. "Why do you fear the Anointed Ones?"

I froze, my tongue going numb.

"I mean, everyone is *generally* afraid of them," he added dryly. "Seeing as they're mentally bonded freaks with supernatural abilities that rule our entire known world. But your fear seems . . . personal. Why?"

I swallowed hard, visions of firelight, and feathers, and beautiful, terrible faces swimming before my eyes.

You must understand that for years, I had tried to forget the night had ever happened. I had to bear the shame in secret. Tried to embrace that terrible lesson—*know your place*—without feeling the scars behind it. But it had not worked. And now here was the Crocodile, staring at me as though I were blameless. As if I didn't deserve what had happened to me since.

As though, through a single act of rebellion, I had not killed my own mother.

I inhaled shakily. Maybe if I confessed, he would leave me alone. If I finally said everything out loud, perhaps this god who filled my heart with impossible fantasies would come to his senses and leave my side, and my life would be dull, and safe, and ordinary again.

So I sank back down onto the stool and retrieved the comb and needle, gesturing for him to sit again. "I'll have to start from the beginning," I said.

And so I did.

PART III

CHAPTER 15

BEFORE I WAS BORN, MY MOTHER WAS CALLED FOLA.

I never met my father, though Mamasade called him *trifling* so often that as a small child, I mistook it for his name.

Whenever I asked about Trifling, Mamasade told me that some people are only kind until they find a better way to make you stay.

And his way, she said, had been me. For once Trifling found out that my mother was with child, his kindness had winked out like a lamp in a gust of wind. His kisses had soured into snarls. His embraces into slaps and punches, and he grew worse every hour until she fled in the dead of night, delivering me alone in the shadows of the Haunted Bush.

Mamasade always told this story with a silly, growling voice for Trifling, and dramatic gestures for her labor in the forest, as though her living nightmare had been nothing more than an entertaining cookfire tale. She had a knack for that—giving me the truth plain while stripping it of terror as best she could.

"It was as though," Mamasade would say, placing my small hands on her belly, "that man felt you growing inside me and thought: 'Ah! Here is a pin to pierce Fola and keep her by my side forever.'"

"But it didn't work," I would pipe up, adding to the story.

"No, my Clever Sade. Because you were not a pin. You have always been my strong, gutsy girl, and when you kicked, I heard you whisper: 'Go, Fola, go!'"

"I wouldn't have called you that," I would object, crossing my arms with mock seriousness. "I would have called you *mama*."

"Very well. 'Go, Mamasade!' you said, and I heard you. So we ran for miles—*patah-patah, patah-patah*—until my sandals were worn, and we had to stop, for you were eager to come out."

"The nearby villages weren't safe," I'd put in. "Because we had to go somewhere that Trifling wouldn't follow us."

Mamasade would explain how the Bush was one of many stretches of land across the continent, each affected by a centuries-old enchantment, which had thinned the lines between this world and the malevolent realm of spirits.

"The only way to protect yourself in the Bush," she said, "is to stick to the path near the kiriwi flowers. The blossoms are kind to mortals, shielding our senses from the glamour of spirits, who would otherwise lure us deeper into the wilderness, tempting us with visions of our greatest desires."

"So you ate flowers by the fistful," I said, quickly coming to my favorite part of the story. "And all the while, I leapt in your belly, saying 'Mama, I want to come out!'"

"And I followed a trail of kiriwi that led to a cave. Then I uprooted the plants, making a bed of petals and rushes, and that is where I laid your head, when hours later . . ."

"Singing *waa, waa*!"

". . . you, my Sade, were born."

That is where she ended the story. But we both knew that the kiriwi—whose scent had coated my newborn lungs, and whose essence had filled my belly, when Mamasade put me to her breast—had done more than protect us that night. In that enchantment-soaked nest of Mamasade's love and despair, the kiriwi had opened a window in my tiny mind's eye, allowing me to see the silt and hear songs that no one else could.

Still weak from childbirth, days later my mother had staggered back out of the Bush with me in her arms. But that unnatural forest bent the rules of time and distance. Though Mamasade had retraced her steps as best as she could, the Bush spat her out hundreds of miles from where she entered. Instead of the muggy farmlands where she had lived with Trifling, she now found herself looking at the sea, overlooked by a cliff with a sparkling fortress.

"It was something out of a dream," she told me later. "I looked at that castle and thought, *Surely, no evil can find us here.*"

She would later learn that the castle was Yorua Keep, where young Raybearers and their councils lived and studied for years, awaiting the day of their continent-wide coronation. Flanking the sacred fortress was Yorua Village: a town of artisans and fishermen supplied the keep with all they needed to live in gilded isolation.

When townspeople saw Mamasade stumble into town from the haunted Bush, clutching me to her chest in a blood-soaked wrapper, they had brushed their chins with their thumbs, making the sign of the Pelican to ward off evil.

"Bride," Mamasade gasped, before the strangers could chase her off. "In the name of Am the Storyteller—I wed myself to the village, and invoke all the rights of a Village Bride."

The strangers had grumbled but took her in, bathing me and Mamasade in a nearby stream and granting her sanctuary in the crumbling shed of a town elder.

The custom of a Village Bride or Groom is a very old one, predating the Realmhood and even the Arit Empire. Back when Oluwan was a splintered plain of clans and tribal territories, marriage was the only way to leave one tribe and join another. But if due to exile or natural disaster, a person found themselves without tribe or spouse . . . they could then "wed" an entire clan, binding themselves as a lifelong servant to the village and doing whatever menial tasks the tribe saw fit in exchange for food and shelter.

Once a Village Groom or Bride declared marriage, a clan could not annul the match unless the person committed three vices—that is, acts of dishonor against the community.

"Your first vice," the Yorua Village elders told my mother, "was coming out of that Bush. Who knows what ill spirits you have brought with you? See that you do not dishonor our town any further."

Mamasade had gritted her teeth and nodded, keeping her head down for my sake.

And that is how we lived for years. Mamasade gutted fish and scrubbed chamber pots, dodging the scorn of gossips and the wandering hands of town lechers . . . while I padded beside her, clueless of our precarious position in the village, and basking in the cool, generous shade of my mother's love.

Once she had served the village faithfully for three years, custom obliged the community to build us a hut of our own. It was there—in our one-room mudbrick house, with its tiny gated yard of fragrant lemongrass—that my Mamasade began to smile again. From our years in the shed, she had developed a dry, persistent cough. As a Village Bride, she could never marry, nor pursue any profession that the townsfolk did not choose for her. But in giving up her freedom, she had won mine. For once Yorua Village had accepted my mother as their bride, honor bound them to treat her offspring as true children of the village.

"So you hold your head high," Mamasade reminded me every morning, dressing me in crisp, clean linen and twisting my hair with shea until every coil shone. "Do you hear, my Strong Sade? In the eyes of the elders, you are no less respectable than any other child. So don't let anyone treat you different."

And I didn't. When the children skipped rope in the market, I counted myself in and jumped alongside them. At the crowded village school, I sat in the very front row, and when bullies pushed me in the yard, I pushed them right back.

And at the end of every day, after jeers and side-glances had covered me in spirit silt, I splashed in the stream behind our hut, singing at the top of my small lungs, as I scoured my neighbors' fears and cruel expectations from my skin.

Say what you like! The water knows—
Yell all you want! The water knows—
Call me your names! The water knows—
I'm Sade, ha, Sade, ha, Sade!

When I was five, my spots began to appear.

"This is what happens," intoned an elder, staring with distaste at the milky patches on my face and arms, "when you whelp out a child in the Bush."

"Her looks do not come from where she was born," Mamasade snapped. I buried my face in Mamasade's stomach, confused by the elders' stares. I liked my spots, most days. They looked like clouds, floating across the sky in the lazy shapes of my favorite animals. Why didn't the elders like them too?

As the eyes of the village pressed around us, Mamasade forced a smile at the elders, fixing her tone to be sweet. Swallowing her pride, as always, to protect me. "Sade's skin runs in the family," she explained patiently. "My sister had skin like hers, as did my grandfather. They had to avoid the sun a bit more than I did, but beyond that—they were perfectly hale and healthy. Nothing came of it."

The elder's eyes narrowed. "Only time will tell if your Small Sade is unlucky. But in a village such as ours, built to honor the Anointed Ones—appearance is everything. If such irregularities run in your family, you should have told us before binding your bloodline to ours in marriage. As punishment . . . this community finds you guilty of a second vice."

Mamasade sobbed in our bedroll that night, which worsened her persistent cough. I still was not exactly sure what a vice was. But I did know that if Mamasade was ever to smile again, I had to show the whole village that we belonged. And if Yorua Village existed to serve the Anointed Ones, then I would serve them best of all.

Every school day began outside, where we children would line up to face the cliff over the sea. Yorua Keep sparkled against the horizon, smiling down at us, and we would pray to each of the Anointed Ones by name.

"Lead us, Ekundayo of Oluwan, blessed prince and Raybearer undying. Judge us, Tarisai of Swana, High Lady Judge Apparent. Heal us, Kirah of Blessid Valley, Priestess of the Realm. Protect us, Sanjeet of Dhyrma, heir to the High Lord General . . ."

Whenever we named Sanjeet, a nervous giggle would ripple through the line. Parents often cited the actions of Anointed Ones as examples for children to follow, but Anointed Honor Sanjeet was both loved and feared. They said he could grow twenty feet tall, and sniff out weakness in the body of any living thing, and grind his foes to bone using nothing but his fists.

We knew Sanjeet to be the future High Lord General, leader of our continent's vast Army of Twelve Realms. But legend also claimed him to be Prince Ekundayo's personal protector. As a result, he was often called "the Prince's Bear," and Yorua Village invoked his name to chasten their children into good behavior.

Pipe down and go to sleep, or the Prince's Bear will carry you off in the night! Stay out of those honeycakes; the Prince's Bear will snap your fingers in two. Fix your tone, or the Prince's Bear will gallop down from Yorua Keep and fix it for you!

I needed no such threats to behave, at least not in public. I had now learned that our place in the village depended on others thinking well of us. If we lost our house, nothing would stop that raging man from my birth story, Trifling, from finding us. My toddler's mind began to conflate Trifling with Sanjeet the Anointed One, until I was half convinced that some half-father, half-general ogre skulked the plains between Yorua Keep and the Bush, eager for the chance to devour me.

The year I turned six, the Anointed Ones of Yorua Keep visited the village.

It was the night of a holy festival, Nu'ina Eve, and we had prepared for months. The Anointed Ones were to provide a feast for the entire village, and in exchange, we were to entertain them, training dancers to act out stories of the gods. The highest ceremony of the evening would involve a select few of the village children crowning each Anointed One with palm wreaths. The honor of this task was so great, it would follow the child to adulthood, shielding them from reproof—for what dishonor could stain hands that had *touched* a living god?

If I crowned an Anointed One, I realized, throwing myself into my school studies with fervor, I could save me and Mamasade from exile. We would be more than saved—we would be *popular*.

The elders held a contest in the square: Whichever child could recite the full genealogy of five-hundred years of Raybearers, as well as their councils of Anointed Ones, would be allowed to participate in the Nu'ina Eve Ceremony.

When I stepped up before the elders, chuckles peppered the square. I was well known, even at this early date, for being hopeless with letters. I could not pore over scrolls of names, nor could my equally illiterate mother help me.

Still, I had a very good memory, aided by my unique ability to pull songs from the air. Whenever the schoolmasters read out the names of Raybearers, I tapped my foot quietly, tacking a rhythm to each dynasty. I would volunteer to dust the genealogy scrolls, singing all the while and inhaling the spirit silt that tended to rest on anything having to do with the Anointed Ones. The hopes and fears of countless Arit citizens whispered in that silt, and sometimes, those whispers held names.

I sang those names in the market square. And out of all twelve children selected for the Nu'ina Eve Ceremony, only I recited every Raybearer and Anointed One without error.

The night of the festival—which we held in a starlit valley just outside the village, yards from the ocean—felt like something out of a cookfire tale. Mountains of rice. Rivers of stew. Mamasade and I stuffed our faces with golden plantain and fried *chin-chin* dough until our bellies stretched taut, which was wise—for once the Anointed Ones arrived, I could not have eaten a single bite for nerves.

They did not glow with divine light, or fly into the village on celestial wings, as half the children had rumored they would. Still—

They were the most beautiful creatures I had ever seen.

I had a vague idea of what each Anointed One looked like, from the handmade shrines and effigies scattered throughout the village. But the crowd pressed so tall around me, I barely had time to see the Anointed Ones' faces. I knew there were twelve, of course—one for each realm of Aritsar—with the myriad of clothing, skin color, and hair styles of their various homelands. But somehow, they filled a space the way a single person might—a presence so united, I was surprised they did not move and speak in tandem.

Those people seemed full adults to me, back then. I am startled to realize now they would have been younger even than I am today—some barely fifteen. At one point, Raybearer Ekundayo—the holy prince undying, direct descendant of Enoba the Perfect!—joined a sweaty throng of dancing village children, purposely dipping and weaving to make us laugh.

I would not get to choose which Anointed One I would crown. But I had high hopes that I would get Kirah of Blessid Valley. According to the stories, she had a blood gift for singing, like me, only her voice cured physical ailments instead of revealing spirit silt. Perhaps I could convince her to take Mamasade's cough away.

At last, the moment came when one by one, the Anointed Ones accepted a token from the elders, and then turned to receive crowns from us children. I held my wreath crown nervously, trying not to crush the green fronds in my sweating hands. The other children who had won the elder's contest jostled me to the back of the line. I could not see over their shoulders, but Prince Ekundayo's warm, friendly voice floated down to my ears as he collected his crown. Then Anointed Honor Ai Ling collected hers, and then, to my despair, Anointed Honor Kirah. I stamped impatiently, quickly losing track of which Anointed Ones had been crowned, and who hadn't. Who would be left for me?

At last, no one stood between me and the raised dais where the Anointed Ones sat side by side. I scampered toward them, dazzled by the firelight glinting off their jeweled circlets and smiling faces . . .

. . . when a giant knelt before me, blocking out the light with his mountainous shoulders, pinning me in place with sad, hooded eyes.

My blood ran to ice. I recognized Sanjeet of Dhyrma, of course, from the tapestries and totems bearing his image, placed around the village as talismans to ward off thieves and invaders. But as the festival drums pounded in my ears, peppered by the villagers' whispers and the distant sound of Mamasade's coughing, my vision began to swim.

The Prince's Bear will carry you off in the night.
We had to enter the Bush, or Trifling would find us.
The Prince's Bear will snap your fingers in two!
Here is a pin to pierce Fola and keep her by my side forever . . .

"Rude girl," hissed one of the villagers from the crowd. "You must crown His Anointed Honor."

But something warm was trickling down my leg. I mewled, mortified; I had wet myself in fear.

"I don't want to," I whispered, trembling as I watched Sanjeet's wide, calloused hands. Did he even need them to crush me? Could he hurt me, as Trifling had hurt Mamasade, simply by willing it in his mind?

"Please," I heard him say. His voice was low and cavernous, like thunder contained in a vessel. "Don't be afraid."

He *reached* for me.

"No!" I shrieked. Visions of faceless men and Bush monsters rose before me, and I stumbled back, dropping the wreath crown. "No, Prince's Bear. Don't hurt me. Don't—"

I turned tail and dove into the crowd for cover. I don't remember much after that, only that Mamasade's arms eventually found me and carried me back to our hut.

She did not scold me as she bathed my brow and pressed her hand to my chest, coaxing me to take deep breaths.

"There, there. Nice and easy." She crooned to me and smiled kindly, though her eyes brimmed with grief I did not yet understand. "Good girl, my Sade. You are safe now."

Then she tucked me into bed and began to pack our things.

Dawn had barely blushed across the horizon when the village elders arrived at our doorstep, bearing torches and grim expressions.

"We need not explain why," one of them intoned to Mamasade, "you have earned your third vice."

Mamasade smiled tightly. "You would cast us out for the tears of a frightened child?"

"No. But we have long recognized your failure to raise that girl in a respectful manner. When you stumbled out of the Bush all those years ago, you did not throw yourself on the mercy of just any village, Mamasade. Our town lives in the shadow of Raybearers—of rulers blessed by the gods. To look in the face of an Anointed One and throw away their crown . . ." The elder shuddered. "The sacrilege! The ingratitude!"

"We both know," Mamasade said, struggling through her coughs, "that this has nothing to do with gratitude."

The elder's features pinched together. "What in Am's name is that supposed to mean?"

"It means that I see how you have watched her all these years. Frowning when she laughs too loud. Or walks too tall. Or bests your bratty children in their games. You never wanted Sade to be grateful." My mother's voice dropped to a hiss. "You wanted her to be *small*. To know always that she is less. To skulk around this town with her head bowed, forever indebted to your cold-blooded charity. But I won't raise her that way. Do you understand? I can't. I won't."

"You may raise that girl any way you like," the elder replied, lip curled. "But you will not do it here. Mamasade, born Fola: Let it be known that as of today, Yorua Village officially discards you as its wife."

That evening, when the sun dipped low on the horizon, I rubbed my aching feet and asked Mamasade, "Is it storytime yet?"

"Not yet, my Sade," she panted. "Almost there."

We had returned to the Bush and walked for hours, the meager content of our Yorua Village hut strapped to our backs.

All the while, I had chewed the side of my cheek. When that didn't hurt enough, I found a small pebble with slightly sharp edges and sucked it until the top of my mouth drew blood.

"What's that?" Mamasade asked with a frown, hearing the stone as it clacked against my teeth.

"It's a prayer pebble," I mumbled, turning my head so she wouldn't see the blood. "So the Goddess of Earth will help us find a new home."

We had lost everything because of me.

Mamasade had insisted it wasn't my fault, but I had heard what she said to the elders.

You wanted her to be small.

Somehow my largeness had cost us our home. My voice. My *no*.

I had to punish myself. I had to prove to the gods that I was sorry. So I'd scrape that *no* out of my mouth, all day. Every day if I had to. And if I did it well enough, Mamasade and I would find a new village. She would get better, and the elders would want to marry her forever.

I would never again forget my place.

When the Bush path guided us to a cave covered in kiriwi flowers, Mamasade laughed and sobbed at the same time, wheezing around a knot of phlegm in her lungs.

"Don't worry," she said, once she had calmed down. We had lined the cave floor with rushes, unpacked our bedrolls, and struck up a quivering fire for light. "It's just for tonight. Until I get my strength back."

Tonight became many nights, for Mamasade's cough worsened. She needed my help to stagger to a nearby stream, where we scrubbed our clothes and relieved ourselves. We boiled the Bush water with kiriwi leaves, so we could drink it without risk of enchantment, and rationed the handfuls of rice we had brought from the village. Mamasade told me stories every night, until her voice weakened to a whisper. Then I told the stories, making up songs to go with them, and jiggling her shoulders whenever she grew too still.

"No sleeping, Mamasade!" I scolded, fear spiking in my voice. "The story's not over yet!"

Slowly, her eyes would flutter open, and she would smile. "Of course not, my Sade. I was only trying to dream a better ending."

On the night she didn't wake up, I sucked the jagged prayer pebble until my mouth grew so swollen, I could not swallow. Then I wove kiriwi blossoms into her soft black hair, lay down beside her, and went to sleep.

CHAPTER 16

THE CROCODILE SAT MOTIONLESS, MY HANDS IN HIS HAIR. Even restless Clemeh had gone still, clinging protectively to my shoulder.

"There isn't much else to the story," I said, unhooking the needle from the Crocodile's locs. "Eventually, I ran out of food. So I walked for a few days—or hours, you can never be certain in the Bush—and the kiriwi path spat me out near Dejitown, where I got my job at the sweatmill."

Before I could hook the needle to start a new row, the Crocodile turned and cupped my cheek.

"Spit it out," he whispered.

I quailed at his touch. "What do you mean?"

"The pebble. You still have it." His features contorted. "I've seen it beneath your tongue. I didn't know what it was at first, but . . . Am's Story, Sade." His voice broke. "How could you want to hurt yourself?"

"It doesn't mean anything," I mumbled, trying to squirm away. "An old habit. And it's . . . a different stone from when I was little. Not as sharp. And I do not use it all the time. Only when—"

"Out," he growled, and I reflexively pressed my mouth shut.

"Please," he added, sounding tired.

The pebble floated across my tongue and pressed against my lips, before at last I sulkily allowed it to plop into his palm.

"There," he breathed. And for some reason I could not explain, his relief made me want to cry.

I shoved him away instead, standing and busying myself by putting hair tonics I had borrowed back in their places.

"Dejitown was known for paper and bookbinding," I said. "Before I started working, an urchin gang took me in. We stayed together for a while, until traffickers started picking us off for pleasure bazaars. I got lucky: They picked me for a sweatmill instead. Then the Raybearers passed that edict about children, the cart brought me to Oluwan City, and, well . . ." I wiped my hands on my wrapper, avoiding his gaze. "Now you know why I can't go near Anointed Ones. Yes, it is unlikely they remember what I did to them, but—"

"Remember what you *did to them*?" the Crocodile cried, clutching a fistful of his newly locked hair in disbelief. "When you were a frightened child who backed out of a silly crown ritual? The Anointed Ones would not punish you, Sade, they would *fight* for you. And if their benevolent shadows loom so large that without trying, their mere presence ruins the life of a little girl, then perhaps Anointed Ones should not exi—"

"Stop," I rasped, rounding on him. "Please. Just . . . stop, all right? I don't know what the world is like where you come from. Some realm of gods, or sorcerers, or—swamp alagbatos, I don't know. But this world, the one that made me, does not care what people deserve. It cares about rules. At least, it cares about rules for people like me, and I know too well, oga, what happens when we break them."

He watched me for a moment. "Are you doing the Sin Salon to punish yourself?"

"No," I shot back. "I am doing it because some of us must work to survive. Some of us need jobs."

"But why *that* job?" he pressed. "What if we could get you another one?"

I paused, considered. While I would never love those horrid stairs, I had grown attached to the Balogun Inn. Especially mournful was the idea of leaving the Amenities. Wafa and Kanwal, Hanuni and Onijibola—even Finnric had burrowed a small, strange place in my heart.

"I do not know," I said. "The Sin Salon is in seven days, and we will be preparing the inn day and night. I do not have time to look for something else, and if Mamadele finds out I have been offering my services elsewhere, she will fire me on the spot."

"That would not matter," he said slowly, "if you had somewhere else to go. What if you came and lived at Bhekina House? That's what it's called, by the way. The villa behind my shrines."

"Oga." My eyes grew to the size of moons. "Are you asking me to be your cleaning lady? Or . . ." I swallowed hard. "Or something else?"

"Neither," he blurted, raising both his hands, as if to reassure me. "The house is not mine, so I would not be your boss. You could do as you liked. And . . ." He sighed, pinching the bridge of his nose. "Look. While it is fairly obvious I have wanted to kiss you ever since you scolded me on that rooftop, I would never touch you unless you asked. That villa is massive. I could stay in an entirely different wing if you like. And you need only stay until you find a place you like better, though—" He rocked on his feet. "In the spa, you said you wanted a home you could get lost in. A place that always changes, yet somehow stays the same. And I cannot think of any place more like that than Bhekina House."

He stopped then, anxiously scanning my face.

I opened my mouth. Closed it. At last I murmured, "It . . . was not obvious."

"What?"

My face burned. "What you wanted on the rooftop. It was not obvious."

"Oh." He raised an eyebrow. "That surprises me. I am known for many things, but subtlety is not one of them."

"I do not understand why you are helping me at all," I began, and then palmed my forehead with realization.

The bond.

"You said my needs would be hard to ignore," I exclaimed. Had I enslaved him by accident? Was our body-bond forcing him to try to find a home for me? My heart pounded with guilt. It was all starting to make sense—even his supposed urge to kiss me in the rooftop garden. I should not have been so reckless with my attraction. "I am sorry," I moaned. "I did not mean to make you feel things; that is not fair. I can try to stop."

His confused expression turned mirthful.

"Sade," he asked, "are you under the impression that you forced my attraction to you?" When I nodded miserably, he said: "I am . . . confident you did not." His voice softened to a rumble, his eyes falling to my mouth. "Suffer no anxiety on that point. And I wish you would stop calling me oga. I am not anyone's *sir* or *boss*."

"But you used to be," I said, "didn't you?"

He face closed up, blank with caution.

I pressed: "I barely know anything about you. How did you come to be cursed? Where is your home—your people? I mean, aside from the realm of Djbanti. I cannot trust you until I know more."

He straightened in alarm. "How did you know I am from Djbanti?"

I gave a small smile. "I did not," I admitted. "But you pronounce certain words like Hanuni, and she is from Djbanti too. She has a commoner's accent, though." I paused, proceeding carefully. "You sound more like Lady Injaana. I heard she fled from Djbanti after the commoners' revolution. A lot of nobles did."

"I am not fleeing from anyone," the Crocodile said through gritted teeth. "And any gentry who fled Djbanti are likely warlord leeches who should be caught and brought to justice by the people they exploited."

"Then you weren't one of those gentry?"

He said nothing.

"How do you know Ye Eun?" I demanded. "She said you were murdered, and then you disappeared. And how—"

"I cannot tell you more than you know already."

"I will only consider staying," I told him, "if you tell me your name."

We watched each other for a moment. His features shaded with stubbornness, undercut with a deep, simmering longing.

"If you move to Bhekina House," he said quietly, "you will be safe, Sade. I have made sure that when my curse progresses and I grow into something I do not recognize, you will never see me again." Dread stole into his gaze as he touched the green scales on his arm. "For I dare not hope that this beast, whoever he is, can be tamed."

We remained at an impasse, even when the Crocodile returned me via rickshaw to the Balogun Inn's back gate.

"My work with the cultists will keep me busy over the next few days," he said. "But if you change your mind about the Sin Salon, you know where to go. My shrines will always be open to you." He hesitated. "In the meantime . . . I would like to see you. If that's all right."

"As a plumber?" I asked. "Mamadele is unlikely to have the spa serviced this week. She is too busy preparing for the salon."

The Crocodile's brow furrowed. "I could send notes."

I laughed lightly. "You can send them," I replied, "but I cannot read them."

He had the decency to look embarrassed, and then he frowned again. "I'll find a way," he murmured to himself, and then disappeared with Clemeh.

Moments later, Mamadele burst through the double doors, fawning as she folded me into her arms. I thought she had been concerned for my safety until she started blubbering into my hair.

"I worried you had been poached," she sobbed. "That you'd whored yourself out to one of my rivals, like some sneaky little traitor. But here you are, my good girl." She sniffled and tapped the tip of my nose. "My darling, loyal Small Sade."

The next day, Mamadele announced that I was to have a raise: four kirahs a month instead of two. I was also to stop being Dele's lady's maid and become hers instead.

"A new life," she told me, eyes growing misty. "No more sleeping in that creaky garret. You are to have your own private room, just like Simple Hanuni. I treat her like family, you know. And if you keep being my good girl, why . . . you might almost be a daughter to me. And families do not turn their backs on each other. Do they, Small Sade?"

She pinched my chin and smiled, not letting go until I smiled back.

My new room was a converted closet, right around the corner from Mamadele's room.

"You will get much better sleep here than in that creaky attic," Mamadele said, lining the closet with woven mats and dotting it with plush tasseled pillows. "Some peace and quiet at last, after having to share the floor with those chattering Dhyrmish sisters."

At the thought of never again sitting up with Wafa and Kanwal—giggling and trading stories until we drifted asleep to the chorus of *Feather Pillow, Breakfast Tray, Baby Rattle*—my heart sank.

"I suppose we should call you Fancy Sade now," Kanwal deadpanned as I helped her and Wafa decorate the front hall great room for the Sin Salon.

"I am still an Amenity," I protested. "And I want an Amenity name." Secretly, I felt guilty asking for one, now that I had considered leaving the inn altogether. But the Crocodile's offer still felt like a far-far dream. And the more tirelessly everyone worked to prepare for my debut at Mamadele's Sin Salon, the more selfish that dream seemed.

Wafa sighed as she teetered on a stool to drape the eaves with festoons. "When I said I liked musical performances," she said, "this isn't what I meant."

"It is a *little* like a dreamscape," I said with strained cheer, filling lamps with perfumed oil and placing them in nooks around the hall. "We will have lighting and music, and I will sing, and people will tell their stories—"

"You know it is not the same," snapped Kanwal. "Small Sade . . . after you ate Mamadele's sins, you were sick for days. For Am's sake, you couldn't even eat Kanwal stew."

"And that's its own kind of sin," Wafa put in.

"The worst kind," I joked, but Kanwal's scowl only deepened.

"How do you plan to survive this? Suppose the salon kills you?"

"It won't," I said, though silently I added: *At least, not my body*.

I thought of cowering on the floor of Mamadele's room, feverish as I clasped my mouth, begging for the guiltworms to stay down. In the worst moments, I had not felt pain but emptiness. As though Small Sade was no longer there and never had been. There had only ever been Mamadele's misdeeds, her despair, and her resulting malice, turning in an endless cycle, over and over like the water-powered wheel of a sweatmill.

For the next day, I had become one with that wheel, going through the motions of my chores without thoughts for the past or future. I had needed to keep moving so the despair would not catch up with me.

"If anything, it will make me a better worker," I said with forced laughter as I trimmed the lamp wicks. "Scrubbing floors will not seem so bad after eating guiltworms for a few hours."

Before Wafa and Kanwal could respond, something bumped across the hall's floor, causing all three of us to jump. A small intruder barreled toward me, then skidded to a stop, tiny belly panting with effort. It was Clemeh, dragging a long, stoppered gourd by a piece of twine tied to his body. He opened his mouth—no doubt to announce *Small Sade*—but I cleared my throat loudly, cutting him off.

"It is a wonder how these creatures keep getting in," I said in a shrill, scooping up both the gourd and Clemeh and willing him to stay quiet. "Fifth lizard I have seen this week. They must be left over from the rainy season."

Wafa and Kanwal were not fooled.

"Small Sade," Wafa said, wide brown eyes growing even wider. "Did that gecko . . . *deliver* something to you?"

"No," I blurted, clutching the gourd to my chest.

"A beast whisperer as well as a Curse-Eater," Kanwal mused, unflappable as usual. "You might have told us, Small Sade. If you can talk to animals, it will save me a lot of trouble setting rat traps."

"I cannot," I said, cupping Clemeh and edging to a side door. "I mean, I am not. It is complicated. Look, I will just . . . let this critter out in the garden, shall I?"

"Tell him we have a beetle problem," Wafa called after me. "If you are to have reptile gentlemen callers, they might as well make themselves useful."

CHAPTER 17

I ESCAPED INTO THE YARD BEHIND THE INN, SCOLDING Clemeh as he squirmed in my hand. "Am's Story, Clemeh. You've got to stop showing up out of nowhere. How am I supposed to explain—"

"Crocodile," Clemeh croaked indignantly, indicating the gourd with a flick of his tongue before escaping my grip and climbing to my shoulder.

"Are you errand boy as well as messenger now?" I sighed. "What is this?"

I weighed the gourd with both hands. It was long and pale, and the stopper made me think it held liquid. But when I shook it, nothing sloshed inside, though a faint pressure strained the rubbery walls. Cautiously, I took out the stopper. The gourd vibrated as a voice thrummed out at me.

"*Hello, Sade, assuming that this works. I have never tried containing a voice but in the end, it is no different than—*"

I gave a little shriek, stoppering the gourd again.

Then I glanced around in a panic. The yard was empty, so I could not have been overheard. That also meant, to my chagrin, that the voice—the *Crocodile's* voice—had to have come from that gourd. You will think that I am a madwoman, but I held up the gourd and examined it, searching its smooth ridges for signs of life.

"Hello?" I whispered. "Crocodile, are you trapped in there?"

No response. On my shoulder, Clemeh made an impatient sound but offered no further clues. So I unstoppered the gourd again, this time peering inside as the voice poured out. Nothing but blackness stared back, though the voice picked up exactly where it had left off.

"—*containing a breeze in a bottle, which is one of the first ways Ixalix showed me how to use my power. I have created a vacuum, so when this message ends, you can send one back. You said, in that adorably indignant tone of yours, that you would not come to Bhekina House unless I told you my name. I propose a compromise: My name shall be whatever you say it is. Have you any suggestions? I am fond of descriptive epithets, like 'That Glorious Flying Man,' or 'Sorcerer with the Very Good Hair.' But these are a mouthful, and as I hold your lips in highest regard, I would not tire them. This gourd is beginning to bloat, so I conclude—speak your reply, stopper the gourd, and send it back with Clemeh. Did I say please? Please, then. I await your judgment, Sensible Sade.*"

And with that, the gourd grew still.

I began to laugh. "You want a name, do you?" I shouted into the gourd, not believing for a moment that my words would be contained. "How about Stubborn Fool Who Interrupts My Chores for No Reason? Though I admit," I muttered to myself, "you do have very good hair."

I replaced the cork, set Clemeh on the ground, and reattached the gourd to his string. He skittered off, and I returned to the front hall, hoping the Crocodile had appeased his boredom.

Clemeh reappeared the next day as I hung clothes to dry in the yard. This time, he toted a bright green calabash, tied with a glistening string of freshwater pearls. Huffing with exasperation, I took out the stopper.

"*Stubborn Fool Who Interrupts My Chores,*" purred the disembodied voice. "*Alluring, though the syllables sound foreign—I am unable to place the name's origin. Is it from Moreyao or Swana? I will bow to your judgment, but I think we should go for something less exotic. Also—about the day we met. I recall you wore beads in your hair. Back when I lived with Ixalix in her rainforest swamp, I coaxed these from some mussels. They have grown lonely, confined to the drawer of an undead bachelor, and I strongly suspect you would make them look lovely. As always, Shrewd Sade, I await your response.*"

The pearls gave off a rainbowed sheen, even covered in the mud of the inn yard. I ran my calloused fingers over each bead, shaking my head ruefully, though my breath caught at their beauty.

"And who will admire me in such finery?" I asked the calabash. "The rats as I sit in prison? For that is where maids go when they are caught wearing jewelry they could only have stolen. You are right: *Stubborn Fool* does not suit you. *Reckless Oga*, I think, has a much better ring to it." Then I put down the pearl-studded gourd and dispatched Clemeh once more.

The next evening, cicadas chorused around me as I sat guarding the cookpit with a palm frond, chasing fire sprites away from the coals, where a pot of Kanwal stew simmered for supper. Poor Clemeh barely managed to haul a small pumpkin across the courtyard before collapsing with a wheeze by my sandal. I had to scoop him up by the tail to keep him from falling into the cookpit.

"Do you get tired of indulging the Crocodile like this?" I asked Clemeh, untying him and placing him on the edge of a water cistern. His tiny pink tongue lapped gratefully at the surface.

"Ixalix," he responded with a tiny shrug.

"Right," I said, picking up the pumpkin. "You were made to be a messenger. Well, Ixalix the alagbato might have given you a few more tools to work with. Longer legs, for one. And a tongue that can speak in sentences. Then the Crocodile would not have to prattle on using vegetables."

I removed the stopper, expecting another flowery speech. But this time, the words that tumbled from the gourd were soft and desperate.

"*I will be anyone you like, Sade. Please don't do the Sin Salon.*"

My pulse raced. Fire sprites floated around me, tiny orange flecks illuminating the pumpkin's hollowed insides. I tipped it over, and a new string of beads fell into my palm. This time, they were made of clay, glazed vibrant green, and hand-sculpted with tiny reptiles.

I suspected he had made them himself. The beads were the same color as the cup he had conjured for me that day in the shrine, when he had shaped the clay and fired it midair, before my very eyes.

I slipped the string of beads around my wrist, a shy smile playing on my lips. But before I could send a response, Mamadele burst through the back door, bosom heaving.

"Ah! There you are, Small Sade. There's a special visitor for you."

"For me?" I echoed. Would the Crocodile truly be so bold as to ask for me directly?

She offered no further details, only checked my face for soot smears before marching me into the inn. She steered me through the front hall and into a prettily decorated side chamber meant for guests who wished to dine in private.

But instead of diners, a silk-robed man with sagging jowls lay sprawled across the floor cushions. A wooden basin rested at his elbow as he idly ran a finger around its edge. I froze in the doorway, but when he looked up, he smiled.

"Small Sade," Mamadele announced, "you remember Lord Liao."

"If it isn't the eater of sins," Liao said jovially, reaching up to kiss my hand. "I look forward to your performance at the Sin Salon, but my curiosity could not wait. So Mamadele arranged this little preview."

"Preview, ma?" I breathed, swiveling to stare at Mamadele. "You— you want me to clean for him? Right now?"

"But of course." She nodded at a nook behind the door, where someone had relocated my cleaning supplies. "I've told Lord Lao how to fill his basin. And you'll take very good care of him, won't you?"

"Guard the doorflaps," Liao told Mamadele, peering at me. "To make sure we aren't disturbed. I will not have anyone eavesdropping on my business."

Panic spiked in my belly as I seized Mamadele's arm. "Surely," I whispered, "surely it is not quite . . . proper, ma? To leave me alone with a guest?"

She shook me off with a tinkling laugh. "Don't be so skittish, my dear. I'll be right outside. Though I will be wearing these to protect Lord Liao's privacy." She produced two gobs of wax from her wrapper, which she jammed into her ears. Then she patted my cheek, winked at Lord Liao, and slipped outside.

"Now, I am told," he murmured, beckoning me with one finger to kneel beside him, "is the part when you sing."

So I did. And as he vomited a barrage of spirit vermin into the basin, I wished with all my heart that Mamadele had given me wax too.

At first, he listed the names of women, fellow scholars from his days at the Academy of the Realm, interspersed with how grateful they should have been for his aid; how much of their success was owed to those salons in his private rooms, and how cruel they were to avoid him afterward; how seldom they mentioned his kindness in discussions among their peers. But in the end he simply uttered one phrase, over and over as thick, veiny guiltworms plopped into the basin, glistening with iridescent mucus.

At least I always waited until they were sleeping.

Pouring salt was not enough this time. These worms were evasive, so as I wailed, I had to catch them in fistfuls. Salt crystals stung my fingers as I kneaded each slimy, wriggling mass. When I came to the stubborn ones that would not shrivel away, Lord Liao watched with interest as I choked them down. He could not see the worms but still craned his neck to observe as I keeled over, chin tucked to my chest, both hands pressed to my lips as my throat heaved.

"There, there," he purred excitedly as my eyes burned with tears. "Keep it down. Breathe through it. Good girl."

I did not look up but heard the clink of coins as Lord Liao paid Mamadele. Before he left, he came to touch my trembling shoulder.

"Thank you, my dear," he said, voice soft with real gratitude. "You have made me a new man. For years, I could not show my face in my Academy haunts of old. But now, I believe I have the courage to try again. After all . . . a new crop of eager young minds await."

Then he was gone.

When Mamadele entered the room and found me curled on the floor, I expected her to scold.

Instead, she made low, soothing noises and cradled me in her lap, stroking my head as I hiccupped with shock. I had not been held at length since I left my mother in that cave.

Against my will, my body relaxed in Mamadele's embrace.

"I know it was hard," she said, voice warm against my ear. "Hearing all of those unpleasant things about Lord Liao and his pupils."

I blinked up at her in surprise. She had been eavesdropping. She continued to caress my brow, making my eyelids droop.

"But you did a good thing, Small Sade. You have the power to comfort people who are suffering. And if you ever withheld that power . . . well. That would be prideful, wouldn't it? To decide who gets to be happy, and who doesn't? That would be cruel. And you aren't cruel, Small Sade. Tell me you aren't proud and cruel."

"I . . ." I swallowed hard, feeling as though she had murmured my brain to mush. "I do not want to be cruel."

"Good," Mamadele breathed. "I am so glad to hear you say that working here, with me, is what you want. Please remember that you said that. That here, just now, you said that this life is what you want."

My brow furrowed in confusion. "I . . . madam? I am not sure I said—"

"Now we'll have to work on strengthening that stomach," she said, patting my belly with a maternal smile. "Because in three days, there will be twenty Lord Liaos. And you will serve them all at once. You are so generous, Small Sade."

After Lord Liao and Mamadele left, Hanuni made me rest in the storeroom, grimly excusing me from chores for the rest of the evening. Kanwal plied me with ginger tea until my stomach stopped heaving while Wafa cocooned me in blankets. Onijibola lit incense, promising to intercede for my health in his prayers to the Idajo. Even Finnric, who had looked forward to a night of wealthy patrons filling the inn, awkwardly patted my shoulder and mumbled that upon further reflection, he found the idea of a Sin Salon "rather unsustainable, as a business practice."

But Mamadele's words had tied my mind in knots, and that night I tossed as I lay alone in my pillow-lined closet.

Would I truly be proud if I ran? What if by running from the Sin Salon, I was committing the same vice as when I ran from crowning an Anointed One? What if by refusing Mamadele, I was killing Mamasade all over again?

But the thought of doing for twenty people what I had done for Lord Liao sent my nerves into a crackling fit, like oil on a brazier. Where my mind could be tamed, my body rebelled, and after an hour in that windowless tomb of a closet, I had half decided to flee to the shrine of the Crocodile that very night.

Then I remembered the kindness of the Amenities and decided to wait until morning. They deserved a proper goodbye, and in any case, the guilt-worms had sapped my energy.

I nestled into my pillow of ferns, which had wilted since the night the Crocodile appeared at my window. But when I buried my face in it, the faint scent of his skin and the timbre of his low, genuine laughter filled my senses, sending soothing ripples of warmth down my spine. I fingered the dark green beads on my wrist.

Perhaps life in Bhekina House would not be so bad. It seemed unlikely that the Crocodile's offer was a trap. He could have imprisoned me, after all, the first day we met, and I had been at his mercy several times after. So if against the odds, he *was* a maiden-eating monster . . . he did not appear to be very good at it.

An enchanted villa stranded in a magical nowhere was a far cry from the bustling city I had dreamed of living in. And traveling using the tooth portals would take getting used to. But it didn't have to be forever, I mused, shifting on the fern pillow. Perhaps I could still see Wafa and Kanwal on their days off from the inn.

"Ixalix," peeped Clemeh's voice in the darkness, and I sat up, startled from sleep.

"Is the Crocodile here?" I asked. My stomach fluttered, and I found myself glancing hopefully at the doorflap. "Waiting outside?"

Clemeh crawled across the wall and waited by the door, barely visible in the weak light glowing from the hallway. "Ixalix," he said, and sounded more timid than usual.

It was then I heard a second voice.

Throaty and slick, it was unlike any I had heard before, somehow confined to my head while seeping up through the floorboards and clinging to my skin like cold evening dew.

Greetings, Small Sade. Our meeting, I believe, is long overdue.

My heart leapt into my throat.

"Ixalix," Clemeh repeated grimly, and at last, I understood.

CHAPTER 18

I SLIPPED FROM MY ROOM, THE CLOTH-WRAPPED BOTTOM of my cane thudding on the floor as I walked. The voice appeared to radiate from the spa. But when I reached those narrow descending stairs, wonder froze me in place.

The steps had disappeared beneath a thick layer of lily pads and glistening moss pierced with vines that crept up and across the landing. One of the tendrils reached for me.

An invitation.

"Is it going to eat me?" I asked Clemeh, who watched the vines from above the doorframe. When his tiny head shook *no* . . . I held my breath, closed my eyes, and reached back.

The vine curled around my shoulders, joined by another that held my waist. In a careful lattice of slithering tendrils, they bore me swiftly down the stairs and into the mist-filled chamber of the ladies' spa.

Sconce light dappled the hazy surface of the bathing pool, where a vast lily pad had grown overnight. In its center, a woman with green-brown skin banded by turquoise stripes lounged on her stomach. She cocked her head as I entered, resting her chin on webbed hands as she watched me with yellow eyes. If she stood, the rainforest alagbato could easily have been twelve feet tall. Her limbs spilled over the lily pad, and when she sat up, her headdress scraped the ceiling, feathers splaying about her silky dark hair in a vibrant quill halo.

The vines receded from my limbs. With a gulp, I knelt on the spa tiles.

"Good evening, Great Lady Ixalix," I said, in the calm, reasoning tone that always seemed to take over when I was most frightened. "I am sorry I did not bring an offering. Perhaps next time, with a little notice—"

"Hush, child." Her laughter whispered around the room, like sheets of rain hissing through leaves. "I am not one of your minor stoop and stream spirits. I care little for offerings, and I do not like flattery. Nor do I like being summoned."

When I stammered in confusion, she waved impatiently.

"I know it was not you but the boy-king who summoned me. But I did not wish to speak with him. I wished to speak with you. Tears?"

She produced a handful of translucent fish bladders from the layers of moss that served as her clothing. Each of the corked bladders sloshed with liquid, and she held one out to me.

"This one is a delicacy," she sighed. "The tears of a child who has lost its favorite toy. Not too sad, though a little whiny. A drop in each eye does wonders for the nerves."

"As lovely as that sounds," I squeaked, "I think I will pass, Great Lady."

She shrugged, holding the bladder over her brow and squeezing a few drops for herself. When the tears splashed onto her reptilian eyes, she hummed in pleasure.

"A hobby of mine," she explained, patting the bladders. "Harvested from my worshippers over thousands of years. Eternity dulls the emotions, and the tears of mortals lend perspective. But I fear that the habit has made me soft. A thousand years ago, I would never have come all this way simply to warn a foolish girl. To tell her that she is swimming in a pool beyond her depth, and she should return to the shallows."

I blinked at her. "I never learned how to swim, Great Lady."

"What I mean," she said, "is that despite your face appearing in some prophetic tapestry, you will never break the curse of Zuri of Djbanti. The boy you know as the Crocodile."

The name stirred a faint memory in my mind, though not for long. Something of court politics and revolutions, whispered on the streets of Dejitown. I had not paid them much mind. The rise and fall of dynasties generally had little effect on girls in sweatmills.

"Zuri," I repeated, and despite my fear of Ixalix, an involuntary smile lifted the corner of my mouth. "It suits him."

"Then you really don't know," murmured Ixalix, chuckling in a way I did not like. "His name will not be so charming, I think, when you realize he is what you most fear. Zuri of Djbanti is an Anointed One. Or at least, he used to be."

I shook my head, ignoring the pangs of warning prickling across my chest. Spirits often spoke nonsense, I told myself. And though I knew I should have indulged Ixalix, if only to survive the encounter, the words *Anointed One* and *Zuri* filled me with such dread that my tongue rebelled.

"You are mistaken, Great Lady," I said. "I have seen the Anointed Ones. There are twelve of them. They all live at the palace, and none of them are named Zuri."

"There *were* twelve Anointed Ones," Ixalix purred, helping herself to another dose of tears. "Just as once upon a time, there was only one Ray-bearer—Ekundayo Kunleo. But when it was revealed that women could also possess the Ray, Tarisai Idajo arose to rule alongside Ekundayo. She anointed a second council of her own, composed of the kings and queens of all twelve realms of Aritsar."

I frowned. "But that would mean—"

"That your darling Crocodile is King of Djbanti? Yes. Or at least he would be . . . if he had not been the first ruler in human history to purposely dismantle his own monarchy. You have heard of the Great Commoner Uprising of Djbanti? Well, while pretending to fight against them, Zuri was helping the peasants all along. He had never wanted to be king, you see. Come here, and let me show you."

Ixalix dipped a turquoise finger into the spa water. The pool rippled, then stilled to dark glass, and on its surface, figures began to move. A throne room had materialized on the water, where a family—king, queen, and three young princes—sat on gilded stools. The youngest boy, no more than six or seven, had a tilt to his eyes that I recognized immediately: the Crocodile. The round openness of his features—not yet hardened into the angular, calculating face I now knew—made my heart ache, though I did not yet know why.

Ixalix narrated: "The Wanguru family, the royal dynasty to which Zuri belonged, had been puppets for generations—controlled completely by Djbanti warlords, who commanded the realm's military as well as its resources."

Warpainted lords entered the throne room, bowing mockingly to the king and queen. The oldest prince bristled with offense and made to stand—but the king put a hand on his son's shoulder, bidding him sit. The warlords looked on, smirking.

"The warlords allowed the Wanguru to remain as figureheads," Ixalix continued. "But any time a Wanguru tried to act as a true ruler—especially when he attempted to improve the lot of their subjects—the warlords had him assassinated."

The water rippled again, showing a series of funeral pyres. At each one, Zuri had grown taller, round face slowly replaced by hollow, grief-stricken lines. When the pool returned to the throne room, it showed a coronation. Zuri, jaw clenched, was made to kneel as chortling warlords placed a circlet on his brow and draped his shoulders with a gold-edged lion pelt.

In the next scene, a man covered in jewels and shimmer powder gestured drunkenly at a banquet, tossing coins at feather-clad dancers who gyrated before him. When he swayed and crashed into a tower of fruit, a gaggle of courtiers caught his arms for balance. Their mouths gaped so wide, I could almost hear their wine-soaked brays of laughter.

Shock turned my stomach when I recognized the drunken fool: Zuri.

"After watching every member of his family die," Ixalix explained, "the boy-king realized the only way to survive in that den of murders was to play the court idiot. He cultivated an empire-wide reputation as a brainless fop. In return, the warlords deemed him too stupid to be a threat, and they left him alone."

The pool showed the gaudy courtiers helping a drunken Zuri into bed. Circlet crooked on his brow, he collapsed on the pillows, limbs splayed, still gripping his wine chalice. The courtiers smirked down at him with derision as they retreated. But the moment they left the room . . . Zuri's kohl-lined eyes opened.

His gaze shone cold sober.

"While playing the fool, he plotted in the shadows for a way to avenge his family and his home realm. Stirrings of revolt had begun throughout Djbanti, but the people had little access to money or weapons. Zuri, of course, had access to both—but the warlords watched his every move. He needed a way to move throughout the empire and incite revolution, all while maintaining the illusion that he rarely left the Wanguru Fortress in Djbanti, where warlords kept him nearly under house arrest. So he raided the Wanguru family vaults, stealing artifacts from the Underworld."

In the vision, Zuri stole down into a gilded crypt, holding a torch as he searched shelves of artifacts recessed in the damp stone walls. He stopped when he reached two small chests, opening them to reveal stones: one gray and metallic, and the other lurid green.

"The first stone," Ixalix said, "was a fragment of a lodestone—those dangerous transportation totems scattered across the continent. By themselves, however, lodestones only enable travel to a single fixed destination, which was far too limiting for Zuri's purposes. He needed a way to enhance the fragment's power. So he turned to the most powerful form of enchantment he knew: the bond of an ehru.

"Ehru bonds are Pale Arts: a power that is evil by nature, leeching life from all it touches. To make someone an ehru is to make them a slave; to deny them the freedom to live or die until your wish is fulfilled. But an ehru is also imbued with great power, which slowly corrupts them until they are released from the bond.

"To bind someone as an ehru, all one needs is an Underworld idekun stone . . . and this too lay among the Wanguru family treasures."

She pointed to the sickly green stone.

"Now all Zuri needed was someone to be his slave. He could have chosen anyone to serve his purposes, even a creature as powerful as myself. He could have won justice for his realm without ever leaving the Wanguru Fortress. It is what most pampered boy-kings would do . . . but Zuri is not most boy-kings.

"In an act so audacious, even I did not believe it when I first heard . . . Zuri chose to enslave himself. He bound his ehru power to a single wish: *For the old rulers of Djbanti to cast down their crowns, and for those they exploit to rise up.*"

I gaped at the pool's surface, where Zuri's lips moved feverishly as he used a dagger to draw slits in his bicep. Then, with a cry, he shoved the stones into his arm. The stones blazed with malevolent light, growing needles that bore into his skin. After the light died away and Zuri appeared to recover, he flexed his hands experimentally. The movement made him vanish out of sight. When he returned, he looked stunned . . . and then he grinned with excitement.

"It was an act that could only destroy him. But after seeing his family murdered and playing the idiot while his subjects suffered, Zuri no longer had interest in his own future, or any purpose beyond burning that exploitative regime to the ground.

"And so he did. Donning the anonymous mask of the Crocodile, he incited protests throughout Djbanti, a movement that in turn spread throughout the Arit Empire."

The water revealed riots in different corners of the continent, demonstrations of commoners surging back against liveried noble forces. Leading them all was a figure in a mask made of crocodile skin, crowned in ivory teeth. It was the same mask I had seen hovering in the courtyard at the Bhekina House villa.

"In secret, he even won the aid of then-Empress Tarisai Idajo, one of the few Arits who knew his true identity and who chose him as one of her eleven Anointed Ones."

You will guess the next thing I saw in the pool. For that reason, it is difficult for me to speak just now, even as you encourage me to go on.

In a scene that made my heart sink to my sandals, the Crocodile drew into his arms the most beautiful girl I had ever seen.

Her features were otherworldly and defiant, and her smooth, dark skin shimmered with power. He slit his palm, pressed it to hers, and wrapped a cloth around both of their hands. Then they stared into each other's eyes like twin gods: statues of polished obsidian, and when the space closed between them . . . I looked away.

You tell me it happened a long time ago. That his true feelings for that girl were muddy and complicated and that I should not feel jealous in the slightest.

But in that moment, I felt about two inches tall: too puny even for a name like Small Sade.

"With Tarisai's help," Ixalix continued in a drone, "the commoners successfully toppled the warlords, ending the rule of both gentry and Wangurus over Djbanti. Zuri could have gone into hiding then, living a life of comfortable obscurity beneath the protection of the empress. But at the last moment, he thrust himself into the battlefield of revolting commoners, allowing his Crocodile mask to be removed in the fray."

A charging army of commoners flickered in the water's reflection. Fighting on their side was the Crocodile with a club and battle pole, mowing down warlords with unearthly grace. Just as the Crocodile dispatched a final foe to the Underworld, the dying warlord wrenched away Zuri's mask, revealing Zuri's face to the commoners. I cried out as, in a wave of confused fury, the commoners turned on him, piercing his chest with spears.

"It was an intentional suicide on Zuri's part," Ixalix said briskly. "Zuri had sullied his own name—the royal line of the Wangurus—among the commoners, so that after revolting they would rule themselves instead of falling again into another cycle of monarchs. Consequently, once the peasant rabble recognized Zuri's face . . . they fell upon him with spears. The boy-king died with a smile on his face, having achieved the only goal he ever wanted: to be a tool for justice. A weapon to bring down empires.

"But the boy-king did not *stay* dead. Instead, his body disappeared before the commoners' eyes. You will remember what I told you of ehru bonds: Until the wish is fulfilled, the bond denies the enslaved even the freedom of death. But as far as anyone could tell, Zuri's wish *had* been fulfilled: *For the old rulers of Djbanti to cast down their crowns, and for those they exploit to rise up.* Well. The exploited had risen up. The warlords had been dethroned. And Zuri, the only remaining Wanguru, had cast down his crown in the most final way imaginable.

"Yet the ehru enchantment mysteriously remained, preserving his body by casting it out of time, then restoring it nine years in the future. He realized quickly that this new world was one he had no place in."

The next scene in the pool wrenched my insides with pity. Zuri gasped to life in the middle of a bustling town street, still gripping his weapons. Palanquins and mule-and-boxes nearly trampled him as he stumbled out of the way, head swiveling in confusion. The Crocodile mask hung at his side. His clothes looked worn and out of date, and keloid scars now covered his chest—the only signs that he had been killed in battle. Townspeople shied away from him in fear as he approached them, hands outstretched in entreaty. I could not hear the words he spoke, but I knew he must be begging them for information. To know where—and when— he was.

"Firstly," Ixalix said, "he could let none of his friends know he was alive. If word spread that the king of Djbanti still lived, royalists might rally to reinstate the monarchy, using his existence as an excuse to delegitimize the new Djbanti Commonwealth. He even hid his return from Tarisai Idajo. As one of her Anointed Ones, his mind should have been linked to hers. But his body's death, though temporary, had broken their bond, so even her Ray could not find him.

"Secondly, the empire was now the Realmhood. Uprisings and reform movements had successfully continued in his absence. Revolutions had died down, and those that remained had no use for him as a leader. For all his charisma as the Crocodile, his understanding of Aritsar was nine years out of touch, and he no longer had access to the resources he once had as king of Djbanti.

"So he attempted what many men do, once devoid of friends or purpose. I will spare you the images of all the ways he tried to die, each more despairingly flamboyant than the last. But of course, none of them worked. Every time, the ehru curse revived him. So he took to transporting himself recklessly around the continent, hoping the excess use of Pale Arts would corrupt his organs, killing him at last.

"That, by chance, is how I met your Crocodile. The stones embedded in his body dumped him in my rainforest in Quetzala."

In the reflection, a swamp teeming with leaves and lily pools shimmered in the evening. Then, with a flash, the Crocodile appeared from thin air, slipping in the damp leaves and landing face down in the muck. He looked haggard and did not move for several moments, letting flies crawl across his cheek as he wheezed a bitter laugh. Nearby, Ixalix's slitted yellow eyes glowed from the shadows.

She continued: "I watched him squelch around the mud for a few days, too weak to transport himself back to wherever he came from. Then I noticed the scales developing on his arm. Apparently, as punishment for not fulfilling his wish, the ehru curse was transforming him into something mindless. Something *glorious*.

"I am fond of beastly creatures, you see. And Zuri's would be a refreshing new addition to my forest menagerie—a novelty I have not enjoyed for some thousand years. So I took him under my wing. Showed him how to use his powers. Encouraged them to grow, for the more he used his abilities, the sooner he would transform into . . . whatever beauty awaits, beneath that boring human skin."

"You tricked him," I gasped accusingly at Ixalix as the pool depicted the Crocodile by her side. He stood almost naked but looked less starved and more determined now, waving his hand to make flowers bloom and conjuring bowls and cups from the clay of the swamp.

"I did not," Ixalix retorted, silencing me with a frown. "Zuri knew what I wanted. He even agreed to it, once I assured him that transforming into a beast would dull his memories, alleviating the pain of his past. Had he stayed by my side, we both would have gotten what we wanted. The trouble is . . . spirits gossip. Other alagbatos heard of my pet boy-king and reported his existence to the Raybearers. Raybearer Tarisai is part alagbato herself, you see, and so many spirits possess an . . . inconvenient loyalty to her. Pressure from my peers forced me to drag Zuri to An-Ileyoba Palace, delivering him in secret to the Raybearers. They were beside themselves with relief that Zuri lived, though the fragile state of politics in Djbanti made them conceal his existence from the general populace."

The water had rippled to reveal a brightly decorated palace receiving chamber. There sat the Anointed Ones, as lovely and terrifying as when I had seen them in my youth, though of course they were older now. When the Crocodile, now dressed and clean shaven, stepped forward, the Anointed Ones rushed to embrace him—especially Raybearer Tarisai, who burst into happy tears.

"Zuri was relieved," Ixalix admitted, "to be among those who had known him before. But the torture of his cursed state, as well as the disorientation of now being nine years younger than everyone else, made him want to leave the palace. The Raybearers and Anointed Ones did not allow it at first, throwing the weight of their divinely gifted abilities into trying to break his curse. Their attempts at healing did not work . . . but one of the Anointed Ones, Umansa of Nyamba, has a gift of prophecy. He sought a cure for Zuri while he wove his prophetic tapestries, and one face stood out on the loom: yours."

The Anointed Ones, now in a different room of the palace, crowded around a tall loom. When they parted to reveal the tapestry, my breath caught. The threads depicted a girl in a high-rise window, chin propped on her hand as she gazed wistfully out at the city below.

It was me—daydreaming as I often did in the Aanu Meji Street orphan house, trying to imagine my life as Sade of Oluwan City.

"The Anointed Ones wanted to organize a search to find you. But Zuri was against it. He did not believe he could be cured, and what was more, he saw no purpose in living as a human in obscurity. Tarisai agreed not to pursue you. But she also made him promise he would stop trying to die. Zuri agreed, on the condition that he would not live in the palace and that Tarisai would allow him to be useful. Hence, he became her agent in disrupting the movements of cultists, setting up his portals around Oluwan City for ease of movement."

The Crocodile's voice echoed in my ears: *I run errands for someone. The Boss Almighty.*

My pulse raced. The Crocodile had never been talking about Ixalix. All along, he had been working for the most powerful, feared, and beloved woman on the entire continent.

The Crocodile's Boss Almighty, I realized, was Tarisai Idajo.

"It was a setback for me, of course," Ixalix said with a sniff, squeezing more tears from a fish bladder. "But I knew it was only a matter of time until Zuri's transformation was complete. I need only wait, and so in the meantime, I gifted Zuri the gecko spirit—the one you saw fit to name *Clemeh*. I told that gecko to keep the boy-king out of trouble. But the creature interpreted my command as an invocation to break Zuri's curse . . . which is why it decided to find you. Tiresome creature." She glowered at Clemeh, who shrank in fear where he perched on the far wall of the spa. "Serves me right for endowing a gecko with intelligence. You are lucky that I am too proud to kill anything I have made."

The pool rippled a final time, then faded. Ixalix fixed me with her yellow gaze, causing me to step back instinctively.

"But surely," she murmured, "now that I have explained all . . . you may see how fruitless your attachment to Zuri is. His curse is unbreakable, and any attempt to change him will only delay the inevitable. For what have you—poor, simple girl—to do with old rulers of Djbanti and their crowns? My motivation in telling you this, of course, is quite selfish. I want a new beast. But as I have said before: The tears of humans have made me soft, and so I also wish to spare you pain, if possible."

Shame sealed my throat as she finished, a mocking pity softening her features.

"I know," she said, "of your past humiliation with the Anointed Ones. All the spirits do. You were not meant to intersect with higher things, my dear. On the contrary—you know better than anyone what happens when you step outside your sphere."

CHAPTER 19

"YOUR LIZARD SUITOR IS HERE AGAIN," ANNOUNCED KANwal the next morning, as she, Wafa, and I hung sheets in the courtyard, beating them with cinnamon powder to rid them of mites and silverfish.

No one knew of Ixalix's visit. The moss and lily pads had vanished from the spa overnight, but not without leaving mildew streaks on the walls and tiny, iridescent water beetles that wriggled in the eaves. These mysterious appearances made Mamadele, who was already on edge as the Sin Salon drew nearer, believe that pipe had burst, so she had demanded that the Amenities air every linen in the house.

In addition to the beetles, a buzzing swarm of dragonflies appeared outside the inn. I did not realize that they were spies of Ixalix until one swooped close as I did chores outside, and I shivered to see that its bulging eyes looked like human irises. The creatures, though eerie, were much stupider than Clemeh—apparently, Ixalix had learned her lesson about creating messengers with free will. So mostly they hovered and left me alone, though they grew angry when I spoke to Clemeh, darting past my ears and buzzing "*What do girls know of gods? What do gods know of girls? Girl, not god. God, not girl*" until I batted them away. I did not need the reminder.

Now, when Clemeh scampered into the courtyard with another gourd in tow, I did not even look down.

"I am not going to open it," I grouched. That morning, I had found a new prayer pebble: one with sharp, gratifying ridges. I churned the stone against my cheek as I beat the linen. "So you might as well go away."

Clemeh croaked in protest, climbing onto my sandal. I shook him off, seized the gourd, and dropped it into the well behind the inn. It sank with a gurgle, letting the murky water drown whatever the Crocodile had tried to tell me. For a moment, I fingered the intricate clay beads on my wrist, considering hurling them in the water as well. Instead, I rounded on Clemeh.

"Go," I ordered. And with a final protesting chirrup, he retreated from the yard. Ixalix's dragonflies danced in triumph.

Kanwal and Wafa paused at their clotheslines.

"Small Sade," Wafa said, large eyes crinkling with concern. "Are you feeling all right?"

Kanwal's thick brows furrowed. "Maybe Mamadele has been picking on her," she said. "Small Sade looks the way I did when Mamadele told me to 'stop experimenting' with the inn's boring dinner menu."

"Well, maybe you should not experiment," I snapped, using my cane to beat wrinkles from a sheet with more malice than the cloth deserved. "She does not pay us to be creative. Have you ever considered that all of us might be happier if we just kept our heads down and remembered our places?"

I was tired of dreams. Angry at foolish fantasies that made girls gaze out windows and smile into fern pillows and think that just maybe, they might not be so small. That they might deserve something vast and unimaginable. Only for them to wake up and realize that the window has bars and they might as well be an ant staring up at the moon.

Wafa and Kanwal gaped, recoiling at my tone.

"You did not seem to mind my creativity," shot back a wounded Kanwal, hands on her hips, "when you had Kanwal stew for breakfast this morning."

I sighed, lowering my cane from the sheet and rubbing my face. "I am sorry. I . . . did not sleep well last night. Here, I will make it up to you." I nodded at the pile of yams stacked by the cookfire pits. "Let me skin those for dinner tonight. Then you and Wafa can take a break. Go watch those mummers in Unity Square you've been wanting to see."

They eyed me doubtfully. "Perhaps *you* should take the break," Wafa suggested. "You've barely sat down all morning."

"No, thank you," I mumbled, marching over to the yams and brandishing a paring knife like it was a weapon.

The trick to knowing one's place is to remain in the present, never making time to imagine some place better. So I scraped yams until my fingers went numb, and when another gourd arrived with Clemeh that evening, I tossed that one into the well too.

The next morning, Clemeh found me in Mamadele's room, scouring oil stains from the floorboards: the most thankless, mind-dulling task I had been able to think up for myself. Against the odds, he had managed to drag an entire hollowed calabash up the stairs. When he wheezed to a stop on the rug, he stared up at me with pleading eyes.

I untied him, patted his head fondly, and then flung the gourd from Mamadele's window, watching it land with a gratifying splatter on the dirt below.

Faintly, snatches of the Crocodile's frantic voice scattered on the wind. *Sade, please . . . can explain, if you only . . . am sorry you found out that way, but Ixalix . . . have my word, please do not . . . that salon, you are better than—*

I left the window and heard nothing more.

Clemeh did not appear the next day. I assumed that the Crocodile had given up, and so with grim satisfaction, I continued to drown my thoughts in chores. The inn grew gaudy with guests and decorations, all in preparation for the Sin Salon.

The day before Mamadele's grand event, I climbed the stairs as usual to spirit-clean Dele's room, forgetting to knock as I wrestled my bucket and broom through her doorflap.

Ye Eun was lying on the floor with Dele, tangled in a violet-embroidered coverlet with her head in Dele's lap. Dele smiled down at her wistfully, playing with Ye Eun's cropped hair.

"Oh," I shrilled, almost dropping the bucket. "I . . . did not mean to interrupt."

Over the past week, I had made a sizable dent in exorcising Mamadele's expectations from Dele's room. I had boiled away the despair-mold from her sheets and curtains, scalding the linens with cheery songs and hot water, and I had dusted every surface, trilling battle marches as I knocked fear webs from ceiling corners. A few nights of sleep in her increasingly spirit-cleaned room had emboldened Dele. Her mother's barbs seemed to slide off her more easily, and now she openly left the inn whenever she liked instead of sneaking through the window. But having Ye Eun in her bedroom was a level of boldness from Dele even I had not expected. I retreated back into the hallway.

"Wait!" Ye Eun scrambled after me, extricating herself from Dele's blankets and grabbing a satchel from the floor. "Small Sade, I have something to tell you!"

"Don't take long," Dele called after Ye Eun, sounding playfully petulant. "You never let me baby you."

Ye Eun shushed Dele over her shoulder, then hurried me farther down the hallway, balling up the coverlet and stuffing it under her arm.

"Sorry about that," she muttered.

"Don't be sorry." I smiled tiredly, putting down my wash bucket and leaning against the wall. "It was nice to see you resting for once. With all the flowers Mamadele ordered for the Sin Salon, you have been as busy as me."

Ye Eun blushed. "Yes. And Dele disapproves. The other day, I made the mistake of telling her that I wasn't coddled as a kid. No parents, the usual tale of woe. And . . . it's a long story, but I basically raised a bunch of refugee infants when I was barely more than a baby myself. Ever since, Dele's been obsessed with swaddling me. Literally. She insists that it will heal 'the wounds of my inner orphan child.'"

I opened my mouth, then closed it, unsure of what to say.

"Rich girls," Ye Eun monotoned.

"Rich girls," I agreed.

Ye Eun and I exchanged a look . . . and then burst into giggles. I had not laughed since Ixalix lured me down to the bathing spa, and I nearly melted at how good it felt.

"She really does mean well. And I did enjoy it a little," admitted Ye Eun, once she had regained her breath. "In any case, I'm glad it was you who caught us."

My eyebrows rose to my hairline. "Wait. Does Mamadele still not know?"

Ye Eun nodded glumly. "I told Dele it was risky to meet in the house, but she wouldn't listen. You know, sometimes . . . I think she hopes we'll get caught." She rubbed the back of her neck. "I suppose that *is* the easiest way for people to find out."

"Easiest for Dele," I murmured. "But what about for you?" I thought with a shudder of what Mamadele had said about Dele and any commoner that Dele might pursue.

You are far more dangerous to her than she ever could be to you.

Ye Eun sidestepped the question, producing a squash from her pocket instead. "I chased after you to give you this. Seeing as he's resorted to using me instead of the gecko, I . . . probably don't have to tell you that he's desperate."

I recoiled.

"I'm not talking to the Crocodile anymore," I said, refusing to take the gourd.

"So I've heard." Ye Eun put the squash back in her pocket. "You've really done a number on Croc, you know. I've never seen him so distraught. He's filled about a dozen gourds with those sappy letters. And when he found out that Ixalix told you who he was, well . . . I had to convince him that challenging a ten-thousand-year-old alagbato to fisticuffs wasn't a good idea."

My gaze narrowed. "How do you know the Crocodile?" I asked, and then took a step back, bumps rising on my arms. "Are . . . are you one of them too? An Anointed One?"

Ye Eun scoffed.

"Me?" she sputtered. "Royalty? No." She cast a nervous glance at Dele's room, then pulled away. Her voice lowered to a murmur. "But I do know the Raybearers."

"How?" I demanded, and she shushed me, glancing over her shoulder again.

Then she sighed, brushed the faint purple glyphs on her skin, and asked, "Are you too young to remember what a Redemptor is?"

My brow furrowed. "Isn't that what they used to call those children? The ones the old empire used to sacrifice to the Underworld?"

"Yes. Well, I was one of them. One of the last, in fact. We are born with maps on our skin to help us navigate the Underworld after we're sacrificed. Don't feel sorry for me," she added sharply when my eyes widened. "It was a long time ago, and I don't like thinking about it anymore. Anyway, I survived. And my story convinced Raybearer Tarisai to make the journey herself. I returned to the Underworld with her, and we battled the spirits of death. Together."

Once again, I felt small—though not in the same sinking way I had felt learning that the Crocodile was an Anointed One. Instead, I wondered to think someone so ordinary—Ye Eun, with hands as rough as mine, with whom I could make silly jokes in a hallway—could have already lived a life so full of adventure. I could barely imagine leaving Bhekina House, let alone visiting a different world.

Ye Eun's eyes shone with tears as the memory took her. She loved Raybearer Tarisai, I realized. Of course she did. Who would not love that young woman I had seen in Ixalix's vision, claiming the Crocodile with all the beauty of a muraled saint?

"Tarisai's journey ended child sacrifice to the Underworld forever— that's why they called her the Empress Redemptor. And after she returned, well . . . she sort of adopted me. She took in my sister, Ae Ri, too. She's twelve now and still lives at the palace. But though the Raybearers were kind to us . . . I couldn't stand that place for more than a few years." Her nose wrinkled. "It's hard to take gossip and garden banquets seriously once you've been to hell and back. Besides, having the affection of Raybearers is like . . . like standing beneath a sweltering, beating sun that never goes down. Not *ever*. Some plants thrive in relentless sunshine. Ae Ri seems to, anyway, and I'm happy for her. But I'm not like that. I need shade and space or I shrivel up and burn. So I struck out on my own, and I've lived at my shop in the Ilemalu District ever since."

She ran a hand through her cropped hair.

"Look . . . don't tell Dele about this, all right? She knows I was a

Redemptor, but I left out pretty much all the rest. She's never understood why I love my grubby little flower shop so much. She'd never admit it, but she's always wanted me to be more ambitious. And if she knew I had connections to the wealthiest people in the Realmhood . . ." Ye Eun grimaced, exhaling through her teeth. "Am's Story. I'd never hear the end of it."

CHAPTER 20

THE DAY OF THE SIN SALON, I DECIDED TO CLEAN THE SERvant's garret.

I waited for late morning, when the Amenities were preoccupied with their chores downstairs. I climbed up the stairs, dragging my cleaning kit up with me. Then I spat out my prayer pebble, just for a little while, so I could sing.

> *Feather Pillow, comfort me!*
> *Yes, oga.*
> *Breakfast Tray, belly's groaning!*
> *Here, madam.*
> *Named or not, here we run—*
> *Come, bow, serve!*

> *Baby Rattle, wipe my tears.*
> *Don't cry, lady.*
> *Chamber Pot, bathwater!*
> *We'll scrub you clean.*
> *Named or not, here we run—*
> *Come, bow, serve!*

It had been days since I found happiness in cleaning. As I brightened the rooms of my friends, the familiar warm trance spread though my limbs. I told myself that I was grateful for my place at the Balogun Inn. That I was only spirit-cleaning to warm up for the Sin Salon this evening.

But if you had searched my heart in earnest, you would have seen that cleaning the garret was my quiet way of fighting back. Tonight, Mamadele's fine guests would use me as they liked. But at least if I used my gift for my friends, my voice would not belong completely to the Lord Liaos of the world.

I entered Hanuni's chamber first. It was nice for a housekeeper, if modest: her bedroll was stuffed with down instead of rushes and lay on a frame instead of on a mat on the floor. A small mirror and washstand rested in the corner. Over everything, however, rolled a thick, damp cloud of rue-fog.

Hanuni did not speak much of her life before the inn, and I knew she had been serving the family since Mamadele was a child. My only clue into what could cause Hanuni these choking clouds of regret was what Mamadele had let spill during her guiltworm confession.

Of course Simple Hanuni had children of her own, but my family paid her salary, and I needed her more. It's not my fault her children don't talk to her anymore . . .

As I sang, I took a sheet from Hanuni's linens, folded it in half, then waved it like a sail, coaxing the rue-fog to float out the window before melting away on the city skyline. I did not know what kind of mother Hanuni had been to her children. But I did know it could not have been easy to have a rich girl's nanny for a parent. To watch your mother spend all her daytime caresses on another, shinier child, leaving you only with the nightly dregs of her exhaustion.

But I also knew that poor women gave birth into a world of impossible choices. Stewing in a haze of regret each night, I thought, helped no one. Perhaps with a little fresh air, Hanuni could accept the choices she had made . . . and the space her children now needed.

Next, I took on Onijibola and Finnric's room. Their bedrolls lay on opposite sides of the bare, low-ceilinged chamber, and the wall hangings smelled stale, a mix of an old man's shaving oil and a young man's unfortunate body odor.

On his side of the room, Onijibola had erected a rickety shrine. A tiny Idajo effigy stood atop a low wood block, surrounded by offerings of coins, dry rice, and wilting flowers. I was not surprised to see despair-mold creeping over the altar, spreading like fetid carpet over a depression in the floorboards, where the old man must have spent hours kneeling before the shrine, begging for the Anointed Ones to heal his arthritic hands. I tied a kerchief over my mouth, trying not to inhale any mold, and scrubbed the altar as best I could without disturbing the offerings. I could not soothe the pain in Onijibola's fingers. But I hoped that when he knelt in this space newly cleared of despair, Onijibola's prayers might bring him peace.

Strangely, Finnric's side of the room made me even sadder. For all his waxing about prosperity, his possessions appeared to fit into a single rat-gnawed basket by his threadbare bedroll. Nothing decorated the cracked plaster wall above his pillow. One of the floorboards squeaked, under which I suspected he had hidden a stash of money, because skid marks of greedgrime covered the area in thick, shimmering tar. A depression showed that he had knelt by that floorboard as often as Onijibola had knelt by his altar. The greasy marks, to my chagrin, marred most of his things, which I cleaned with a long-handled brush, cringing away from handling the grime directly.

Finnric had left a life of shoveling sheep dung only to bury himself in a sort of muck that was harder to escape from. He would have to do most of the work himself. But perhaps a clean slate could help him work toward a new, less mercenary imagination.

Finally, I reached the chamber I had shared with Wafa and Kanwal. Ambition-spores floated around Kanwal's bedroll, and I readied my duster to banish them . . . then hesitated. I knew where those spores had come from: Kanwal's desire to be head chef of the inn.

If I sang the spores away, Kanwal might sleep in her bedroll tonight and awake the next morning with her ambitions cooled. Perhaps she would let go of that far-fetched chef fantasy, embracing the humbler, more certain life of a kitchen maid. I could help her be content. Happy, even.

I lifted the duster.

But as I watched those spores drift above Kanwal's pillow, arranging themselves in iridescent patterns, hazy in the morning light . . . my arm lowered. The patterns were lovely. And even if those ambitions were far too grand for a servant's garret . . . I would not rid that chamber of any more beauty than I had to.

A blanket of downy dream-moss covered Wafa's bedroll, sprouted from her wistful desire for a place to produce her dreamscapes. I could have scraped the moss away with a razor and vinegar, but in the end . . . I left that alone too.

Instead, I took a sharp comb to both of their beds and stripped them of worry-lint, which fell in itchy balls from their blankets and clothing. Wafa and Kanwal had left their home city of Vhraipur to work for higher pay in Oluwan City, allowing them to send money home to their relatives. A week ago, a letter had arrived at the inn for Wafa and Kanwal, with word that an aunt and small cousin were sick. The sisters had whispered all night, heads pressed together as they whimpered about how to convince Mama-dele to give them an advance on their pay.

Ever since, they had tossed and turned on their bedrolls, tortured by prickling balls of worry they could not see. I could do nothing for their aunt and cousin. But at least I could grant them the soft, guiltless sleep of loving sisters who were trying their hardest.

Some nights, Wafa, Kanwal, and I had stayed up chatting in hushed voices, even after Hanuni had snuffed out our bed lamps. We stifled giggles as we traded stories of the silliest things we had ever seen, converting them all into dramatic dreamscapes, complete with songs and elaborate set dressing. Hanuni, Finnric, and Onijibola sometimes complained about the noise, but just as often they listened through the thin walls, chiming in with their own silly tales.

Evidence of our late-night games now fluttered in the garret, beating the rafters with golden translucent wings: joy-moths, making shimmering loops in the sunshine.

I climbed atop a crate, balancing on both my strong and weaker foot. To my delight, I spied a row of silvery cocoons hanging from the rafters— unhatched joy-moths. I left half of them in our maid garret, then collected the rest, rehoming them in the rooms where Hanuni, Finnric, and Oniji-bola slept. Finally, I climbed the crate again and sprinkled a few bits of melon rind on the garret rafters.

I had never tried to feed the creatures of spirit silt before, and mortal food was unlikely to work. But I had to try. Perhaps the joy-moths, feeling my intent, would feed on the rinds and multiply, ensuring the Amenities would have many nights of golden laughter to come.

I did not place any joy-moths in the closet Mamadele had made for me, as I was not sure they would survive. I had not touched my own spirit silt since I was a girl. And after tonight, I suspected as I descended from the garret . . . I would not feel like laughing for some time.

⊚⊚⊚⊚⊚⊚

"You look resplendent," Mamadele gushed, tucking my arm beneath hers, and engulfing me in a wave of honeyed perfume. We stood together in the anteroom to the great hall, waiting to make our entrance to the Sin Salon.

"So do you, madam," I croaked.

In truth, we both looked unnatural, as overdone and lurid as the now heavily decorated inn. This time, instead of reserving the gold powder for my arms and collarbone, Mamadele had gilded my entire body, so that I could not move without shedding sparkles. Over my sand-colored servant's wrapper, she had draped an ashoke shawl that matched her own, shot through with silver threads.

A new circlet of eucalyptus sat on my brow, intertwined with gold wire and cowrie shells—symbols of love. Mamadele had made sure that if her guests looked upon me, they would not see a young girl eating worms to have a roof over her head. They would see a pampered angel, absolving their sins with a smile on her face.

After cooing over me a final time, Mamadele glanced down at my cane.

"And you're sure you can't get rid of that?" she wheedled, for the fifth time that evening. "I know your poor little foot hurts, but tonight is about purging and *renewal*. And your injury, well . . . it's not quite on theme, my dear. Surely you understand."

Impatience surged in my already taut chest, but I measured my breaths.

Know your place. Know your place. Know your place.

"As I told you before," I said quietly, "I cannot walk far without assistance, madam. And if I am to clean for twenty people, I must move as best as I can."

Through the doorflap, the voices of excited guests hummed over the tinkle of kora harps, the rattle of shekeres, the throaty *go-gun* of talking drums. Mamadele had hired live musicians to accompany my wailing, though I had warned her my songs were unpredictable.

"It will be festive," she had countered. "This is a celebration, after all."

As the music swelled, my chest began to heave, and my hands shook. Visions of retching on the floor, first at Mamadele's feet, then at Lord Liao's, flashed before my eyes.

Knowyourplace, I told my heart in a scolding rush. But it was no longer listening.

"Ma," I gasped. "I think . . . I need to sit down for a moment."

But Mamadele did not hear me. Her eyes misted as she looked toward the great hall doors, as though beyond them lay the rest of her life: Her return to high society. Her ascent to grace.

She wheeled to grasp my shoulders, lightly, so as not to smudge my powder.

"Small Sade," she said, voice sweet but shaky, "after tonight, things might . . . change for you. A lot of people—greedy, unscrupulous grifters, not nice mothers like me—may tempt you away from the inn. Try to convince you that you would be happier elsewhere. But do you remember the day I took you in?"

"Of course, madam." I barely registered speaking, so hard was I trying to focus on not fainting. The guests' voices had raised in pitch, roiling with anticipation of my entrance. Mamadele's words clattered against my ears, sharp hail on a rooftop.

"You were a stranger. You could have been a thief. A murderer. But I took you into my home, and fed you, and clothed you, made you everything you are now. So remember that, Small Sade. Remember that in a world as cruel and discerning as this one, no one will ever love you as I do."

Then she secured my arm under hers again, and we swept into the great front hall.

The hanging lanterns that usually lit the hall had been extinguished, so the only light came from standing candelabras and flickering floor lamps, bathing the faces of guests and musicians in shifting orbs of light and shadow. Curling incense hung in the air. Outside the inn, a storm brewed, causing the ground to tremble with every clap of thunder.

The guests sat on floor cushions in two lines of ten, facing each other across a long, low kneeling table. The table was bare of refreshments, for the guests had come not to dine but to purge.

I spotted many faces from Mamadele's previous salons, like Lady Injaana and Lord Liao, and even Dele, who must have been threatened into attendance. But many of the guests were new, and they varied in complexion as well as clothing, though wealth united them all. Apparently the salon had attracted patrons from every region of the Realmhood. A milk-skinned, balding old baron draped in furs gave a hacking cough, marring the otherwise sultry atmosphere. He must have traveled here all the way from the northern realms, where Finnric had once lived.

But despite their differences, every silk robe, sweeping agbada, and crisp linen wrapper glowed chilling white: the color of death. Tonight, I supposed, they intended to put their old selves—the ones who had done all those horrible things—to death. They would emerge as new creatures, absolved of their burdens, which would then rest on my thin, unimportant shoulders.

Everyone, even the musicians, wore a strip of white cloth around their eyes: blindfolds. I knew from our rehearsals that Hanuni would have distributed the folds as each person entered, so that no guest could put a face to a voice when they spilled their dirtiest sins. When Mamadele and I entered, the sound of unknown new arrivals sent a delighted ripple of shrieks and whispers down the room.

In that moment, I realized why Mamadele had held the salon in the first place.

Every noble in that room, after all, could have booked a session with me privately, as Lord Liao had. It would have been far more practical, and much more effective, as I could not clean for twenty nearly as well as I could for one.

But Mamadele, with her twisted genius, had understood that most nobles would not *want* to confess in private. For the only thing more soothing than being cleansed of sin was to know that everyone else was as dirty as you are. Worse, even. And what a thrill to guess who had confessed to what. Why, it was enough to broil the entire Ileyoba District in gossip for months.

So would a single tawdry night transform the Balogun Inn and Philosophy Salon into the most fashionable destination in all of Oluwan City.

"Good evening, my friends," said Mamadele, in a tone throbbing with drama. "And welcome to your redemption."

CHAPTER 21

NERVOUS LAUGHTER RIPPLED ACROSS THE HALL, ALONG with another clap of thunder. The music shifted to a low, pulsing rhythm.

"I am your Mistress of Ceremonies," Mamadele intoned, launching into the flowery speech she had performed at our rehearsals. "And this is a sacred space. A place to confess your sins. To lay down your burdens all, and be forever—"

Phlegmy hacking erupted from one of the guests: the balding old baron. Dele snickered as the man scrambled to find a handkerchief, clearly disoriented by his blindfold. Mamadele cleared her throat.

". . . forever reborn," she continued, maintaining her otherworldly voice. "Once the Curse-Eater begins her song, the cleansing will—"

"Could you repeat the instructions please, Mamadele?" Dele interrupted loudly. "Between the rain outside and the coughing, I could barely hear."

"My apologies," rasped the baron, though a rattle of mucus that made his neighbors cringe away. "Old lungs and old ears. What was that you said?"

"Do you mean what I said, or what Mamadele said?" Dele replied, tone dripping with innocent confusion. "Because I said, 'Mamadele, could you repeat the instructions?' And before that, Mamadele said—"

"Enough!" Mamadele snapped. She glared at her daughter, whose face contorted with laughter beneath her blindfold. "As I said before . . . this space is sacred. Before you stands a creature who delights in eating your sins. As you confess, she shall raise her voice and dispense your healing. At the sound of the bells, let us begin!"

The musicians beat a pair of iron *agogo* bells, and when the guests began to murmur as though in prayer, it was my cue to climb onto the table.

The kneeling table was low, so I mounted it with one step, my legs trembling so hard that I had to grip my cane to stay upright. My feet were bare, except for the bandage on my weak one. A satchel hung heavily across my shoulders. I was to walk back and forth across the long, cold table, sowing salt as I crushed the guilt of Mamadele's guests beneath my feet.

"Maybe you could even sway your hips and arms a little," Mamadele had suggested gaily when we rehearsed it. "Like a dance. Give a fun little show, in case any of the guests are peeking."

Once the salt stopped working, I was to crawl atop the table on my hands and knees, devouring as many of the surviving guiltworms as I could before fainting from revulsion.

"Wait," coughed the baron, voice rasping in protest. "Don't start the ceremony. My blindfold is coming loose. And I still don't understand the instructions. Perhaps if you explain again . . ."

But already the air thickened with scandalous confession, drowning out the old baron. As more of the guests spoke and their words blended together, their voices rose in volume, seduced by the illusion of anonymity. Dele had removed her blindfold and sat in silence, eyes locked pityingly on mine as nobles caterwauled around her.

"It was not my fault," screeched a noble, over and over. "None of it. Not the bombs. Not the massacre. Not my fault . . ."

". . . and the children were listless before we employed them," wailed another. "We gave them a sense of direction. In truth, they *yearned* for the mines."

"A wife must be chaste," declared a lord, "but surely, no man can be satisfied by a single mate. It goes against nature. And to honor her, I never brought them in the house . . ."

"So what if their shacks burned?" protested a lady. "We had to smoke them out. They were like cockroaches! Filthy, job-stealing, land-squatting—"

My mouth ran dry. I could not yet see the worms from that volley of ugly words, but I knew they were there, filling the table, teeming around my ankles in a squirming layer of silver. Already, I felt invaded—a presence flitted through my body, like the ghost of a worm I had not yet eaten. On that table, my future seemed to writhe before me, an endless ocean of wailing and salons and moonless closets, and all I could do was open my mouth and let the sound come out: a song of raging despair. A song that would free everyone in that room, except for me.

But when I tried to sing . . . nothing came out.

I swallowed and rubbed my neck, thinking I had gone hoarse from the smoking incense, and tried again. Still, nothing.

I turned back to look at Mamadele, who was gesturing impatiently at me. I shook my head with wide eyes, opening my mouth to say, *Perhaps I need some water, madam* . . . But the words seemed to stick in my throat. I could not so much as rasp. This was no reaction to smoke, or even a sudden head cold.

The moment I stepped on that table, my voice had simply vanished.

Mamadele came to stand beneath me, leaning up to hiss in my ear. "What's going on?"

I gestured helplessly, and her eyes glinted with panic as they darted around the room. The spew of confessions had begun to lull, fading into confused murmurs.

"Isn't there supposed to be singing?" someone asked.

"That's what they promised," said another. "When exactly is the healing supposed to start? Is the Curse-Eater even here?"

More voices spiked with suspicion. "Should I feel better yet? Because I don't. By all the Anointed Ones, if I've come all this way for nothing . . ."

"Sing!" Mamadele shrilled at me, fingers digging into my arm. I nearly toppled as she dragged me from the table and grasped my chin, her expression livid. She raised her hand to slap . . . but to her gasping shock, I deflected the blow, wrenched her wrist until she howled, and shoved her away.

I was not sorry, but I had not meant to do it.

It had simply been a reflex from my years in the gutter. Snide looks and cruel names rolled off my skin. I could bear all manner of verbal abuse without flinching. But the moment any person laid their hands on me, be they urchin or empress . . . my numbing armor of humility crumbled to dust.

Mamadele regarded me with pure, frothing hatred, any hint of maternal sweetness gone from her face. I wished then that she had tried to hit me earlier.

If she had, I would have known that I would never be Sade of the Balogun Inn. Sade who belonged. I would only ever have been a Village Wife, wrung for every last drop of my usefulness before being tossed back into the wilderness. I would not have wasted my time hoping for anything different.

I still might have chosen to stay, for being a Village Wife was better than having no village at all. But now my body had made the choice for me, and all I could do was watch with horror as my future unraveled.

Dele watched me fight back against her mother, dazed, as though I had performed some kind of miracle. Then her shoulders braced with determination. Most of the guests had already stopped confessing, but Dele decided then to announce her own secret:

"My confession is that I, Dele Balogun, am in love with a girl named Ye Eun. She owns a flower shop on the west end of the Ilemalu District. She's only a commoner, but then, so am I. The Baloguns have no title, despite my mother's attempts to make the world forget it."

The room froze. Then it burst into louder chaos than before. Mamadele looked like she might faint. The clamoring guests began to stand and take off their masks.

"Wait! Stop! It isn't time yet," Mamadele shrieked, her protests drowned by the rising tide of scandalized gasps and feverish gossip.

"There was never any Curse-Eater. This evening was a scam all along, didn't I tell you—"

"I also knew there was something *unusual* about that Dele girl . . ."

"What a waste of an evening . . ."

One lady looked especially hunted. "How do we know that everyone covered their eyes while we confessed?" she demanded. "Suppose someone peeked?" Her stare landed on Mamadele and me. "I don't think those two ever had blindfolds," she accused. "Suppose they spill our secrets?

"I would never," Mamadele sputtered, blinking rapidly. "This is a sacred space."

"You promised that nothing would be heard over the singing," the guest retorted. "You said a song would make everything better. So when is it happening?"

"On . . . on another night, perhaps," Mamadele stammered, and cries of protest erupted around the room. A few guests, including the old baron, grumbled and left immediately.

When the complaints turned into demands for refunds, Mamadele's features steeled. I wondered, taking in her new clothes and jewelry, how much of the Sin Salon money Mamadele had already spent.

She inhaled, composing herself, and her tone turned sweet and placating. "My dearest friends: I am not a common thief. I am a lady—"

"Former lady," Dele monotoned.

"I am," Mamadele amended, only just managing to suppress the murder in each syllable, "a person of enlightened society. And every person here will be satisfied—they need only come back another night. My Curse-Eater appears to be having . . . difficulty . . ." Her eyes rested briefly on mine, and I shivered at the flash of feral rage. "But her voice exists. I assure you."

"We know her voice exists," droned Lady Injaana, dropping her blindfold on the table with two bony fingers. "We heard it that night she stammered through our debate during the salon. The question is whether or not she has a gift."

"But she does," Mamadele insisted. "You haven't heard her sing." Her frantic gaze sought out Lord Liao, brightening when she found him. "My dear lord," she said, reaching for him with both hands. "You have experienced Small Sade's gift. Won't you testify to her rejuvenating abilities?"

Lord Liao recoiled. He had been hovering in his usual possessive position over Dele. Since the moment of Dele's announcement, however, his mouth had grown increasingly tight, until I was surprised it could open at all.

"Madam," he said coolly, "regardless of what I may or may not have experienced . . . I find I have lost confidence in the intellectual integrity of this salon."

"I beg your pardon?" Mamadele breathed.

Lord Liao shrugged, beginning to collect his things and head for the door. "There can be no enlightenment in a place where one is promised one thing"—he slid a petulant look at Dele, who looked as though she might gag—"then denied it, without any consideration for one's feelings. I have lost trust in this establishment. Good night, madam."

A final pulse of thunder shook the inn as Lord Liao left the hall, taking with him Mamadele's last hope of returning to society.

"Well?" asked one of the remaining guests. "What about getting our money back?" The other guests echoed the question, slowly moving toward Mamadele. Cornered, Mamadele leapt behind me.

"It wasn't my fault," she wailed. "I'm a victim too. It's *her!*"

She pointed at me.

"She's cursed," Mamadele insisted, pupils dilated. "She bewitched my daughter. Why else would Dele confess such a thing? She tricked me. Tricked us all . . . ask *her* where the money is."

And suddenly, all the ire of the room centered on me.

Dele ranted against the crowd in my defense. "Small Sade didn't steal anything. And I was telling the truth. Don't listen to Mother. For Am's sake, won't anyone here with half a brain stop and *think*—"

But no one seemed to hear her. A roar filled my ears, drowning out the guests' barrage of voices, though a few sharp phrases pierced the fog.

"*Arrest the Curse-Eater . . . Call the Raybearers' Guard . . . She'll answer to the district judges—no, to the Anointed Ones.*"

And so I did what all gutter girls do best: I ran.

Mamadele made a swipe for me, but I dodged, lurching across the room with my cane. The guests parted before me, out of surprise and not a little fear. I shed both the satchel of salt and Mamadele's ashoke shawl, then ripped the crown of wire and eucalyptus from my brow, discarding them all on the marble tiled floor. Gold powder trailed after me as I fled through the front hall doors, past the foyer, and across the inn's front courtyard, which pooled with rain, flagstones slick with mud. The gates of the Balogun Inn and Philosophy Salon clamored shut behind me as I plunged into the wet, moonless night.

PART IV

CHAPTER 22

RAIN PELTED THE SIDE OF MY FACE. I BEGAN TO LAUGH IN heaving sobs . . . for of course then, after I already had left the inn and lost everything, my voice chose to return. My feet prickled with cold as they squelched through the flooded streets, mud soaking my bandaged injury. I had left my only pair of shoes back at the inn. No rickshaws could be hailed in foul-foul weather, but even if they could, I had no money. My meager pile of earnings from my month of spirit-cleaning remained in the inn, hidden in a pouch beneath the floorboards of my room.

What a good joke, if a cruel one, that I had left my first job in Oluwan City with less than when I arrived.

I had no direction in mind, but my legs kept moving. So I bustled with false purpose through the shadowy district, roads lit only by the glow of high-rise windows and lanterns that spluttered in the torrent from the sky. The wood of my cane grew rough and swollen with water, chafing my hand.

When I was little, Mamasade had invented a game called *At Least*. We had last played it together in the Bush as we hiked away from the village that had discarded us.

"Chin up, Small Sade," she had said in a silly gruff voice as we trudged over rough, wooded paths. "At least we stink so bad, the mosquitoes could not bear to bite us."

"Don't worry, Mama," I had panted, taking up the game. "At least no lions will chase after us. Our bellies are so empty, the growling will scare them all away."

She had nodded with mock seriousness. "At least we will save money on cocoa butter. We are so sweaty, our elbows will never be ashy again."

At least . . . at least . . . at least . . .

Now, as rain ran down my face and into my mouth, I said aloud, teeth chattering: "Chin up, Mama. At least this weather is so bad, the streets have no thieves or scouts for pleasure bazaars."

I chuckled bitterly.

"At least if a thief cornered me, they would have nothing to steal. At least after tonight, Mamadele will sully my reputation so completely, I will never have to work for a rich family in the Ileyoba District ever again."

As a child, I had thought the point of the game was to cheer up. To focus on the bright side, no matter the situation. That, after all, is what the Mercy Aunties always told me to do.

But as that storm soaked my wrapper, I knew my mother had not played *At Least* to soften our pain but to honor it. She had taught me to yowl our trials out loud instead of hiding them like something shameful. We aired our dirty laundry in the public sunshine of humor.

I stopped when I reached a dead-end street, and the cold white walls of the Crocodile's Ileyoba shrine rose in the darkness, glittering with rain. As I mounted the steps, offerings of wilted flowers and waterlogged balls of rice squashed beneath my toes. The resin crocodile head on the door stared down at me dolefully, water beading like pearls on the tips of its teeth.

From the head's mouth, a swarm of wet, buzzing things dove at my face. I yelped and slapped them away, catching one against my neck. It was a maimed dragonfly of Ixalix, staring up at me with empty, humanlike eyes.

"*Girl, not god,*" it buzzed. "*God, not girl—*"

"If your mistress has a problem with my being here," I scolded, "she can blame a world in which gods have power and serving girls have none."

I crushed the creature to put it out of its misery, then pushed open the shrine door, stepping over the chalk tooth line.

The roar of the storm ceased.

I now stood beneath a clear, serene purple sky, quilted with twinkling stars. The night air was warm and tasted of mango blossoms. If I had thought the Crocodile's villa unnaturally quiet before, it seemed even more so now. For in Oluwan, night is when creatures come alive. But though it lacked the click of cicadas or throaty coo of wood owls, the Bhekina House courtyard glowed with cheer.

Flickering lanterns crowded on every surface: the well, the windowsills, even the benches and tops of barrels. Green silk streamers hung in festoons across the yard. Even the crocodile mask, which floated in midair above the well, had been trimmed with ribbons. At my entrance, Clemeh did joy loops on a nearby wall.

The Crocodile did not see me at first. When I entered, he was gazing at the floating crocodile mask, his expression worshipful, creased in memory.

Then he roused from the trance, bounding across the courtyard when he saw me. A triumphant grin split his face in half. Over his bare chest and trousers, a dressing robe of finespun linen swept the ground as he walked. When he reached me, he shrugged off the robe and wrapped it around my trembling shoulders.

I flinched to see that the scales on his arm had tripled in number, shining uneasily against his smooth, dark skin.

"You came," he sighed, breath hot on my brow. "Thank Am. I was beginning to think you wouldn't, especially when that storm grew teeth." He frowned at something on my shoulder—the remains of a dragonfly carcass, which he brushed off with a chuckle. "I see Ixalix has been keeping tabs on you. Don't worry—lodestone travel confuses her weaker spies, and so they are unlikely to follow you here."

I noticed faintly that water beaded on his locs, as though he had recently been out in the rain.

"The food will be cold now," he said. "But I can warm it up again. I managed to buy meat pies from the street vendors before they closed for the night. Stop it, Clemeh," he scolded playfully, glancing behind him. "You know very well those are not meant for you."

Dazed, I followed the Crocodile's gaze across the courtyard to a lantern-lit picnic blanket, where Clemeh slunk guiltily away from a basket of golden pastries. The blanket was set for two, with ceramic plates and green-glazed goblets, napkins folded cleverly to resemble a pair of crouching reptiles.

It was only then I realized—taking in the picnic amid the lights and festoons—he had decorated the courtyard for me.

Heat flooded my cheeks. But my heart remained brittle, as though I had left it behind to shiver in the storm.

I removed the robe and gave it back to him. Then I put distance between us and bobbed in a wooden curtsy.

"Good evening, Your Majesty," I monotoned. "I am here to be your maid."

The smile dropped from his mouth. "Sade," he growled, "for both your safety and that of the realm, do not call me that ever again."

"As you wish," I said, and curtsied a second time. "Oga."

He sucked in an angry breath through his teeth but decided for the moment not to argue.

My bare feet prickled, and my wrapper clung wetly to my hips and torso, making me regret giving back his robe. I crossed my arms.

"You will catch cold," he said, and waved a hand. In an instant, the water vanished from my clothes and reappeared in a puddle at my feet, leaving my body light and warm. Even my cane felt bone dry, water leeched from the grain.

The puddle dispersed, replaced by a patch of violets that grew beneath my toes, shaping themselves around my feet into a pair of soft purple slippers.

"You will find proper shoes in your room," he said. "But these should last you through dinner."

"My room?" I echoed blankly, but he ignored the question, gesturing instead for me to join him at the picnic blanket.

I lied: "I am not hungry, oga."

"My stomach has been growling for hours," he observed. "So yes, you are."

Caught out, I eyed the basket of meat pies peevishly and said, "I am a Person of the Clay. I do not eat land animals." My tone held childish triumph, as if to say: *Body-bond or no, you don't know everything about me.*

He swore softly, scowling at the basket . . . and then rallied. "I did buy something else. A backup plan."

He opened a tureen on the blanket, and steam rose from a mouthwatering pile of moi moi bean pudding. It was the kind they usually only sold at festivals, stuffed to the brim with peppers and onions, with an entire boiled egg in each piece.

"Judging from the drool that just pooled in my mouth," the Crocodile monotoned, "I'm guessing this option is acceptable. Sit, if you please. Though I'll need that prayer pebble you're hiding under your tongue first."

I obeyed sulkily, though the scowl melted from my features with my first bite of moi moi. Anticipating the Sin Salon had tied my belly in knots, and so I had barely eaten all week. Any shyness I had felt about being in the presence of the former king of Djbanti vanished temporarily as I ate, smacking my lips and grunting with relish like the gutter girl I was. He watched with boyish smugness, as though he had cooked the dish himself.

Once I had finished the last bite and licked my fingers, however, I folded my hands on my lap, fixed my gaze formally on the ground, and said, "Thank you for the meal, oga. Please know that in the future, I will not expect to share your dinner. But in exchange for my keep, I—"

"Why are you doing this?" he demanded, running an exasperated hand through his locs. "You know I do not want you as my maid. Forget what Ixalix told you. I am not your boss, your oga, your king or anyone else's. Please, Sade . . . can we not be as we were before?"

"Before?" I breathed. "When I did not know your name? Did not know you were an *Anointed One*?"

Even saying it sent chills up my spine. I stumbled to my feet and backed away from the picnic blanket, my soft blossom slippers rustling with each step. He stood too, holding up his hands, as if to show they held no weapons. The scales on his arm glinted in the lamplight.

"What difference does it make?" he pleaded. "The world believes me to be dead. I rule over nothing. Even if I did, you know I would not hurt you."

"Anointed Honor Sanjeet did not mean to hurt me either," I said quietly. "Any more than a giant means to crush an ant. Don't you see, oga?" I met his eyes for the first time since I had entered the courtyard. "It does not matter what we want. We were born on opposite ends of the mill wheel. And try as you might . . . you will always be the hammer, and I the pulp pressed into paper."

He launched into a stream of protest, which washed over my head without seeping into my ears. I watched his lips, absently admiring their dark fullness as he shaped words like *revolution,* and *equality,* and *the inherent worth of every soul, regardless of the state of their birth.* The Crocodile's beauty seemed less dangerous to me now, because he felt less real. I observed him as I would a statue on a turret, high above me on the lofty domes of An-Ileyoba Palace. He still made my heart pound. But now that I knew who he was, a chasm had grown between us so wide, I could no more dream of touching him than I would the moon.

I waited until he had tired himself out, pausing for breath in his impassioned speech. Then I asked, gesturing at the villa, "Where am I to sleep, oga? I must rest soon, if I am to clean in the morning."

He laughed through his nose, shaking his head in disbelief. Then he sighed and gestured for me to follow him.

We entered the villa through a side door. It opened soundlessly with another wave of his hand, making the hairs on my arms stand on end. A smooth plaster hallway stretched out before us, lit with old-fashioned torches nestled into the walls. Despite the house's austerity, evidence of the owner's wealth lay every few yards: doors. Real, carved and polished wooden doors, instead of the more economical waxed cloth doorflaps most center realm homes employed. In warm climates like the center realms, flaps allowed for better airflow in interior rooms, so real doors were reserved for exteriors only. The only people who filled the inside of a home with *doors* had too much money and many more secrets.

"This was Raybearer Tarisai's childhood home," the Crocodile explained. "It was built by her father, a powerful alagbato from Swana, at the command of her mother, a woman known only as the Lady. The villa's official location is a remote savannah in Swana, though when it comes to enchanted buildings, pinning down an exact temporal location is complicated."

"But she knows I am here?" I asked in a panic. Immediately, I imagined the walls growing porous with eyes: the same gaze from the terrifyingly lovely girl in Ixalix's vision who the Crocodile—*Zuri*—had embraced.

You will think I am silly. But you must understand that in the circles where I grew up, just as the phrase *Sanjeet of Dhyrma* scared children into good behavior, the words *Tarisai Idajo* scared everyone into keeping their thoughts virtuous. We avoided thinking of the worst things we had done, lest the Idajo peek into our minds and ride from the palace on her crystal-horned Underworld beast, spear poised to dispense the justice that was her namesake.

"She does not," the Crocodile said, reading the terror on my face with dry amusement. "Nor can she read your mind, at least, not without touching you, and even then, she mainly looks at what you want to show her. Do not worry. She would not mind that you are here. The Boss Almighty's childhood was . . . isolated, to put it mildly, and she has little interest in seeing this place ever again."

A pang of sadness rippled through me as I imagined that girl from the vision as a child, creeping alone down that cold, elegant hall. Perhaps the young Idajo had been treated like one of her mother's many secrets: to be kept, polished, and locked away behind a thick wooden door.

"But won't she find out?" I asked. "When her servants come to clean?"

His expression grew perplexed. "Sade . . . there are no servants. Not in either wing of the villa, or any of the facilities on the grounds. No one has lived here for years."

My brows shot up. "But that is not possible," I said, scanning the hall to try to determine what felt uncanny. I realized then that aside from a slight stale smell, the hall was too clean. A thin layer of dust coated some surfaces, and leaves we had tracked in from the courtyard skittered on the ground, but beyond that . . .

"Where are the cobwebs?" I asked. "The rats and roaches?" The surest part of cleaning, I had learned over the years, was that when humans moved out, other creatures moved in.

He looked thoughtful. "I have noticed that while animals can come here, they generally choose not to. Even the insects. When the Lady forced that alagbato to build this place, she stipulated that she must always be safe. That included, among other things, an invisible barrier allowing only creatures she approved to sense the villa's existence. The villa is visible to most now, as that part of the enchantment wore off when the Lady died. But I think animals can sense that the villa does not want to be seen. Perhaps they avoid it out of politeness."

"Polite roaches?" I said dubiously.

"Are those any less likely than girl-eating gods?"

"Much less," I deadpanned. "Especially in this infested neighborhood."

His mouth twitched, and I must have been very tired then, because I smiled too and met his gaze as we chuckled softly, our voices blending together in the echoing hallway.

"Your room is here," he said, pushing open the first door on the right. Then he backed several steps down the hallway. I realized, after a moment, that he was trying to demonstrate that I was in no danger of him following me in. A corner of my heart melted when he began to babble, sounding suddenly much younger.

"I will be staying in the opposite wing, across the courtyard. I can give you a tour of the grounds in the morning, but in the meantime, send Clemeh if you need me. Not that you will need me. The ceiling is an illusion. I made it because of your difficulty sleeping in tall buildings. If it disturbs you, I can change it . . ."

I entered the bedchamber and looked up.

He had turned the ceiling into a replica of the night sky: an indigo dome awash with shifting clouds and tiny, winking stars. The illusion must have taken a massive deal of enchantment, which explained the worrying increase of scales that now covered the Crocodile's arm.

The illusion sky stretched above a chamber twice the size of Dele's room at the inn. Though sparsely furnished, the room was strewn generously with rugs, and a down bedroll rested on a real raised frame. He had taken a few of the green festoons from the courtyard to drape the plaster walls, and instead of oil lamps, purple *tutsu* sprites flickered in tall, swan-necked jars.

His deep voice echoed from down the hall.

"Well? What do you think?"

I swallowed hard, frozen in place by the peace that had flooded my limbs the moment I looked up at that marvelous not-sky. An army of joy-moths fluttered in my stomach, threatening to swarm up my throat in the form of tears.

"I think," I said, "that it is too fine-fine for a maid."

He was quiet for so long, I wondered if I had hurt his feelings. Then he said, with a passion that unnerved me, "The world has hampered your potential. But that ends tonight. Now that you are rid of that horrible salon, it is the dawn of a new age. A new Sade."

To which I responded, "I am tired, oga. May I have my prayer stone back?"

He winced but produced the pebble from his pocket and floated it down the hall on an invisible current.

I plucked it out the air, said good night, and closed the door. Before lying down, I dragged the bedroll from its fancy wooden frame so the mattress lay on the cold floor. Then I watched those false stars as they spun, begging the gods, for once, to let me dream of nothing.

CHAPTER 23

WHEN THE CEILING OF STARS BRIGHTENED INTO A GRAY morning sky, I told myself in my best Mercy Auntie voice: "All right, Small Sade. You have had your cry, and now it is time to make a plan."

I told myself that despite everything that had happened at Mamadele's, nothing had changed, really. I had been penniless and unemployed before, and I was penniless and unemployed now. Mamadele would do her best to sully my name in the Ileyoba Luxury District, but that left several other districts in which to ply my trade. I need only trespass on the Crocodile's hospitality a few days longer. All I had to do was find a new employer. I could still be Sade of Oluwan City.

Until your employer blames you for something that is not your fault.

The thought pierced me as though I had stepped barefoot on a pottery shard. I recoiled, and when I tried to think of working for another madam, a new, hot sensation thrummed through my body.

Rage.

The sensation was not truly new, not entirely. But I had worked for years to keep it in check. Even now, I summoned all the phrases I had kept close since leaving Yorua Village, flinging them like water to dampen the burning coals in my chest.

There will always be maids and masters. Ants and giants. It is the way of the world. The only pain comes from expecting more. All will be well, Sade, so long as you keep small and know your place.

Only . . . knowing my place at the Balogun Inn had not mattered, had it? The moment I had lost my voice, Mamadele had been quick to turn on me, just as she would on Onijibola, once she learned that she could wring no more use out of his loyal hands.

But I had not known my place, I was quick to remind myself. It may not have been my fault that I lost my voice, but I had struck Mamadele.

Only because she was about to strike you.

And for all my prayer pebbles, and lowered gazes, and determination to know my place . . . I could not quite convince myself that I deserved to be struck for losing my voice. I had too much of Fola in me for that. Too much of the woman who would rather give birth in the Bush, sprouting a garden of life in the wilderness, than accept the looming shelter of a balled fist.

But I have always been practical to a fault. So after letting the emotion boil, I shelved it like a can of preserves: destined either to rot with time or pickle into something sharp and new.

Rage, I could do nothing with at present. Soap, on the other hand . . .

I could see the room better, now that the false sky had lightened. A wash pitcher and tureen stood out on a low vanity table, along with a pile of clothing neatly folded atop a chest. I washed, pausing to blink at a hunk of soap that someone—presumably the Crocodile—had carved cheekily into the shape of a frog. Rummaging through the table drawers yielded a jar of chewing sticks, so I cleaned my teeth and then investigated the pile of clothes.

The clothing clearly came from the villa, as each garment was luxurious but outdated. I pictured the Crocodile rummaging through the chests of this grand, haunted abode looking for clothes my size and wanted to laugh and shiver at the same time.

"What part of *too fine-fine for a maid* does he not understand?" I grumbled to Clemeh. The gecko had spent the night dozing on one of the posts of the abandoned bed frame, and now he watched me with interest. With growing wariness, I leafed through the pile of watery silk, shining ashoke, and a spidery ghost fabric I suspected was called *lace*.

It might surprise you to know that I am fond of pretty things. Some make a tiresome show of disdaining them, but sweeping gowns and shining wrappers make me sigh in the same way that sunsets and birdsong do. I have never had the patience to pretend otherwise.

The problem here was, I had only ever touched such clothing to wash it. Every maid fears being caught trying on the garments of her betters, and these were pieces that lords and ladies, perhaps even *you*, had worn. But the only outfit I had was the one from last night: that pale livery from the Balogun Inn. Staying in that felt equally as dangerous as dressing above my station. So in the end, I picked the plainest thing in the pile: an airy gown of guava pink linen with no sleeves. It wrapped around my neck in a soft spun halter, leaving my shoulders bare.

The linen was so finely woven that when I took a few steps, the fabric floated around my legs, making me feel naked. The sensation made me giggle. I dared glance in the oval vanity mirror . . . and my laughter soured to a snort.

For all my new riches, I had forgotten my hair. It could have been worse, I supposed, after walking in a storm and then tossing all night with no protective sleep scarf. Still, half my twists had come undone, and the rest stuck out in spongey blobs around my head. I retwisted the strands as best I could without the aid of flaxseed gel, then wrapped the lot in a square of gauzy linen.

"You are not," I told myself as I braided the cloth, "trying to look attractive for the Crocodile."

But I lingered at the mirror.

I wet the coils at my brow and the nape of my neck, so they shone in neat, glistening spirals. Then I turned swiftly away, pretending I had not noticed that strands peeked out from the linen turban, framing my face in a fetching fringe of curls.

My violet slippers from the previous night had wilted, but as the Crocodile had promised, a line of sandals in varying trims and sizes lay neatly on a shelf. I picked the smallest pair, feeling vaguely as though I were robbing a shop. Then I hurried out into the courtyard, with Clemeh scampering after me.

After all his talk of dawns and new ages, I had expected the Crocodile to rise with the sun, and so I half expected him to be waiting impatiently just outside the door, ready to lecture me about my new purpose. But the courtyard was empty.

The festive lanterns from last night, now burnt out, still littered the surfaces. Dawn bathed the drooping streamers and tinted the edges of the Crocodile mask.

The mask hung like a forlorn star above the well, forever grimacing. When I had seen it all those weeks ago, that fateful day I had first entered the Crocodile's shrine, I had not questioned its presence. Hanging an object in the sky, after all, made about as much sense as anything else an immortal being did. But now the sight of it filled me with dreadful awe.

It was *the* Crocodile mask—the one copied by hundreds of vigilantes and peasant protesters throughout the Realmhood, all inspired by that first revolutionary: Zuri of Djbanti, the mad boy-king who dismantled his own monarchy. As I stared up at it, I thought, the boy who wore that mask should be enshrined in a tomb somewhere, a noble relic of history. Instead, he was here, lurking in empty hallways that smelled of stale air and lost time.

"Unless he has gone out," I wondered, and bumps rose on my arms as I imagined him gliding through the city streets in disguise, no doubt on some important errand from the Raybearers.

Crocodile or not, I thought, hauling up my whispering skirts to walk more easily—my first order of business was to explore the villa until I found the privy.

I had not relieved myself since leaving the Balogun Inn, and my bladder was near to bursting. There had been a chamber pot in my room, but the thought of running into the Crocodile at the crack of dawn while carrying a sloshing pot had mortified me so much, I had not used it.

A scalloped archway led from the courtyard to the manicured fields surrounding the villa. Careful to avoid stepping on the tooth portals, I left the yard and rounded the left wing.

An orchard of mango trees sprawled before me, ripe fruit twinkling with morning dew. Their loveliness made me shiver. Not a single weed or rotting spot blighted the fruit, and the trees remained perfectly spaced, though they could not have been tended for years.

The most beautiful thing in the orchard to me, however, was the whitewashed outhouse, which stood out among the abandoned gardening sheds. I used the outhouse gratefully, though unnerved by how little it smelled—did the same enchantment that cared for the mangoes whisk all the dung away?—and then marched back toward the villa, determined to find the kitchens.

It did not take me long. Around another corner, a breezy awning stretched over a line of dusty coal pits, supplied with several stew pots. It even boasted its own water source: a well some paces away. But when I checked the barrels and larder, they were all empty.

"There must be another kitchen where the Crocodile cooks his food," I thought aloud to Clemeh, who rooted the ground fruitlessly for insects. "This place has not been touched in years."

"Crocodile," Clemeh replied in his cryptic way, and I raised an eyebrow at him.

"Do you mean to say he is still here?" I asked uneasily. Clemeh nodded once, then made quick tracks back to the courtyard. Once there, he gestured with his head, guiding me to the wing of the villa opposite my own.

When I hauled open the tall carved doors and entered, I half expected a hallway floating with fantastical objects: the colorful robes of his many disguises, perhaps, or a library of weapons poised to strike. Perhaps even a collection of those torture objects called books, pages darting around the eaves like birds. If I had been immortal like the Crocodile, after all, even I who hated reading would have tried to learn. How else would a former king spend eternity, if not to learn as much as possible?

But when I entered the wing, not only were the halls as bare as mine, they also . . . stank.

My nose wrinkled. The smell was not urine, thankfully, but something sweet and sharp. Juice turned to vinegar. I tried to walk quietly but had to catch my balance with my cane when my toe collided with a jug—one of many carelessly dotting the hallway. I bent down and sniffed, then ran my finger around the rim and licked it with a grimace.

Mango wine.

"But he has only lived here a year," I wondered aloud, dodging jugs left and right. "He could not possibly have drunk all this alone."

Clemeh made a sardonic chirruping sound, as though I had underestimated the capacity of gods to feel sorry for themselves.

A repeated clashing sound echoed from the end of the hall, where a door lay slightly ajar. Clemeh stopped outside of it. With a gulp, I leaned to peek inside.

Amid a jungle of wine jugs and standing candelabras, the Crocodile lay fast asleep. His dark, sinewy body sprawled across a giant nest of faded cushions, tasseled blankets, and thousands of paper scraps. Overhead, several spears darted to and fro in the air, beating against each other—the clashing I had heard from the hallway. The items rose and drooped in tandem with the Crocodile's snoring chest, as if acting out his dream as a play in real time.

Alongside the skirmishing spears floated an empty suit of leather armor studded with brass rivulets and draped with the lion pelts of a Djbanti king. Suddenly, the spears paused, turned, and hurled themselves in unison at the suit of armor, piercing it repeatedly. I gasped . . . then the spears and armor reset themselves, telling the short, gruesome story over and over again in a seamless loop.

In his sleep, the Crocodile smiled.

Scraps of paper from his nest drifted toward the door, and I stooped to pick one up. The edges were torn and yellowed. While I could not read the script, I could tell that they were WANTED flyers, emblazoned with the image of a man in a crocodile mask. I was better at numbers than letters and just managed to make out the faded date glyphs in the corner. These flyers were more than ten years old.

Considering that he had been dead nearly as long, he would have gone through great lengths to collect them . . . and for what? To remember a time when people feared his revolution across the empire?

My brows knit. So much for spending his eternity learning new things.

Despite his grand speech the night before, the Crocodile's plans to make a "new Sade" did not appear to involve him getting out of bed before noon. So I began to back out of the room, but Clemeh charged across the paper-littered floor, tiny body wriggling with sass. Before I could stop him, he crawled onto the Crocodile's face and flicked his tongue, mercilessly, into the Crocodile's ear.

"*Grah*—!" The Crocodile sputtered awake and sat up, slapping at his head. The green scales covering his arm and shoulder stood on end. With his dazed expression and face swollen by sleep, he looked more his age—a forlorn nineteen-year-old boy—than he ever had before. The floating spears and armor clattered to the ground. Reflexively, the Crocodile held out his arm for a weapon, and a club sailed across the room into his hand. He lowered it when he saw Clemeh.

"There are more polite ways to ask for breakfast, you know," said the Crocodile, rubbing his eyes as the gecko escaped back to the floor. "Though I should not expect much from you in the way of manners. You were raised by Ixalix, after all."

Grumbling, the Crocodile swayed to his feet and rummaged across a nearby table until he found a jar full of wriggling grubs. He did not yet notice me standing uncertainly in the doorway.

With a gentleness that belied his grumpy expression, he shook a few grubs onto a plate and placed the plate on the floor.

"Eat up, old friend," he sighed, patting Clemeh's head. "I am sorry you cannot hunt. Bugs are hard to come by in Bhekina House. But tell you what: Once I am a senseless beast, we will return to the swamp and hunt together. Unless of course, Sade decides to save us."

My breath caught at the sound of my name. When he said it, his voice grew low and warm, as though he had dipped each syllable in honey and savored every bite.

"The girl with worlds on her skin," mused the Crocodile. "I did not think it possible before, but if she is as powerful as she is stubborn . . . she might break my curse out of sheer spite. That would put a hitch in our hunting plans, eh Clemeh?"

He trailed off, staring with a sad, wistful smile at the cluttered floor. I recognized then that among the jugs of mango wine lay gourds—dozens of pumpkins, squash, and calabashes, all stoppered like the ones he had tried to send to the inn. The Crocodile's room was full of unsent letters.

To me.

A vision played on my heartstrings then: a disheveled boy, composing letter after letter before tossing them to the ground in despair.

"I wonder if she's awake yet," he murmured, then frowned, putting a hand on his stomach. "She's certainly hungry. We'll have to buy more food. Aside from the leftovers from last night, there's nothing in this wretched place but mangoes."

I blurted, unable to hide any longer: "I can cook for myself, if you will show me where your kitchens are."

The Crocodile jumped three feet in the air, scattering a pile of gourds as he whirled to face me.

"Sade," he croaked, seizing up a robe from the floor. He tossed it over his broad shoulders. "Ah. Good morning. I trust you slept . . ." He hitched in an appreciative breath, taking in my guava-colored gown.

My face heated. "Good morning, oga."

"It suits you," he said quietly. "I am not surprised."

"I will have to find something plainer," I babbled. "I cannot look for a new maid's job in clothes like this. And I am sorry for disturbing you. Only I was trying to prepare breakfast and did not know where to go."

His eyebrow rose. "Prepare? With what?"

"Your larder," I said, as though it were obvious. "In addition to being a maid, I can cook to earn my keep. If you have rice and the basics for a stew—tomato, pepper, onion—I can whip up something that will last a few days, though if you want meat, I am only good with fish—"

"But there is no larder." He laughed, looking quizzical. "That is why I bought all those dishes from vendors last night."

I blinked. "Why didn't you just buy the ingredients instead? It would be much cheaper, and from what I have seen of your kitchens, there is plenty of coal to cook with."

"Ah," he said after a pause, looking a little sheepish. "The thing is . . . I do not exactly know how to use a cookfire. Usually when I get hungry, I will pluck some mangoes from the orchard and call it a day."

"But you must cook sometimes," I insisted. When he continued to stare blankly, I snorted in exasperation, surprised by the sudden return of the hot, livid feeling I had awoken with that morning.

"Do you mean to tell me," I said, "that in the year since you returned from the dead—a year in which you had the power to read anything and go anywhere—you have not learned a skill as simple as frying an egg?"

The Crocodile's dark eyes glittered. "You are angry with me," he observed in fascination. "That is good. Much better than bowing and scraping and calling me *oga*. You should be angry, no, *furious* at anyone remotely like me. Didn't I tell you I was useless?"

I opened my mouth. Closed it. Then, once my blood had stopped boiling long enough for me to speak, I smiled and said through gritted teeth: "Get dressed, oga. And bring your purse. We are going shopping."

CHAPTER 24

"I TOLD YOU WE ARE GOING TO THE MARKET," I SAID, WHEN the Crocodile finally met me in the courtyard some twenty minutes later. "Not to a *wedding*."

He had insisted on bathing, dressing and—apparently, from the whiff of floral agave now filling my nostrils—perfuming himself before we left the villa.

"I wanted to match you," the Crocodile said, as though our appearance had even the slightest bit in common.

To be fair, he *was* wearing trousers in the same guava hue as my plain dress. But that was where the similarities ended. The trousers were shining silk, slung daringly low on his tapered torso. Silver thread shot through the crisp, thin robe that hung open over his bare chest. The sleeves only just covered the parts of his skin colonized by the green scales, which had now grown up his arm to graze his neck. Cowrie shells dotted his locs, and a dangling gold earring shone in his ear. When I squinted, I could have sworn that metallic powder shimmered on his contoured cheekbones.

I scoffed, even as my heart quickened. He looked so immaculate, it was hard to imagine the boy from moments earlier, sleep-addled and nesting in a pile of musty flyers.

"At least take off the jewelry," I grumbled. "The vendors are already going to rob us blind once they see how you are dressed. I would rather we avoid getting mugged by street urchins as well."

"Very well." He leaned down, offering his ear, and that warm, complicated scent of flowers and spear polish washed over me. "Since I am clearly the amateur here, why don't you hold it for safekeeping?"

I swallowed hard but assumed a blank expression as I reached up to unclasp the pendant from his ear. My hand grazed his jawbone in the process, sending a thrill up my arm. Then I tucked the earring away in the folds of my bodice, where it pricked against my heart.

"Now, which portal?" asked the Crocodile, glancing cheerfully around at his teeth embedded in the red courtyard dirt.

"I am most familiar with the Lower Market in Ileyimo," I admitted, "but that is near Aanu Meji Street, where my old orphanage is, and . . . I would rather not see it again. Not for a while, anyway." His expression creased with concern, but I did not explain. The truth was, my dream of being Sade of Oluwan City felt further away than ever, and returning to my old neighborhood a month after leaving would feel too much like permanent failure. I frowned, considering. "Perhaps we should try Ilemalu. Eggs will be freshest in the Agricultural District."

"Yellow Molar Door it is," said the Crocodile, and we crossed the courtyard to the chalk line where a mottled yellow tooth stuck out of the ground. "If you please, Clemeh, won't you check if the coast is clear? We can't be seen leaving the shrine in broad daylight."

The gecko shimmied over the line, which glowed red as his tiny body disappeared. After a moment, his disembodied head reappeared on the ground, chirruping his approval. I raised my foot to cross the threshold, bracing myself for the inevitable wave of nausea as the enchantment whisked my body through the portal.

The Crocodile cleared his throat. "The side effects of lodestone travel tend to be easier when one is touching the source," he said, and held out his hand.

I took it, and together, we reentered the relentless sprawling din of Oluwan City.

Almost as soon as we stepped out, a cohort of dragonflies began to tail us. The sight of me and the Crocodile hand in hand appeared to distress them, and they buzzed "*Girl, not god, god, not girl*" until the Crocodile waved at them irritably, and a breeze sent the creatures wheeling away.

The Ilemalu District reeked in a way I found oddly comforting, after the still, sterile air of Bhekina House. This part of the city, while crowded, boasted far more tanneries and cow pens than it did high-rise buildings, a fact I hid away in my head when considering my future employment. Scrubbing entrails from the floor of a prosperous meat merchant sounded considerably less pleasant than working at an inn alongside the Amenities, but it was easier than dealing with stairs and much better than doing nothing. And I couldn't stay with the Crocodile forever.

Could I?

With a jolt, I wrenched my hand from his, pretending to adjust the woven sack I had brought from the Bhekina House kitchens on my shoulder.

Of course I could not stay with him. These streets—smelly and loud, where every shoulder jostled another as we clawed to make our livings—this was reality. This was what living *meant* for a girl like me. Whatever peace I felt in Bhekina House, sitting across from him on that picnic blanket beneath a dome of stars . . . it could only ever be a dream.

"We should go for the inner stalls," I told the Crocodile, once we reached the Lower Market. I had to yell to be heard above the cries of vendors.

"But why?" He was swiveling in awe at the maze of stalls, standing out in his clothes like a peacock in a flock of geese. His features shone with childlike curiosity as hawker women jostled around him, balancing towers of wares from baskets atop their heads. "Everything we need is right here."

"Because you never buy goods sold at the entrance to a market," I said, rolling my eyes and grabbing the corner of his sleeve to drag him farther along. "The vendors will think you are in a hurry and will charge you more for the convenience. And for Am's sake, would you stop looking so *happy*? You will attract every peddler for miles."

He grinned down at me. "Should I scowl like you, then?"

"Yes," I said. "The grumpier you look, the less likely you seem to part with your money." I paused, eyeing him with sudden horror. "Oga, when I told you to bring your purse . . . you did bring *small* coins, didn't you?"

If we stopped at a vendor and he shook out a pile of solid gold tari-dayos for all the market to see, we would be lucky to make it back to the shrine alive, let alone with the clothes on our backs.

His smile widened. "I did not bring anything larger than a silver kirah. I said I'm useless, not stupid."

"Thank Am for that," I muttered, and pulled him aside when I spotted a promising produce stall. "All right," I said. "Time to barter. Rule one: Never use your hands to point at what you want. Use your lips instead, like this." I pursed my mouth to gesture at a nearby tower of oranges.

"Like this?" He made a face that looked constipated.

"No," I groaned, them demonstrated again. "Like this. The idea is to seem so uninterested in the product, you cannot even bother to move your arms."

"This?" He bit his bottom lip, eyes dancing wickedly.

"Now you are not even trying."

"Perhaps you should demonstrate again," he said, gaze dropping to my mouth. "I don't think I quite got it the first time."

"Behave, oga." But a smile crept across my face. "Rule two is to never accept the first price. Listen closely and repeat after me."

He cocked his head, watching with increasing delight as I screwed up my features and sucked my teeth in a show of disgust.

"Ah-ah!" I exclaimed. "Two kamerons for a bag of rice? Hayyy, you must be joking. Look at my face. Look at me laughing at your bad-joke price!"

I dropped the mask and nodded seriously at the Crocodile. "Your turn."

He mirrored my performance exactly, including a high flutelike voice clearly meant to sound like mine.

"Five zathulus for a cassava? Ah-ah!" He clapped for emphasis, scrunching his face in a girlish glare. "Do not make me come back there. I march into the shrines of gods, do you think I am afraid of you, a mere produce seller?"

"Stop," I protested, whacking him lightly with my cane as I began to giggle. "I do not sound like that."

"I really mean it, o!" he went on, winding his neck. "Give me your best price, or I will come back there and spirit-clean your insides until you forget your own mother's—"

"You are making people stare," I warned, but by now my cheeks hurt from grinning. His talent for acting should not have surprised me. After all, this was the same boy who had fooled an entire royal court into thinking he was a fop, all while growing an armed revolution beneath their noses.

Once the Crocodile had succeeded in making me laugh, he grew obsessed with doing it again. Wherever we shopped, he stood behind the vendor and mimicked them so well, I fumbled my haggling as I tried not to giggle.

After a while, I insisted he be serious, making him listen as I explained which ingredients went into a pepper stew, and how to check rice for signs of weevils, and where to bend a plantain to test if it was ripe for frying. When he bought me a cup of fried chin-chin dough as a treat, I made him watch the cook, pointing out how she kept the oil hot so the dough fried to a golden crisp instead of getting soggy.

He nodded, attentively at first, and then with a distant, indulgent smile, as though he enjoyed watching me lecture him more than he enjoyed learning anything. This bothered me. But before I could say why, a girl shopping at a nearby booth caught the corner of my eye.

A vendor was leering over her, expression dripping with amused contempt as the girl struggled to count out zathulus for a meager sack of beans, which the vendor had placed on a scale.

My body reacted even before my mind did. "I will be right back," I told the Crocodile over my shoulder, as my feet were already marching toward the booth. When I arrived, I kissed the air around the confused girl's cheeks, as though we were old-old friends.

"Ah, there you are my sister! I have been looking for you everywhere." I sang out, beaming as she blinked at me. Swiftly, I blocked her from handing over the money to the vendor. I turned, pretending to register the booth only then, and let my hip bump the scale.

"Ah-ah!" exclaimed the seller, as the beans tumbled from the scale. "Watch where you are stepping, you stupid girl . . ."

But he trailed off when the girl gasped, pointing at the scale, which had remained weighed down even once the beans were removed. Some passersby glanced over before the merchant could cover his booth, and cries of indignation rang through the crowd.

"*Cheat! Cheat! See this useless man . . . scamming people for their hard-won money . . . I knew it all along, o! He has that look about him . . .*"

The vendor shielded the scale with his body, ranting about being framed, but the quickly forming crowd shouted over him. In the shadows, the dazed girl scurried away . . . but not, I noticed with satisfaction, without pocketing some of the spilled beans for which the vendor had tried to overcharge her.

"Let's go," I told the Crocodile, who had watched the whole exchange with a stunned expression. I seized his wrist and led him down another maze of stalls. "The more that man denies it, the angrier the crowd will get. His stall will likely not be there tomorrow."

"But how did you know the scales were rigged?" asked the Crocodile, once we stopped in a feathery alcove of poultry vendors.

"I did not know," I replied. "Not for sure." The vision of that bean seller, contempt filling his eyes as he leaned over that bone-thin girl, seared in my mind. "It's only . . . some people are like cats. The ones allowed outside instead of kept indoors will kill birds and small-small animals by the hundreds. Even when they are not hungry. It is as though the very existence of creatures weaker than themselves makes them restless. I have gotten good at spotting them—Outside-Cat People. Those who see smallness and poverty as a crime to punish."

"Sade," the Crocodile said after a moment, staring at me with a strange heat, "do you realize the magnitude of the skills you just displayed? A nudge from you . . . and an entire crowd of people united in common purpose. Organized, to rally against injustice."

The excitement in his voice made me uncomfortable. "I made a lucky guess," I mumbled.

"No. You spurred a community to action," he insisted. A manic light had stolen into his eyes. "Don't you see? You are the opposite of useless. You can be everything I can't be."

He began to pace back and forth in that alleyway littered with chickens.

"I am nothing but the ghost of a washed-up royal family. But you—you could be leading movements. Changing the fabric of society. Someone who truly understands what it is to have nothing. A person of the people. Do not let that potential go to waste."

A small corner of my heart lifted, like a vine peeking up to face the sun. But I felt tired just listening to him. In all his speeches, he seldom mentioned what I had told him I wanted: to simply belong. To live each day in calm assurance of what I must do and where I must go, all while being part of this living, breathing city that did not know my name but claimed me as its own. Was it so wrong to want that?

Wrong, after being an orphan, a gutter girl, an edict brat, a Curse-Eater, to want to just . . . *be*?

Besides, I was called Small Sade for a reason. If my voice was good for anything, then it would not have killed my mother.

"We are not here to change the fabric of society, oga," I said, changing the subject. "We are here for you to learn how to buy groceries. And we still need eggs."

"Very well." The Crocodile's stance grew cocky, his gaze calculating. "But if must I learn away my uselessness, then you must learn your revolutionary potential. Agreed?"

I eyed him warily. *It is just until I find another maid job.* "Agreed."

He flashed a grin so radiant, it made me step back a little. I wondered how many teeth he would have, once that curse transformed him into a beast.

"Excellent," he murmured. "Your first lesson starts now: Acknowledge your enemy. Now, where did you say we can buy eggs? I have a feeling we will need quite a few."

CHAPTER 25

I SHOULD HAVE KNOWN HE MEANT TROUBLE WHEN, AFTER my suggestion of buying six eggs, he instead bought three dozen.

I did know he meant trouble when he strapped our bundle of groceries to his back and asked, "About your fear of multistory buildings . . . does it have anything to do with heights?"

My eyes narrowed at him suspiciously, but I gave the question genuine thought. "No," I said after a moment. "At least, I do not think so. It is not being high that frightens me, but the idea of the floors caving in."

"Excellent," he murmured.

And in a movement so fluid I barely felt my feet leave the ground, he scooped me up, cane and all, and lifted into the air.

We shot into the sky so quickly, the scream did not leave my lungs until we were skimming the high-rise rooftops. I clung to the Crocodile's neck as my pink skirts billowed around us, calling him *kolo-head, madman, yam-for-brains,* and . . . some less polite words that I will not share, as *your* ears are more well-bred than my own.

"Keep up that anger!" he told me above the rush of the wind. "We can use it! Nearly there!"

And despite my filthy mouth and hammering pulse, as we glided across the skyline . . . awe, warm and quiet, blossomed inside my chest. Because there she was:

My Oluwan City.

You will think me bold for calling it mine, but that is truly what it felt like. From the sparkling gold domes of Palace Hill, to the muraled turrets of the Watching Wall; the teeming patchwork of markets, to the long-sailed boats of the Olorun River docks; the colorful web of laundry lines connecting each high-rise, to the sun-worn statues of obsidian, towering in every palm-dotted square . . . every inch was as glorious as I had imagined, back when I was only Small Sade the country bumpkin, stuck between the stinking mudbrick walls of a sweatmill.

A sigh escaped me . . . but my wonder quickly cooled when I realized we were descending. I recognized the pristine neighborhood and the garden-covered rooftop coming toward us: the Balogun Inn and Philosophy Salon.

At the sight of Mamadele's high arched window—the memory of her arms around me, stroking my hair as I retched on the floor—rage rose inside me so quickly, I nearly saw red.

"What are you doing?" I demanded, seizing the Crocodile's collar. "Don't you know Mamadele will go mad if she sees me?"

Though in my current state, I was slightly more concerned about what *I* might do to her.

"Oga," I rasped, "why on Earth would you take us back here?"

"Do not worry," he murmured into my hair. "We are not going to land. But I thought you might like to do a little . . . decorating. For old time's sake."

Then he reached into our bag of groceries and handed me an egg.

My fingers trembled as they closed around it. *Know your place.* "I . . . I can't."

He cocked his head, staring down at me through dark, cunning lashes. "But do you want to?"

I swallowed hard, tasting, for just a moment, the salt of worms as they slid down my throat.

"Yes," I said. And I hurled the egg, gasping when it splattered against the lattice.

The Crocodile whooped in victory, dipping out of sight of the window so we would not be caught. His heart thrummed against my cheek as I laughed, first softly, then with my whole belly, shoulders shaking as I chortled. When no one came out to investigate, he looped back toward the inn, placing another egg in my hand.

"This time," he growled, "say what it represents out loud. With your whole chest, Sade. What is this egg for?"

"This," I whispered, gripping the egg so hard it almost shattered, "is for making me eat worms."

Another yolk stained the lattice. The Crocodile handed me another. "And this?"

"This is for leaving me alone with Lord Liao!" I hollered. *Splat!* "And making me climb deathtrap stairs!" *Splat!* "And Hanuni's children. And Onijibola's fingers. And treating the Amenities like they are nothing, when you owe them everything!" *Splat-splat-splat!*

At this point, I no longer saw Mamadele's window. Instead I saw a face, yawning and featureless, smirking with all the greed of a dozen sweatmill owners. The smugness of a hundred Mercy Aunties. The contempt of a thousand village elders. The looming, indifferent shadow of countless benevolent Anointed Ones.

"And this is for *my mother*," I roared. "*Fola, called Mamasade!*"

Then I seized an entire packet of eggs and threw them at the inn, reveling in the sound as they burst above the casing and dripped down the sill . . .

Right into Mamadele's open-mouthed face.

I had not even noticed her come to the window. With a shriek half horror, half delight, I squeezed the Crocodile's neck and yelled, "Go, go!"

And we hurtled away through the air, our pulses hammering in tandem, lungs breathless with laughter.

"You, oga," I said hours later, "are a bad influence."

We lay in the Bhekina House courtyard on opposite sides of the picnic blanket, rubbing our taut bellies. The aftermath of our enormous midday meal—remains of my cooking, and the Crocodile's attempts at it—littered the blanket in pots of oil-slick stew, heaps of fufu, skewers of crispy fish, and crumbling hills of seasoned red rice.

"Did you have fun or not?" he asked, grinning languidly as the gold cuffs on his locs twinkled in the sunlight.

"I did," I admitted. "Only . . . I am thinking of the Amenities. That's what we—what the inn workers call themselves. They will have to clean up what we did."

He shrugged, throwing an arm over his face. "It's a small price to pay for your first Giant Lesson. When you become a leader, you will make a better world for all 'Amenities.'"

The casualness with which he dismissed the discomfort of the inn staff made me frown, but he did not appear to notice, yawning as he rolled onto his side, propping his head up with one hand.

"You're a bad influence too, you know," he teased. "Why did you convince me that deboning catfish and boiling rice would be easy? Because I'll have you know, it wasn't. If I have another bite of undercooked grains or crunchy fish fillets, I just might let my curse take me early."

"You cannot be good at everything," I retorted. "Some things take time. And even when it is boring, you do it to survive."

He gave a wry snort. "I can't die, remember?"

"Even so," I said, staring up at the floating crocodile mask, which cast a narrow shadow across the blanket in the afternoon sun. "That does not mean you should stop living."

When I turned to face him, something pricked at my breast. I picked it out of my dress: It was his golden pendant earring from earlier.

"Here is this back," I said shyly, reaching across the blanket. When he took it, his fingers brushed mine . . . and I gasped.

Beneath his silver-threaded sleeve, lurid green scales now covered his entire arm, from shoulder to fingertip.

He sat up and recoiled, avoiding my gaze. But I seized his elbow, scooting closer to examine his torso. There were more scales there too—at least twice the amount from this morning. I realized then that he had taken pains to hide his arm during our lessons in the kitchen, often using one hand and never letting me watch the other too closely.

"It was the flying," he admitted quietly. "Stunts like that use a lot of power. That is why, most of the time, I use the tooth portals to travel instead. Aside from the initial enchantment, they take less effort. Less . . . out of me."

"Then why on Earth did you fly me across town?" I protested, my chest suddenly tight.

"You need not fear. I have made arrangements to keep you safe . . ."

"Why don't *you* fear?" I demanded. "Oga, aren't you afraid of what your curse is doing to you? Do you really want to return to Ixalix? Live as a beast in her swamp forever?"

"I do not matter anymore," he snapped, with a ferocity that stunned me. "Sade, it does not matter how many cooking lessons you give me. It does not matter how many missions—spying on cultists and their silly demonstrations—that the Raybearers assign me out of pity. I have no more use in this world. But you do." He took my hand in his cursed one, and I felt the ridges of budding scales on his fingertips. "Who better to lead the oppressed against a broken system than one who has experienced it herself? And you could inspire others to change as well. Sade, what if you could use your gift of spirit-cleaning to help those who truly need it? Not wealthy lechers. But people like you. People stuck beneath the roles the world has assigned to them."

I stiffened. "It is not wise to help people forget their place. To encourage behavior that will get them cast out of their homes and villages, like I did to my mother."

"You know," he said, gaze growing solemn, "instead of to the Balogun Inn, I almost flew you to your old orphan house. It would do you good to egg that place as much as Mamadele's. To cut yourself free of the constraints into which you were born."

Slowly, I withdrew my hand from his. "You almost flew me to Aanu Meji Street," I said, "even though I told you I have no wish to go back there?"

"No one wants to face their fears," he replied, expression cool. "But it is the only way to reach one's true potential."

I wanted to throw an egg at his face, just as I had at Mamadele's.

The urge took me by surprise. This new, foreign rage I had so recently allowed myself to feel was developing a life of its own, rearing its head at the most illogical times. How could I be angry at the Crocodile? Hadn't he been kind and generous, offering me a place to stay for nothing in return? How could I think of him as anything like Mamadele?

Because he feels entitled to pick your future for you, just like she did. Just like everyone with power always has.

The thought paralyzed me like a wasp alighting on my arm. But before it could decide whether to fly or sting, the air in the courtyard hummed with enchantment. One of the chalk lines burned red.

"Yellow Molar Door," the Crocodile murmured, and we both leapt to our feet as Ye Eun stumbled across the line into view. Several knapsacks wobbled on her back, haphazardly lashed together in a tower over her shoulders. Her cropped hair was disheveled, naked of its usual flower crown, and circles pooled beneath her eyes. A giant blue bird with death-white eyes perched protectively on her shoulder. To my shock, I could see through the bird's body, as though it were made from water.

"Small Sade," Ye Eun gasped when she saw us. The imperious bird flapped away as she shrugged off the knapsacks and bounded over to squeeze me so hard, I coughed. "You're all right," she wailed. "Thank the Storyteller. Croc, you've made sure that no one knows she's here?"

"Of course," he replied, features shading with concern. "Ye Eun . . . is everything all right?"

Her face closed up, bottom lip growing stubborn as she swiped tear tracks from her cheeks. "It's fine," she said brusquely. "Only . . . I might need to stay here for a few days. Just . . . just until things die down back at the shop."

He eyed the teetering bundle she had brought through the door. The bags burst with potted plants, seed packets, and cuttings of flowering shrubs. "It looks like you *brought* your shop."

"Die down?" I asked, hairs rising on the back of my neck. "Ye Eun, what's going on? And—what in Am's name is that bird?"

Unable to respond right away, she sank onto the rim of the well. She looked like she had not slept all night. Wordlessly, the Crocodile conjured a cup of tea and placed it in her hands while I fetched a plate of rice and stew from the picnic blanket and coaxed her to eat.

When she spoke again, it was to ask me a question.

"Small Sade," she said in a low, breaking voice. "There are rumors circulating about Mamadele's Sin Salon. I won't ask you what happened or why you left. But I have to know: Was it really Dele who told the entire party about our relationship? Did she really tell a room full of malicious nobles where I *live*?"

"Yes," I admitted. "To show she wasn't ashamed. She did it to declare her love for you."

Ye Eun's face crumbled. "She did it," she said through her teeth, "to embarrass her mother. Dele wasn't thinking about me at all. She was doing what she has always done: indulging her own feelings and letting me pick up the pieces."

I paused, confused by the betrayed anguish in her voice. "But didn't you want Mamadele to know? I thought, all this time, you were waiting for Dele to tell her."

"No," Ye Eun retorted. "I was waiting for Dele to choose me. To decide that I was more important than being a Balogun, or getting petty revenge on her mother. I . . . I even offered to support us both with my flower shop. I knew good and well she had never worked a day in her life, but I didn't care. I never needed her to get her hands dirty. Only for her to place them in mine." She stared into the murky depths of her tea. "But thanks to that darling, maddening, impulsive mouth of hers . . . I'm not sure I have a shop anymore. Hwanghu"—she nodded at the bird, which had gone to preen itself on the well—"might be the only reason I am alive at all."

"Hwanghu," the Crocodile explained to me quietly, when Ye Eun did not elaborate, "is Ye Eun's emi-ehran. Her soul guardian. The gods bestow one on any person who has journeyed to the Underworld and back."

"Hwanghu tends to appear when I'm in duress," Ye Eun said, tossing back her tea. She wiped her mouth and slammed the mug down on the rim of the well. "So she hasn't left me all day.

"This morning, just before sunrise, a group of masked thugs with torches started idling around my storefront. I live in the apartment above, and Hwanghu cried at the window to wake me up, or else I wouldn't have seen them. I know the type: hired fists. The type rich folk will not let in their parlors but pay at the back door to run their unsavory errands. I ran downstairs to make sure the store's doors and windows were barred . . . and that's when I smelled smoke. Mamadele had figured out where I lived using Dele's confession, and she hired thugs to set fire to my shop."

The Crocodile inhaled sharply, and I let out a horrified wail.

"Oh, Ye Eun," I breathed. "I'm so sorry."

Her jaw tightened as she continued. "It didn't ignite at first. Everything was still so damp from the rain; and Hwanghu made sure those mouth-breathers barely kept their torches lit. That's when I grabbed whatever I could." She pointed at the sprout-laden knapsacks. "They might take my home, but I was damned if I'd let them destroy eight new strains of drought-resistant *ibembem* flowers right after I'd spent a year learning how to splice them. Anyway. Once the torches didn't work fast enough, they resorted to smashing the storefront with clubs. I escaped through the back door and lay low at a tavern until late morning, which is when I heard the rumors about Mamadele's Sin Salon. I thought of going back to whatever was left of my apartment—see if there was anything else I could save—but that meant I would risk seeing Dele, who had probably run sobbing to my shop the moment she realized what her mother had done. I didn't want to see her. I was afraid of what I would say. So I came here, to hide mostly, and to draw up plans for a new shop far away from anyone resembling a Balogun." She gestured at the villa. "You two mind if I take a bed?"

"Of course not," I said. "You can have the room next to mine."

"Ye Eun," said the Crocodile in a hesitant tone, "have you told the Raybearers what happened?"

"No," she snapped. "And I don't plan to. I didn't leave the palace just to run whining back to them every time I get in a scrape."

"It is considerably more than a scrape," he countered. "Those men could have killed you, and . . . for Am's sake, Ye Eun, you know how much the Boss worries about you. You are the closest thing to a daughter she has. Even if you don't want those men pursued, at least let her know about the shop. She would build you a brand-new one by tomorrow. Hell, she'd build you ten shops if you wanted them."

Ye Eun shot back, "Which is exactly why I can't tell her! Look . . . I know she means well." She paused, chewing her lip. "But there's a reason I left that palace, all right? Every day, I had to live with the knowledge that if I hadn't been born a Redemptor, the Raybearers would never have met me. Would never have adopted me, or showered me in gifts and protection. I awoke each morning knowing that everything I owned—the food, the clothes, the fancy private gardens—was a result of the worst thing that ever happened to me. But that dinky little shop . . . I loved it because it was *mine*. Something I made and worked for, all on my own. So don't you dare tell her, Croc. Promise me right now you won't."

"All right, all right." The Crocodile raised his hands in defeat. "My lips are sealed. I'll go prepare a room."

From the way he shook his head as he disappeared into the villa, it was clear that he did not understand Ye Eun's outburst. But to my surprise . . . I did.

Though I had hid it from the Crocodile, I still grieved the loss of my job at the Balogun Inn. Even when I had gleefully pelted the building with eggs . . . I couldn't shake that small pang of longing to be back inside. It wasn't just that I missed the Amenities, and trading stories in our garret, and eating Kanwal stew.

It was that—unlike Yorua Village, and the sweatmill, and the orphanage—my job at the Balogun Inn was the first thing I had ever truly chosen for myself.

I had convinced Mamadele to hire and pay me. *I* had won the affection of the Amenities. *I* had made a home for myself . . . and even though I could not have stayed and swallowed guiltworms forever, I could not help but feel it should have been my choice to leave. But at the moment I had needed it most, my voice had simply vanished, snatched away by an invisible hand. Some ruthless power had forced me to leave the inn, just as those goons had made Ye Eun flee her shop. Just as I had been forced to leave every place I had ever lived.

"Come on," I told her, helping her up from the well and nodding at her pile of knapsacks. "Let's find a better place for your flowers to bloom."

CHAPTER 26

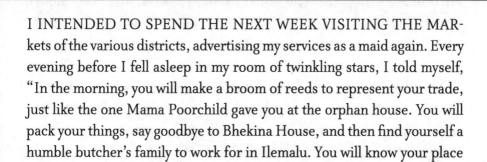

I INTENDED TO SPEND THE NEXT WEEK VISITING THE MAR-kets of the various districts, advertising my services as a maid again. Every evening before I fell asleep in my room of twinkling stars, I told myself, "In the morning, you will make a broom of reeds to represent your trade, just like the one Mama Poorchild gave you at the orphan house. You will pack your things, say goodbye to Bhekina House, and then find yourself a humble butcher's family to work for in Ilemalu. You will know your place and be grateful. You will be Sade, Nobody of Oluwan City."

But always, by the next dawn, I never quite got around to packing my things.

A week at Bhekina House slipped by, then another, days blending into each other in a parade of noiseless nights and crystal skies. The five of us—me, Ye Eun, Hwanghu, Clemeh, and the Crocodile—fell into an odd routine. The Crocodile launched himself into giving me what he called *Giant Lessons*—referring to the time I had called people like him giants and myself an ant.

"If Giant Lesson One was acknowledging your enemy," he said, digging out a stack of books and dusty scrolls from beneath the jugs in his room, "then Giant Lesson Two is empowering yourself with information. You do not challenge the systems that are, because you cannot imagine any different ones."

I had scoffed, pointing at my misshapen foot. "Oga, you have forgotten that books and I are not friends." If anything, books—those opaquely written objects for the wealthy, and the dangerous paper industry behind them—had helped shape my grim view of the world in the first place.

"Only because you were never given the proper material," he countered.

When I pointed out the obvious—that I could not read—his features had only grown more determined. The next morning, I woke to find that the Crocodile had enchanted every object and surface in Bhekina House to display its name in pulsing, shimmering characters.

I rolled out of bed to find my sandals covered in eerily glowing script, which he would later inform me spelled *SHOE*. I rubbed at it until it came off in shimmering dust. The words *COMB*, *MIRROR*, and *SOAP* glowed from the objects on my vanity table. I wiped those off too, only for a *HALL* and *FLOOR* to greet me in massive labels across the corridor the moment I left my room. The courtyard boasted ambitious glyphs of *GROUND* and *SKY*. Even the surface of the well shimmered with calligraphy: *WATER*.

I hunched my shoulders and ignored them all. But the last straw was when I escaped to help Ye Eun plant her garden near the orchard and found every single tree emblazoned with *MANGO*.

"Has the Crocodile always been this annoying?" I demanded of Ye Eun.

"Yes," she said simply, pruning her violets, whose individual petals now glittered with the word *FLOWER*. "I can scold him for you, but in general, it's best to wait until he wears himself out."

When days of enchanted graffiti did not turn me into a voracious bookworm, the Crocodile took to following me around and reading scrolls aloud while I busied myself doing whatever chores the villa did not do for itself. He preached on *the grassroots movements of the working class* while I stripped the linens from our bedrooms and hung them to air in the courtyard. He lectured on *the contradictions inherent to a market-driven existence* while I skinned and deboned the fish we would eat for lunch and peeled the yams for our supper. Even when I coaxed him back to the Lower Market to buy more groceries, he filled my ears with the *exploits of peasant revolutionaries*.

After a day or two of this, I handed the linen beater and yam peeler to the Crocodile and said that if I was to learn Giant Lessons, then he must submit to Ant ones. Among other chores, those lessons would include clearing the empty wine jugs from his wing of the villa—which I insisted he do by hand and not sorcery—and boiling them in water to get rid of the smell.

At first, he obeyed my orders with amusement, as though domestic labor was a curious new game. When the novelty wore off, however, I caught him trying to cut corners. He would scrub the linens for a minute or too, listening half-heartedly to my instructions on laundering silk versus cotton. Then, when he thought I wasn't looking, the sheets would sparkle, grow suspiciously white, and then fling themselves through the air to dry. The jugs did get cleared from his room, but instead of sanitizing the bottles for reuse, he used his powers to melt them down and reshape them into mirrored tiles, which twinkled facetiously across his previously cluttered floor.

Clemeh, who still seemed to think I could break the Crocodile's curse, took it upon himself to bully the Crocodile into matching my routine. His favorite task was to wake the Crocodile at dawn by slithering onto his shoulder, cheerily shrieking "*Small Sade!*" into his ear, then nipping at his ankles until the Crocodile came to help me in the kitchen.

"As much as I am enjoying this lesson, in particular," the Crocodile mused as I pressed my hand over his scaled one, showing him how to hold a knife to dice peppers, "we *could* just slice these using my powers. The work would be done in an instant."

"Absolutely not," I retorted. "Every time you use those nasty Pale Arts, you grow another set of scales. Besides, avoiding basic chores is how you ended up eating nothing but mangoes. Your powers made you lazy."

"That," he yawned, using the top of my head as a chin rest, "is where you are wrong. I was lazy long before I was a sorcerer. Do not give my curse all the credit."

I rolled my eyes, wriggled out from under him, and pointed at the peppers. "Chop."

"Very well," he said, sighing like a martyr.

Ye Eun usually joined us for breakfast, having already been up for hours planting her new garden in the Bhekina House orchards. The mysterious enchantment of the house had made her plants double in size

215

every night, though unlike the mango trees that had come with the villa, Ye Eun's blossoms still needed tending. I volunteered to help her, dragging the Crocodile along as well.

"All this time," I scolded, "you could have been growing vegetables practically overnight. For Am's sake, with a field this enchanted, you didn't even *need* to shop at the market. You could have started a produce stall of your own."

I had not dealt with soil and plants since I was a little girl, helping my mother weed our garden in Yorua Village as we lifted prayers to the Goddess of Earth. Beneath Ye Eun's guidance, my old skills flooded back to me. I sang a child's hymn of the Clay as I weeded rows, feeling the same relaxed trance I felt while cleaning. Ye Eun picked up the melody and hummed along. The Crocodile—likely to distract from how little weeding he was *actually* doing—lent his smooth tenor as well, harmonizing with showy runs and flourishes.

Seasons come and go, the Queen Mother grows
New life from the old, we sow (She grows!)
Rain and rot and wind, still our Mother knows
Life from death again, we sow (She grows!)

I expected my vision to reveal spirit silt covering the ground, like it always did when I sang. As expected, silt covered me, Ye Eun, and the Crocodile, pooling around the earth where we stood. But when I looked around, the rest of the orchard remained unchanged. The sun-drenched fields around Bhekina House had remained vacant of humans for so many years, the lands were free—unburdened by the pulsing layer of silver that covered every other place I had ever lived. A clean slate.

Here, a girl could start again. Here, a girl could be any person she wanted to be.

"You know," Ye Eun ventured when we took a break for water, "it's not a bad idea, Small Sade. What you said about growing things here and selling them in the city. I *am* going to build my old shop back, but there wasn't much space for growing stock—not like here. Still, I would have to figure out how this orchard magic works. The mango trees bear fruit—does that mean there are bugs?"

"I do not think so," I replied, squinting around at the pristine balmy air. "I am usually quite popular with mosquitoes. But since coming here, I have not been bitten once."

"If there were insects, Clemeh would have found some by now," the Crocodile pointed out. "As it is, I've had to buy mealworms from the market just so he doesn't starve."

"Then the enchantment must pollinate the trees on its own," Ye Eun mused, wiping her green-stained hands on her trousers. "I suppose I can't count on it doing the same for my plants, since they're foreign to the area. I'd have to bring in bees from the outside, or butterflies. Still . . . look at the *size* of this beauty." Reverently, she caressed a golden starblossom the size of my head. Only the night before, it had been a bud barely larger than Ye Eun's finger. "These would sell so fast on festival days, I'd barely keep them in stock. Insects from the grasslands surrounding the villa would be best. It might take a day or two camping on the savannah, but Hwanghu could help me track down a hive . . ."

After Ye Eun wandered away from the orchard, muttering excitedly about smoke traps and bee boxes, the Crocodile turned to me, features brightening.

"Ye Eun's right," he said. "Small Sade, why don't *you* start that produce stand?"

I frowned. "What do you mean?"

"It's like you said: Food here would grow overnight. You could set up shop in any of the high or lower markets. Then you'd never have to work as a maid again."

The idea was so simple and inviting, I recoiled from it out of suspicion. Grasping for objections, I said, "I do not know much about gardening."

"You wouldn't need to," countered the Crocodile. "The orchard would do half the work for you, and Ye Eun could teach you the rest. And when you're not selling vegetables," he went on, dark eyes shining, "you could deepen your education. Start organizing, build movements. No more toiling at maid's work. Sade . . . you could start doing things that actually matter."

I crossed my arms. "Oga, are you saying that cleaning homes and selling vegetables do not matter?"

"That is not what I meant," he said impatiently, waving a hand as he began to pace. "Sade, your mind is extraordinary. The problem is, your scope of vision is too narrow. You grapple with individual problems, but you do not see or challenge the systems that create them. You believe everything that you have suffered just . . . *happens*. But in a society, most things happen on purpose. Why not shape the world you live in instead of just existing inside it?"

The arrogance of his tone grated on my nerves so sharply, I nearly turned on my heel to leave the orchard. Still, his actual words—*shape the world you live in*—sent shuttles wheeling in my mind, weaving pictures I had never seen before.

Clearly, some people did shape the world. Gods, kings. Alagbatos and Anointed Ones. But it was not only them who shaped it. The last ten years, in which an empire had given way to a Realmhood, had proven that several times over. Haughty nobles like Lady Injaana expelled from their homelands when commoners rose in revolt. Families like the Baloguns made to give up their mines by the very workers they had driven into the ground. Even orphans like Ye Eun, defying demons in the Underworld and fighting alongside the Raybearers to end child sacrifice forever.

Though I had scarcely admitted it even to myself . . . there was a reason I had not yet left Bhekina House to become a butcher's maid. It was not only that Ye Eun's troubles had made me cautious and that I feared Mamadele may send her goons after me, as well. It was also that, ever since the night I had left the Balogun Inn, a restlessness had simmered inside me. I had not sucked my prayer pebble in weeks.

Could I really work for another person like Mamadele? Even if my next employers were decent, they would still expect me to keep my head bowed. To jump when they barked an order. To laugh along with them when they mocked my skin and cane. None of these realities would have troubled the Small Sade of even a few months prior. But now . . .

I smiled every time I thought of eggs.

The smile faded, however, when I closed my eyes and saw my mother. Mamasade, who was not here. Mamasade, who would be alive in our hut of laughter and lemongrass, if only I had done what I was told and kept my mouth shut.

I stared hard at the clouds casting shadows across that untouched orchard. Without blinking, I told the Crocodile, "Whenever I try to shape my world, I end up destroying it."

He turned my chin so I met his gaze, which had grown uncharacteristically soft, and said, "That is a lie told to subdue slaves who outnumber their masters. It is the lie on which every empire is built."

Despite my anger from moments earlier, I wanted to kiss him then. Badly. And deep down, I knew why.

Because for all my impatience, those silly, exasperating Giant Lessons had *meant* something to me. They had been nothing like Mamadele's philosophy salons, where pompous heads had picked away at my mind without expecting to find anything of value. Instead, the Crocodile had encouraged me to be angry. Had reminded me of the ways in which ordinary people rebelled every day. Had shared with boyish excitement every concept he held dear, shining with faith in my ability to understand. Each lesson fanned the flames of my new restlessness—of that eager, curious rage I could no longer bottle away.

The force of my desire, revealed to him by that damned body-bond, seemed to take him by surprise. Then his dark eyes grew molten. He swallowed with a longing that looked painful, full lips parting as he closed the distance between us.

"Ask me," he whispered, mouth suspended over mine, "and I will."

I wanted to believe that I should take charge of my fate. I believed it for other people. Like for Ye Eun, and Wafa, and Kanwal, and the girls tossed into the shrine, and all the other children back at my old orphan house. Every ounce of rage I let myself feel, I wielded on their behalf. *They* should not have to accept their place. *They* deserved to fight back. To shape the world and make something new. But . . .

The village elders burned in my mind's eye, followed by Mamasade, kiriwi flowers wilting in her hair.

When all was said and done, I still was not sure that *I* deserved something new.

And until I could be . . . I could not close that final distance between me and the Crocodile. Not while I was still Small Sade and he was still oga.

So I drew back and rasped, "I can't. Not . . . not yet. But—" I squared my shoulders, meeting his gaze head on. "Give me my next Giant Lesson."

CHAPTER 27

"OGA, WHEN ARE YOU GOING TO EXPLAIN WHAT WE ARE DO-ing?" My tone was impressively calm for how close he was. His muscled arm wrapped around my waist, keeping me from pitching over the rooftop railing of the high-rise as a gust of wind billowed my skirts around us. His locs brushed my bare arms, and I shivered.

Get it together, Small Sade.

Close by, a cohort of Ixalix's dragonflies hovered sulkily, though they dared not dive at my face with the Crocodile so near.

"You said you wanted a Giant Lesson," he replied casually.

"What I meant to ask," I said with the patience of a saint, "is why we are back at Unity Square on Balogun Street, where Mamadele's goons could be out for my blood. Why you insisted on flying us here, to this high-high tower, when you know good and well that flying is bad for your curse?"

He had chosen the top of a luxury apartment building bordering Unity Square. Stories below, townspeople swarmed like ants around the looming statue of Enoba the Perfect.

"Lesson three," he said, gesturing down at the teeming crowd. "Rallying the masses."

I frowned. "They look rallied to me already."

"What do you think is happening down there?"

"The same demonstrations that have been going on for months." I pointed at one side of the square where nobility and cultists had gathered. The nobles shouted *Order and beauty! Save our city!* amid peals of *Praise the Idajo!* from the cultists. The metallic tops of their headdresses and masks bobbed and glinted in the sun. I said, "The nobles want to take back control of Unity Square, and the cultists have sided with them. They say that ever since the Raybearers opened the square to the public, it has grown uglier and less safe." I pointed at the opposite end, where a larger group of workers and families milled in confusion and babbled in protest. "But the commoners are not convinced."

"And just why," the Crocodile asked, "would commoners resist things like beauty and safety?"

Because common people are foolish and uneducated and have no idea how to care for themselves, let alone a society. The thought darted through my mind like a snake through grass. It was certainly how those fine-fine nobles at the salon would answer the Crocodile's question. *Foolish* was how I had been taught to think about myself, and others like me, since I was very small. But now I thought of Hanuni, expertly organizing the inn stockroom and managing the guests' moods. I thought of Onijibola and Kanwal running the chaotic kitchen at high speed, and Finnric rapidly settling the inn's accounts, Wafa hanging laundry with the grace of a dancer. I thought of all those revolutions from the Crocodile's stories, where ordinary people starved out their rulers simply by refusing to farm and weave and fish, tasks all lords needed to survive but did not do for themselves.

"Because the common people do not trust the nobles," I replied at last. "They know that these lords and ladies do not want to share that space at all."

"Exactly," the Crocodile purred. "So 'order' will mean guards with spears, whom the nobles will bribe to harass unwanted commoners. 'Beauty' will mean removing benches where people could sleep and erecting statues in any open space in which a large group could *loiter*, especially for the purpose of protest. Now, when you look at that rally . . . which side seems like they are winning?"

Even from our far-far rooftop, the answer was clear. "The cultists and nobles," I said. "They are shouting over everyone else, and so some commoners are starting to listen."

"But how? The nobles and cultists have few weapons, and the commoners outnumber them. So why is the smaller group dominating the space?"

I thought hard, a reed broom brushing the corners of my vision, beating down cobwebs until my mind was clear.

"The cultists claim to speak on behalf of the Idajo," I said slowly, "a name that most people respect. So even though the commoners do not trust the nobles, they are tempted to listen."

"True, but anyone can yell out names. What else?"

"The cultists look strange. With their masks and dyed hands, they capture people's attention."

"Good catch. They have set themselves apart visually, so they present a united front to observers. What else?"

I paused to observe again, my focus narrowing over the square, watching bodies and faces until I gasped, turning to face the Crocodile. "The cultists and nobles know what they want," I said. "They are all saying the same thing. Everyone else is—messy. Disorganized."

"Well observed."

"But a lot of those commoners *do* know what they want," I pointed out. "A place to catch up with their neighbors that is not a back alley. A place to hear news and music, and for their children to play without getting trampled by carts and palanquins. Structures that catch the wind, where they can hang their laundry, and awnings where they can rest without burning in the sun."

"Yes. But it is hard to say all those things at once. Do you know what it's much easier to say?"

"*Order and beauty*," I said, mimicking the reedy voices of the cultists. "*Hail the Idajo*."

"Precisely."

The broom behind my eyes beat faster until a rhythm made its way to my fingertips, which tapped against the rooftop railing. "They need a song," I said. "A chant, something easy to remember, to remind them what they want and drown out the other voices. A song to unite."

I felt the Crocodile's eyes sharpen on me, and his heartbeat quickened where his chest pressed against my back. But instead of saying anything, he only waited.

"*Our hands built it*," I murmured, in a breath so long it sang. "*We are the beauty*."

And the square below erupted with spirit silt, the silver spores covering the sea of bodies and shifting beneath their feet. As the hopes, fears, and winged dreams of a thousand stubborn-hearted laborers filled the air, my eyes stung with happy tears.

"*We are the beauty*," I repeated. "*A city belongs to its people*."

But this time, something strange had happened in my throat. My voice came out so loud, the vibration numbed my chin, and the song ricocheted off the high-rise turrets. Below, confused heads looked up and around, trying to find the source of the echo. I stumbled back from the railing, hands clapped over my mouth, and whirled on the Crocodile.

He grinned with the full array of his pointed teeth. When he gestured at my neck, the scaly tips of his fingers shimmered. "I gave you a little boost," he said. "To make you harder to ignore."

"Make it stop!" I hissed through my teeth, in a whisper so loud it shook like thunder on my tongue.

The Crocodile pouted, but reluctantly waved his fingers again. The buzz in my throat disappeared. "Those people need guidance," he scolded. "The point of these lessons is that you learn to use your voice—"

"I am using my voice now, oga: Shut your mouth and listen," I snapped, which stunned him into blank-faced silence.

I paced the roof. Why didn't I want the Crocodile to amplify my song? It would certainly make it easier to unite those people. But . . .

"I am too far," I explained at last. "Too high above them. They will look up here instead of marching with each other."

"Why shouldn't they look at you?" the Crocodile countered. "Stand tall, Sade. Be the giant they need."

I took a moment to examine him—beautiful, scale-marred features, and the lost glory of his battle scars—before turning to watch the milling crowd. "I am beginning to think," I said, "that standing tall is less useful than standing together."

I closed my eyes, feeling the ghosts of a million stubborn dreams, silver spores, tickling my cheeks and collecting like pollen on my lashes.

"What if there is nothing wrong with being an ant?" I wondered aloud. "What if together, we could be stronger than any giant?"

When I opened my eyes, the Crocodile was watching me, for once looking a little lost. I smiled at him and pointed at the square. "You may use your Pale Arts on my voice. But only for a moment, and only if we leave this silly tower. We should be with those people, not above them."

He let us down in a nearby alleyway, stopping only for the Crocodile to conceal his scaly features with a cowl. When we rounded the corner into Unity Square, the reedy voices of the nobles filled our ears even as commoners booed and heckled from every side.

"You must remember, good citizens, what brought you to this square in the first place. Was it not the beauty and order? Do you wish to see this square fall into the disrepair and squalor of the districts you came from? Ileyoba is lovely for a reason: elegant leadership, rather than mob rule . . ."

The Crocodile and I snorted in unison. We knew that Ileyoba's loveliness came from places like the Baloguns' slave-run marble mine. Its cleanliness came from underpaid and calloused hands, and its culture from ogas and madams who had rebranded their greed as cleverness.

But whenever the crowd's unrest began to grow, the cultists would step in, leading a round of hymns to the Idajo and the Anointed Ones, which cowed onlookers into a reverent silence.

"Those fanatics do not speak for the Idajo," the Crocodile growled. "But if you shout a beloved name and a poison message together long enough, even intelligent people will mix them together."

"It does not matter what they say," I said, touching my throat and shooting him a daring look: *In a moment, no one will hear them at all.*

His gaze sparkled. "As you command," he said, and waved his fingers.

I kept my head down and chanted as softly as I could: "*Our hands built it. We are the beauty.*"

When a gaggle of heads turned to find the source, I darted as fast as I could with my cane to another section of the crowd, and spoke again in my soft-loud voice.

"*We are the beauty. A city belongs to its people.*"

Again I hurried away, sowing my song like seed in a coop until, like an answering echo, the chant rose across the square: disjointed at first, then unified as the rhythm took hold.

Our hands built it! We are the beauty! A city belongs to its people!

And it grew so strong that my heart swelled against my lungs, and I sang full volume—sang so the words thrummed through my teeth and vibrated the tip of my nose and filled every inch of my belly—but not a single person turned to look at me, for that music now filled the square whether I sang or not.

Our hands. Our hands. A city belongs to its people!

The chant changed in pitch as the crowd surged toward the elevated platforms in the square, where the nobles quailed, demanding assistance from their guards. Another wing of the crowd charged the towering statue of the old emperor Enoba Kunleo, climbing its obsidian limbs as they yelled obscenities at the cultists below.

In the rising tide of people, someone bumped my cane, and I nearly toppled—but strong arms connected around my shoulders, tugging me firmly upright.

"Almost lost you," the Crocodile panted. "Time to go."

But before the Crocodile whisked me away, I looked back at Unity Square.

The people had covered the statue. Lithe dark bodies, reckless with song, had buried Enoba the Perfect until you could not see his face, nor the upright disc of his crown, nor the proud lion mask on his chest.

Our hands built it. We are the beauty. A city belongs to its people.

"Your way was better," the Crocodile said quietly as we flew back to his bone house shrine.

"Oga?"

"Singing from below instead of above. You were right." Something in his tone sounded conflicted, as though he was untangling a mire of thoughts he did not like.

"Ye Eun was excited about getting those bees for the orchard. I doubt we will be seeing her anytime soon," I mused as we stepped back through the Ilemalu shrine portal, hand in hand.

"She could be gone for days," the Crocodile agreed. "With her prized starblossoms at stake, I wouldn't be surprised if she smokes out the whole savannah."

I chuckled softly, and then our voices trickled to silence. As the courtyard plunged into the hazy lavender of twilight, we seemed to realize at the same time that we were alone in the villa. Not even Clemeh skittered across the courtyard walls, having apparently decided he deserved a break from babysitting the two of us.

I let go of his hand immediately. The air around us seemed suddenly charged, and the villa estate very small, despite it being the same sprawling acre it was when Ye Eun and Clemeh had been present. I cleared my throat and rubbed the back of my neck. In contrast, the tension between us did not seem to ruffle him at all, though when I had removed my hand from his, a wounded shadow passed over his angular features.

My heart twinged, unsettled as it always was when the Crocodile let his charming mask slip, revealing the depths of boyish grief and insecurities underneath.

"I suppose we had better prepare supper," I said, avoiding his searching gaze. "In case Ye Eun comes back after all. I left some beans to soak, and if I boil them now, they'll be soft in time for—"

"Is it because I am getting worse?" he asked suddenly.

"Oga?"

"The reason you do not act on how you feel." He reached to take my wrist, then held it up like a trembling bird between us, his long fingers pressed against my traitorous, galloping pulse. Blood rose to my cheeks.

He had not needed to touch me, of course, to know how I felt. How my poor Sade mind seemed incapable of getting *used* to his voice and person. How every time I looked at him, it was like seeing those chiseled features and curtain of waist-length locs for the first time. I realized with chagrin that he knew my desire—could *sense* it through our bond—at all times. Even when we lay on opposite ends of Bhekina House, with him in his bed and I in mine—soaked in sweat as I dreamed of a certain rippling torso and teasing dark eyes.

"You are not afraid of me," the Crocodile continued, in a quiet, even tone. "You are quite possibly the bravest person I have ever met. So is it because my curse is getting worse? You are repulsed by what I am . . . becoming?"

He pulled off his cowl and let his cloak hang open, displaying the state of his scarred body. I inhaled sharply. Half his torso and the sides of his neck now glistened with green ridged scales. And it was not only his body that had worsened in the last few days. Sometimes, when he grew animated, his pupils narrowed to slits, eyes flashing briefly yellow. Even his teeth had changed slowly each day, sharpening subtly to spear-shaped points.

"No," I said. "It is not that."

And I meant it. I had not resisted the Crocodile because of his changing appearance but because of my unchanging smallness. Because gutter girls did not kiss former boy-kings. Because no matter how many Giant Lessons he taught me, I could not believe that the same gods who had punished my childhood defiance would allow me to woo an Anointed One.

But I must not have sounded convincing, because his expression grew determined. "It's time I told you my plan," he said. "For when I take a turn for the worse and can no longer sort the man from the beast. Come."

He strode to a pile of wine barrels at one end of the courtyard. With unnatural strength that made me shiver, he picked up the massive barrels one by one and tossed them aside. On the ground shone a chalk line, clearly newer than the others. Instead of a tooth, a larger triangular bone stood out from this line's center.

"The tip of my tailbone," the Crocodile said. "A tooth would not have been strong enough for lodestone travel of this distance. Don't, ah, ask me how I got it out."

Then he reached for my hand, which I gave him, and we stepped over the line together.

Immediately, a wall of humid night air enveloped us, and my ears roared with a concert of cicadas, frogs, and howler monkeys. The ground beneath my sandals was soft and spongy: a forest floor, thickly carpeted in moss and ferns. When my eyes adjusted, a jungle draped in vines rose around us, and a waxy canopy blotted out the distant sky. Through the trees, I could just make out a marshy lake, from which the smell of fetid water mixed with the scent of lilies. I had smelled that perfume before.

"Ixalix," I gasped, seizing the Crocodile's arm.

This must have been her swamp, in the far southern realm of Quetzala. The lodestone portal had brought us to the other side of the Arit megacontinent, thousands of miles away from Oluwan City.

"Oga . . ." My palms grew clammy. "Why would you bring us here?"

"So you know what to do," he replied. "When the time is right. Sade . . . no matter what that tapestry said, we both know my curse cannot be broken. But I will shield you from the worst of it. When I feel the last of my humanity slipping away, I will come here . . . and you need only remove that bone from the chalk line to close the portal behind me."

"But then . . . you'll be trapped here with Ixalix."

"Yes. And Bhekina House will be yours to live in, for as long as you want it. Before I go, I'll show you how to lock the tooth portals so no one can disturb you without your permission. You can grow vegetables in the orchard. Start that produce stall. You'll be safe from me, Sade—and from anyone else who would wish you harm. So you see . . ." He smiled down at me and gave a small, grim wink. "You need not worry that by kissing me, you will be saddled with a beast forever."

"Stop it," I rasped. "Stop talking like that right now." Then I seized him by the elbow and dragged him back through the portal. Once we were safely back in the courtyard, I rounded on him, surprised to find my cheeks wet with tears. "You are a hypocrite, oga," I shouted. "You lecture all day about how I shape my destiny, while you stand there and refuse to shape yours. Well, I can lecture you too! As long as I live at Bhekina House, you are not allowed to give up. Do you hear me?"

"Sade—"

"No. No more of your sad, pretty speeches. Promise me, oga. Promise right now you will not give up."

But before he could respond, across the courtyard, one of the tooth portals glowed red.

"Fat Molar Door," the Crocodile murmured, frowning in confusion. "The Textile District. But why would Ye Eun come in from Ileyaso?"

Then a body lurched, kicking and screaming, over the line, and my blood ran cold. Because of course, it was not Ye Eun who had come through the portal.

It was a sacrificed girl.

PART V

CHAPTER 28

THE GIRL—OR WOMAN—WAS ONLY A FEW YEARS OLDER THAN me, with a mucus-streaked round face and wide, indignant eyes. When she fell into the courtyard, her lips were moving in a rant we had not heard the beginning of, spitting and hissing as she struggled at her bindings.

". . . and I may be the sacrifice," she roared, "but you will always be the failure! You will always be the man who killed his own child and failed to make its mother love you! Always! Always—"

She trailed off when she took in her surroundings, clearly confused by the courtyard. But when her eyes fell on the Crocodile in all of his scaly, sharp-toothed glory, she froze.

"No," she shrieked. "Away from me, Nameless God. You shall not have my child." Then she began shrieking Clay prayers of protection, struggling to shield her belly with her bound hands. "Life from death, birth to soil, if you touch me, may the Queen Mother of Earth swallow you up; may her fingers rise in roots and grind you to the ground . . ." Every few lines, she broke off to cry out, grimacing as she doubled over. My mouth grew dry.

This woman was in labor. *Now.*

I expected the Crocodile, who had dealt with sacrifices before, to leap into motion, soothing the woman's cries with grandiose speeches and suave assurances of her safety. Instead, he tensed beside me, eyes widening with fear. The Crocodile looked . . . helpless.

"Normally, I would approach to cut her bindings," he croaked. "But considering how monstrous I look now, and her—condition"—he eyed the girl's swollen belly as though he might faint—"suppose I disturb her so much, I make it worse? I—Sade . . ."

In that moment, a focused calm washed over me—a calm that came when the only hands available were my own, and time was a matter of life and death.

I shoved past the Crocodile, marched over to the moaning, thrashing girl, and knelt by her side, placing my cane on the dirt beside us.

"Hush now," I said, in the same crooning murmur I had used on my mother in the Bush, when the fever had made her delirious. "Peace, my sister. It is all right. There are no angry gods here. No one is going to hurt you."

Her protests turned to confused hiccups, brow furrowing as she took in my fine-fine clothing and spirit-touched skin, then glanced furtively past me toward the Crocodile.

"He is harmless," I told her with a dry smile. "I promise. Now, if you hold still, we are going to cut those ropes. Oga," I called over my shoulder, "find us a knife."

The woman watched in horrified wonder as he unsheathed a knife from his belt and flew it gently across the courtyard, all without coming a step closer. I caught the knife midair and sawed carefully at the woman's bonds.

"Who are you people?" she demanded, scrambling to put distance between us once I had freed her. "What is this place?"

I hesitated. There was no possible way to describe Bhekina House, or my relationship to the Crocodile, without sounding like I had lost my senses.

"A safe place," I said at last. "I am called Small Sade. And that, over there, is Oga Crocodile. This house—it took us in when we had nowhere else to go. And it will take you too, for as long as you need it. Can you stand? My foot's bad, but if you get on my other side, I can help you."

I retrieved my cane and offered her my shoulder. After a moment, she accepted, and together we struggled to our feet. Then with her leaning on me, and me leaning on the cane, we hobbled to my bedroom in the villa, the Crocodile using his enchantment to clear all obstacles from our path.

She swore under her breath when she saw the ceiling made of sky, which had grown dusky with moonrise, deepening to depthless violet.

"Does it bother you?" I asked. "We can find you another room. This one is closest to the courtyard well, though, and we should probably keep you near a water source."

"This is your room?" she said, and I nodded. Her pained, intelligent eyes scanned my face fervently, looking for what, I did not know. But whatever she found there seemed to make up her mind.

"If this is your room, Small Sade," she said, "then I will stay. Thank you. And—I'm called Kwabena."

A Nyamban name. She, or her family, hailed from the realm neighboring Oluwan. I wondered how long ago she had arrived in Oluwan City, fresh-faced and full of hope for a new life.

I led her to my bedroll and made her sit, propping her up with every cushion I could find, fighting the panic clawing its way through my mask of calm. I had seen birth before. Most gutter girls have—the doorless tenements of slums rang often with screams of labor, haunting us even when we played in the alleyways as children. I knew she would need to stand and sit, to pace and squat and writhe on her side, a dance that would last anywhere from minutes to countless hours. I knew there would be tears and dung and urine, and that blood was normal, but too much meant death. But beyond that . . . I felt scarcely more useful than the Crocodile, cowering outside.

"You are safe here," I repeated, holding her hands, which gripped mine so hard, my fingertips turned numb. "But—I am not a midwife, my sister. Is . . . is there anyone I can go and find for you? A healer, or even just a relative?"

She shook her head fiercely. "No one can know that I'm alive. No one near the shrine, anyway. I can't let him find me. Though . . . I do have a sister in the Academy District. That's where I was going, when Uwagbo— that man who calls himself my husband—caught me trying to leave."

"I'll get her. Or send the oga."

Fear set her features alight, and her grip on me tightened. "Do not leave me alone," she rasped. "Please. Anything but that. And she would not trust . . ." She gestured uneasily toward the courtyard, indicating the Crocodile.

I swallowed hard, then nodded with what I hoped was a brave smile. "Then the two of us will welcome your child together."

She told me her story in between contractions, letting it distract her from the pain.

"I came from Nyamba with my sister, Efia," Kwabena said. "We had outgrown our weaving business back home and hoped to expand in the big city. Soon after we arrived, Uwagbo found me.

"It is the story of many girls, I think. A man is always kind and charming for those first few months, when you are still able to leave him. He showered us with gifts. Showed us the ropes of the city. I enjoyed the attention." She paused to wheeze through a contraction. "But he could tell that Efia did not trust him. So he put distance between us, encouraging her to move to the other end of the city and study trade at the Academy in Ileyimo. I stayed behind in Ileyaso, managing our fabric shop. But without Efia, I grew busier than ever, which made Uwagbo sulky. He began to say that I did not appreciate him. He pointed to all the gifts he had bought and accused me of using him. So I cut back on my work. Soon, he asked me to give up on the business altogether. 'Do not be proud,' he always said. 'Let a good man take care of you. Don't you trust me, Bena?' When I threatened to leave, he said no more on the subject . . . until five months later, when I realized I was as many months pregnant.

"I had been careful. We chewed the herbs to prevent children every time we lay together . . . or at least, I had. It turned out that after our last argument, he began spitting out the herbs in secret.

"By now, Uwagbo had driven such a wedge between Efia and me that we had not spoken in months. She already hated Uwagbo for causing me to neglect our shop, and she would be angrier still when she found out what he had done. So I kept everything to myself. I moved into Uwagbo's flat and made preparations for our child. That, of course, is when the beating started."

She paused for another contraction, and I hurried to bring my wash basin, mopping her brow with rosemary water. "Rest," I begged. "You need not finish the story if it distresses you."

"No—I must," she gasped, with a smile that was half grimace. "It helps to be angry." And so she went on.

"As my 'husband's' tiny flat grew crowded with baby blankets and nappies, he acted more and more frantic. Uwagbo looked at me and my belly and began to see the end of his youth. A weight around his neck. For of course, he had never truly wanted the baby. He had wanted to be the center of my world. At that, at least, he had failed miserably, for I hated him more and more each day.

"He did not want me anymore. But his pride would not allow me to flee, and he punished me every time I tried. At last I left in broad daylight, announcing to our entire neighborhood how he had treated our unborn child. Humiliated, he yelled over me, declaring me a witch, a seductress who had got herself pregnant by some stranger and had tried to pass off the child as his own.

"I do not know why the neighborhood believed him over me. Perhaps because I had no friends, and he, many. Perhaps because to them, I would always be the foreigner, the migrant whore, here to take their jobs and flats and men. Whatever the reason . . . I found myself bound, carried in a mob to the shrine of the Crocodile God."

As Kwabena spoke, I felt somehow that she told a hundred stories at once. As though the fate of every girl discarded to a shrine could be told to the same tired song, with only the chords rearranged.

A knock sounded on the door, and Kwabena jumped.

"Don't worry," I told her. "He will not come in."

And when I went to investigate, the Crocodile was not there at all. Instead, he had left in the corridor an earnestly folded pile of clean linens, several steaming buckets of hot water, and a humorously large selection of medical salves and potions—mostly useless for childbirth, but he clearly had not dared to leave a single bottle out.

I laughed softly. "Thank you, oga," I told the air of the corridor, in case he was listening. "And if you would like to be even more useful, you can run to the market and get some raspberry leaf tea. And . . ." I swallowed hard, unable to wrap my mind around the idea of a baby arriving, perhaps in a few short hours. "We'll need nappies too."

Then I brought in the supplies, closed the door, and surveyed the room. The enchanted ceiling had darkened to midnight purple, quilted with gossamer clouds and twinkling stars. As Kwabena rocked and moaned beneath it, I realized that I had lived this scene before—not as the midwife, but as the unborn babe.

A tingling determination washed over my limbs.

"Kwabena," I asked, "I am going to clean up in here a little. Do you mind if I sing?"

"Please," she said, and I did.

CHAPTER 29

YOU WILL REMEMBER THAT I NEVER CLEAN SPIRIT SILT FROM myself or from my own chambers. But my room had never welcomed a brand-new person before. And while I may have resigned myself to sleeping beneath that silvery mantle of the world's expectations . . . I would be damned if that new soul was born smothered by it.

It was another song with no words, like the one I had performed for Mamadele. Only this time, my voice lifted not in a mournful wail but a battle cry.

I scoured despair-mold from the tiles around Kwabena, crooning with each breath the promise of a new day. I struck down grief-gnats from the air using a towel as a whip, singing through their swarms with a trilling staccato. I tore down vines of apathy-ivy—those whispering tendrils that bid souls to *know your place, stop trying, accept your lot*—with my bare hands, snapping the stems in two so they could not grow back.

When I found a single joy-moth, fluttering shyly in a bed of dream-moss . . . I cupped it carefully with both hands and held it over Kwabena's sweat-soaked brow. I sang until that moth swelled in size, doubling, tripling its wingspan until it made a song of its own, a high, pure whistletone that filled the room as wind passed beneath its vast, golden wings.

Hours later, when Kwabena gave birth to a perfect tiny girl, her healthy cries rose to match the joy-moth's song in pitch, as though celebrating her own fearless, blood-soaked journey to being alive.

I held the child as Kwabena slept, rinsing the mucus of birth from her small head of soft black curls. The baby stopped fussing when I toweled her dry, instead taking me in with wide, curious eyes. Her fist groped the front of my chest, closing around my prayer pebble, which I had taken to wearing on a string around my neck.

"Do not touch that, small one," I cooed at her, hurrying to move the sharp-edged pebble from her reach. "You will hurt yourself."

And just like that, a door burst open in my brain, as though someone had taken a hammer to an iron lock, long rusted over by grief, guilt, and fear.

I had selected my first prayer pebble—had let it cut the insides of my mouth to ribbons—when I was scarcely six years older than this infant.

Yet when I looked down at that round, birth-bruised face and imagined a rock slicing her rosy brown skin, for any reason, at *any* age . . . my mind recoiled in horror.

Because she would never deserve it. Not ever.

No matter how low-born her mother was, or how base her father. No matter how boldly she ran from an Anointed One and refused to crown him. No matter how many times she made mistakes, or said *no*, or demanded *why* . . . she would always deserve to be housed, and clothed, and fed, and taught to imagine a better world for herself and everyone in it.

Always.

I broke the string around my neck and hurled the prayer pebble into the shadows.

Later, when Kwabena roused from slumber, I put the baby to her breast and said, "Congratulations, Kwabena."

She shook her head. "But I am a mother now. You must call me my new name," she said, smiling at me, then down at her daughter. "You must call me Mamasade."

I encouraged Kwabena to rest for as long as she needed. But the new Mamasade—still unnerved by the Crocodile and eager to reach her sister, Efia—would not stay for longer than a day more. So I loaded her and the newest, smallest Sade with food from the kitchen and money from the shrine steps, hired a rickshaw, and delivered mother and baby to a tenement in the Academy District. A tearful Efia welcomed them both. They made me promise to return and visit my namesake, and in exchange, I swore them to secrecy about the Crocodile and his shrine. By the time I left, the sisters were already plotting a new business as weavers of fine scholar's robes.

"Well done," said the Crocodile, applauding lightly when I returned through the Pointy Molar Door of Bhekina House. He conjured a clay goblet in the air, flew a jug of mango wine into the courtyard, and poured me a drink. "To your first experience as a god of the Bhekina House shrine."

I laughed but accepted the goblet when it floated into my hand. "And when exactly did I become a god?"

"You meet all the criteria, where legend is concerned," he pointed out, and counted items on his scaly fingers. "You accepted a sacrifice made to the shrine where you live—"

"I do not live here," I protested. "At least, I have not decided yet."

"You performed a miracle on request . . ."

"Kwabena did all of the real work."

"And you passed on your name. What is that, if not immortality?"

This made me blush. "Kwabena was kind to name that baby after me," I admitted. "But it is not the same as living forever. I will die, oga, just as the newest Small Sade will too someday."

"But not," countered the Crocodile, "before she tells *her* children the story of her birth. How her mother stumbled into a realm of the gods and labored in a chamber of stars. How a kindly goddess with worlds on her skin watched over the birth, cleansing the room of ill spirits, so the baby was born to the sound of divine music. And so the story will be told to her children, and her children's children, until Sade the Singer, spirit of the Ileyaso Shrine, is never forgotten . . . for that is the true divinity of gods." When he finished, he grew quieter, looking suddenly earnest. "If you had not been here when that woman arrived . . . I truly do not know what I would have done."

"Take heart, oga. After you finished panicking, you were very helpful fetching supplies." I lifted my goblet in a toast. "If you ever get tired of being a god, you have a bright future as a midwife's errand boy."

A corner of his mouth lifted, and I smiled up at him. We looked both exhausted and on edge: My clothes were rumpled from the rickshaw journey, and circles pooled beneath his dark eyes. We were once again alone in Bhekina House.

That heated tension between us returned in full force, ringing in my ears like the ping of that prayer pebble skipping across tiles, disappearing into the shadows, and taking every inhibition I had with it.

He had felt it, of course. Just as he had felt every surge of my desire for him, since the moment we first met. I expected him to smirk and lean closer as he had several times before, running a hand through his locs, and biting the corner of his lip in invitation.

Instead, he remained where he was, regarding me with a calm seriousness that made my pulse hammer. He said not a word. But his eyes held the promise he had made in the orchard days earlier.

Ask me, and I will.

I almost asked *Oga?* But caught the word before it left my throat, and I instead murmured, "Zuri."

He took in a sharp breath, pupils dilating with hunger. "Yes?"

I set the goblet down on the well and drew close, boldly resting my hands on his broad, scarred chest. "Zuri," I repeated, "I would like you to kiss me."

His heart—that wild, undying thing—beat beneath my palms as his arms closed around me. He lowered his face to mine . . . and then hesitated, features growing suddenly conflicted.

"Sade," he rasped. "I want this. I do. But if we are to be this way, truly . . . there is something I have to tell you."

He stepped back, looking more self-conscious now than I had ever seen him. The places where my skin had touched him felt cold, and I longed to close that distance again. I waited, unease growing in my veins as the silence stretched on.

At last he said, "Do you remember what I told you about our body-bond? That it was . . . unequally weighted?"

"Of course," I said, shrugging. "You are burdened with my needs, but I am not affected by yours."

"That is not what I meant." His tone was labored. "Unequal means I can take things from you. Possess them, without you knowing it."

The Crocodile was changing before my eyes, donning an illusion, as he had when posing as a plumber in the Balogun Inn spa, and a cultist in the High Market Square. Unlike those disguises, however, this one caused his back to hunch, his hair to thin and gray, and his skin to bleach and sprout wrinkles. It took me a moment to place where I had seen that man before.

"The coughing baron at the Sin Salon," I gasped. "It was you."

My mind reeled. Like Dele, the baron had constantly interrupted the salon, trying to stop the proceedings. But when that hadn't worked . . .

Cold realization washed over me as the Crocodile returned to his true form.

"You stole my voice," I rasped. "You are the reason I lost my job at the inn."

He took a step toward me, but I backed away, hands flying to my throat.

"I felt you," he said. "Sade, whenever you swallowed the guilt of those monsters, I felt you, here." He clutched his chest, expression tortured. "Clawing at your own insides. I could not bear to watch you sing for those monsters. To debase yourself and let them *use* you like that—"

"Because you wanted to use me instead."

"No! I wanted to free you—"

"By taking away my choice, *oga*?"

My use of his title hit him like a slap, and he recoiled. But I continued on, breathing hard, letting all the anger I had kept bottled and pickled away burn through my chest. With every Giant Lesson, I had lost by ability to let someone else choose my place. To let anyone, oga or madam, shape my world for me.

"You have never cared about what I wanted," I roared. "Never valued my freedom, except when it aligned with your grand words and plans. Do you know who acts like that, oga? A *king*."

"I wanted what was best for your future." Despite the pain in his voice, stubbornness bled through his tone. His features sprouted rapidly with scales. "Yours, and the future of everyone like you. You could make a difference, Sade, if only you would—"

"Everyone like me?" I shrilled. Colors swirled in my head, each shade a different memory of the Crocodile, a different snippet of his life, all coming together to form a picture I had not seen before. "You look *down* on people 'like me'! You helped lead a revolution for commoners, and then refused to live among them! You were given a second chance at living. You could have studied a trade. Learned to fry an egg, even. Instead, you holed yourself up in a mansion, hoarding relics of your glory days, and puppeting me into living them for you. Because for all your praise of commoners, oga . . . you would rather be dead and a hero than alive and *nobody*."

He looked stricken. But before he could reply, footfalls echoed on the flagstone, alongside a wet fluttering of wings. Ye Eun and Hwanghu had returned from their quest to bring bees from the savannah. Judging from the welts dappling Ye Eun's arms and the bird's ruffled feathers, it had not been successful.

"Croc?" Ye Eun asked, her gaze sliding uneasily between the two of us. "Small Sade? Is everything all right?"

The Crocodile began to explain, but I spoke over him. Invisible flames licked around my ears, a searing anger that drove me to *do* something. Fix something. To change a fate for once, instead of grimly trudging through whichever swamp fate plopped me in.

"Ye Eun," I demanded, "have you really given up on getting your shop back?"

She frowned uncertainly. "Well, no. I just thought I'd lay low for a while. But it has been a few weeks, and I have missed it . . ."

"We need to get your shop back," I said, brandishing my cane like a fighter's club and gesturing toward the Yellow Molar Door. "The longer you wait, the more likely some entitled oga will try and take it over. Do not let them claim what is yours, or tell you what to do with it . . ."

"Are you sure you're talking about my shop?" she asked at the same time the Crocodile said, "Sade, that could be dangerous. Do not put yourself in danger just to spite me—"

"Not everything is about you!" I snarled, at which his face crumpled with guilt.

As I pushed past him to the Yellow Molar Door, he breathed a final, "Please."

And though I felt his gaze, searing and broken, I did not meet it. Instead I told Ye Eun, "Do you want your shop back or not?" and the lattice of birthmarks across her face stretched into an intrigued smile.

"I *like* this Small Sade," she said. "All right. Let's go."

We stepped over the chalk line . . . but just before the door could whisk us away, I shot a glance back at the Crocodile. Chills ran up my spine when I saw that his eyes had turned lurid yellow, doubling in size and tilting toward his temples. Talons emerged from his fingertips before the tooth door enchantment plunged my vision to black.

CHAPTER 30

ONCE OUTSIDE THE SHRINE, YE EUN AND I HIRED A rickshaw while Hwanghu kept an eye on us from the sky. My ears rang with the Crocodile's warning, but I assured Ye Eun out loud that Mamadele's goons had likely collected their money and lost interest.

"Besides," I said with unearned certainty, "they will not risk attacking in broad daylight."

We passed by the Ilemalu Lower Market I had visited with the Crocodile. Amid the stalls and milling vendors, girls and boys not much older than me held tools above their heads: brooms and shovels, hair combs and cooking spoons. They shouted to be heard above the crowd, and though they all trilled different things—"*Let me be your maid, oga . . . House boy, errand boy, see how fast I run, madam . . . Never-greedy kitchen girl, here to scrub your pots! Feed me a little, and I'll feed you a lot . . .*"—my heart twinged with a familiar ache. Because in the end, it was all the same song, and one I knew well.

Please oga, let me have shelter, if only for a night. Please madam, my belly is empty, and I will starve if you do not fill it.

Ye Eun followed my gaze to the singers and sighed. "I don't understand it," she mused. "Why so many people still age out of those orphan high-rises with nowhere to go. The Raybearers worked on the Lonesome Child Edict for nearly a decade. It was supposed to help children, not abandon them."

"It did help a lot of us," I said quietly. "Mostly younger children, who were adopted or fostered with families willing to teach them a trade. But for us older orphans . . . the edict came too late. And apprenticeships cost money. So when we leave the high-rises, we are not suited for anything but grind work."

"Don't worry," said Ye Eun. "If the Crocodile has his way, you will never have to do such work again."

Those words bothered me even more. Because there was nothing wrong with being a maid. Buildings had to be cleaned, after all, and food cooked, clothes washed, goods fetched. If maids and servants disappeared, the Realmhood would collapse overnight. I squirmed in my seat as the flagstone road bumped beneath us. None of it made sense.

Since you are listening, let me ask you: If labor like mine is so crucial to the Realmhood, then why are workers like me treated so badly? And why do we put up with it?

Because if we didn't, of course, we would end up on the street. Because there would always be another orphan, another desperate, hungry soul to take our place.

So the Lord Liaos and Mamadeles of the world treat workers however they like. And people become Amenities.

Even as I seethed with rage at the Crocodile, a line from one of his speeches rang in my ears: *In a society, most things happen on purpose.*

As my mind worked, a roaring filled my ears, like water churning the wheel of a sweatmill. If the wealthy could not survive without menial laborers, I realized, then they would create a world where such workers were always available. Always desperate. Plentiful and ripe for the picking, like fruit at a produce stall.

As that gaggle of hollering boys and girls grew distant behind us, I craned my neck to watch them for as long as I could.

What would this world be like, I asked them silently, *if we shaped it instead?*

"My shop's just around this block," Ye Eun said minutes later, voice trembling with anticipation as the rickshaw driver began to slow. We had entered a bustling neighborhood fragrant with flowers and herb cuttings. Bundles of greenery teetered on the backs of passersby, and the carts of mule-drawn wagons burst with blossoms.

"It will be the third building from the right," Ye Eun whispered.

We tensed in our seats, expecting to see a smashed-in storefront covered in rubble, and perhaps a goon or two lingering in the shadows.

We rounded the corner . . . and Ye Eun gasped.

While remains of the break-in still littered the street, the third shop from the right was not only intact but colorfully—if awkwardly—repaired. New boards, slightly off center, had been hammered onto the front, and the door rehung crookedly on its hinges. The ripped awning had been patched with blossom-embroidered fabric. An elaborate mural of flowers curled over the shopfront window. And there, balancing on a ladder with her tongue stuck out in concentration, stood Dele Balogun. She wielded a paintbrush and a bucket of varnish, her cloud of black hair bursting from beneath a kerchief.

When she saw us, she shrieked in surprise, catching her foot on a rung. Her arms windmilled.

In a movement so swift it was a blur, Ye Eun leapt from the rickshaw and plucked Dele from the air just as Dele tumbled from the ladder.

"Ye Eun," Dele breathed, frozen for a moment in Ye Eun's arms before wobbling to her feet. "And Small Sade. You're both all right." Then her doe-black eyes pooled with tears. "Ye Eun, I'm sorry. Am's Story, darling, I'm so sorry. This is all my fault. I was self-absorbed, and an idiot, and I've moved out from the inn and cut off Mother and I understand if you never want to see me again but I need to know that you're all right . . ." Both women were crying now, though Ye Eun refused to look at Dele, staring stiffly over her head as Dele wrung her hands. "I looked for you everywhere, but after that night it was like you just . . . disappeared. So I guarded your shop. I didn't know where else to wait. I've been coming here every day, and I'm sorry I couldn't fix it up better, but I'm not done. I know it's not the same, but once I get a better handle on the shutters and sweep up a bit more inside, maybe you can reopen and . . ."

For the first time, Ye Eun noticed Dele's plump tapered arms, which were covered in splinters. Stains marred Dele's elegant linen blouse and trousers, and tools dangled from her belt, in addition to the usual embroidery hoops.

"Dele," Ye Eun asked, her voice gone strange. "Have you been fixing the shop . . . all by yourself? With your bare hands?"

Dele nodded, wiping her nose. "I . . . I didn't think you would want anyone else touching it. Including me, at this point, but . . . I couldn't just leave it like that. Not your shop that you worked so hard for, and besides, sanding wood and sharpening nails and hanging doors isn't so difficult once you've gotten the hang of—"

Ye Eun took Dele into her arms and kissed her.

I looked away, pretending to be absorbed in the floral mural over the shop. When they parted, it was only a hair, and Dele exhaled a shaky breath. "I need you to know that you're safe from my mother," she said. "She's left town. For good."

Ye Eun blinked in astonishment. "What do you mean, 'for good'?"

Dele's lips pressed into a line. "It means, she finally got what she wanted: to be a lady again. Once the Sin Salon venture went belly up, she visited Lord Liao and forced him to marry her. Apparently, Lord Liao preyed on the daughters of some powerful people at the Realmhood Academy, where he gives his precious lectures. Mother listened in when he confessed his sins to Small Sade, then threatened to expose him to the families, risking the Academy's grant money. So now they're married and removed to some manor in the country to strangle each other in peace. I can't think of a couple that deserves each other more."

"But what about the inn?" I cut in. If Mamadele had left, did that mean the Amenities would lose their jobs?

"Oh," Dele said, looking dazed. "Legally . . . it's mine now. Mother lost her rights to Father's property the moment she became Lady Simi Liao instead of Madam Balogun. But I'll probably sell. I'm tired of being a Balogun, and that building is the last pillar of my family's legacy—all those quarry workers they exploited. Once it's gone, the past will finally be over." She looked dreamily at Ye Eun. "I'll be free."

I told myself to stay quiet. To nod, smile, and let Dele shut the door on her fine-fine lady life and skip blithely with Ye Eun into her happy-ever-after. But that pulsing restlessness with which I had left Bhekina House had not quieted. So I blurted, "You'll still have the money from the sale of the inn. The money your family made off of those workers."

Dele flinched, looking suddenly uncomfortable. "Well . . . yes. I suppose you're right."

"I think," I said in a rush, as though the words were so dangerously hot that I had to spew them out, "that if you really wanted to be free, you would give the inn to the Amenities instead of selling it. They ran it while your mother collected the profits. Just like the miners who worked that quarry, when it should have been theirs all along."

Then, I bobbed once at a stunned Dele and retreated to the road to hail another rickshaw. Ye Eun followed after me, laughing.

"Small Sade, just where do you think you're going?"

I shrugged, fidgeting. I had not planned my next move beyond saving Ye Eun's shop. But my anger at the Crocodile had not cooled. "I . . . I do not know. But your shop is all right, and it seems like you and Dele have a lot to talk about, so . . ."

"So what? I've never seen you so angry with Croc. That angry, period, come to think of it. You're in no shape to go back to Bhekina House."

"I was not planning on it," I said sharply, scowling at the bustling road, then squaring my shoulders. A familiar numbness washed over me. "And it does not matter. Do not worry about me, Ye Eun; I will find a new job, like I did before. There is always a floor to be scrubbed. Dishes to rinse clean."

But even as I said the words, I knew it would not be the same as before. It was not that such labor scared me—being a maid had always filled me with purpose. Cleaning was so necessary, whether you lived as a prince or a pauper, the work seemed to me almost sacred. It was only—I could no longer accept how I would be treated. *I* knew my job was sacred, but the people who hired me would not. I was still suited to labor, but no longer, it seemed, to servanthood.

Ye Eun's brow creased at me thoughtfully. "You do not have to tell me what happened between you and Croc now, if you don't want to. But I live in a room above the shop. You're welcome to share with me and Dele, until you, ah, sort things out."

I drew in a breath, taking in the unfamiliar maze of streets, then looking back at the cheerfully painted shop front. If I had a place to sleep, my job search would feel less desperate. Still, I looked guiltily at Dele, who waited with a wistful expression, clearly longing for a moment alone with Ye Eun.

"Thank you," I said at last. "But—if you will let me—I will sleep in the shop." I wiggled my weak foot. "That way I won't need to climb your stairs."

Or get in the way of you kissing your lady-maiden.

Ye Eun was nervous to leave me alone in the shop that night, in case anyone else tried to break in, but I insisted, making myself a comfortable nest of earth-scented sacks beneath a table of flowerpots. Ye Eun triple-checked the locks on the doors and windows before joining Dele upstairs, leaving an oil lamp to murmur near my head. The night deepened, and the flame cast flickering shadows across the rush-strewn dirt floor. As my eyelids drooped, one of the shadows crept farther across the floor than the others. I recognized the shape and its telltale wriggle but shut my eyes stubbornly. A thumping sound, too low and faint to be a human knocking, sounded from the door. When at last, a tiny rasping "*Small Sade*" rang in the dark, I huffed and scooped up the lamp, illuminating the front of the shop.

Clemeh had broken in through a crack beneath the door but had gotten stuck. Whatever burden he had dragged across town via twine was too large for the crack and so repeatedly bumped the door outside while Clemeh strained against the twine.

"Hush," I scolded. "You will wake the ladies upstairs."

But when I reached down to untie him, Clemeh pulled the burden through with a last mighty heave. A tiny bruised gourd, narrow as a vial and no longer than my hand, rolled across the floor and stopped at my sandal.

I considered stamping it to pieces. But its minuscule size made me curious, a feeling that won out even over my pettiness. After all, the Crocodile adored his own voice over all other sounds. What screed of his could be short enough to fit in that gourd?

I laced my fingers behind my neck, scowled down at the message, and hissed a breath through my teeth. Then before I could change my mind, I scooped up the gourd and yanked out the stopper.

I had been certain that no apology, no speech from his velvet tongue, could convince me to endure the Crocodile's face again. But when I opened that gourd, two words filled the room in a desperate rasp— possibly the only two words in the universe that out of sheer, mad spite could drive me back to the Crocodile's shrine.

"Don't. Come."

I stared at the gourd in my hand, temples pulsing with—what, I was not sure. Shock? Confusion? Rage at his audacity? The feeling was too tangled for a name, but as though in a trance, I retrieved my cane and lifted the bar that locked the front door.

"Don't tell me what to do," I growled at the gourd. Then I hurled it away and marched back toward the shrine.

CHAPTER 31

THE MOMENT MY FEET HIT THE PAVED ROAD, A SWARM OF human-eyed dragonflies dove at my face.

"*Home,*" they whined. "*Go back, Sade. Go home, Sade. Home. Back. Home—*"

I gagged, batting them away as I staggered on and hailed a rickshaw, yelling at the driver to run. We covered a few blocks more before the street filled with jewel-toned frogs, leaping and squeezing out from the gutters, blocking our path in a glistening, croaking sea.

"Well," I sighed. "This is new." Apparently, Ixalix was no longer content with dragonflies.

I paid the trembling driver with the only coins I had—a few zathulus, left in my pocket from my market trip with the Crocodile—and left the rickshaw, setting down over the street by foot.

"You think I am put off by a little slime?" I yelled at the frogs, laughing so my voice would not quail. "I, Sade of the Bush? Sade of the Sweatmill and Sin Salon? Please. I have seen more disgusting things than you on an ordinary morning!"

As I stormed forward, ruthlessly plowing over frogs with my cane arm and shielding my face from dragonflies with the other, foreboding thrummed in my ears.

Why was Ixalix so desperate for me not to reach the shrine? Such a display of power must have exhausted her—an alagbato's power weakened the farther it reached from its source, and Ixalix's rainforest lay thousands of miles away.

"You should not have gone through all this trouble," I panted aloud, though I was not sure if the goddess could hear me. "You have only made me more curious."

When at last I staggered up the steps of the Ileyaso shrine, my limbs trembled with exhaustion. Still, I pushed open the door of the white bone house and stumbled inside.

When the enchantment whisked me to the Bhekina House courtyard, clouds of kicked-up dust stung the back of my throat. Stools and benches lay upended, and the courtyard flagstones had been scratched and broken. Barrels of mango wine gushed in splinters, and cracks dappled the villa's plaster facade, as though some large creature had thrown itself repeatedly against the walls.

I rubbed my eyes, which stung from the debris, and yelled, "Oga!"

A looming shape rose from the shadows: the hulking beast-man I had once known as the Crocodile.

Since I left, he had grown several feet taller, even as he hunched low to the ground. I froze at the sight of him, and when those livid yellow eyes fell on me, the Crocodile let out a roar.

I stumbled back, hands clapped over my ears. His voice had shaken the ground, guttural and cavernous as his chest expanded like a barrel, and his limbs bowed and thickened into trunks of green veins.

"Sade—it's happening," he growled through a mouth that now resembled a glistening snout, bristling with teeth. "You should not have come. Seal—me in—the portal. Get away from here—"

"No," I barked over his snarls. My body was strangely devoid of fear. "No, oga! You do not get to just give up again! I will not let you!"

He screamed as his torso doubled in size, ripping apart his clothing, and a wide, sweeping tail armored in scales burst in snaps from his backside. He writhed, bellowing, and I barely managed to duck for cover behind a bench as his tail swept through the courtyard, shattering a pile of barrels.

He howled in a voice both beast and human, a deafening wail thick with grief. It took me several moments to make out the words as they echoed from the plaster villa walls.

"*I'm . . . useless.*"

The well began to overflow. Water bubbled over the surface and streamed into the courtyard in a pulsing gurgle that sounded suspiciously like laughter. The sickly-sweet smell of lilies choked the air as the water-distorted tone of Ixalix sounded from the depths.

"Did I not warn you, foolish girl, that he was destined to be mine?"

"No," I rasped. Then I stood from behind the bench and faced the Crocodile.

"Who says that you are useless?" I demanded. In his yellow eyes, the beast's pupils narrowed to slits, struggling to find me. Willing my weak foot not to cramp, I heaved myself up to stand on the bench, yelling at him. "Who shapes the world? We do, oga. You taught me that, hypocrite, so start believing it yourself!"

He roared again. *"Too . . . late. Hideous."*

"So what?" I bellowed back. "No one's ever called me beautiful, and you don't see me throwing a tantrum!"

His tail swept again, this time colliding with the stone barrier around the well, causing the stones to cave in. The water surged to a river, and Ixalix laughed harder, her unseen lungs causing the river to shimmer with bubbles.

"Well done, girl," she chortled. *"I have not been this entertained in a millennium. But your tongue will not save him. Leave us, mortal, and go back to the small world you know."*

I ignored her, my focus traveling above the well, to where—despite the chaos underneath—the Crocodile mask remained untouched, hovering haughtily over the yard below. Even in his rage, he had managed not to destroy it.

An idea sparked inside me, flaming to life. I forced my mind to recall the exact wording of the Crocodile's curse: the unfulfilled ehru wish that bound him.

For the old rulers of Djbanti to cast down their crowns, and for those they exploit to rise up.

The Crocodile had led a glorious revolution. The people of Djbanti had risen up, enshrining the name of Zuri of Djbanti in history forever. But revolutions were not about heroes or names that never died. They were about people. The miners and sweatmill workers, the maids and village wives, the aging cooks and flower farmers . . . the work of a million stubborn ants, joining together to topple a gang of giants. The people who used swords when necessary, then put them down to take up plowshares and gardening trowels, laundry lines and soap buckets, mothering the world they had fought to win. Beautifying that world, for the sake of each other.

Most heroes did not have names. And some crowns, I thought as light glinted in the mask's haunted eyes, were not made of gold.

I teetered down from the bench and limped to the well, drawing the Crocodile's lurid yellow gaze with me. I lifted my cane to the sky, pointing at the mask. "You took my choice away," I told him, "but I am giving you yours. *Cast down your crown, oga!*"

The beast's face contorted in confusion. I cried out, exasperated as water chilled by the anger of Ixalix lapped around my ankles.

"Be useful again," I ordered. "Zuri of Djbanti: Join the real rebellion. The one that never ends. The one that means working side by side with the nobodies you chose to fight for, in a world that will never know your name."

He hesitated.

I labored across the courtyard, placed my hands on either side of his massive, scaly temples, and yelled into vein-shot eyes: "*Strike. It. Down!*"

He freed himself from my grasp with a roar, and I stumbled to the ground as he leapt into the air. At the same time, the ground cracked around the courtyard, and geysers of water exploded up from the earth as Ixalix screeched, "*No!*"

But she was too late. The sound of rent leather ripped across the flagstones, along with an earsplitting *boom* and the din of a thousand invisible spirits, lifting their ageless voices in song. A sigh, I would later realize, of healing. Of nature banishing the stolen power of Pale Arts and reclaiming the balanced rule of blood, earth, and clay.

The sound of an enchantment dying.

When I looked up, the mask had vanished from the sky and lay in pieces on the ground. And next to it rested a man—a boy, really, with smooth, dark skin clothed in tatters. For several moments, he did not move, and ice froze in my veins. Then he coughed, and I came to kneel at his side.

The battle scars across his torso remained . . . but all the scales were gone. His full lips parted to reveal an unpointed set of teeth. When his eyes fluttered open, they no longer glowed yellow, and his irises were pure, brilliant black. When I seized his arm to examine it, his skin was clammy to the touch, as though he were fighting a fever. Still, when I removed the cuff from his bicep . . . the festering wound had gone, and the stones vanished with it. A tiny heat that had tugged at my insides for months cooled, then fizzled out—the death of my body-bond with the Crocodile God, for that god was no more.

A guttural moan sounded from the well. When I rose to peer over its ruined walls, I let out a startled yelp. A single massive eye glowered back at me, its iridescent iris filling the mouth of the well.

"*You did not need him as I did,*" Ixalix rasped in a last gush of bubbles. "*You will live your small, dull life and die, as all mortals do. Whereas I must continue to be. He would have been something new, something glorious to hold my interest. But you, selfish girl that you are, denied me even that.*"

As I looked into that immortal pupil, a familiar smallness squeezed at my insides. What right had I, a speck of a gutter girl, to shape a story of a goddess? Ixalix was a force that had existed eons before me, and would remain long after. I found myself wanting to comfort her. To do what I always did in the looming shadow of my betters: shrink from their gaze, making excuses for my own existence.

But I stopped myself. How much of life had I spent making powerful people feel comfortable?

"Too much," I murmured, and then told that ageless eye, "You are wrong, Lady Ixalix. Mortals are not dull, as we are able to change. And I . . . I am not small. Not really. Not where it counts."

"I told you so," murmured the man on the ground.

When I returned to his side, he squinted, peering up at me with fearful wonder. "You came," he sighed.

I scowled, my anger from earlier seeping back. "Only because I was tired of being told what to do."

"You broke my curse," he whispered. "You did what no one else could; the tapestry was right all along. Sade, I—"

He broke off as, all around us, the chalk lines on the ground began to burn and hiss, each tooth glowing crimson as the lines shrank in size.

The Crocodile, now Zuri, scrambled to his feet, pulling me up with him.

"The portals to Oluwan," he gasped, hauling me across the courtyard. "They're closing. Once you broke my curse, my teeth lost their power as lodestones. Quick—we have to get across before . . ."

With a shove that knocked the air from my lungs, he hurled us across the nearest chalk line: the Chipped Molar Door.

When we entered the black box of the Ileyoba Palace District shrine, the ground shook beneath us, and we barely managed to burst through the shrine door and down the whitewashed steps before the entire bone house, kept in place only by the Crocodile's power, began to crumble. On the street beyond the shrine, a crowd formed, shrieking with fear and excitement as we, a spirit-touched girl and mostly naked man, stumbled forth from the god-haunted building. Heavy bricks and sharp roof tiles fell like hail around us. One piece of debris hit Zuri on his shoulder, sending him sprawling on the dirt, but before I could go to him, another piece clipped my temple, and I stumbled to my knees.

The next few minutes are extremely hazy, though I remember the crowd splitting to the sound of armored footfalls.

"Disperse for the Raybearers' Guard!" rang out several voices, and before long we were surrounded by grave-looking warriors, leather breastplates painted with the dual-sun emblem of the Realmhood. By this time, my vision was fading, but I made out a tall figure leaning over me, a band on his broad copper shoulder identifying him as a warrior medic.

"Easy breaths now," the figure murmured in a cavernous Dhyrmish baritone, placing a bandage to my bleeding temple. "You will be all right. I have scanned your skull with my Hallow, and there is no serious damage. But it is best if you do not move at present."

Gently, the figure scooped me up and placed me onto a stretcher. It was only then, in those few seconds before I lost consciousness, that I got a clear look at his face.

Anointed Honor Sanjeet of Dhyrma—the Prince's Bear, the boogey-man who had haunted my childhood—smiled kindly down at me.

Then his brow furrowed, the ghost of a memory stealing into his thick-lashed brown eyes.

"Young lady," he asked, "have we met before?"

CHAPTER 32

"SHE'S AWAKE!" SAID A VOICE, WHEN I STIRRED WHAT FELT like hours later.

A girl of eleven or twelve stood over me with a dripping cloth, fragrant with salve. From the dampness on my cheeks, I supposed that she had been bathing my face. My forehead was stiff, and when I touched it, I found that my temples had been bandaged.

"Not so loud, Ae Ri," said Ye Eun, coming into my hazy field of vision. She placed a restraining arm around the child, who I remembered was her little sister—the one adopted by Raybearers. "You'll make Sade's head hurt."

She was right. My head throbbed, but I sat up anyway, breathing hard as I took in my surroundings. A room so fine, it would make the Balogun Inn look like a rickety tenement in the slums of Dejitown. Dread pooled in my stomach. Because of course, I could only be in one place: the innermost chambers of An-Ileyoba Palace.

I would have known this even without the muraled ceiling, the gilded wax-cloth tapestries, and the solid marble bed dais, where my body lay half consumed by a pure down mattress and silken comforters. I knew it because behind Ye Eun and the child, one more person had entered the room—possibly the only person in the world who could scare me more than Sanjeet of Dhyrma.

You.

The room fell quiet as you entered, standing hesitantly just inside the door. A gold circlet shone on your dark brow, and ashoke garments furled around your tall, lithe form. You wore few adornments, likely because you did not need them. The light of the Ray, of your family's dynasty—that power that had united the souls of millions across a continent spanning half the globe—pulsed visibly across your warm, dark skin and shone from your mirror-black eyes. A lioness mask, shining with twelve vivid stripes, hung as a pendant from your neck, and a talking drum hung from a strap on your shoulder.

I knew, on some level, that you were only ten years my senior, not even thirty—but your spirit felt ancient. When I quailed beneath your gaze, however . . . you seemed as nervous as I did, wringing all nine of your fingers with a self-conscious smile.

"Auntie Tar!" the girl Ae Ri exclaimed, bounding over to you with a casualness that made me flinch. She held up the dripping cloth importantly. "I took care of her, just like you asked. Uncle Jeet stitched her up, so she stopped bleeding, but I'm the one who made sure she didn't catch fever. Is she staying with us now? She can share my room if she wants. Unless she wants to stay with Monster Uncle—"

You snorted with laughter, ruffling Ae Ri's curly brown hair. "'Monster Uncle,'" you sighed, in a voice like silver. "Don't ever let Zuri know you called him that. He has a fondness for absurd nicknames, and he will never let you call him anything else."

"Is he doing all right?" Ye Eun asked, eyeing you anxiously. "Are . . . *you* doing all right, Your Majesty? I know it was jarring, the first time Croc came back. But now that he's not Croc anymore—now that he's back for good . . ."

"Zuri is not back for good," you said with a soft, sad smile. "He is leaving us again. Life as a council member never suited him, and his mental bond with me broke when he died years ago—so I should not be surprised. Still . . ." Your features grew puzzled. "The debris from that falling shrine must have hit him harder than we thought. He keeps on rambling about 'getting a job,' and 'learning a trade,' and 'joining the real world, for once.' If he didn't look exactly the same as he did a decade ago . . . I would have thought him a completely different person."

"You have Sade to thank for that," said Ye Eun, shooting me a sly grin. When your curious gaze fell on me again, I wanted to hide under the covers.

"Ye Eun," you said quietly, "if you and Ae Ri don't mind, I would like to speak with Sade alone."

My tongue turned to lead, growing even heavier when Ye Eun and Ae Ri left, and you sank gracefully onto a stool at my bedside. You set the talking drum on the floor and placed your four-fingered hand—the one immortalized in legend, revered and mimicked by cultists the world over—on my arm.

"Hello, Sade," you said. "I know this must all be very confusing. Do you know where you are?"

"P-palace," I whispered, unable to stop gawking at your ring-adorned hand.

"And . . ." You bit your lip, giving me time to prepare. "Do you know who I am?"

I nodded slowly, as though my head were on a string. "You are the Idajo," I croaked. "I mean, Raybearer Tarisai. I mean, Your Majesty. I mean—"

"Tarisai is fine," you cut in, and poured a glass of water from a crystalline jug at your elbow, holding it to my lips. "Please. You've been sleeping for hours. I'm sure you're thirsty."

I drank obediently, trying not to swoon at the *nearness* of you. You seemed to sense this, and politely settled back onto the stool, folding your tapered arms on your silk-covered lap.

"I'm sorry about your bandages," you said. "Normally, we could have fixed you up in an instant. But healing is my council sister Kirah's Hallow— her blood gift, that is—and she is away in Songland, preparing for her wedding. But Sanjeet is an excellent physician. If he did your stitches, I doubt you'll even have a scar."

My hand rose to my temple, trembling in disbelief. Then I hadn't dreamed it. Anointed Honor Sanjeet of Dhyrma had pulled me from the rubble of that shrine. Had . . . *tended* to me. He, the Prince's Bear. I wondered, guiltily, if some part of him had recognized the little girl who had spurned him so many years ago. The child who had fled from his touch, as though he would rip her limb from limb.

Then I stiffened, scanning your features in terror.

"Can you tell what I'm thinking?" I blurted. "If you can, I didn't mean it. About High Lord General Sanjeet being . . . that is—I was very young. I didn't mean—"

"I cannot read your mind, Sade," you said, in a tired, patient tone that meant you explained this quite often. "Please do not worry. Also, we changed his title. He's High Lord Medic Sanjeet now."

"But you can see my memories," I accused, and after a slight pause, you nodded.

"That is my Hallow, yes. But in your case, I would prefer not to look. In fact . . ." You cocked your head to one side and then drew the talking drum onto your lap. "I would much rather you told your story out loud. How you came to meet Zuri. How you managed to break his curse, when even my most skilled mages could not manage it."

I blinked at the drum. "Are you going to . . . play music, Your Majesty?"

"No." You smiled. "This drum belongs to my personal griot, Adukeh. She is in charge of documenting every important event that happens during my reign, but she cannot be everywhere at once. So I carry this." You tapped playfully on the drum's goatskin hide. "A griot's drum is a powerful thing. Legend has it they can absorb stories themselves, even when their griot is not present."

"And your griot wants to know about . . . me?"

"Of course." Your eyebrows rose in surprise. "As do I. Sade . . . I don't believe you realize just how long I've been waiting to meet you." You crossed the room, to where a loom-shaped object lay covered in a sheet. You tore the sheet down . . . and I gasped.

There it was: the tapestry with my face. The portrait of me in the window of the Aanu Meji Street orphan high-rise, chin resting on my hand as I stared dreamily at nothing. The tapestry looked enormous in person—much more so than it had in Ixalix's vision. And as you stood beside it, you—Tarisai Idajo, the most powerful woman in our sprawling Realmhood—looked small.

You asked, "Will you tell me your story, Sade?"

I stared into the eyes of that tapestry Sade—the one who, while she did not know it, had always been a giant. Then I held out my hands for the griot drum.

You placed it on my lap, and I cradled it in my arms. And of course—I told you everything.

◎◎◎◎◎◎

Many hours later, I end my tale—or at least, the one I tell you out loud. I describe losing consciousness in the Crocodile's collapsing shrine before waking up here, in the palace. But even when I finish, and we sit together in silence . . . I continue addressing my thoughts to you. I find I cannot help it, even though I know you cannot hear me, for you are more woman than god.

In a way, I believe I have always been trying to tell you my story. Ever since I emerged from the Bush, a babe in my mother's arms, and our weary eyes fell on Yorua Keep—that lofty symbol of hope, where you would one day sleep and study, shaping the world with your giant words and pen.

Perhaps when we ants learn to shape the world ourselves, we will pray to you giants less.

But you have shared my story this far. So I do not mind taking you along with me, if only in my head, for a little longer.

"Brilliant girl," you say, black eyes burning over me with admiration, and then righteous anger. "Sade, that Nu'Ina Eve festival . . . I am so sorry. I was there. All those years ago—if I had known . . ."

"But you did not," I say, with a grim shrug. "You could not. You were too big, and I was too small. That is the world you rule, Your Majesty."

Your lips press together in a firm line. "We are working to grow smaller, Raybearer Dayo and I. Someday, this world will not need keeps or palaces, Village Wives or nobility. You must tell no one, but our dream is to grow a Realmhood that will not even need Raybearers. At least, not in the same way. It will take time. Decades. Centuries, perhaps. But until then . . . promise me you will never stop telling your story."

"Agreed, Your Majesty." I smile at you wearily. "If you help us build a world that listens."

You pause, gazing thoughtfully at my hand. My face heats. Even after all that has happened, the Crocodile's string of painted beads remains on my wrist.

"About Zuri," you say, your voice cautious. "He . . . has requested to see you. Before he leaves the palace. You have every right to be angry with him," you add when I recoil. "But ever since he woke up, he has done nothing but speak of you. He is . . . a complicated man to love. Believe me, I know." You smile wryly. "But he is sorry, Sade. And if you can find it in your heart to see him, I know he would—"

"I do not want to talk about Zuri, Your Majesty," I interrupt, and you straighten in surprise. I imagine you are not interrupted often, and I am shocked at myself for doing it. But I realize, all at once, that I have the ear of the most powerful person in thirteen realms. And here is the thing about us ants: Even when we are only one, we carry the colony with us. We carry its memory in our veins, the burden of its scars and dreams.

Whether we crawl on the sandal of a pauper or an empress, an ant fights for the colony.

"Your Majesty," I say, taking another long sip of water, "let me tell you about the orphans on Aanu Meji Street."

And so I do, describing the gaps in your Lonesome Child Edict. I lecture you about the children who slip through the cracks, and how those who are not adopted are preyed upon by madams and ogas. I press on you the need for shelters and community kitchens, so that employers like Mamadele could not frighten their staff into submission with the threat of a night on the streets. I even tell you about my idea—the one I have been forming in my head ever since I saw Unity Square. An idea I had not shared even with the Crocodile.

"What if there was a new kind of academy?" I say, voice pitching with excitement. "One where a person need not know how to read. We have griots who tell stories in city squares—crowds gathering to hear histories of heroes and emperors. But what if crowds could gather just like that, for free, and learn something . . . useful? An open-air market of skills. Where the point was not to buy but to learn? A place where anyone—from an orphan to a middle-aged scullery maid—could drop in for an hour and watch lessons on smithing, baking, pelt-tanning, carpentry. Could put their hands on tools and be tutored by experts hired by the Realmhood, without needing to buy an apprenticeship or be adopted by a benevolent family? What if . . . everyone was just a little less bound by the lot into which they were born?"

Your features grow increasingly animated, and by the end of my idea, you have risen and begun to pace. "It would be an excellent use of public space," you say, gesturing as though surveying a map of the city. "An excuse to build *more* public space. The nobles and more exclusive trade guilds won't like it, but if the idea takes hold of the populace, they'll have a hard time shooting it down. It's brilliant." You pause to regard me, and light enters your eyes as you make a decision. "Sade . . . I know these past months have shown you a great deal and that you will need time to rest and recover. But once you've had time to think about it . . . how would you like to work as an advisor, here in the palace?"

I sit back, gaping like a fish. "An advisor, Your Majesty? To . . . who?"

"Me, of course." You dimple. "And my court, when we discuss such matters."

"You want me," I say, palms growing clammy, "to live here among nobles, and . . . talk to them? *All* the time?"

My mind flashes back to that night in Mamadele's salon, when her friends circled me for interrogation, poking fun at my answers and brandishing words I did not understand. Part of me wants to tell you *no, thank you* and flee from this dazzling jewelry box of a chamber, escaping into the familiar muggy air of Oluwan City. Another part of me knows that if I am truly to fight for my colony—to lead the charge of ants shaping our world—then I could hardly do better than staying here, at the heart of the Realmhood's power, bully nobles and all. A third part of me stares truth in the face and states the most pragmatic fact of all:

"I have nowhere else to go." I say it aloud, though I regret it. It sounds very ungrateful. But it is true, and I find I am too tired to soften the truth's edges. Now that the Crocodile's shrines are demolished, I have no way of reaching Bhekina House, and so farming enchanted vegetables to sell in the market is no longer an option.

"Are you certain?" you ask, looking perplexed. "But your friends have come to see you. Once Ye Eun found out you were brought here, she told them right away. They've been in the antechamber ever since, waiting for you to wake up. I will have a servant send them in."

"My . . . friends?"

You rise and glide for the exit. "You called them 'Amenities.'"

CHAPTER 33

WHEN WAFA, KANWAL, AND FINNRIC CREEP INTO THE CHAM-
ber, I barely recognize them—they look so small and cowed in this room,
with its tapestried walls and towering painted ceilings. I imagine I look
just as drab wrapped in these silk blankets, like a sparrow drowning in
peacock feathers. But once they see me, the Amenities transform into the
cheerful gang I know so well, surrounding my bed and speaking all at once.

"Small Sade," Wafa gushes, taking both my hands in hers. "Thank
Am you're all right. When Ye Eun brought us here, we could scarcely
believe it—"

"Is it true the Crocodile God took you hostage?" Finnric asks, sounding more impressed than concerned. "Does that mean you're blessed
now, instead of cursed? Considering how swanky this room is . . . I'd say
blessed. Good for you, Sade. I always sensed in you a kindred spirit of
ambition—"

"You might have told us your lizard boyfriend was a *god*," exclaims
Kanwal. "Or was the lizard his messenger? Ye Eun tried to explain it, but
she wasn't very clear on that point . . ."

I am so happy to see them, my eyes prick with tears. "I'm . . . not sure
how much I can tell you," I tell them, once they pause for breath. "I did
stay with the Crocodile, but I was not a hostage. And he is not a god. Well,
not anymore. He's a man who was cursed, and I helped him. The Anointed
Ones took an interest, and so next thing I knew . . . I was here." I gesture clumsily as I babble, doing my best to explain without revealing Zuri's
true identity or his connection to the Raybearers. As far as most of Aritsar
knows, the king of Djbanti has been dead for years, enabling Djbanti's

new commonwealth to flourish. The truth can only complicate things, and so I quickly change the subject. "How are all of you? Do you still live at the inn? I hear Mamadele got married and Dele inherited everything."

Both Wafa and Kanwal brighten, inhaling in tandem. Even Finnric looks squeamish with happiness.

"Not only do we live there—" begins Kanwal.

"It's ours!" squeals Wafa, dancing in place.

"Ours," Finnric drones, "and Hanuni's, and Onijibola's." He frowns as he counts on his fingers. "Personally, I think we should have split the property into competing establishments. But as always, my sensible idea was voted down . . ."

"One inn. Run by workers, owned by workers. Like it always should have been, yam-for-brains," Kanwal retorts, and then she turns to me again, her gaze softening. "And Dele told us it was all your idea. So we had to come see you when Ye Eun told us what happened. Onijibola wanted to come too, but he kept fainting at the idea of *breathing the same air* as the Idajo, and so Hanuni had to stay behind to keep an eye on him. Anyway . . ." She draws her solid body up to full height. "Small Sade, on behalf of all the Amenities, we would like to make you a proposal."

"We promised we wouldn't just spring it on her," Wafa reminds Kanwal, gently tugging her sister's braid. "Look at her bandage. She's had a shock. Maybe we should wait and come back when she's had more rest."

"You really think the palace guards will let us back in here twice?" Finnric asks, staring with reverent lust at the marble bed dais and gilded end tables. "I'm surprised they haven't kicked us out already. Tell her now, Kanwal."

So Kanwal clears her throat and declaims, "Sade, as we hold to the creed of 'once an Amenity, always an Amenity,' we hereby invite you to be fellow staff member and co-owner of the newly titled Tall Tale Inn of Balogun Street: home to legendary stew and marvelous dreamscapes."

I sit up, joy-moths fluttering in my belly. "Then you're really doing it?" I ask Wafa. "Your idea for telling people's stories?"

"It's not just mine now," Wafa explains, breathless with anticipation.

"We're converting the salon into a stage. It'll be like those mummer shows at festivals, only instead of tales about gods and emperors, we'll collect stories about ordinary people. We'll even have themes for each week: comedy, tragedy, first love, unsolved mystery . . ."

"We're already the talk of the city," Finnric says, attempting to sound bored, though he bounces as though he were a child. "Once word got out, people started shouting from windows and bickering in the streets, trying to decide which of their neighbor's stories they should submit for a performance. I'll give it to you, Wafa . . . I was wrong all these years, making fun of the idea. It is an effective way to ensure repeat revenue from multiple districts . . ."

"But we can't open yet," Kanwal says to me, pointedly. "Because even though we're collecting stories and refreshments and dyed bottles for lighting . . . we don't have a singer. Or at least, someone to hear people's stories and turn them into songs for us to sing."

"Of course," I say, my voice choking up as I grin at them. "Of course I'll do it. With all my heart. Only . . ." I pause, thinking suddenly of you.

Living with the Amenities, having a job, a home at the heart of Oluwan City . . . it is all I have ever wanted. But if I stay at the palace and act as your advisor, I have a chance at making a difference. To make the world better for people like Kwabena, and Smallest Sade, and all those orphans begging for work in the Lower Markets. How could I choose to live as an ant when you have offered to let me sit among giants?

Then, as I scan the hopeful faces of the Amenities, their humble inn livery stark against the glittering palace walls . . . a new thought settles onto my shoulders.

Why should I have to choose at all?

Why should anyone?

It is the same mistake Zuri made, thinking the only way to fight the powerful was to reign among them.

So when the Amenities leave the chamber, and you return hours later to hear my decision . . . I tell you that I will help lead your projects to improve the Realmhood, but not from the palace.

"I am happy to visit sometimes," I say, "when I can be of service. But perhaps your Anointed Ones could learn something more by coming down to Unity Square. Hear the people come to their own minds on what they want, and enforce their decisions. See what they see in their daily lives. And if your Anointed Ones are fond of our stories," I add, with a streak of boldness, "they might drop by the Tall Tale Inn."

When I move back to the inn, I am finally given my Amenity name. After hours of deliberation, the servants of the Tall Tale Inn christen me Hand Bell . . . because when guests have need of anything, I am likely to come singing.

We have many kinds of guests now, not just wealthy ones, for we offer an experience unlike any other in Oluwan City. People travel from the corners of every district, and at first, I think it is because we have decorated the former salon so beautifully. Unlike outdoor performance stages, after all, our dreamscape space is intimate, with embroidered tapestries for backdrops, hidden soundmakers beneath the stage, and suspended lamps tinted by colored glass, dyed pink or blue to portray the time of day in the story. But eventually, I realize that people come to see themselves. Or rather, everyday stories of heartbreak and triumph, told with a reverence previously reserved for the lives of gods and kings.

Our dreamscapes are part play, part concert, with dance interludes from Wafa as a treat. We do our best to tell the stories as we hear them, but sometimes an audience member rises in protest, insisting that they witnessed the real event and that our performance got some detail wrong. Often, we humor them and make up new songs on the spot. But we have learned to ignore certain interrupters. Many folk, you see, complain that a story is incorrect, when they really mean it is not comfortable.

Now that the shrines of the Crocodile have fallen to rubble, the city burns with rumor. Some claim that the Crocodile's appetite for Oluwan girls has been sated, and so he has left to sample another realm's store of maidens. But through a few well-placed songs, I cause another rumor to circulate: that the Crocodile God never wanted girls at all. That he had destroyed his shrines in anger at a city that discarded its women and expected blessings in return. Over the months, I track down the stories of every person sacrificed to the Crocodile, enlisting the help of those who lived nearby the now-destroyed shrines. Hanuni advises me not to sing of what I learn, as such stories will surely lead to a rowdy audience. But I convince the Amenities to perform the stories anyway, and together, we end each dreamscape with a sung entreaty:

> *Will you eat them yourself?*
> *Those hard and pretty girls?*
> *Now that your god is gone?*

As each story ends with some horrid injustice, wails of protest rise from the audience, demanding that we perform a new ending. But we do not change it. Instead, we invite the audience to stay for Kanwal stew and discuss how they might have prevented the tragedy from happening. On such nights, our guests cease to be the audience and instead become the players. They go away knowing that no single person, but all of us together, decide if our city produces dreamscapes or nightmares.

Our rooms fill quickly. Not only with travelers from outside the city, but with devoted admirers of the inn, eager to reserve their seats for the next performance. Even those who live nearby stay so late laughing, singing, and eating feasts by Head Cook Kanwal, they are loath to go home again. After the first few dreamscapes, the front hall grows so crowded, we have to expand it into the front courtyard and add an extra wing to the back of the inn. To serve our new influx of guests and handle our inn's expansion, we hire more Amenities, bestowing on each a share in the inn's ownership once they have passed an initial trial.

When I am not meeting with townspeople to compose their story songs, I help you supervise the new Realmhood projects being built in Unity Square: an open-air market for learning trades, a community kitchen, and my favorite of the three, a night shelter for new releases from the orphanages, newcomers to the city, and women who simply have nowhere else to go. During the day, when no one is there, I walk the rows of bed singing, mopping up silt, and dusting away despair, watering moss for dreams to grow.

When I have time, I hail a rickshaw to the Academy District to visit Smallest Sade or to the Agricultural District to chat with Ye Eun and Dele as they bustle about their thriving flower shop, which has expanded to offer same-day embroidery services. Mostly, though, I work the inn with the Amenities, attending to the needs of guests by day and performing stories by night, on a stage lit by sprite lamps to a crowd of breathless listeners.

I try not to scan their faces. I try, with all my heart, not to look for one with cobalt-black skin and haughty cheekbones. For a man with full, smirking lips and locs that fall in sheets past sinewy shoulders.

It was I who left without saying goodbye. It does not make sense to resent him for staying away, and even if he came, I have little reason to trust him. Curse or no curse, he is still the oga who stole my voice.

Still . . . he must know where I am. You would have told him, and even if you had not, he could not hide from the fame of the Tall Tale Inn, at least not in Oluwan City.

Sometimes, out of the corner of my eye, a Clemeh-sized streak of green skitters across a rafter. A pumpkin or calabash turns up where it has no business being: on the sill of a window, for example, or at the bottom of my laundry basket.

And every now and then, a brand-new cane appears outside my bedroom door. They are simply whittled at first, the mark of an amateur craftsman. But as time passes the handles grow more and more elaborate, shapes of birds and toothy beasts, with celestial patterns of stars and moons carved down the shaft, until I have a menagerie of canes—more than I could use in a month. Always, they are perfectly suited to my height and sanded whisper smooth, so as never to leave a splinter. I have acquired a number of secret admirers since becoming the Story Singer of the Tall Tale Inn, and gifts are not uncommon. So I wield my new canes in public, praising their beauty aloud, but no one comes forward to take credit.

The Crocodile does not appear. And so, little by little, as the months stretch into a year . . . I stop looking.

One morning, Ye Eun and Dele request my aid for a cleaning emergency. Apparently Ye Eun's newest import of starblossoms arrived with bog-rot, infesting the rest of her stock. As the shop has enjoyed an especially prosperous season, Ye Eun suspects foul play, perhaps a curse from one of her floral competitors, and hires me to spirit-clean her apartment shop from top to bottom. It is the work of several days, and they refuse to let me return to the inn between cleanings, insisting I be their guest and plying me with stories and distractions. When at last I declare the shop curse-free—and the flowers looked suspiciously healthy to begin with—they allow me to return to Balogun Street.

When I arrive in the evening, just as the moon begins to rise, all of the Amenities are standing in the front yard, whispering and furtively watching the road.

"Has something happened?" I ask. "Did the sprites from the stage lamps get loose again?"

But they jump when they see me, eyes bright with held-back grins and giggles.

"Surprise!" Wafa bursts out at last. "We've been planning this for ages, but we couldn't keep you away from the inn long enough."

"Ye Eun and Dele were in on it," Kanwal says, looking devious.

"And I helped supervise the craftsman," Finnric puts in, causing Hanuni to roll her eyes.

"The craftsman did not need help," says Hanuni. "He approached us with the plans all on his own. In fact, I think we should take him on full-time. Am knows we'll be swimming in renovations, now those dreamscapes are getting more elaborate."

"Give Hand Bell room to go inside, now," Onijibola says, his rheumy eyes twinkling. His hands have become less gnarled over the past year, as the inn's prosperity allowed him to rest. "Let the girl see what we're babbling about."

When I pass the stage in the front courtyard to enter the inn, I find the front hall blazing cheerily with lanterns. Beside the spiral staircase stands a new tower of pillars and polished latticework, stretching from the ground to the second-floor landing. Inside the pillars, a platform lies suspended by rope pulleys.

Once I see it, the Amenities crowd in behind me. "Well?" they demand. "What do you think?

I smile but shake my head, perplexed. "I . . . do not understand. What is it? Where did it come from?"

"It's called an elevator," Wafa announces grandly. "It can hold the weight of ten men. You operate it by pulling the ropes. It's very strong—go on, try it."

Speechless, I sit on the platform, placing my cane beside me. When Kanwal shows me how to work the pulleys, my stomach does a loop as the platform sails upward, counterweights sinking from the ceiling. When the elevator delivers me safely to the second floor, the Amenities cheer, and I laugh breathlessly, heart rising to my throat.

"The goal," Hanuni says sensibly, "is for you never to use stairs again."

My eyes blur with tears as I let the elevator descend. "But . . . how? The expense—"

To my surprise, it is Finnric who waves away the objection, though he tries his best to look nonchalant. "You are a co-owner of the inn, as well as a valuable asset. Letting you sweat climbing stairs every day is bad business."

"And even if it wasn't," Wafa puts in, "this is your home, Hand Bell." She drops a kiss on my temple. "A home should be easy to live in. That's what the traveling craftsman said, and we all agreed with him."

"Where did that pretty man go, anyway?" asks Beauty Bisi, one of our newest Amenities and my old friend from the orphanage. "Wasn't he just here a second ago?"

"He went out back," says Kanwal, pulling a face. "Bit strange, that one. Speaks a little too fancy for a handyman."

"I believe the young man is finishing another project in the yard," Onijibola muses. "Free of charge, he said. Something to keep our Sade from having to use those slippery stairs down to the spa."

And that is when Clemeh, who I have not seen in a year, creeps out from the pulley system of the elevator, licking his beady eyes in a wink.

Hanuni has been watching me keenly, and she hides a smirk as my features slacken. "I think," she monotones, "that Sade might want to meet that craftsman alone."

◎◎◎◎◎◎

He must have heard the tap of my cane, for when I enter the inn's backyard, he does not startle, only stands at attention. He looks hopeful and nervous. The deepening twilight bathes his dark skin in deep, luminous blue.

Despite his worker's clothes and lack of adornments, he still has the bearing of a boy-king. Posture a little too straight. Movements swift and graceful. A twinkling amber pendant—just a hint of remaining vanity—dangles in his ear. But his face and body have filled out with a healthy padding, no longer the over-toned muscles of a body running only on mangoes and enchantment. His locs have grown longer, shining and well-kept, tied away from his face with a practical leather ribbon.

Beneath his workman's shirt, open at the chest, the keloid scars of his past life have finally begun to fade.

"You are back, then," I say, in a voice that barely carries.

He nods once, takes a step toward me, then steps back, swallowing hard. He says, "I am sorry."

"For coming back?"

"For taking your voice. I never said it. So I suppose I'm also sorry for waiting this long, but I was not sure you would want to see me. I . . . am not sure even now." His tortured dark eyes scan mine, in search of an answer he will not yet find. So he soldiers on: "I have been on apprenticeship for a year, with a guild of craftspeople outside the city. They are about to leave on a five-year tour of the countryside and have offered to let me join them. I am still learning, but they are decent, and there is work to be done in the outer villages. I would rather not go. I would rather not live a day without you in it ever again. But I will leave and not return if you say the word."

I do not answer right away. Instead I cross the courtyard and say, "Thank you for my canes." I lift the one I have chosen today: one with a shaft of notched scales and a smooth handle shaped like a long-tailed gecko. "This one is my favorite."

His breath quickens when I draw near, but he dons a neutral mask. "Mine too."

I notice then that the amber pendant in his ear is made of resin. Inside the golden drop floats a single black spiral of hair.

"It does not bind us anymore," he says, following my gaze. "But I could not part with it."

I say nothing, moving instead to the structure beside him, at which he brightens. It is a narrow, three-walled, roofless room of polished wood, over which he has erected a grate-covered rain gutter. A linen sheet covers the room's entrance.

He hurries to explain. "It's called a shower. I could not build you an elevator down to the spa, and those steps are lethal. So I drew up plans for an alternative. It's an idea I've been working on since Bhekina House, back when I still had powers. In that version, of course, I would have summoned a storm cloud for water, but I think a rain cistern will work just as well . . ." He dusts off his tool-scarred hands, then reaches inside the chamber to pull a handle. A lid beneath the cistern pulls back, and I gasp as water rains down—an enclosed waterfall in the center of the inn courtyard.

When I laugh in delight, a grin splits his face in two. As the water trickles to a stop, I fix my features, crossing my arms in a mock scold. "I thought you had given up sorcery."

"Alas," he sighs, "woodworkers, maids, and gardeners perform such magic every day. And they do not incur decade-long curses to do so."

A lump rises in my throat. "Did you really learn how to do all of this for me?"

For a moment he falls quiet, and nothing sounds but the clicks of cicadas slowly waking around us and the distant music of a city that never sleeps.

"No," he says at last. "I did it to make a living. Because—whether you send me away or not—that is what I intend to do. Live."

I nod slowly as joy-moths rise in my stomach. "Zuri?" I ask.

At the sound of his name on my tongue, he grows very, very still. When he speaks again, his voice is rough with desire. "Yes, Sade?"

I lean my cane against the outside of the shower wall, then step inside. "I would like to bathe. But you will need to show me how it works again."

"Shall I tell you?" he asks quietly, and I shake my head, stepping back to make room in the narrow chamber.

"No," I say. "Show me."

He moves to join me, clumsy with eagerness. I reach to draw the sheet across the door, closing us both inside. When he pulls the cord again, water runs down our cheeks and shoulders, soaking our clothing as the heat of our bodies draws us closer. I place my arms around his neck and say, "Ask me, oga, and I will."

"Please," he whispers, and so I close the distance between us, kissing him as beneath the water, two lifetimes of spirit silt run unseen down our limbs and disappear forever into the earth beneath our feet.

"We will need to give you an Amenity name," I murmur when we part for air. "And as the dreamscapes are getting more elaborate, you will have to be more than a handyman. We may make you act on stage."

He nudges my nose with his. "You will recall, my love, that I am excellent at playing a part."

TALL TALE INN: GROUND FLOOR

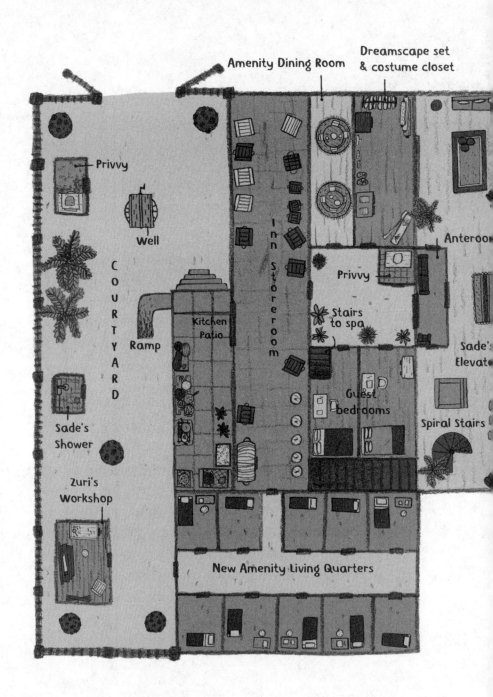

Amenity Dining Room

Dreamscape set & costume closet

Privvy

Well

COURTYARD

Ramp

Kitchen Patio

Inn Storeroom

Privvy

Stairs to spa

Anteroom

Sade's Shower

Sade's Elevator

Guest bedrooms

Zuri's Workshop

Spiral Stairs

New Amenity Living Quarters

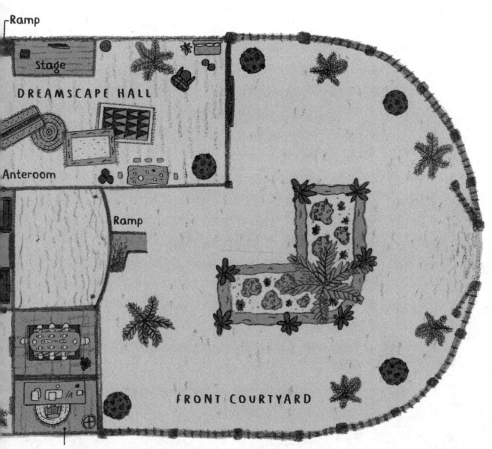

Ramp

Stage

DREAMSCAPE HALL

Anteroom

Ramp

Hanuni's Office

FRONT COURTYARD

HOW TO SPIRIT-CLEAN
YOUR BEDROOM

A beginner's guide by Sade,
called Hand Bell, of the Tall Tale Inn

As dictated to me: Zuri, called Hot Shower, of the same.

Acquire the following items:
   a broom
   cleaning cloths
   an old towel for mopping
   a bucket of hot water
   a bowl of vinegar, diluted with three parts water and scented with an oil of
      your choice
   lemon juice
   optional: alcohol, and an atomizer, known in some regions as a spray
      bottle

Step One
Befriend a charming, stubborn, lovely, perplexing, and utterly bewitching housemaid. (I jest. This is my suggestion, not hers, as Sade suspects that one does not require Hallowed sight to spirit-clean. Spirit silt reacts to one's intention, regardless of whether or not one can perceive it. Sade adds that if you have physical disabilities that would make deep cleaning difficult, you are free to skip to the last and most powerful step of this guide.)

Step One, in Actuality

Start high, with ceiling corners, and the tops of shelves, light fixtures, and wardrobes. Use your broom for high corners, and use your damp cloth of scented vinegar to rid surfaces of dust and spirit grime.

Step Two

Strip your bed of linens. Wash away worry and nightmares with hot water and a splash of lemon juice, either in a tub or in your favorite enchanted device.

(Sade's bedroom, when I am lucky enough to be invited, smells of rosemary and lavender. You may achieve a similar effect by spraying your clean, dry sheets with those oils, diluted in alcohol.)

Step Three

Remove all objects from remaining surfaces, and cleanse each surface with your damp cloth of scented vinegar.

Step Four

Return the objects you use at least once a week to their places. Consider giving away the objects you use less often. Store as many things as possible in plain sight, so you are mindful of their existence. This will help prevent you from acquiring more than you need.

Step Five

Sweep the floors, then swab on hands and knees with hot scented water. Most importantly, during all of your actions above:

Step Six

Sing, out loud if you can. The song you choose will depend on how your room makes you feel. Your chamber may fill you with peace or worry, restlessness or pride, quiet joy or crippling shame. There is no right or wrong feeling. You may sing whatever you like, but you will know you have chosen a cleansing song when a weight lifts from your shoulders and a ray of warmth travels from your belly into your mind.

If you struggle to think of a song, I have included my favorite of Sade's infinite melodies below. I sing it often in my new workshop behind the inn, though I greatly prefer her voice to mine. It goes like this:

I will make my mind a safe place
I will hold my dreams and yours too
I am all the seeds we planted
May we always own our multitudes.

I have learned that with the last line, Sade means two things at once. First: that each person is many things, and always will be, no matter how often they are pressured to fit one role or to pursue one future. Second: that there is power in numbers, and a sea of ants can change the world more in a day than a giant can in a lifetime.

May you grow to love your ordinary as I have grown to love mine.

May we always own our multitudes.

AUTHOR'S NOTE

Aritsar and its comprising realms are imaginary, with Easter egg references to popular fairy tales (many readers will recognize Zuri's door system as a loose tribute to *Howl's Moving Castle* by Diana Wynne Jones, a great favorite of mine). However, the realms of Aritsar are casually inspired by real-world places throughout history. Oluwan, for example, shares aspects with the Oyo Empire of West Africa, a wealthy and vast civilization that lasted from the thirteenth to the nineteenth century. If you're interested in learning more about West African civilizations, one beginner-friendly read is *The Royal Kingdoms of Ghana, Mali, and Songhay: Life in Medieval Africa* by Patricia McKissack and Frederick McKissack. If you're a fan of films, I greatly enjoyed *The Woman King* (2022). Alternatively, if you're wondering why you've never heard of these civilizations, I'd recommend reading *How Europe Underdeveloped Africa* by Walter Rodney.

Many negative aspects of Arit society, unfortunately, are also based on real-world problems, ones just as present today as they have ever been. The tragic stories of both Mamasades in this book are based on modern-day statistics, not historical ones. In the United States, where I live, the *most common cause* of death for pregnant women is murder by their male partners (*BMJ*, 2022; 379:o2499). You read that right: A pregnant woman is **less** likely to die from high blood pressure, infection, or birthing complications than she is from *the father of her child*. Many abusive men know that a pregnant woman, being both physically and economically vulnerable, is less likely to leave them, and so they coerce their partners into pregnancy (refusing to use condoms, tampering with birth control, etc.)

and begin abusing them soon afterward. Instances of reproductive coercion are higher in states with laws that limit a woman's access to birth control and reproductive freedom. If you or anyone you know is at risk of pregnancy coercion or intimate partner violence, you can access help through RAINN.org (24/7 phone hotline: 800-656-4673).

Other aspects of Sade's story are current-world problems as well. As of 2023, factory child labor is **legal** in the United States and in many other parts of the world. Your smart phone runs on a battery made from cobalt, an element that comes almost exclusively from the Democratic Republic of the Congo. As of 2021, forty thousand children as young as six years old mine cobalt in harrowing, often lethal conditions, a fact known by corporations like Apple, Microsoft, and Tesla, who continue to buy the element anyway. In 2023, American meatpacking facilities like Tyson, as well as giants of many other industries, use workers as young as thirteen who have then sustained permanent or lethal injuries involving factory equipment (US Dept. of Labor, dol.gov/newsroom/releases/whd/whd20220729). While those injuries may have been an accident, the decision to hire children was not. Company owners know that children cannot demand the same pay as adults. They also know that child workers come from desperate families, which means they are unlikely to quit. Crucially, American company owners purposely hire children who are undocumented, which means these children cannot report dangerous working conditions to authorities for **fear of deportation**. If you or anyone you know is being exploited by a US employer, you can access information about your rights by contacting the toll-free Dept. of Labor helpline at 866-4US-WAGE (487-9243).

Finally, if you'd like to read another fictional book about class inequality, I highly recommend *Munmun* by Jesse Andrews, as it's one of the most unique, hilarious, achingly spot-on satires of money inequality in the United States that I've ever read.

Thank you for reading, and I hope you use your voice.

ACKNOWLEDGMENTS

In the acknowledgments of my previous novel, *Redemptor*, I wrote a tear-stained tribute to all the people who helped me write a book while it felt like my world was falling apart. Someday, I would love to break my streak of "writing books while having a mental breakdown," but that day is not today. *Maid* was written during an entirely new, *shiny* set of world-melting circumstances (deconversion from my religion of thirty years, life-threatening medical emergencies, a cross-country move, and a sea of deadlines, just to name a few). I absolutely could not have finished this book without my own family of Amenities. Thanks to:

- Becca Seidler, who (I promised I would yell this part) *SAVED MY BEHIND* keeping me company and accountable as I wrote this book. May a lifelong stream of boba, curly fries, and rare Disney pins flow eternally to your doorstep.
- Kim-Mei Kirtland, my agent extraordinaire, who took late-night panicked calls and advocated for both my health and the quality of this book.
- Maggie Lehrman, my insightful and ever-game editor, who has journeyed with me through three books and counting. (She also wrote *The Last Best Story*, one of the most unique, ambitious, and timely YA stories I've ever read.)
- Fran Wilde, my cane-use sensitivity reader, and Lid'ya C. Rivera, my vitiligo sensitivity reader, for the emotionally taxing and intellectually rigorous work of ensuring healthy representation.

- Madina Nalwanga, an actress (*Queen of Katwe*, 2016) I have never met but whose soft, enchanting mannerisms directly inspired my early drafts of Small Sade.
- Charles Chaisson, the talented cover artist for all the US editions of my novels so far.
- Micaela Alcaino, the incredible artist behind all the UK editions of the same novels.
- Micah Fleming, the cover designer at Abrams who worked tirelessly to make this book shine.
- Namina Forna, my friend and fellow bestselling author, who talked me off many a metaphorical ledge as I navigated delaying this book's release for health reasons.
- Wafa and Kanwal Azeem, for being lovely friends and letting me use their names in a book.
- Uncle Femi, Auntie Monica, and Auntie Lisa, for their unconditional love and support.
- Adetinpo Thomas, talented actress (*Hawkeye*, *The Color Purple*) and excellent friend, for adopting my introverted self as I entered the disorienting new chapter of my life in Atlanta.
- Belle, Darian, Isis, Terrence, and Des, for embracing the nerd in me.
- Tara Newby, my soul sister, for many hours of "friend-church" and for riding the roller coaster of my numerous identity crises.
- Rachael, my blood sister, for being my beta reader and meme-explainer and wine-mom simulator and favorite baby-bug.
- David, my life person, for the words, and the tearstained nights, and the arroz caldo, and the ever-changing story of us we choose to keep writing. I love you so.

"Dazzling . . . All hail RAYBEARER."
—*Entertainment Weekly*

BEHOLD WHAT IS COMING

RAYBEARER.

JORDAN IFUEKO

The *New York Times* bestselling novel that
introduced readers to the world of Aritsar

★ "Ifueko's writing is nothing short of transportive, whisking readers to far-off worlds while employing gorgeous imagery and prose."
—*Kirkus Reviews*, starred review

SEQUEL TO THE *NEW YORK TIMES* BESTSELLER *RAYBEARER*

REDEMPTOR

JORDAN IFUEKO

The story of Aritsar and the
Raybearers continues . . .

ABOUT THE AUTHOR

JORDAN IFUEKO IS THE *NEW YORK TIMES* BESTSELLING author of the Raybearer series and the Disney-Marvel comic *Moon Girl & Devil Dinosaur: Menace on Wheels*. She's a Nebula Award, Ignyte Award, Audie Award, and Hugo Lodestar finalist, and she's been featured in *People* magazine, NPR Best Books, NPR Pop Culture Hour, and ALA Top Ten. She writes about magic Black girls who aren't magic all the time, because honestly, they deserve a vacation. Ifueko lives in Atlanta with her husband and their tripawd dog.

Follow Jordan on Instagram @jordanifueko.